PAYING THE PRICE

BOOK FIVE OF THE EMPIRE OF BONES SAGA

TERRY MIXON

BOOK FIVE OF THE EMPIRE OF BONES SAGA

PAYING THE PRICE

No good
deed...

...goes
UNPUNISHED!

TERRY MIXON

BESTSELLING AUTHOR OF *GHOSTS OF EMPIRE*

Published by Yowling Cat Press ®

Digital edition date: 7/11/2020

Print ISBN: 978-1947376045

Large Print ISBN: 978-1947376199

Cover art - image copyrights as follows:

BigStockPhoto.com/molodec

DepositPhotos/innovari (Luca Oleastri)

Donna Mixon

Cover design and composition by Donna Mixon

Print edition design and layout by Terry Mixon

Audio edition performed and produced by Veronica Giguere

Reach her at: v@voicesbyveronica.com

ALSO BY TERRY MIXON

You can always find the most up to date listing of Terry's titles on his
Amazon Author Page.

The Empire of Bones Saga

Empire of Bones

Veil of Shadows

Command Decisions

Ghosts of Empire

Paying the Price

Recon in Force

Behind Enemy Lines

The Terra Gambit

Hidden Enemies

Race to Terra

Ruined Terra

Victory on Terra

The Humanity Unlimited Saga

Liberty Station

Freedom Express

Tree of Liberty

Blood of Patriots

The Imperial Marines Saga

Spoils of War

The Fractured Republic Saga

Storm Divers

The Scorched Earth Saga

Scorched Earth

Omnibus Volumes

The Empire of Bones Saga Volume 1

The Empire of Bones Saga Volume 2

The Empire of Bones Saga Volume 3

Humanity Unlimited Publisher's Pack 1

The Vigilante Series with Glynn Stewart

Heart of Vengeance

Oath of Vengeance

Bound By Law

Bound By Honor

Bound By Blood

Want to get updates from Terry about new books and other general nonsense going on in his life? He promises there will be cats. Go to TerryMixon.com/Mailing-List and sign up.

DEDICATION

This book would not be possible without the love and support of my beautiful wife. Donna, I love you more than life itself.

ACKNOWLEDGMENTS

Once again, the people who read my books before you see them have saved me. Thanks to Tracy Bodine, Michael Falkner, Cain Hopwood, Kristopher Neidecker, Bob Noble, Jon Paul Olivier, Tom Stoecklein, Dale Thompson, and Jason Young for making me look good.

I also want to thank my readers for putting up with me. You guys are great.

1

"Admiral, do you have a few minutes?"

Jared Mertz looked up groggily from his lunch in the officers' mess to find Doctor Jerry Leonard standing beside his table. The fog of exhaustion that hung over him had dulled his edge. It seemed like a year since he'd slept a full night.

He gestured for the scientist to join him. "Pull up a chair and order something to eat."

The older man sat down primly. "I had something in the lab an hour ago, but thank you. I'd like to take one more try at traversing the weak flip point before we pull out."

The strange variants of the standard flip points were new to all of them, and the scientists were still struggling to understand them. Some only allowed one-way passage. Others were just as hard to find, but two-way. They knew so little about the new stellar phenomena.

The one in the Harrison's World system had eaten every probe they'd sent through it. Not one had returned. Not even when programmed to return as soon as the flip capacitor recharged.

Of course, no enemy had followed them home, so that was good news. Jared thought whatever was happening to them was probably natural. Perhaps this flip point was one-way for even the smallest of vessels.

"The fleet is performing the final checks before we leave for Pentagar," Jared said. "We're on a tight schedule."

"This won't take long. We've devised a new probe. Well, actually, we built one that looks like Frankenstein's monster. The core is a standard probe, but we added an external battle screen generator and bolted on the power system from one of the defunct war machines. We even added a second flip capacitor to speed its return.

"If the environment on the other side of the flip point is hostile— which at this point seems a given—that should allow it time to return with some readings. We'd like your permission to send it through."

Jared shrugged. "Why not? Let me wrap up my lunch, and I'll join you on the flag bridge. Say fifteen minutes?"

The scientist beamed. "Thank you, Admiral."

Jared finished his meal and returned to the bustling flag bridge. Over the last few months, he'd selected a full-time staff of officers to assist him in overseeing the fleet he'd assembled. They sat at their stations all around the circumference of the large control center, monitoring the preparations for departure.

No one called out when he entered the bridge. That had been one tradition he was happy to dispense with. Everyone had work to do. They didn't need to stop what they were doing just because he'd walked off the lift.

He sat at his console. It swept a full 270 degrees around his command chair, giving him the ability to multitask like nobody's business. It had taken him months to get fully accustomed to it, but now he was thrilled at how much data he could keep track of at once.

Jared pulled a headset from the niche in his console and slipped it on. His implants could interface without it, but the headset allowed for much greater data throughput. When linked to his flagship, he could access anything at lightning speed and in tremendous detail.

Part of his attention went to the scanner readings. The superdreadnought *Invincible* floated in a wide orbit around Boxer Station. They'd captured the Old Empire Fleet base from the Rebel Empire AI that had once ruled this system.

The rest went to the fleet he was taking back home. It consisted of his superdreadnought, a Fleet carrier, six battlecruisers, eight heavy cruisers, twelve light cruisers, and two dozen destroyers. It also had ten colliers with extra missiles and supplies, six Marine troop transports, sixteen fast couriers built for speed, twelve scouts built for stealth, a dedicated science vessel, two hospital ships, four factory ships, *New York*, and *Persephone*.

The factory ships would be particularly useful back home. They had all the tools needed to make the high technology items they'd need, like the cranial implants. They couldn't make the Marine Raider equipment because *Persephone* didn't have the details on the manufacture. That had been one of the Old Empire's most closely guarded secrets.

Once they figured out how to manufacture the Raider hardware, he suspected they'd have a crash course in bringing as many marines up to those specs as possible. They'd have to impose some stringent psych exams to keep that kind of power out of the wrong hands.

Those factories could also duplicate themselves. With more manufacturing capability, they could build advanced shipyards and simultaneously lift themselves up to Old Empire tech levels. Arguably, they were the most important ships in the fleet he'd gathered. Two just like them would go back to Erorsi and Pentagar with his compliments.

It would take a lot of reverse engineering or recovering the plans at some future point, but the factory ships could probably also build new AI hardware. The Empire would need additional sentient AIs on their side for the coming fight. Though, he admitted it would probably take the emperor a while to come around to that point of view.

All the ships were severely undermanned and only functional at the most basic level. Not even Boxer Station's construction bays could perform miracles. They took in battered wrecks and repaired the critical systems. The rest would need to happen by hand, because there was an almost unending line of derelicts waiting their turn.

They'd brought more people in from Pentagar and Erorsi, but that barely made a dent in their needs. They'd even begun careful, limited recruiting from Harrison's World. They had to be certain those people were trustworthy before they told them the truth about the Rebel Empire.

After a lot of thought, Kelsey had decided that the people there had to know the truth. They couldn't just hide it from them. That was wrong, and the truth would get out. That would be damaging. They had to stay on the moral high ground.

Plans were in development to roll out the knowledge once they were sure they had the existing implants scrubbed of the viral code. There would be resistance, but that was natural. They'd be upsetting the existing layers of society.

They'd be giving the lower orders implants and medical nanites. The higher orders, used to being the lords of all they surveyed, would scream bloody murder. They'd deal with it. Learn from it. This process would eventually play out in many other systems, so they had to refine the process while they could.

In the end, everyone would be better for it. The hard part was convincing them of that. Kelsey had recorded a number of speeches that the leadership could play when the time was right. Jared hoped they'd help explain the situation and keep the inevitable violence to a minimum.

Back to his current situation. Even understrength, the ships he'd gathered represented more fighting power than the rest of the New Terran Empire. Hell, *Invincible* alone could conquer his nation. The rest was overkill.

They also had thirteen Fleet transports for cargo and an upgraded cruise liner to carry civilians. *Best Deal*, the freighter that had housed their scientists, was far too slow to keep up. They'd be leaving her here.

Captain Anton Keller, *Best Deal*'s civilian skipper, was thrilled with the larger and much faster ship Jared had given him. It had military grade defenses, systems, and engines. It also carried many times more cargo than his old ship. He'd lost no time renaming her *Best Deal II*. The original one would go to Erorsi to help rebuild the system.

They'd even found a luxurious yacht to take home as a gift for the emperor. The current Imperial yacht was a fine vessel, but this one was much faster, had real defenses, and was armed. Jared was sure Karl Bandar would like it.

They'd done a few modifications to *New York* as well. They'd added battle screen generators and a second set of flip capacitors. The Old Empire versions of the capacitors were small enough to fit beside the current ones in engineering. They'd had to stash the battle screen controls in a conference room, but Captain Kaiser was happy to have the extra protection.

Jared had arrived with a small, old destroyer and a slow freighter converted to do science. He was going home with more than a hundred ships. Even with the surviving officers and men from *Spear*, *Shadow*, and *Ginnie Dare* helping to fill needed roles—both on his fleet and on Boxer Station—that left them with few Imperial personnel. Wallace had lost the light cruiser *Titan* and the destroyer *One Bullet* with all hands.

He'd robbed the destroyer *New York* as much as he could, but Captain Kaiser needed her core team. Her ship didn't have the same level of automation as the Old Empire ships. He'd considered leaving *New York* here, but he knew the woman would refuse that order, and Fleet Command wouldn't be happy, either.

Jared had insisted that everyone get Fleet implants. That way they could work on any ship, if required.

It amazed Jared that they'd been able to repair so many badly damaged ships in such a short time.

This wouldn't have been possible without the oversight of the AI on Boxer Station. Carl Owlet had used clean code to make a new personality for it that would be loyal to humanity and the Empire. It was able to juggle repairing multiple ships much better than a human team could have.

That was possible because the AIs were truly sentient. That was the last big shock the New Terran Empire would have to accept, and Jared had made it hard to ignore.

With the desperate need for command personnel, he'd reassigned Zia Anderson to command the Fleet carrier *Audacious*. He'd considered his original executive officer, Charlie Graves, but Zia was the more aggressive of the two. Besides, Charlie was completely happy commanding *Courageous*.

Zia's previous slot as his flag captain went to *Invincible* herself. Or rather the AI that resided inside her. The AI knew the ship better than anyone else possibly could. Kelsey had made an Imperial ruling that the AIs were people and so entitled to give oaths of service.

Invincible's AI, who'd decided to take the name Marcus, now had a commission as a Fleet captain. Boxer Station's AI—which had chosen the name Harrison—had one as well. That would give Fleet Command apoplexy and cause the Imperial Senate to implode.

The crew had been a little spooked to have an all-seeing captain, but they were adjusting. They'd even found a crash test dummy somewhere, made it a uniform, and strapped it into the command chair on the bridge so they'd have someone to look at when reporting.

Marcus used the speaker in the chair, and he didn't use what he heard or saw in his oversight of the public areas of the ship in his captain persona. He kept it segregated, and the crew knew how the subroutines maintained their privacy. It was working surprisingly well.

With the three flip-point jammers the scientists at the Grant Research Facility had built, they could lock down Harrison's World, Pentagar, and Erorsi from Rebel Empire incursions. Except for when they needed to perform maintenance on them.

That didn't account for the weak flip points, though. They'd have to be very careful using them.

Commodore Sean Meyer had two battlecruisers, four heavy cruisers, and six destroyers to guard Harrison's World. He'd work hand in hand with Coordinator Olivia West to ease the planet into the New Terran Empire without letting most of the people know about the change in management.

Someday, the general population would learn the truth. Just not right now.

Pentagar was getting a number of ships, as well. They'd watch over the base on Erorsi, too, until more ships arrived. Since Jared was taking a long, unexplored path home, they'd only accompany him partway.

By his best guess, it would take another six months to finish the final repairs on all the ships in his fleet. It would take even longer to get them fully manned with trained, enhanced personnel. He shuddered to think about how long it would take to work through the remaining tens of thousands of derelicts.

They'd brought the mines in the asteroid belt back online, reestablished the automated fabrication units, and now had a mobile station to disassemble ships too badly wrecked to fly again. They called it the breaker. It salvaged what parts it could and melted the rest down. The critical and rare elements went into new parts.

The crew there also pulled the dead from the wrecks and sealed them in body bags. If the medical teams could reactivate the person's implants, they made note of their names and copied the data stored in implant memory.

The cargo holds on several of the transports held the tens of thousands of bodies they'd recovered so far. Fleet was going to have to come up with a new means of burying their honored dead. The Spire couldn't hold the many millions of corpses in these ships.

The lift doors slid open and Doctor Leonard walked onto the flag bridge. Kelsey was with him.

She smiled at Jared. "I hear we're about to go exploring."

* * *

KELSEY EYED her brother critically from behind her cheerful expression. He looked exhausted. That was understandable. He'd been putting in twenty-hour days for the last nine months.

His implants and medical nanites reduced his need for sleep, but there were limits. Four hours a night wasn't enough. Not over that long a timeframe.

She'd tried to put her foot down and discovered there were some things she couldn't order him to do. She shuddered to think about how he'd have been without teams of people working behind the scenes to take tasks off his plate.

Maybe once they started back toward Avalon he'd get some rest.

"I don't think exploring is quite the right word," Jared said.

"We're only sending a probe. Another probe, actually. This makes what? Eight?"

"Nine," Doctor Leonard said. "Perhaps we'll get this one back. If not, we'll have to ponder over what we missed on the long trip home."

"We're leaving on time," Jared said sternly. "You have sixteen hours. Any more than that and you're out of luck."

"I'm quite certain we won't need that long," Doctor Leonard said. "This will either work or it won't. I took the liberty of sending the probe out earlier today. A second probe will monitor this side for us. We can signal it whenever you're ready."

Kelsey linked her implants to *Invincible*'s scanners. The weak flip point was only fifteen light minutes away. She saw the system layout in her mind and noted the delayed readings from the probes.

She had been working hard over the last few months and had mastered the basic operation of her Raider implants. She could now process data as quickly as it came in. Using the processors in her head to spin off tasks was becoming second nature. She'd even gotten used to the ghostly voice of Ned Quincy in her mind.

Mostly.

Thankfully, he didn't seem inclined to speak much unless she spoke to him first. Once she had time, she was going to have to figure out how to move him somewhere else, if they could figure out how. Perhaps he could be of use on *Persephone*, like Marcus was on *Invincible*. He wasn't nearly as complex, but he seemed to be a sentient AI.

"Send the go signal, Marcus," Jared said.

Kelsey felt the transmission leave the ship.

"Command sent, Admiral," the AI said. "It's programmed to make the trip and immediately return. We'll know in half an hour if it was successful."

She leaned up against Jared's console. "While we wait, I have a few things to run by you."

They talked about last-minute loading details until her implant timer indicated the probe would have made the transit and the data was about to arrive at their location. She could see Doctor Leonard was busy reading the full data stream from the probe staying in the

Harrison's World system, but it made no sense to her. It was focused on the flip point and too technical.

The first probe vanished... and reappeared a few seconds later. It immediately indicated it was in distress. The battle screen had failed, and many of the systems were offline.

"What the hell happened to it?" she asked. "Was it fired on?"

"I'm getting the scanner recording now," Marcus said. "I'm forwarding it to you."

The view from the probe was of deep space. It saw the weak flip point in its scanners. When the signal came across to flip, it did so.

Intense radiation bombarded it from every angle on the other side. The battle screen held up almost as long as it took the flip drive to cycle and take the probe back to their side.

The view of the system beyond the flip point was indistinct. It was as though space was foggy.

"What the hell was that?" Jared asked.

"I believe I understand," Doctor Leonard said as he stepped up beside Jared's console. "The other system's sun has gone nova. The destination side is far too close to either a neutron star or perhaps even a black hole for the probes to survive more than a few moments."

Kelsey shook her head. "Well, that certainly explains why none of them came back. It means we're not going over there, either."

"Actually, that's not a given," Marcus said. "I've analyzed the strength of the radiation, and a ship's battle screens are capable of protecting it. Only the probe's lack of power caused its premature failure."

"Admiral, might I mention that this is an unprecedented opportunity to study such a phenomenon?" Doctor Leonard asked. "We have no records of anything like this in the Old Empire databases, and we might not be back this way again anytime soon. Might we use one of your ships for a few hours? Other than the natural dangers, the system probably doesn't pose any additional risk."

Her brother looked between the scientist and Kelsey. "Okay, but only if you make the trip on *Persephone*. Her scanners are more than capable of getting you the data you need. You only have half a day. We're leaving on schedule. I'm serious."

Kelsey was more than a bit surprised Jared was allowing her to go. He must be even more exhausted than he looked. Still, it sounded interesting.

"We can do that," she said. "Doctor, what are the chances you can detect other flip points in that system?"

"Slim, but not impossible," he ventured. "Weak flip points are out of the question. We'll be able to find the one linking to Harrison's World again because we know precisely where it is, but the chaotic environment there will overshadow any others.

"We can use the ship's scanners to locate gravimetric anomalies like planets and regular flip points, though. If they aren't too far away from us, that is."

She grinned. "Well then, what are we waiting for? We have a supernova to explore!"

2

"Is that thing safe?"

Carl Owlet looked over at Fleet Captain Aaron Black. "It should be. Why?"

"It could go right through you—and the wall behind you—if it malfunctions. You don't have Princess Kelsey's strength. Hell, I'm not even sure *that* would be enough if it went rogue."

The graduate student gave the Fleet officer a suitably unimpressed expression. "Don't be ridiculous, Captain. Everything will be perfectly fine."

"Famous last words," the other man said. "I'll just watch from behind this handy blast shield."

The two of them were down in one of the ranges used for testing weapons inside the Grant Research Facility. It had plenty of protection for observers and the labs around it. If it could handle plasma weapons, Carl thought it should be safe enough.

Probably.

He took a deep breath and tried to put the worries Black had raised out of his mind. Yes, he only had normal human strength. Well, maybe a little less. He was only seventeen and a bit on the scrawny side.

His latest creation sat on the table in front of him, looking like the prop from an old play. He'd taken some artistic license with it, admittedly. That old pre-Empire vid Kelsey had insisted he watch had influenced both his stylistic choices and some of the programming he'd designed for it.

As a weapon, it looked... short, but that was kind of the point. Thor's hammer was a unique sort of thing.

After she'd raved about the rather primitive special effects and acting in the vid, he'd sat bolt upright that night with the idea fully formed in his head. It was straightforward engineering using the newly discovered grav technology from the mobile weapon systems the AI had been using.

Since it had both power generation and grav capability all wrapped up in one package, the real challenge had been making a shell that could protect the controls and designing the programming to make it work.

That had taken four months of robbing his sleep cycle to solve. An hour or two stolen between working like a dog to get the new ships up and running. He couldn't complain, though. Everyone had put in the same amount of hard work, and it was about to pay off in a big way.

Captain Black had come into this project late. While Carl could design the parts, he wanted someone with experience in robust weapon systems to do the final construction.

The staff here had really come through. He'd never have thought of some of the things they included as a matter of course. Some of the design changes they suggested were brilliant. They had access to the highest technology of the Old Empire, and they'd been working with it their entire lives. He had a lot of work to do just to get into their league.

They'd created a custom shell for the hammer that was both a stunning replica of the weapon from the vid and virtually indestructible.

The Old Empire had been working with some very cutting-edge hull metals using partially collapsed matter. While nowhere in the same neighborhood as something like neutronium, it still weighed a wickedly large amount. Without the built-in grav generator, he'd never be able to pick the hammer up.

With the grav generator working to keep it stationary, not even a Marine Raider could move it if the wielder didn't want them to. That also fit with the myth behind the vid.

That left the control functions. A normal set of Fleet implants could only work within fifteen meters. That's why the Old Empire had used headsets to amplify them.

He'd solved that by learning how the headsets worked and building an additional transmitter they could add to an existing set of implants. Since it was going to go inside a person, he'd spent a great deal of time ironing the bugs out. It had to be perfect.

Then Captain Black's people had gone over every aspect of it and suggested a number of modifications. That only proved to Carl that he still needed a lot of polish, even though they were uniformly complimentary of his work, calling it groundbreaking.

Once he was done with this project, he'd submit the long-range communicator to Admiral Mertz. He'd already worked up a modification to add it to the basic implant set for future recipients. Those would give someone the range of a headset. They could even give it to people that already had implants with an outpatient procedure.

Still, that wasn't enough range to control the hammer in combat, so he'd created one with even more range for Princess Kelsey. Rather than present her with an untested device, he'd had Doctor Stone implant it inside himself. It was too large for the cranium, so it went behind his lungs. He'd figured it wouldn't interfere with anything there and Doctor Stone agreed.

The matching equipment in the hammer linked and communicated with the wielder via a channel so heavily encrypted that he doubted even he could hack it without his personal knowledge of the algorithms. Good luck to the outsider that wanted to tap in.

Avoiding jamming was ridiculously simple, in theory. The actual hardware and new scientific theory was a lot more complicated. The execution was fiendishly difficult, and he'd had to create an entirely new branch of science to make it work. Well, expand one that existed into something that was actually useful, rather. That had taken the last two months to get working.

Everyone knew about Einstein's pre-Imperial work. Pre-spaceflight, really. Specifically, spooky action at a distance. Quantum entanglement of photons so that changes in spin replicated on the linked pair without regard to distance or transmission time.

A curious scientific oddity. Nothing had ever been created that could successfully harness the effect in a meaningful way. He'd torn up the databases at the research facility and a few separate projects had smashed together in another dream. The work on that had been so intense that he'd once yelled at Doctor Leonard for interrupting him.

He'd been mortified later, but the older scientist had just beamed at him. He'd acted as though Carl had passed some kind of test.

Older people were weird.

The quantum validation unit worked in tandem with the long-range communicator. It used an expected sequence of photon spin changes to validate the commands. Someone might tap into the encrypted communications frequency, he supposed, but they wouldn't even be able to know there was a second signal required to validate any instructions.

It also kept the two units linked. The hammer and wielder would always know where the other was, within the range of the quantum unit. Whatever that ended up being.

Now that he'd brought it all together in this device, it was time to see if it actually worked. He'd test the range later.

Quantum theory said it was unlimited, but nature didn't behave that way. Even flip points had limits. There would be a maximum useful range. He just hoped it was enough to prove workable with Mjölnir.

He linked his implants to the hammer and hefted it. With the grav assist, it seemed light enough. It would collapse the table if he turned that off.

The target was a set of the Old Empire marine armor on a stand at the other end of the room. It looked imposing as hell. Part of him expected the hammer to bounce off, leaving him looking like an idiot.

"I'm ready," he said after taking a deep breath.

"The recorders are on," Black said. "You're clear to go. I have a med team standing by. Just in case."

"Thanks for the confidence booster," Carl said in the same dry voice he'd been practicing after hearing how good it sounded on Admiral Mertz.

The hammer had a strap to wrap around the wrist, but this wasn't the time to use it. He drew the weapon back and awkwardly threw it while designating the armor as its target. It left his hand and flew toward the armor at maximum speed.

In retrospect, that was a rookie mistake.

The hammer brought up its miniature battle screen, broke the sound barrier just in front of Carl, and blasted into the armor with the force of a speeding pinnace.

It blew through the chest of the armor as though it were tissue paper. The reinforced plascrete behind the target faired just as poorly. Carl had a clear view of the room next door as the hammer screamed around in a tight turn and howled back toward him, generating two more sonic booms right together as it reversed course.

The first blast had deafened him, even with the protection of his implants, and blown him into the wall. It thoughtfully slammed the table on top of him. He'd ended up sitting with his back to the wall as the hammer arrowed toward him like a freight train.

He had just a moment to get his hand up, and the hammer abruptly slowed, creating a fourth sonic boom that almost knocked him unconscious. The handle slapped into his hand as gently as one could ask for.

Carl lay there, stunned, staring at the hammer and at the devastation it had wreaked on the range and the surrounding labs.

He couldn't hear Captain Black shouting for the medical teams, but he saw them rushing in with their trauma gear and expressions that told him he looked pretty bad.

"I think I might need to tweak a few settings before I present it to Princess Kelsey," he said faintly as they surrounded him.

* * *

CROWN PRINCESS ELISE ORISON stood beside Admiral Walter Sanders on the bridge of His Majesty's battlecruiser *New Wales*. It was identical in every respect to Jared's old ship, *Courageous*, and it was all theirs.

There was still a lot to do in refitting her, but this ship represented more power than the rest of the Royal Pentagaran Navy combined.

She could see the pride in Walter's expression. He was very pleased with this as his new flagship. At least until Boxer Station completed basic repairs on the superdreadnought *Great Britain*.

"Well, Admiral," she said. "The time has come for me to say my goodbyes. You'll be on your way back to Pentagar shortly, so my cutter will take me to *Invincible*. I'm going to miss having you around."

The older man smiled. "Not so much, I'll wager, Your Highness. You want more time alone with Admiral Mertz, and I'm too much like a chaperone."

She grinned. "You've found me out. Well, it's not as though I've let that stop me so far. He and I *are* sharing quarters, you know."

"What a scandal that would be, if word ever leaked back home. The heir to the Pentagaran crown shacking up with some foreigner."

She cocked her head. "Shacking up? Have you been watching those old movies Kelsey favors again?"

"Every chance I get," he admitted. "Princess Kelsey says the twenty-first century was some kind of touchstone to the Old Empire. They supposedly enshrined it in a kind of collective consciousness.

"She attributed a Captain Jack Harkness in saying that was when everything changed. I suppose it's a reference to that being the last truly common sense of humanity before they went interstellar and forged their own societies. Perhaps that explains some of her madness for the era, and that of a number of other people.

"In any case, Jared is a fine man. I'd rather not see either of you hurt."

"Why should I hurt him?"

"You shouldn't," the old admiral said gruffly. "But, you need to keep in mind who you are. You'll inherit the Throne one day. He's a serving officer in a foreign navy. Do you have a future together?"

She'd been pondering that question for a while. She loved Jared, but her duty was clear. That wasn't going to be an easy decision to make. Give up her soulmate or her people. A stark choice indeed.

"We're both aware of what lies ahead of us," she said gravely. "I'm hopeful this trip will settle it for us."

She checked her internal chronometer. She'd never get used to the capabilities of her new implants. It had been nine months, and she still wondered how Kelsey did it.

"I need to be on my way. I promise I'll uphold the dignity of the Pentagaran people. Be safe, Admiral."

"Screw dignity, Elise. Do what's right for you, and damn anyone who lifts their nose."

"Now there's some advice I can surely follow," she said with a laugh.

* * *

MARINE MAJOR ANGELA ELLIS stared at the destruction with wide eyes. "One little guy did all this? The kid from the science department? Seriously?"

"You have no idea, Major," Fleet Captain Black said. "You're selling him short. Way short. My people tell me the work he did on this project is breathtaking."

She nodded as she walked over to look through the hole in the plascrete wall. It was three meters across. "So I see. Breathtakingly stupid and he wants to give this thing to Princess Kelsey. Not happening."

The Fleet officer smiled. "Even the commander of her personal protective detail might find that difficult to enforce."

Nine months ago, she'd commanded the destroyer *Ginnie Dare*'s marine complement. With the loss of her ship and far too many of her people, they'd assigned her to keep an eye on Princess Kelsey. Which was more of a challenge than it sometimes appeared. Even with a double squad of men and women working diligently to make it happen.

Such as when Kelsey took off through an unexplored weak flip point without summoning Angela back to the ship.

"What did this?" she asked, gesturing toward the shattered armor and ruptured wall.

He pointed to an innocuous hammer on the floor. It sat handle up, as though someone had just set it down.

"That. He threw it at the suit of marine armor you see scattered around the chamber. The recorders say the hammer broke the sound barrier less than five meters in front of him. It reached Mach 7 before it hit the armor. It was still accelerating. Don't ask me what its top speed is. I have no idea.

"It wrecked the lab on the other side of the wall with a double sonic boom when it reversed course. He ate a table and took another sonic boom when it decelerated on the way back. Even behind a blast shield, four sonic booms all on top of each other felt like being on hand for the apocalypse."

She bent down and grasped the handle. The hammer didn't even twitch. Not even when she put her back into it.

"Jesus. How much does this thing weigh?"

"Somewhere in the ballpark of three tons. Imagine that with the full power of a grav generator pushing it to that kind of speed."

She tried and failed. "That makes the anti-vehicle weapons we have look like a kid's popgun. Even the new plasma ones."

Black righted the table and sat on its corner. "My chief of weapons design locked himself in his office right after Carl wrecked his lab. He has this idea for a new set of implant-controlled ground assault weapons. Something with 'real heft,' he said."

"Jesus." She ran her hand through her hair. "This kid is a menace. Why haven't your people made something like this before?"

"Because we didn't put everything together. Even if we had, we couldn't have solved the communications issues. Mister Owlet came up with the theories needed for these breakthroughs in days, though it took months to create working prototypes. You call him a kid, but that's not what I see when I look at him."

She sat down beside the Fleet officer. "What do you see?"

"You can never tell him this, but he's the kind of man who redefines the course of entire civilizations. Like Einstein on old Terra. The man was such a giant that his shadow still falls across us today.

People might mention him and Carl Owlet in the same breath one day, too. Assuming, of course, that he doesn't kill himself before then."

Angela felt an expression of disbelief steal onto her face. "You're kidding me. I've met the kid. He's not all that."

"Forgive my saying so, but you couldn't be more wrong if you tried, Major." His voice had gone hard. She felt her spine reflexively straighten. When a Fleet captain used that tone, you'd screwed up big-time.

Black waved his hand, dissipating the cloud of tension. "Sorry. I just don't think you can see the forest for the trees. I work with geniuses every day. Everything from the quiet, brilliant men and women to the screaming and shouting prima donnas that throw things when they don't get their way. That kid is brighter than all of them.

"The best minds in this research facility simultaneously worship and hate him. Once he gains the experience of age, I expect he'll probe the very secrets of the universe. With medical nanites pushing our lifespans to centuries, the mind boggles."

She shook her head. "We *can't* be talking about the same person. He's not old enough to drink. Hell, he couldn't get a date if he tried."

The Fleet captain smiled. "I expect that will change with time. Meanwhile, we're going to rebuild this room with a lot more protection. I imagine he'll also put some more stringent limits into the hammer when the medics release him."

"What's his condition?"

"Shattered eardrums and a concussion. A few scrapes and bruises. He got off light. We both did."

She felt her lips tighten. "He won't feel that way once I get ahold of him. If he thinks he's giving that damned hammer to the princess, he's got another think coming."

Black laughed. "Good luck with that. The boy has spine."

3

K elsey guided *Persephone* deeper into the radiation-filled void of the new star system with a hint of disappointment. She'd expected there to be more excitement running around the remnants of a supernova.

Instead, she could barely see anything. The intense radiation made a hash of scanner readings in a ridiculously short distance.

That wasn't stopping Doctor Leonard from chortling over whatever it was he was seeing.

She'd tried sampling the data feed, but didn't have the background to understand it.

"Captain," Lieutenant Jack Thompson said, turning away from the helm console. "I think we're closing in on a large planet. The ship is veering slightly off course."

She leaned forward and looked through the ship's scanners. Other than seeing the course deviation, she wasn't getting anything. Not even on optical. Frankly, they weren't really even sure of how close they were to whatever was left of the sun.

Kelsey frowned and did some comparisons in her head. "I'm not sure it's a planet. That might be the star remnant or the black hole.

We should try to triangulate it. Take us on a divergent course, and tell me how far away that thing is."

"Aye, ma'am."

She returned her attention to Doctor Leonard. "Can you give me an update? We might have found the central body in this system."

He looked up from his borrowed console, blinking owlishly. "What? Of course you have. I spotted it five minutes ago."

Kelsey restrained her initial response. "Don't you think you should share little details like that, Doctor? We're flying blind here."

"Ah. Forgive me. The gravity pull you're seeing is coming from the central object in the system. A black hole, I suspect, based on the type of radiation we're seeing and the amount of stellar matter we're flying through."

"Why so?"

"If the sun were still intact, its solar wind would've pushed all these energetic particles clear. We'd see a starkly bright object where the sun once was. A star without its mantle of gas would be unmistakable.

"Since we're not seeing anything like that, it must be because the solar mass collapsed into a black hole and it's drawing the remaining stellar matter inward without the corresponding push of the solar wind."

That made her sit up. "We're not in danger of falling into it, are we?"

"Oh, no. We're still quite distant. The space around it will clear to some degree as we get closer. We won't see it optically, of course, but we should have an unparalleled view of the event horizon. Which we also won't see directly."

"You make it all sound so exciting. We should have Christmas cards made."

Doctor Leonard smiled. "That's clever. Indeed, we should. What we *will* see shortly is the accretion disk. It's spinning around the black hole and generating the radiation ahead of us. I imagine it will be quite spectacular."

He returned to his data, and she had the ship move back into a course that would take them closer to the black hole. Slowly.

Space cleared until they could see the vast emptiness that was the central system. The titanic blast had vaporized the inner planets, leaving only husks to circle what might have once been a life-giving star.

The charged particles hid any gas giants in the outer system from view. The nova would have stripped them of their atmospheres, but their cores should be mostly intact. She imagined they would be very educational to the scientists.

In the place of honor was a spinning disk of glowing dust. It was very beautiful, and quite deadly, if the radiation levels were to be believed. As they grew closer, those kept going up. At some point, the radiation would be a threat even with their battle screens.

"That's it," Doctor Leonard said. "The black hole at the center of the system." He turned to face her. "It's so powerful that even light cannot escape its clutches. The ultimate prison. Well, technically, the matter inside eventually evaporates, but I'll stand with my analogy."

"If we can't get close, how are you going to get more data?"

"I believe we can get excellent readings from a safe distance. We'll have to devise dedicated probes the size of cutters to get into close ranges, but that won't be happening anytime soon. Rest assured, though, what I get here will revolutionize our understanding of black holes."

"Captain, what's that?"

She returned her attention to the helmsman. "What?"

He highlighted part of the scanner readings. It was some kind of debris orbiting around the black hole. "An asteroid? Something blown off a planet?"

"No," Doctor Leonard said after a moment studying his console. "Lieutenant Thompson is quite correct. The orbit is unusually stable for such a small object near the mass of a black hole."

Kelsey made some measurements. She'd really rather not get that close, but they could get nearer to the object and determine exactly what it was in relative safety.

"Take us in," she ordered, "but only until we get better readings."

"Aye, ma'am."

He took *Persephone* in closer. It took almost an hour before they were seeing details optically. The object wasn't as irregular as she'd expected. In fact, it was far too regular to be natural.

"That's artificial," she said. "Nature abhors consistent lines like those."

Leonard frowned. "Who would put something out here? How could they? Is it another Old Empire relic?"

Kelsey shrugged. "I have no idea, but we're going in for a close look. If this is something we need to explore before we head home, I want to take as much data back to Jared as I can. Get me the cleanest scanner readings you can, Doctor."

He nodded and bent back over his console.

This little adventure was showing signs of adventure after all. Hopefully, without the kind of destruction that usually meant for everything around her.

* * *

MAJOR RUSS TALBOT looked up from his console when someone knocked. Angela Ellis stood outside his office aboard *Invincible*. He gestured for her to come in.

"I thought you were down on Harrison's World, Major. What brings you here?"

Nine months ago, he'd been a senior sergeant and Angela had been a lieutenant, the same rank as his now-dead boss.

Kelsey had waved her magic finger—yes, that one—and made him a major. He hoped to God that someone didn't convince her to make him a damned colonel before they got home. His career was already screwed to hell.

If the recent changes in their rank bothered her, she didn't allow it to show. "I've got a big problem, Russ. Carl Owlet."

The marine grinned and leaned back in his chair. "Your idea of big differs from mine. I'm not sure he even shaves regularly. He hitting on you?"

"What? No. No! He's doing something much worse. Look at this."

She sent him a vid through his implants that made him sit up abruptly at the destruction.

"Holy cow!" he muttered. "Is he okay?"

"I'm told he'll make a full recovery, but he built that damned thing for Princess Kelsey."

"Ah. All becomes clear. You're worried he's trying to kill your principal."

She sighed and sat abruptly in one of the chairs. "No, not really. He's just not thinking, and I'm worried about what something like this would mean for the princess. What if he makes it more dangerous?"

"I've known Carl for over a year. He's damned bright. Perhaps not as grounded in common sense as I'd like, but not a menace. You're not giving Kelsey enough credit. She doesn't usually grab the biggest weapon handy to smash a problem."

Not recently, anyway.

"So I should just let him give her that thing? It can blow holes in this ship."

He smiled a little. "I understand you want to keep Kelsey safe, but you can't just shoot everyone who might give her something dangerous. For Christ's sake, she routinely wears powered armor and has an arsenal in our closet."

It was common knowledge that he shared Kelsey's palatial quarters and her bed. He'd overseen the installation of the armory. It had everything from two spare sets of armor—one Marine Raider and the other an upgraded general marine assault suit—to an array of every weapon they'd found to date.

If their commander had been anyone other than Jared Mertz, he'd have had a coronary.

At some point, she'd end up moving to *Persephone*. The captain's quarters there were significantly smaller. He had no idea where she'd put her toys. Maybe they could rip out the adjoining cabin and provide the two of them some extra space. If, of course, his duty didn't take him elsewhere.

"Look," he said after a moment. "Talk with her about it. She'll listen to your concerns."

"Yeah," Angela said glumly. "She'll listen and then do whatever she likes."

"Welcome to the Imperial Guard in everything but name. Thank God it isn't me keeping her from doing crazy stuff now."

Angela sighed. "The universe hates me."

* * *

JARED WALKED into *Invincible*'s briefing room and nodded to the various officers and scientists gathered there. It was early in the morning, and most of them looked a bit out of sorts.

"Good morning, everyone. There's coffee and a buffet against the wall. Please indulge yourselves."

He suited words to deeds and filled a plate. If this turned into anything like some of Kelsey's other discoveries, it might be hard to find time for food later.

Kelsey had an even larger plate than his, but didn't look nearly as discomfited by putting all the food away as she once had. His sister was adjusting to her new condition.

"I told you not to do anything to wreck my schedule," he growled as he sat beside her.

She smiled. "I didn't put that thing there. It's not my fault."

Once everyone had taken their seats, he nodded toward his sister. "Tell us what you found."

The screen came to life. An image of a large space station showed against a bright swirl of dust. It was difficult to make out the surface details, but it was undoubtedly artificial.

"We found this station orbiting the black hole in the other system," Kelsey said. "Due to its proximity to the event horizon, we were unable to approach as closely as I'd have liked. *Persephone* told me our drives and screens were up to the task, but it would put us at almost ninety percent of capacity. I decided that was cutting it a little too close."

Jared nodded. "Good call. We don't want a failure to send you falling into a black hole. Your father's already going to kill me for everything you've been through."

The people gathered around the table rumbled with laughter.

Even Kelsey. They'd achieved enough distance from the events to see the humor in something like that now.

"That's what I was thinking, too," she said. "So, while we couldn't get close, we did creep up enough for the scanners to get some data. The layout is nothing like what we've found in any of the Old Empire databases. With Doctor Leonard's concurrence, I'm declaring this as probably nonhuman in origin."

That set off a murmur around the table.

"Wait," Jared said. "You mean as in alien? Not just one of the other human polities that existed back then? The Old Empire never found any evidence of sentient alien life."

"I submit that we just did," she said seriously. "We attempted to communicate with it, but the station didn't respond. It may be that our methods are so different that it didn't recognize our message. It's also possible it isn't completely functional. In that environment, I wouldn't be surprised."

Doctor Leonard cleared his throat. "The design elements of this station are markedly different than what we've seen before, Admiral. Rather than a sphere, this is more like a massive ring with the center aligned toward the black hole. That means very little in and of itself, but combined with its survival in the most hostile environment imaginable and its lack of battle screens, that has to mean something."

Jared considered that. "Kelsey thinks the station's protection might have failed. Perhaps it once had screens."

The older man shook his head. "The orbit is far too precise for it to be a derelict. If it were being flooded with radiation, the drives that kept it in place would have also failed. It's protected by something we're unfamiliar with."

"We'll have to send a ship in more closely to find out," Kelsey said. "That decision falls to you, Admiral. Do we look now or let others follow up at a later date?"

"I can send a few ships in to take a closer look after you head out," Commodore Sean Meyer offered.

The man had recovered from the injuries he'd sustained nine months ago and settled into commanding Boxer Station with more ease than Jared had expected. His cadre of officers from the wrecked heavy cruiser *Spear* was working out better than Jared had hoped.

"I could even task my exec with that," Meyer said with a grin toward Captain Paul Cooley. The man's injuries had been far worse than Sean's, and he was only now getting used to the artificial legs the doctors on Harrison's World had built for him.

The emotional damage from losing his ship and many of his crew would take far longer to heal.

Cooley nodded. "I can take some ships in to check it out."

Jared shook his head. "We should look before we head back for home. I'll leave the follow-up exploration to you two, though."

He leaned back for a moment and thought about it. "I'll take every ship in my fleet through. We'll search the system thoroughly and get as many readings as we can. Then we'll head for home."

"That's a little bit of overkill, don't you think?" Kelsey asked dryly.

"I want to know if there are other flip points there and where they let out. Nothing in the Old Empire records indicates a system like this one, and I doubt it went nova in the last five hundred years. The aliens that built that station came from somewhere. I'd like to have an idea of where that might be."

He checked the time. "Everyone, head back to your ships after you download the data Princess Kelsey brought back for us. We'll move into the Nova system in half an hour. And that's a capital Nova, as in the new official name."

Kelsey waited for the others to start leaving before she spoke. "I honestly didn't mean to delay our departure."

He smiled. "As if I were going to go home without as much information about a potential alien species as possible. This won't take long."

Jared hoped it actually worked out that way for once. It would be a refreshing change of pace.

* * *

CARL ARRIVED BACK on the science ship *Pallas* just in time to avoid any awkward questions. He'd brought the hammer with him, safely tucked away in his gear with the grav drive making it almost weightless.

He'd spend some time reevaluating the settings before he presented it to Princess Kelsey. Thankfully, she wouldn't need it anytime soon. They wouldn't be fighting hostile AIs or Pale Ones on this adventure.

He hurried into the lab and dropped his bag on the table.

Doctor Leonard frowned at him. "What's wrong with your ears?"

Carl reached up to touch the sterile cotton sticking out from his ears. "Just a little accident. The doctor down there said I should keep these in until the nanites do some catch up work."

In actuality, the doctor had blistered Carl's damaged ears for his carelessness. She'd regenerated his eardrums in the base medical center, but told him that he was in danger of infection, even with his nanites. She'd also told him he was an idiot several times.

He pretty much agreed with everything she said. He'd really screwed up.

Doctor Leonard gave him a look that said he was less than convinced, but he allowed the explanation to stand. "You made it back in the nick of time. We're heading through the weak flip point to explore the Nova system. That's what Admiral Mertz named it. We've found something very exciting there."

His mentor sent him the data through his implants. It only took Carl a moment to realize what he was looking at. "Aliens?"

"Possibly," Doctor Leonard allowed. "We'll take point on making that determination. Are you able to wear a pressure suit?"

"Of course!"

He had no idea if that was true, but he wasn't going to miss this opportunity.

4

Angela found Kelsey Bandar in her office. Admiral Mertz had decided his sister needed one, and it wasn't as if there wasn't room on the superdreadnought. Someone had decorated it with furnishings from Pentagar, Harrison's World, and Erorsi. It looked nice.

There were some odd additions she suspected came from somewhere in the Old Empire. No doubt salvaged from the graveyard. That was a little creepy, but Angela supposed that might just be her.

The princess smiled at her. "Angela! We found aliens. Isn't that exciting?"

"I suppose," the marine admitted. "Though I'd have liked it better if you'd kept me in the loop."

"Somehow, I knew that was going to be your takeaway from this," Kelsey said wryly. "I was on a Marine Raider ship. What additional safety could you have provided?"

"If aliens had boarded you, I could've kept shooting them till I went down."

Angela knew that sounded ridiculous, but she couldn't help it. Kelsey thought her guards were an inconvenience to someone built to be one of the deadliest fighters in the Old Empire. She didn't say that, but Angela knew that's what she was thinking.

Her boss sighed a bit theatrically and gestured for Angela to sit. "I'll try to remember. At least get comfortable while you rip my head off."

Angela took her up on the offer and sat in one of the comfortable chairs. Unlike the ones in Major Talbot's office, these actually encouraged someone to stay awhile. She still sat in a posture of attention.

"I'm not going to belabor the obvious, Your Highness," she said, "but it's true. Your protective detail is here for a reason. Even if it doesn't make much sense to you. Besides, you made a deal."

When Angela agreed to enter the princess's service as guard commander, she'd extracted a few promises from the woman. Within the basic parameters of Kelsey's activities, the guards would be low-key.

They trusted that the princess was relatively safe on *Invincible* or one of the other Fleet warships. But she was still supposed to inform Angela of where she was and what she was up to.

Looks could be so deceiving. Kelsey was half a meter shorter than Angela and so damned slender that the marine imagined she could break the tiny woman in two without much effort. The reverse was true, as one bout in marine country had decisively proven.

If they ever gained access to the materials to make more Marine Raiders, Angela was going to be the first person in line. That was the other promise Kelsey had made.

"I'm sorry," the smaller woman said, looking a little contrite. "I got caught up in the moment. I'll do my best not to forget again. I promise."

After a moment, Angela nodded. "I appreciate that, Your Highness. In any case, that isn't the reason I'm here to see you. It's actually a completely different kind of security issue."

Kelsey folded her fingers on her desk and gave Angela her complete attention. "Tell me. What threat to life and limb is next on your hit parade of value?"

Angela shook her head. "Where do you get those sayings? Never mind. I don't want to know. This time, it's Carl Owlet."

The princess blinked. She opened her mouth and then closed it again. Finally, she spoke with a bit of a smile playing about the corners of her lips. "If I had to rank my friends as threatening, he'd be buried somewhere in a footnote. How could that young man possibly threaten me? Or anyone? He's a scientist."

"With science," she said firmly. "Or rather, what he builds using it. He's working on something he intends to give you, and it's dangerous."

Kelsey rubbed her hands together like a little kid. "Oooooo! I like presents! What is it? And how is it dangerous? You can tell me. I'll still act surprised."

"You're going to be the death of me yet," Angela said glumly. "Let me put this into perspective. He destroyed a weapons range down on Harrison's World and almost killed himself with it."

That wiped the gleeful expression right off Kelsey's face. "Oh my God! Is he okay?" She surged to her feet. "We're going to see him right now. Why didn't someone tell me he was hurt?"

Angela kept her seat. "He only caught a few minor injuries. He's already back at work on *Pallas*, but that's only because he got lucky. Damned lucky. His creation could very easily have killed him and dozens of other people in the area. I don't want you accepting that gift."

She probably shouldn't have phrased it so bluntly. She realized that as soon as she'd said it.

Kelsey's eyes narrowed. "That's a strong statement. I'll consider it when *I* make *my* decision on the matter. Now, enough dancing around. What the hell is this weapon?"

"Something he calls Project Mjölnir."

The princess's eyes widened. "Seriously? Like Thor's hammer?"

"It is a hammer. I have no idea about it belonging to someone else. It's based on a vid."

"Which is based on an ancient myth from pre-Empire Terra. Hell, before modern technology. And he destroyed a lab with it? What happened?"

Angela sent Kelsey the vid she'd uploaded to her implants.

The princess frowned as she watched it in her head and then twitched violently. "Holy shit! That thing just vaporized a set of marine armor and the wall behind it. I couldn't even do that with a plasma rifle. Oh, it really messed him up. He should've been in armor."

"That isn't the right takeaway from this fiasco," Angela said repressively. "He was incredibly reckless, and that weapon is far too dangerous for you to use."

Kelsey shrugged. "I thought the same thing about my implants before I learned to control them. Practice and refining the skills needed are key. Come on. We're going to pay him a visit and let him explain this for himself."

She took one step toward the hatch and stopped. "You aren't to tear into him about this. I'll handle that. You've delivered your warning and I've heard it. I'll decide how to chastise him about this. Clear?"

Angela sighed inside where it was safe. "Of course, Your Highness."

This wasn't going to work out well at all. The little blonde maniac would take the weapon and gleefully put herself in the medical center. Angela just knew it.

* * *

CARL WENT over everything Doctor Leonard had recorded about the alien station with a fine-toothed comb. The interference of the radiation combined with the distance of the ship from the object made the small details difficult to make out, but he had a good general feeling for it.

It was somewhat larger than Boxer Station, but a lot of that area was empty space in the center of the ring. The structure itself was a mighty circle. He couldn't tell, but there were probably instruments on the interior of the ring.

The station was at least several decks thick but looked fragile because of the empty space. It wasn't rotating, so the purpose wasn't to generate artificial gravity. Frankly, he was at a loss as to what it really did.

The most obvious guess was that it was there to study the black hole. Certainly, the Empire would want to do the same thing. The opportunity was unprecedented.

That still didn't explain who had built the station. It didn't look Imperial, but there had been other human polities before the Fall. He wasn't quite ready to jump on the "aliens" bandwagon.

Humanity had never found a single example of nonhuman sentience. Not even the remains of a long-dead civilization. Nothing.

Well, arguably the AIs were sentient nonhumans. He should be more precise.

Yet, this station wasn't using battle screens to filter out the deadly radiation. In that environment, it would quickly fry an unprotected Imperial facility, so there must be something there shielding it.

Or, perhaps not. Maybe the screens had failed long ago and the station was a dead hulk. They wouldn't know until they got a chance to examine it more closely.

The hatch to his lab slid open, and Princess Kelsey walked in. Her guard dog was at her heels.

Perhaps that was being too harsh, but he'd never seen Major Ellis smile. Of course, perhaps having her ship shot out from under her had something to do with that.

In any case, he wasn't really a fan.

Kelsey came over to him. "I heard you got hurt, and I wanted to see you for myself. Why do you have cotton balls in your ears?"

He tried to give a nonchalant shrug. "Just a problem testing something out. The docs fixed me up and put those in to help speed the healing."

She gave him a stern look. "You should know me better than that. I want the real story, and I want you to trot it out right now, young man."

He sighed. He should've known this wasn't going to be easy.

"It's a surprise."

"Congratulations. I'm surprised. Now, let's have some details."

He shot a look at Major Ellis. The woman had obviously tattled on him. His opinion of her plummeted.

"I'm not sure what you heard," he said as he walked over to his desk, "but I'll wager some important details were left out."

He pulled the hammer out of his pack and handed it to her. "This is Mjölnir."

She hefted it with a frown. "It's kind of light. After watching that vid, I expected something with a bit more heft."

So, she'd already seen the vid. He considered turning off the grav support, but that might cause an injury. He'd already done enough to give her the wrong opinion about this.

"Set it down, please."

She placed it on the deck and he stopped the miniature grav drive from neutralizing the weight. "Try it now."

Kelsey went to pick it up and her eyes widened in surprise. "Wow. Okay, that is heavy."

She lifted it, but he imagined it had taken a significant percentage of her Marine Raider artificial muscles to do it.

"The shell is made of partially collapsed matter," he said. "It weighs about three tons, and that's not all. Set it back down."

Once she did, he engaged the grav drive to resist motion. It didn't precisely make the hammer weigh more, but it added resistance to movement. If someone tried to lift it, it quickly adjusted the drive to counteract that pressure. It could stop a dozen Marine Raiders acting in concert but still not damage the floor.

When combined with the neutral buoyancy function he'd worked out, it wasn't dangerous to set it on a glass table and yet still prevent others from moving it. One of his more clever ideas, he thought.

This time Kelsey couldn't budge it.

She stood and shook her head. "I suppose I'm not worthy. Impressive."

"You *could* be worthy, with the right additions to your implants."

Kelsey nodded. "You can tell me all about it, but I want to make something particularly clear first. You're my friend, and we've been through so much together. I don't want to see you hurt yourself. That vid was scary and you were lucky."

He deflated a bit at that. "Things didn't quite go as planned. I didn't anticipate how abruptly the hammer could change speed. To be honest, I didn't realize the destructive scope of a grav drive pushing it like that. My simulations were flawed. I've corrected that and will add in safeguards to prevent something like that from happening again."

"Sit down," Kelsey said.

He sat on his roller chair and she took a handy stool. Now came the ass chewing.

"I'm honored and grateful that you thought I'd like this. The idea of this in my arsenal is exceptionally cool. That said, you don't understand how the mind of a warrior works. And, contrary to some opinions, that's what I am."

He wondered who she was talking about. Everyone knew she was a badass.

"You need to do more testing," she continued, "but that kind of capability might save my life one day. If I had someone in marine armor shooting at me, I'd do exactly what you did. Boom. Problem solved. Sometimes, you have to blow shit up.

"Still, you're not a warrior. You're more like that guy Q in the Bond movies. You come up with all the cool toys."

He felt his lips quirk at her cursing. It still seemed so out of place. Talbot was rubbing off on her.

"I thought Batman had the cool toys."

"Don't quibble," she said with a smile of her own. "Both of them can have cool toys. Now, I want you to explain the capabilities of this hammer to me."

"Well, it can obviously power through heavy armor and thick walls with ease. It's a combination of the partially collapsed matter shielding it, a miniaturized battle screen, and the grav drive."

Kelsey blinked. "Battle screens don't work in atmosphere. Besides, the equipment to project one takes up a lot of room."

He nodded. "For a full-strength one, yes. This one is somewhat lightweight in the protection department. It doesn't need to shield you from a ship's missile. Flechettes and plasma are more in line with the threats I envisioned you facing."

"Captain Black didn't mention anything about a battle screen," Major Ellis said with a frown.

"It was a last-minute addition," he admitted. "I didn't think I'd be able to make the hardware small enough, but I had a last-minute breakthrough. It's very short range. Just a couple of meters, at most."

Kelsey seemed impressed. "Is it only good in a single direction, or is it omnidirectional?"

"Single direction only. The smaller the coverage area, the stronger the protection. That's what made the hole in the plascrete. I wanted it to be useful against threats as well as in flight."

The princess cocked her head. "Flight?"

"Sure. The grav drive is pretty powerful. See the strap? It can secure around your wrist and pull you along. Not like dragging you, because the grav drive affects you, too. It's more a way to keep you inside the field. You and your armor will slow it down, but not that much, I'd imagine."

She sat back. "I could fly. Now *that* is cool. We'll come back to that. Could you add this to marine armor? Or to my Raider suit?"

He nodded. "Sure. It would take me a while to design something to fit into an appropriate place inside the armor. Space is somewhat at a premium. It would drain the power cells fast, though.

"It would be better if the suits were redesigned to use the grav/fusion power packs. It would also give them new capabilities similar to yours."

That last didn't exactly make him happy. He'd wanted to give her something unique.

Still, anything that kept the marines alive was a good thing. Part of his mind was already starting to work over how he could do that.

Kelsey snapped her fingers. "Hello in there."

He came back to reality. "Sorry. I was thinking about how I could make that happen."

"You've got the entire trip home to work that out. Back to the hammer. So, it would really allow me to fly? How fast?"

"I've never really opened it up. With the extra load a person adds, I suspect somewhere around Mach 15."

She looked stunned. "Are you pulling my leg? That's insane."

Major Ellis looked like she shared that opinion. Only she wasn't so happy about it.

"That's incredibly irresponsible," the marine said. "That could kill an unprotected person."

"Angela," Kelsey warned.

"I'm sorry, Highness, but that's madness. Not even you could survive a crash at that speed, armored or not. You're tough, not invincible."

The marine focused her attention on Carl. He shrank back a little at her intense expression. "Princess Kelsey told me I had to let her do the ass chewing, but I'm putting you on notice. If your antics hurt her, I'll hurt you. Am I clear?"

"Angela!" Kelsey said as she surged to her feet. "I think you've said enough. Perhaps you should wait for me on my pinnace."

The marine gave him one last, hard look before she bowed her head toward Kelsey. "Perhaps I should, Highness. My apologies to you."

The large woman stalked to the hatch and spoke briefly with the marine there before she left.

Carl noticed that she hadn't taken back any of what she'd said. If something went wrong, the woman could break him in half.

Kelsey sighed and resumed her seat. "I'm sorry about that. She's a bit overprotective. She means well."

"I don't disagree with anything she said." He rubbed his face. "I don't usually build things that have the potential to kill. Not so easily, anyhow. I need to keep that fact firmly in mind."

He'd test this hammer to levels that combat equipment would envy. He'd die before he allowed it to hurt his friend.

"As for the flying," he said, "the grav drive and battle screen keep you protected. I'll obviously need to test it very, *very* thoroughly before there are human trials.

"A collision would hurt, but the battle screen would absorb most of the kinetic energy and deflect all the debris away from you. You could fly through a pinnace, but I'd recommend you wear armor. Something still might bounce back. If you somehow became separated from the hammer, it will come back by the shortest route unless you've ordered it elsewhere."

She nodded slowly. "How could I do that? My implants have the same fifteen-meter limit as everyone else's. The armor boosts it to several hundred, but that's pretty short for something like this."

"I designed and built an extended range communications implant. I've tested it out to ten kilometers. The hammer has the same range, but can track the user from even further away."

"Like with a beacon?" she asked. "That's a bad thing in combat. You don't want your enemies to be able to track you."

"Actually, it's nothing like a beacon. It uses aspects of quantum mechanics to track the wielder. There are no detectable signals at all. In any case, I had Doctor Stone put the matching unit inside me. It works great at the ranges I've tried. I'll narrow down the maximum useful range before I turn the final version over to you."

He held up his hand and the hammer flew from the table into it with a slight singing sound. "Just like in the vids."

"Whosoever holds this hammer, if he be worthy, shall possess the power of Thor," she said. "Or, I suppose 'she,' if this was intended for me."

"It seemed easier to go gender neutral," he said. "Unlike a magic hammer, I can't change the inscription on a whim. So, I went with 'they.' It seemed simpler."

"You even put the inscription on it? Damned impressive, Carl. Damned impressive. Still, you're going to need to convince a very skeptical audience before I try it."

Carl set the hammer down beside him. "Whatever it takes."

She smiled. "I'm glad you're being so understanding. I want you to work with Major Ellis. She's going to vet every aspect of this hammer before I accept it."

He felt his mouth drop open. "Seriously? The woman hates me. You'll never get it if that's the bar I have to meet."

Kelsey stood, her expression sympathetic. "I understand, but that's the way it is. I'm fairly certain she doesn't actually hate you. She'd give her life to protect me, and I won't dismiss her concerns. Even when expressed in such an abrupt manner. Sometimes you have to overcome tremendous obstacles to get what you want."

"She's not an obstacle, she's a mountain. With wild animals ready to rip me apart."

She headed for the door. "I'll be rooting for you. As I said, I'd really like to have something like Mjölnir. I hope you can make that happen. Good luck."

Carl sat there long after she'd left, trying to imagine how he could please the impossible woman. No scenario he envisioned worked.

He was doomed.

5

Elise sat up when Doctor Lily Stone lifted the headset off her temples. "Everything good?"

Stone nodded. "The update went smoothly, and the hardware replacement checks out, too. Congratulations, Your Highness. You're no longer hackable by the Pale Ones or the Rebel Empire AIs."

She hopped off the examination table. "I can't begin to tell you how good that makes me feel, Doctor. My people have a cultural fear of forced reprogramming that you newcomers just don't understand. Being immune to having these implants suborned is a huge relief to me."

"I saw what those things put Kelsey through, and the poor bastards on Erorsi. They'll need modifications, too."

"Won't that be fun?"

Elise could hardly imagine how difficult it was going to be to track down every single Pale One on Erorsi. Especially now that the planet was going through such a brutal and semi-permanent winter. The asteroid impact had thrown enough debris into the atmosphere to obscure the sun, and living was tough.

Current estimates put the timeframe before the weather patterns returned to some semblance of normal at fifteen to twenty years. Even then, the long cold streak was going to alter things permanently. Many species were going to die. The biosphere was going to change, and not for the better.

At least they didn't have to obey the mad AI anymore.

Perhaps that was how they'd get them fixed. They could use the equipment the AI had used to control the Pale Ones to summon them to a central area and sedate them. Part of her cringed at forcing them to obey, but this would be the last time. Then they'd be free forever.

"Could you explain again what changed in the hardware?" she asked as Stone walked her to the door.

"Certainly. We replaced the central node in your implants with a new model designed by the folks at the Grant Research Facility. This one is not subject to external overwriting without the person's consent and active cooperation, and it includes a number of improvements thanks to other research they've done over the centuries. They tell me the performance is even faster, but it already seems like lightning to me.

"The core kernel's programming is now hardwired. A sentry subroutine will monitor the implants for aberrant behavior and overwrite any new code. Or if the user tells it to."

"That's reassuring. So, no more people under the control of their hardware?"

Stone nodded. "Precisely. Kelsey still has what she calls combat mode, but that's not *quite* the same thing. Her implants control her body in combat, but she's always in the driver's seat.

"Also, Carl Owlet put a nasty surprise in there for anyone that tries to overwrite the implant code. Your implants will hack a rogue unit that attacks you, taking control of it instead. I don't know the details, but I understand the program is wickedly subtle. The AI won't even know what's happening until it's too late."

Elise grinned. "Payback is a bitch. I assume it won't work against a true AI."

"No," Stone said. "They're immune in much the same way you are. That's where Carl got the idea. On the plus side, those things are rare. The odds you'll ever run into one are pretty slim. Not counting Marcus and Harrison, of course."

"Why didn't the Old Empire do this? It seems so straightforward."

Stone shrugged. "We may never know for sure, but Kelsey thinks that critical people were killed by whoever was behind the rebellion. Carl says that the old implants have something that is supposed to allow only a restricted few to update the code. Something about private keys. Without them, the Old Empire was powerless.

"We captured those keys when we rescued Princess Kelsey. With them, we can easily update the old hardware. The people at Grant have come up with new keys, and we'll make sure that trusted people in many places have a way to get it, but not have it taken from them. I don't know the details and I'm happy with that."

Elise nodded. "We're sure they're secure?"

"They had Marcus try and hack someone. He failed. That works for me."

"Me, too." Elise shook Stone's hand. "Thank you, Doctor. When will everyone have this update?"

"We're focusing on your people now. The change is quick, and your doctors can handle the process now that we've trained them. I figure all of the people in the task force heading to Pentagar will be done before they get home.

"Commodore Meyer will have his people done in about the same timeframe. Then he'll assist Coordinator West in getting Harrison's World done."

Elise felt the corner of her mouth quirk up. "Those two have been working together pretty closely these last few months. I think their relationship might be changing from a purely professional one."

Stone raised an eyebrow. "You think? They seem pretty professional to me."

Elise waved her hand dismissively. "I have an eye for that kind of thing. He might not know it yet, but Coordinator West is interested in deepening their relationship. She's good at keeping her cards close to her vest."

Considering the woman had been running an underground movement for most of her life, conspiring against the AIs while infiltrating their puppet government, that was something of an understatement. Elise had played poker with her, Sean, Jared, Kelsey, and Talbot. That had been an eye-opening education. An expensive one, too.

The woman didn't have a single tell. Not one. Her bluffs were indistinguishable from the rest of her hands.

Kelsey was by far the best player Elise had ever met, and she was outclassed. Worse, Elise was almost certain that Olivia West had thrown a number of hands to play down her advantage, and she'd still trounced them all.

Elise had made a number of notes to improve her own skills in that arena. In fact, she'd gotten together with the coordinator several times and sat at the feet of the mistress. Those skills would serve her well as a stateswoman. Particularly now that she was on her way to the seat of the New Terran Empire.

Based on everything she'd heard, and some of the things she hadn't, there was going to be trouble. She'd need to work hard to turn that situation around before it bit them all in the behind.

"I'm not saying that her intent will necessarily mean anything," Elise added. "It takes two to dance, after all. It really depends on what Sean wants. What about the people in Jared's task force?"

Stone smiled. "We have a lot of people to work through, but we'll be done before we reach Avalon. Keep an eye on things over the next few days. I don't expect that you'll have any issues, but if you do, call me at once."

"I will. Thank you, Lily."

Elise made her way to the ship's library. With all the electronic books, most crewmembers never saw it, which was a shame. She'd found it amazing and fascinating, and that was before they'd put any books in it.

Just the idea that a modern warship would have a two-level room of that size dedicated to the printed page was astounding to her.

She'd lost no time sending a message home for books to fill it with. Word had spread to Coordinator West's friend and mentor, Lord William Hawthorne. He'd found many tomes to add to the haul.

Between the two of them, and the various finds in the graveyard, this library was now worthy of the name.

In fact, Lord Hawthorne was the one she was coming here to meet. She found him standing beside a tall shelf with an old book in his hand. He wasn't alone. Reginald Bell sat in a chair nearby, examining a portfolio of some kind.

"Gentlemen," she said as she came over. "Thank you for taking the time to meet with me."

William Hawthorne slid the book back onto the shelf and bent low at the waist. "Elise. It's a pleasure as always. May I say you look stunning?"

"Flatterer. No need to rise on my account, Reg. Your knees aren't as young as they used to be."

The older man gave up on standing and bowed his head. "Princess Elise. It's good to see you again. The trip here was a trifle more tiring than I'd imagined. Though these new nanites are helping some."

Kelsey had Doctor Leonard remove some of her Marine Raider nanites and examine them. The little machines were markedly more advanced than the ones given to regular Fleet personnel, but the scientists could reprogram them to work in others.

They'd need periodic replacement, but they might keep the old gentleman with them a few more decades. He had so much to tell them and so little time left to do it. They could harvest enough Raider nanites from her for that.

Reginald Bell was the only person alive who'd seen the Empire before the Fall. Even his ancient appearance belied his true age. The Terran Empire had gone down fighting more than five centuries ago. That was far longer than even Fleet nanites could extend someone's age.

And that was a blessing. The poor people the AIs had enslaved during the Fall were all dead. God rest their souls.

He'd spent more than two centuries in a stasis unit. Generations of men and women had watched over him as they were born, grew old, and finally passed on. They'd done so solely in the hope that, one day, his intimate knowledge of the Old Empire would once more prove valuable.

Now that Jared and Kelsey had freed Erorsi from the thrall of the crazed AI, the people that had survived in the old planetary defense center could finally live their lives out in the open. Now they could save Reg's knowledge of the Old Empire.

That wasn't to say that he hadn't recorded a lot before he'd gone into stasis. Only, he hadn't known what those outside would lose over the years. He'd stuck to large events, but current day anthropologists and historians wanted to know the minutia of his life. He spent hours every day telling stories and answering questions.

He'd also decided to record his memories in the same way Ned had. It probably wouldn't result in an AI of him after his death, but it would save the only direct memories of the Old Empire they had left. Other than Ned, of course.

"We've just been amusing ourselves while we waited," William said. "Please, join us."

She sat in the chair he held for her and waited for him to sit. Then she launched into her semiprepared speech.

"I appreciate you both taking the time to meet with me. Marcus is also in attendance, though the subroutine is not going to report our conversation to his main memory unless we decide that's appropriate."

"What's the old saying?" Marcus asked from a speaker under the table. "Four people can keep a secret if two of them are dead and one is an AI that isn't talking to itself?"

"I'm fairly sure that's almost correct," William said with a smile. "This is all suitably mysterious. What, if I might ask, can we help you with?"

"Something very important," she said. "Jared is going to need our assistance when he gets home. Crown Prince Ethan Bandar has a very real and very deadly grudge against him."

She leaned forward. "Jared is intensely loyal to the Empire, and Kelsey has blinders on when it comes to family. That means it's up to us to protect him. Ethan Bandar will try to kill Jared. I will not stand idly by and let that happen, and I want you to help me stop him."

* * *

Kelsey sat in the command chair on *Persephone*. She'd been studying her ass off and now had what Jared charitably called an ensign's skill set. She was hoping to bump that up to at least lieutenant by the time they got home.

Ned said that was really all she needed for a ship this size. Yes, there were some specific skills required for operating a Marine Raider strike ship, but he was helping her learn those.

She'd never be as good at piloting as someone that started learning a decade ago. She'd be happy if she learned enough to be competent.

That was why she had primary on the ship's helm as they prepared to flip to the Nova system. Lieutenant Thompson would be watching her like a hawk from his console, though he'd never say so. She felt like a kid riding her bike for the very first time. The mental image of a powerful warship with training wheels almost made her laugh.

"All Fleet elements, this is Admiral Mertz. Flip in sixty seconds and report to *Invincible* upon arrival. You all have your assigned sectors, so get about it. Remember, you'll be out of direct communication once you move any distance at all into the radiation, so you'll have to use your discretion on approaching anything anomalous.

"Be careful and rendezvous at the Harrison's World flip point in twenty-four hours. Good luck. Mertz out."

She took a deep breath as the timer counted down. She had the helm on manual, so this wasn't just pushing a button. She was adjusting the power output and frequency of the flip drive by hand. If she got it wrong, the ship might not flip at all. Wouldn't *that* be embarrassing?

Thompson hadn't said a word about her settings. She wasn't sure if that was because she had them right or he wanted her to learn something. When the timer hit zero, she activated the flip drive.

Thankfully, *Persephone* flipped.

"Good settings, ma'am," Jack said. "A trifle low, but within the margin of error. Watch out for *Ajax*."

"Thanks, Jack."

The destroyer in question had appeared just in front of them and was cutting across their bow. Kelsey adjusted course enough to be certain they'd miss one another. In the radiation field, it wasn't easy to see everyone at a glance.

She sent a message to *Invincible* and then eased the ship away from the flip point. Once they were clear, she headed off toward their assigned search area.

"Doing this all by hand is complex," she said. "It's a lot simpler to have *Persephone* do the fine details."

"True, but then you wouldn't know what to do if you ever had to do it yourself under pressure. For example, what if Captain Baxter had blown his attempt when *Athena* was running from the Pale Ones?"

She'd been unconscious for that, but she'd heard the story. Once Jared had rescued her from the Pale Ones, they'd chased the ship back to the Pentagar flip point. *Athena* had lost power and bridge control seconds before flip, and the engineer had calculated the settings in his head.

If he'd screwed it up, they'd all be slaves to the Pale Ones right now. She made a mental note to see that he received the Imperial Cross for that. Her father wouldn't argue. That was over and above whatever Fleet Command and the Imperial Senate decided to do.

The highest award for valor in the Terran Empire came with a few perks that only the emperor could bestow. A small plot of land somewhere and a knighthood. Sir Dennis. Wouldn't that tie his trickster tongue?

It also bumped someone up the chain when it came to salutes from his fellows. All Fleet personnel owed a holder of the Imperial Cross a salute, regardless of their respective ranks. Admirals saluted sailors if they held the Imperial Cross.

Since the Fall, they hadn't had an opportunity for anyone to earn that high award. Peacetime wasn't the kind of forge that created moments that earned one.

This mission was going to change that. She wouldn't be surprised to see a number of people receive the Empire's highest honor. It saddened her that all too many of them died doing so.

"Well, yes," she said after a moment. "That would've been awkward. As an engineer, I'm not sure how he knew what to do."

"It's part of their training, just because it might prove necessary. Score one for the training weenies. I never thought I'd say this, but I may have to buy some of them drinks when we get home."

"Your secret is safe with me. I'm transferring the helm back to you, Lieutenant Thompson."

"Aye, ma'am. I have the controls."

Once he'd accepted the helm, she brought up a display of the Nova system. They were going about a third of the way around. They'd be looking for planetary bodies and flip points. If they hadn't found any in twelve hours, they'd circle around and come back via a different route.

Part of her was disappointed that she wouldn't be exploring the strange station, but the rest of her was thrilled to avoid being at the sharp end for once.

That's violating the Marine Raider code.

"Use your outdoor voice," she subvocalized at Ned.

He laughed. This time it came across as an actual sound. Of course, it only came through her auditory implants, but this was better than the disembodied voice in her head.

It had taken her quite a bit of practice to learn to speak without others either hearing her or seeing what she was up to. Or being so incomprehensible that Ned couldn't understand her.

They'd come to this compromise because she needed the privacy of her mind left intact. The shade of Marine Raider Major Ned Quincy, the previous commander of *Persephone*, was a resident in her implants.

It was ludicrous on the face of it. Her implant processors were far inferior to the most basic of Old Empire computers. At least the ones that were of any size. Yet, somehow the memory recordings that he'd left had come into a life of their own. He was an AI. A real one, similar to Marcus, but different enough to be unique.

That had sent Doctor Leonard and Carl Owlet into a tizzy. That was the only word for it. Yet, so far, they'd been unable to recreate that lightning in a bottle. They were still hopeful, though. It had worked once, so they could do it again. All they needed to do was figure out the critical elements they were missing.

Even Marcus was at a loss to explain it. All he could do was confirm that Ned Quincy was undoubtedly sentient.

She hadn't needed anyone to tell her that. The man's odd sense of humor didn't allow for any other possibility. He was a real person, even if he wasn't the man who'd created the recordings before the Fall.

Living with him in her head had proven... challenging. She wanted her privacy, too. So, they'd made a pact. She was the arbiter of when he could use her senses. As he was resident in her implants, she had to trust that he would respect her wishes.

Otherwise, she'd go crazy.

So, he was on his word that he didn't monitor her when she told him to get lost for a while. Like when she and Talbot retired for the evening. Or when she had to use the restroom.

Since he lived in her implants, he could interface with the ship and do any number of things. Watch entertainment vids, read, and visit with friends. Of which he had some. How that worked, she wasn't precisely sure.

He even claimed he was able to sleep. That involved putting part of one of her implant processors into a low powered state that he claimed allowed him to dream.

Ned also wasn't normally supposed to monitor her thoughts. She'd given him permission while she was flying the ship today. That way, if she was about to screw up, he could warn her. A second safety net.

That meant, under normal circumstances, he only heard what she said to him, and she only heard his "voice" in her real ears. That made things bearable.

"Now that we're in the Nova system, no more monitoring my surface thoughts. Was my transition for crap?"

"I wouldn't say that. It could've been a little steadier, but you made it. Just keep working the sims, and you'll get better. Practice makes perfect."

She didn't need a lot of sleep, so she spent a fair amount of time in various sims. Some for the piloting, others for combat. She'd also visited a number of Old Empire worlds via recordings.

Ned's input on combat was immeasurably helpful. He'd made complete copies of all his training in his implants. They'd been among the files she'd taken over when they recovered his body.

Having the files didn't directly translate to her being able to use the skills. It did make her processors' use of combat mode significantly more effective.

That wasn't good enough for her, though. Kelsey coveted his skills. She wanted to be the badass that he'd been.

Direct access to his memories of using the techniques gave her a leg up, though. The style of fighting favored by the Raiders was a distilled compilation of many different Old Empire martial arts. Almost all of which had been lost during the Fall.

With him in her head, she was the last remaining practitioner of this dead art. One day she'd have to teach others, and she wanted to be able to do that. She felt like that kid in one of the old vids with the quirky master. Wax on. Wax off.

"That reminds me," she said. "I have a question for you."

"Since I'm not reading your mind, you'll have to clue me in."

"Sorry. I was thinking about an old martial arts vid. Pre-spaceflight. What degree master were you?"

He projected a mental image of himself standing beside her. It was spooky really. He could overwrite her optical input and add himself to the scene around her. It was just like what he did for her auditory implants. No one else could see him, unless he chose to go wide, so he was like a ghost.

"We didn't use the black belt rankings a lot of the civilian martial arts favored," he said. "Those got all funny once you made black belt. We made an intentional break with that tradition. We use the colored belts for lower levels and a black belt to indicate mastery. The only level we have above that is sensei. One capable of teaching."

"I'd imagined you were some super badass. What a letdown." She smiled to take any sting out of her joke.

"Well, if it's any consolation, I was the Raider's unarmed combat champion six years in a row. And the woman that broke my streak? She cheated."

"Uh-huh. Well, that does make me feel better. Where do I fall on that ranking?"

He made a show of thinking about it. "Not black belt. Sorry. It's not second nature to you, yet. You haven't caught a fly with your chopsticks."

"You *did* see that movie!"

"Which movie, ma'am?"

Kelsey blinked a moment. She'd said that out loud. "Sorry. I was talking to my resident ghost and got carried away."

Lieutenant Thompson and the rest of the bridge crew knew about her guest. Jared had decided that they had to. If something went wrong, they might need that knowledge.

It had taken some doing to convince them she wasn't crazy. Sometimes, she still wasn't sure.

The officer's eyes moved to her right. Ned must've made himself visible to everyone. Through the ship, he could do that. Maybe that was how he had friends.

"Sorry," Ned said. "I was teasing her."

"You still didn't answer my question."

He smiled. "You're a brown belt for sure. Keep working and you'll make black by the time we get to Avalon."

"I hope so. I'd like to have that part of my training squared away. I'm getting tired of Talbot throwing me around the mat when we fight. Well, when my augmentation is turned off, anyway."

She checked her chrono. "We've got almost a full day, and it looks like we won't be stumbling across very many surprises in the next twenty-three hours. Jack, I'll be in the gym if you need me."

6

Carl Owlet exited the pinnace and floated over to the strange station with light pushes from his grav unit. Because of the extreme radiation, he wasn't wearing a normal vacuum suit. Not even the marine versions would last more than a few moments here.

Instead, they'd raided the engineering section for suits designed to operate near an exposed fusion plant. That wasn't the same level of radiation, but tests had shown they'd allow the team to survive in this environment.

The heavy suit restricted his movements but protected him from the intense radiation flowing from the black hole.

Which wasn't that far away, really. He had a fabulous view of the accretion disk through the center of the alien ring. It was stunning. He made certain to get some good shots of it with his external vid recorders. They were more powerful and had much higher resolution than his implants.

He wasn't the first to make the trip. The marines were waiting for him on the surface of the construct. Still, it felt as though he was first on the scene.

"Stop lollygagging and get your skinny butt down here, Carl," Talbot said.

"On my way, Major. Your exaltedness. Sir."

"Someone is looking for a round on the mat, I see."

Carl smiled. His big friend was so easy to predict. His promotion still had him in an odd mental space. Still, he'd best not tease Talbot too much. He didn't want another marine ready to tie him into knots.

Up close, the station really did look different. The hull material was nothing like what they'd used in the Old Empire. Not only was it completely black, it absorbed every form of radiation they could detect. Discovering what it was would be high on his list of tasks.

He stopped lightly beside Talbot and the rest of the marines floating near the hull of the station. Its bulk obscured the accretion disk, and they were in shadow, so they all had their suit lights on. The skin of the station absorbed a lot of that, too.

"Did you find an entrance?" Carl asked.

"Not yet. Since no one reacted to our arrival, I have teams making the rounds in both directions. While we wait, I'd like to ask you a few questions."

"Shoot."

Carl changed his orientation so he was looking closely at the skin of the station. Rather than a smooth surface, small bumps covered it like a texture. Yeah, definitely not of Imperial manufacture.

Talbot sent him a private message to switch to channel six. Carl opened it, but also continued monitoring the general channel.

"What the hell were you thinking?"

He rolled his eyes. "Is this about the hammer again? Make one damned mistake and you never live it down."

"Don't curse."

"Hello? Pot, this is kettle, over."

"Yeah, well I'm a grizzled adult and you're ruining my preconceptions. No, this is about Angela Ellis. You're getting on the bad side of the wrong person, and you need to take a step back before she hurts you."

Carl shook his head, even though the marine couldn't see him. He unhooked a small scanner from his belt and began taking readings from the surface of the station.

"I haven't done anything to that woman. She's frothing all on her own. I'll get the kinks worked out of the hammer a lot faster without her breathing down my neck."

Talbot floated next to him. "You have no idea. She's a good person, but she has issues when it comes to losing people. We all do, really, but hers are more like an obsession. She's convinced you're out to kill Kelsey with your supposed incompetence."

The marine held up a hand. "I've told her you're the brightest guy on the block, but she got a bad first impression. You need to stop banging heads with her and try a different approach. You're not going to bulldoze your way through her objections."

The scanner readings were very odd. Part of the beams never came back. The hull must be absorbing them, too. What he was getting told him two mutually exclusive things.

First, the hull was made of collapsed matter. Not the partial stuff that he'd used on the hammer, but something a lot closer to neutronium. So much so that the beams weren't penetrating the surface at all.

If that were true, that explained the lack of a battle screen. No radiation would make it through that. Just cutting it would take a hell of a lot of focused energy. If they could do it at all.

Invincible's beams would be ineffective. It would require more power in a tighter focus. Well, maybe they would work with time, but the designers had never envisioned long duration shots. Their tightest focus would be useless. It required something much finer, yet more powerful.

Assuming the readings were correct, the mass of the station should be incredible. Here he was floating beside it, but it should have enough pull on its own to anchor him. Not like a planet, perhaps, but maybe a large asteroid. A handful of true neutronium would weigh millions of tons. He'd need to do some calculations before he knew what to expect.

Yet there was nothing. No indication at all that the surface was pulling any of them in, and that was damned odd. It really couldn't be both ways. He was missing something.

"I wish I had a clue how to hit the reset button," Carl told the marine. "Major Ellis is all over my ass. Talk about hostile. She threatened to break me into little pieces with Kelsey standing right there."

"I hope you take what she says seriously," Talbot said. "She's pretty pissed about the whole thing."

"I don't understand why. There was no way Kelsey was ever getting that version of the hammer. I have a lot more testing to do on it. Hell, I wasn't even going to tell her about it until the testing was complete. *She* told Kelsey. Now I have to convince the she-bear that it's safe."

He looked over at Talbot as he said that last. The marine was smiling. Bastard.

"Look, kid, I get it. I really do. I tried to tell her what a stand-up guy you are, and it bounced. She's got it in her head that you're a dangerous fellow. It's up to you to convince her she's wrong. I can't help you with that. No one can."

"I'm doomed."

Talbot laughed and moved off to confer with the other marines keeping watch. So much for a helping hand.

Carl sighed and glared at his scanner. It wasn't even giving him a good idea what the texture was for. If they didn't get inside the thing, they might never find out. At least not before they left to go home.

He hated the idea of someone else making the big discoveries after he came up empty. Maybe he could get a more detailed reading on the skin if he boosted the scanner power and narrowed the focus. A sweeping scan that went up and down the potential frequencies would also increase his odds of getting something meaningful back.

It only took a few moments to change the settings. He held the scanner against the surface of the station and started probing it.

The hull underneath him sank with astonishing speed, yanking him inside the station. He didn't even have time to yell before the darkness engulfed him.

* * *

Angela finished going over the data Owlet had given her about Project Mjölnir. It was insulting. He'd tailored his summary as though she was four. And slow.

His opinion of marines in general, and her in specific, had to be pretty dismal.

Perhaps he didn't know that officers in the emperor's service had to have university degrees. Admittedly, hers was in military studies, but she had the ability to grasp other advanced subjects.

She set the summary aside and opened his write-up about the quantum validation theory.

That might have been a mistake.

It quickly arrowed off into science that she didn't have the background to understand. Not without a lot of study. Time she was unwilling to waste on this one project.

Maybe the computer could help her grasp it. "*Persephone*, if I send you a file on a scientific subject, can you help me understand it?"

"This unit may be able to assist, Major Ellis. It depends on the nature of the theory and how specific your question is."

She sent the files. "This is classified under my seal. Only Princess Kelsey, Carl Owlet, Doctor Leonard, Admiral Mertz, and I are cleared to know the contents."

"Understood. Which theory are you looking for clarification on? There are a number of fields that are mentioned."

"Quantum communication. How does that work?"

"It doesn't, at least as far as this unit's databases are concerned. This unit has located several mentions of failed experiments in that line, but none that were able to meaningfully use the quantum entanglement of photons."

"Then focus on the files I sent. How does it propose the communication to work?"

She leaned back in the chair behind her desk to await what was no doubt going to be a boring lecture in science. She really didn't need an office, but the privacy would be useful if it put her to sleep.

"The devices use entangled photons and predefined arrangements of spin as authentication mechanisms. These units do not directly communicate, strictly speaking. The standard communications units use the spin of the photons to verify a command is authentic.

"Though not directly designed for communication, it may be possible to use them for such. The photon sets are sizable and would allow for significant data throughput. The quantum devices are only capable of communicating with one another in linked pairs. A working range of ten kilometers is given, but this unit finds that claim doubtful."

Angela sat up, interested. "Doubtful in what way? Are you saying that it doesn't work?"

"Test results indicate that it did in fact work in a lab setting, but this unit is finding a discrepancy in the range Carl Owlet has verified and what the original scientific theory seems to indicate.

"Carl Owlet has set a working range of ten kilometers. That is unrealistic and does not fit the scope of how entangled particles operate."

"Okay, what would be a more likely range? Five kilometers? Less?"

"This unit apologizes. Perhaps it did not adequately explain the original theory. Even prior to spaceflight on Terra, the effect of entangled photons were observable at hundreds of kilometers of separation."

She blinked. "Are you saying someone could control this hammer over a distance of hundreds of kilometers?"

"Negative."

Angela sighed in relief. "Thank goodness. That would be hard to get my head around. What do you hypothesize the maximum range to be?"

"This unit believes the upper range to be unlimited."

She must've misheard what it said. "Could you expand on that?"

"Theoretically, entangled photons are not bound by distance at all. It should not matter if they are in the same compartment, in different stellar systems, or across the observable universe. The artificial range assigned to the communicator by Carl Owlet does not seem supported in theory."

She stood slowly. "Are you telling me that he could control that hammer over interstellar distances? That's ridiculous. If so, why would he only say it worked out to ten kilometers?"

"As designed, control of the hammer requires both the standard communications unit and the quantum validation device. So, the normal communicator limits the range.

"That said, this unit believes that Carl Owlet doubted the scope of his breakthrough. It believes that he incorrectly applied an artificial limitation. Only an actual test of the communications potential can prove or disprove that assertion, however."

Angela tried to get her head around what the computer was saying. Unlimited communication range? Absurd.

"We'll leave that aside for the moment. Tell me about the rest of the hammer."

Hopefully, she wouldn't find any other glitches in his presentation. This wasn't looking good at all.

* * *

JARED FELT like he was floating beside Talbot. He was using the vid feed from one of the other marines to have a conversation with him from his flag bridge, but it was just as though he was there.

"How the hell could he just disappear?"

"Damned if I know, sir. I turned my back for a minute and he was gone. I thought he'd floated around the curve of the station, but he didn't turn up when we spread out. *Invincible* scanned the entire area looking for him. Nothing. He has to be inside that thing."

"I thought you didn't find any airlocks."

The former noncom growled. "We didn't. There isn't a single entrance to this thing. Not one seam we can find. Nothing."

"Then we'll need to open the thing up. Try a plasma rifle."

"No dice. As far as I can tell, it had no effect whatsoever. It didn't even discolor the skin. We need bigger guns."

"*Invincible*'s beams are too heavy. Try the plasma weapons on one of the pinnaces. Call me back once you're in."

He turned to Doctor Leonard. "What do you think happened?"

The older man shrugged. "He went over to get scanner readings of the hull on that station. There's no way he would wander off. I suppose it's possible that he had a suit failure, but that doesn't explain why no one can locate him. I think your belief that he's inside that station is an accurate one."

"Then how did he get in, and how do we get him out?"

"I haven't the slightest idea. What's more troubling is that he should've called us. Perhaps we might not be in range to hear a cry for help, but Major Talbot is. I should go over there and take readings for myself."

Jared shook his head. "Not until we know more about what happened. One of the marines can take a reading after they breach the hull on that thing."

"Incoming communication from Major Talbot," Marcus said.

This time the marine had his helmet off, obviously inside the pinnace.

"Are you ready to fire?"

Talbot shrugged. "We already did. No effect that we can see. The damned thing is immune to damage from us."

"Hold on," Jared said. "Are you telling me that our weapons are just bouncing?"

"Literally. I hit it with flechettes, too. Not a scratch on it. You're going to have to use the ship's weapons."

"Not the missiles. That's overkill. Maybe a low-powered beam. Marcus?"

"If the Major and his people will pull back, I can move into range and focus the beam on the hull. At the lowest power settings, it still has the potential to do a lot of damage."

Jared nodded. "Aim somewhere other than the spot Carl disappeared."

It took about ten minutes to get everything set up. Jared monitored the shot when Marcus took it at the lowest power setting.

It had no more effect than the handheld plasma weapons.

"Well," Marcus said. "This is unexpected. Shall I increase power, Admiral?"

"Take it up slowly. When it fails, it might go suddenly."

Invincible fired ever increasingly powerful shots at the station. None had any effect whatsoever. Once they reached full power, they started adding in additional beams. All to no effect. The dammed thing might as well be immune to energy weapons.

"Shall we stand off and try a missile, Admiral?" Marcus asked.

Jared rubbed his face. "Not yet. An explosion or high-speed impact might be completely different from a beam attack. I'd rather not rupture the thing."

He turned to Doctor Leonard. "Suit up, Doctor. You're going to take some readings before we try again. Tell me what that thing is and how to open it. If we can't, we might never see Carl again."

The odds were stacked against the young man. His suit only had air for another four hours. Assuming that was an alien environment in there—if the station was even functional—it would probably be hostile to humans.

The clock was ticking.

7

After half an hour of searching, Carl gave up on figuring out how the station had pulled him inside. He also conceded that he wouldn't be repeating the feat that made it happen. No amount of scanning from the inside was having any effect, though he was getting clean readings now.

He wasn't getting out the same way he'd gotten in.

Which was bad. The interior of the station was dark and cold, and that didn't even begin to consider the "atmosphere" he found himself in.

It was difficult to tell with his suit lights, but the liquid surrounding him certainly had pale blue color. The scanner said it was water, though it had some odd trace elements. The oxygen content was in line with what he recalled about normal water on Avalon, but it had a higher range of heavy metals. Arsenic in particular.

In any case, he wasn't going to be breathing water anytime soon. He needed to find an exit, or he was going to die in here in a few short hours.

A year ago, this might have paralyzed him with fear, but not now. He'd learned a lot from the people around him. When the pressure hit, you had to keep swinging. So, he buried his fear and got to work.

The ring was clear in the center. A tube several dozen meters across seemed to circle the station. Many compartments sat to every side, none with hatches.

He supposed that made sense. With a liquid atmosphere, it probably required better circulation to remain healthy for the occupants.

Not that he'd seen any sign of them. Not in person or through furniture. Though he did see what looked like operational machinery. He had no idea how they kept it functional over long periods submerged like this.

Or even how an aquatic race could learn to forge metal and get into space.

There were a lot of questions he'd like answered, if he survived.

Once again, discovering the purpose of the station was high on the list. Someone had come into the most hostile environment imaginable and built it. Considering that and the materials, the aliens were more advanced than the Old Empire. So, why hadn't anyone found evidence of them or even met them?

Surely, such an advanced people must've left other artifacts.

Unless, somehow, they were located on an unconnected set of flip points. Everyone knew that only a fraction of stellar systems had flip points. What if that theory was flawed? What if there were two or more unconnected—or only barely connected—flip-point networks?

With that, it might be possible for two advanced species to occupy the same volume of space without ever having met. The weak flip point that led here might be a fluke.

It seemed as though one of them would have discovered communications from the other. Unless, of course, the builders were long gone. Swallowed by the mists of time.

Could this station, hidden away in a place no one would come looking, be the only remnant of these people?

That was frightening, when one considered it. What could cause the end of an advanced people like this? Something similar to the Fall? Humanity had survived. Shouldn't they have as well?

A blinking light from ahead caused him to slow down. Something was different.

He approached the small light cautiously. It sat above a hatch—one not that different from the ones used in the Empire, though constructed from what looked like salvaged materials.

What sent a chill down his spine was a message scratched under a button.

Press me.

The implications were staggering. He wasn't the first human to visit this place, and his predecessor had anticipated his arrival.

Carl considered his options. He didn't have anything to lose by trying. He pressed the button.

The hatch slid slowly open, allowing the fluid to flow gently into what was obviously some kind of airlock. One large enough for his suit, thankfully.

He wedged himself inside and found the button to cycle the lock. Unsure of what or who might be on the other side, he pressed the button firmly.

* * *

ANGELA STARED AT THE HAMMER. It sat on her desk without seeming all that special. Yet, after *Persephone* had explained the research to her, she'd realized that it was a stunning technological marvel. Even if some parts of it failed to live up to expectations. Or the designer was a mad genius.

She'd arranged to take it with them against Owlet's wishes. That had really pissed him off, and that was just fine with her. The boy needed to learn his limits.

Taken singly, the quantum validation unit, the partially collapsed matter, the miniature grav drive with the incorporated fusion plant, the tiny battle screen, and the enhanced-range communicator were all groundbreaking in one way or another.

Owlet wasn't even responsible for the partially collapsed matter or the drive/fusion plant combo. The people at the Grant Research Facility figured out the former and God only knew who created the latter for the AIs.

Still, Owlet had managed to create something unique and

dangerous. If only the boy had common sense to go along with his genius.

The true groundbreaker might be the quantum validation system. She completely understood his impulse to limit its range. Faced with the alternative, she'd instinctively rejected it, too.

Perhaps the range wouldn't be infinite. There might be more to the theory than what they knew. Flip points had an upper end. Perhaps this system would, too. Only testing would tell for sure.

None of that changed her opinion on allowing the boy to hand over his toy to Kelsey without changes. Weapon or no, it needed some limitations.

Frankly, she wished she had some method to interface with the quantum setup. Just to see if it bypassed the radiation and distance to Owlet. But she didn't have that implant. Only he did.

But what if she just had the communicator do something to the quantum unit? Could it?

It only took a moment's search of the technical specifications to show that wasn't possible. He'd only wired the hammer to check the spin of the photons in the quantum validation unit. There was no provision to use the validation unit to communicate directly with the hammer or wielder.

Too bad. That might have been interesting.

* * *

KELSEY'S LESSON had gone as well as it could. Ned had the knowledge, but not the body to spar with her.

So, she spent a lot of time doing katas. Dances that drilled the moves into her muscle memory. He was also training her marine guards, so Kelsey could turn her enhancements down to human normal and practice with them.

Even with her skill level, that was more in line with the butt whooping she'd have expected before this grand adventure. She knew the word diminutive was an understatement when applied to her. Particularly when compared to marines.

So she cheated. She kept just a little speed and strength to bring her more in line with them. The goal was to learn how to win, after all. Not how to be stomped into the mat gracefully.

They were the real reason she was determined to make black belt before the fleet returned to Avalon. They had a background in combat and were racing up the ranks. She was determined to be the first one there. She knew she wouldn't be the first sensei, but that was fine with her.

She'd banished Ned from her mind and taken a shower, satisfied with her progress. Maybe another few weeks and she'd get that damned belt.

Angela was waiting for her when she finished dressing. Kelsey schooled her face and hoped the woman wasn't there to rant about Carl or Mjölnir. It was like an obsession.

She got an energy drink out of the refrigeration unit in her office. "What can I do for you, Angela? Drink?"

"I'm good, Highness. I wanted to give you an update on my research into the hammer project."

The marine couldn't even bring herself to name it. Kelsey suppressed a smile and sat down. Not behind her desk, but off to one side in a comfortable cluster of chairs. The marine officer joined her.

"You can't have done any real testing yet, so what new danger have you discovered?"

The large woman smiled wryly. "I hope I'm not always so full of negativity."

"Only when it comes to this project and Carl Owlet. Sorry."

"Then this will be a refreshing change of pace. I think Owlet has made the most important breakthrough in science since the creation of flip drives."

Kelsey choked a little on her drink. "Excuse me? Are you trying to drown me?"

"Not intentionally," Angela said. "I'm being completely serious. This quantum validation system and tracking unit. He told us it was good out to ten kilometers. I think he's allowed himself to doubt the true reach of his discovery.

"I'm no scientist, but it seems to me that the limit he imposed is arbitrary. Quantum theory says it should have no range limitation at all."

Kelsey carefully set her drink down on the handy end table. "You're telling me that he created an intergalactic communicator? The fabled means of one system talking to another without sending a ship through a flip point?"

Angela shrugged. "I can't speak as to the distance, but I'm willing to bet my firstborn child that it will be a hell of a lot further than ten kilometers. I think it has some relation to flip points, so like them, I bet there is an upper end to the realistic range.

"But they can send a ship hundreds of light years. How far could a simple communication go? Twice that? Five? Ten? I have no idea. Until we start testing, we won't know."

The marine leaned forward earnestly. "I can see some obvious advantages and drawbacks. We could send a probe through a flip point and get a view from the other side without it coming back. In real time. There isn't supposed to be a delay in transmission, though there might be, I suppose. This is all new stuff."

Kelsey nodded. "And the downside?"

"Fleet Command could become backseat drivers. Right now, Fleet commanders make calls for themselves. With direct communication, that opens the possibility of micromanagement."

"That would be a negative," Kelsey admitted. "Wow. This is big. Why didn't he admit there was the possibility of something like this?"

"I have no idea. If I could tinker with the hammer and figure it out, I'd ask him. I can't, though. It's not open to use as a communicator the way the hammer is set up."

Kelsey considered that. "I bet one of the techs could untangle that for us. We'd just have to be careful not to break something. It's only a test device, so I'm not worried about taking it apart. Make that happen, and see if you can open a channel to Carl."

Angela smiled. "Won't *that* surprise him?"

8

The situation had Jared stumped. If they used a missile, they might critically damage the station. Or destroy it. Yet, none of the other weapons even made a scratch on the thing's surface. Whatever it was, it was damned good at stopping energy.

He supposed that made sense. That kind of thing was terrific for a station built near a black hole.

Doctor Leonard was over there scanning it now. The initial readings told the tale of why their beams and plasma were ineffective. The hull was some kind of collapsed matter. Perhaps even neutronium.

The scientist was unwilling to guess at how strong the material might be, but he'd already determined that it wasn't as massive as theory predicted. He'd keep working, but time was running short.

Jared would hate to do it, but he'd punch a missile into the station to gain access if he had to. Searching the wreckage might take a while, so he was only giving the man another half hour. If he didn't find a way in before that, Jared would do so on his own.

The scientist had a dozen marines in close proximity, all of them heavily armed and loaded down with supplies. If they got in, he wanted extra air and gear to keep them going while they figured out how to create an exit.

Remotes were recording everything and sending it to *Invincible*. For all the good it seemed to be doing.

* * *

"How's it coming, Doc?" Talbot asked. "You found anything yet?"

The older man gave him an exasperated look. "Not since you asked me two minutes ago, Major Talbot. I'll certainly inform you the moment that changes."

"I'm not trying to rush you or anything, but Carl only has two hours of air left. Admiral Mertz doesn't want to do it, but he'll put a missile into this thing in half an hour if you haven't found the way in."

"I'm quite aware of the time constraints, Major. I'm not seeing anything. Almost literally. The skin of this station is blocking my attempts to get any data."

"So, that was what Carl saw, too. What would he do to get around that?"

The other man nodded. "I'm already doing that. I've increased the power of the scan as much as this equipment will allow. Nothing."

Talbot had guessed as much. "Is there any way you might be able to get a better reading?"

"Perhaps if I modulated the frequency I might find one that gives better results. It will take me a moment to set up an oscillation."

"I suggest you try to mimic what you think Carl would've done."

"Yes, indeed. Thank you, Major Obvious."

Talbot smiled. Some of those old movies and entertainment shows were gaining a cult following. Even the so-called commercials.

Without warning, the hull sank, pulling Leonard, Talbot, and the entire cluster of marines into the cavity. It flowed around them and closed off before he could even kick his own scanners into high gear.

"I believe I replicated the sequence Carl found," Leonard said.

"Thank you, Doctor Obvious. First squad, go left. Second, go right."

Talbot switched to the channel he'd been using to communicate with Carl earlier. "Buddy, can you hear me?"

A moment later, Carl Owlet called back. "I hope you brought something that can get us out of here."

"The jury's still out on that. We're headed your way."

"I have him," Talbot said on the general frequency. "He sounds okay." He consulted his implants and started toward the left. Carl wasn't that far away.

"I'm unable to signal the ship," Doctor Leonard said. "We appear to be just as muzzled as Carl is, even with the higher-powered gear I brought along."

"I'm not that surprised. What's this stuff around us?"

The scientist scanned the liquid. "It's water, with a number of trace elements mixed in. It appears our mythical builders were either water breathers or amphibians. That rules out humanity. Congratulations, Major Talbot. We've discovered an alien civilization."

"Whee. Now all we need to do is get out and tell someone."

He led the marines around the ring until they found the airlock. Carl floated outside it.

"How are you doing, pal?" Talbot asked. "Is your life support good? We have air and other supplies for you."

The boy shook his head. "I'm good for a few more hours. Thanks for coming, but I really wish you'd stayed away. I'm very much afraid we won't be getting back out."

He slapped Carl on the shoulder, an odd feeling in the water. "Don't be so negative. How hard can it be to get back out?"

"Ask the guys that built this." He gestured at the airlock. "They're still inside. They never made it out again.

"That's not all. You need to come in and look at them. There's not a whole lot of room, so I suggest only the three of us go in."

Talbot started to insist he go in first, but decided that was silly. Carl had already been inside the room. He'd have known if there were any dangers. He'd settle for going in before the doctor.

Once they followed Carl through, he saw what the younger man meant. Someone had taken a compartment and sealed it off. They'd managed to pump out the water after they'd built the airlock. Quite a feat on an alien space station.

The down side was that they were still here. One side of the compartment had dozens of bodies in armored vacuum gear identical to their own. Even from here, he could tell they were still inside those suits.

The only one of them not stacked like cut wood was sitting in a makeshift chair. He, too, was suited, but he'd rigged up some kind of screen in front of him. The keyboard looked virtual, but the rest had come from a large communicator, something like what Doctor Leonard had brought along.

"Who are they?" Talbot asked. "Old Empire?"

"It's a *lot* more complicated and confusing than that," Carl said. "Ping his implants."

Talbot was surprised the dead man's implants were still active. That was a first from an Old Empire Fleet body. He pinged them for the man's identity and immediately realized what Carl had meant.

The body belonged to Carl Owlet.

* * *

KELSEY WATCHED the technician disassemble Mjölnir with interest. Some of the parts looked familiar to her—such as the grav drive/fusion combo—but the rest was new. Carl had really packed it tightly. There was no room to spare.

The woman put on a pair of magnifying goggles and looked at the connections. "This is the quantum validation unit here, Captain. It's pretty small, but I don't have any experience to tell me what that means about capability.

"It's wired directly into the central processor and linked to the communicator. The connection is parallel, so I'm assuming that it can operate independently, but the two are somehow both required."

"That's what the technical specifications say," Angela said. "It uses the quantum unit to validate commands sent by the standard communicator."

"Can you isolate the quantum unit and use it for communication?" Kelsey asked.

The tech looked up at her. "I can isolate it, but I'm not even sure how it works. I could probably send a signal of some kind, but I'm unsure what the input is supposed to look like. If it's only built to authenticate the commands, it might just be a code."

Angela nodded. "That's what I gathered from reading the specs. It has a large list of valid codes. It uses one and moves on to the next. All are just different spin states for the various photons."

"That makes sense, if both ends work off the same list and have a means of discerning when a code was missed, for whatever reason. I'll examine the system in a little more detail and determine if I can send some kind of meaningful sequence to Mister Owlet. I have to be sure of the mechanism first."

Kelsey nodded. "Call me when you have it ready to test."

* * *

ELISE WENT over the research she'd gathered about Ethan Bandar. It was scant on details, other than what was in the public record. She resigned herself to the fact she just wouldn't be able to pin him down without actually meeting him. She couldn't really ask the people that knew him best for crucial details.

But, perhaps she didn't have to. Jared must have confided in someone. Captain Graves was his oldest friend and former executive officer. He must have heard an earful. But he wasn't available until the ships regrouped.

He might also have confided in Doctor Stone. Elise had found there were several classes of people that knew the most about someone's life: mates, close friends, priests, bartenders, and doctors.

There was only one way to find out.

She made her way to the medical center. The place was a hive of activity. Elise hoped that didn't mean there was some kind of emergency.

Doctor Stone spotted her from across the compartment and made her way over. "Are you having a problem with the implant updates, Your Highness?"

Elise shook her head. "Not at all. I had some personal questions, but I see you have something in progress. Has something happened?"

"There's an unfolding situation on the alien station, but I can spare a few minutes. Until the admiral gets more information and we get the people back out, we won't know if there's really a problem."

"They got in? That's good, right?"

"Only if we manage to get them back out. Come into my office and we can talk."

Stone led Elise into her office. They sat in a comfortable set of chairs off to the side of the desk. "What kind of personal questions are we talking about? You're not writing my unauthorized biography, are you?"

Elise smiled. "No. I'm trying to make plans for when we get to Avalon. Based on a number of comments, I'm fairly certain that Jared, and to some extent Kelsey, are going to have problems with Ethan Bandar. I need to get a feel for the man so I can make some contingency plans. I've heard some rather dark whispers."

That last made Stone nod. "Well, I've heard a few things, too. Some I'd slot under the doctor-patient confidentiality umbrella, but others I can talk about. What dark whispers have you heard?"

"Jared told me that he was pretty certain that Ethan was responsible for someone's death. He thought it was an assassination attempt gone wrong."

"Yes," Stone said. "The mission's original ambassador, Carlo Vega. He ate something that *really* disagreed with him. There was an investigation, but it proved inconclusive."

"You think the heir to the Imperial Throne is capable of that?"

Stone considered that. "I hate saying so, but I've seen how he feels about Jared. I think it's a reasonable suspicion. No one will ever prove it, mind you, and that doesn't even begin to count the number of rumors I've heard about the man."

Elise sat up straighter. "What kind of rumors?"

Stone leaned forward and lowered her voice. "None of this is more than gossip, mind you. Ethan Bandar has worked hard to get

Jared ejected from Fleet. When that proved impossible, he settled for poisoning his reputation. Whispers about his character here, pushes to keep him out of promotions or better postings there.

"Honestly, Jared was a full grade behind where he should've been. That's all because of Ethan Bandar and the people in Fleet hauling his water."

Elise nodded slowly. "I imagine he's not going to be pleased when Jared returns as an admiral in command of a fleet like this. As the one to have met the Pale Ones and emerged victorious."

Stone's lips quirked. "You have a talent for understatement. Based on what I've seen of the man, he's going to have a stroke. Or die of apoplectic shock. If he somehow survives, he'll come out swinging. If he tried to have Jared killed before, he'll try harder.

"He'll immediately have his Fleet stooges take everything away that he can. Expect a court-martial."

"Seriously? For winning? What does the loser get? A blindfold and the final meal of his choice?"

"They'll charge him for the loss of his ship. For what he did to Captain Breckenridge, too. Ethan Bandar can't allow Jared to emerge victorious. It's like a medical condition, his paranoia. The heir will feel justified doing whatever it takes to stop Jared. Including murder, in my opinion."

Elise sighed. "That matches everything I've heard about the man. What can we do to protect Jared?"

"Make certain the emperor is behind him, which I suspect he will be. The strike will come from the shadows or through proxies in Fleet. We'll need to be in control of Jared's transport. We wouldn't want any unfortunate cutter accidents, would we? That sort of thing."

"There's no way to prove Ethan Bandar was behind the assassination attempt?"

"I've been over Vega's body with every tool this Old Empire ship has to offer. I can say with certainty what killed the poor man, but not who was behind it. But I promise I'll be with you every step of the way making sure we protect Jared from that man's twisted hatred."

After a deep breath, Elise continued. "What about Kelsey?"

"Are you asking if she thinks her brother is a murderer? I doubt it.

Jared kept that theory away from her, and she's never approached me about it. Ethan is her twin brother. I can't imagine she believes him capable of something like that."

"I'll have to talk with her," Elise said. "Just to let her know I'm worried. Especially with the changes she's gone through. He might turn some of his anger on her. If she's not on guard, something terrible might happen."

Stone grinned. "Oh, I do hope he tries something. I remember the vid of the assassination attempt in your parliament building. That's when she could barely walk. Now that she's fully integrated with her implants and hardware, it would be brief and very messy for her attackers."

"I hope it doesn't come to that. A shot from the dark could kill her before she knows a thing."

"Then we'll have to work hard to make sure that never happens."

Elise extended her hand. "Welcome to the conspiracy, Doctor. Let's hope we can keep anyone from making a terrible mistake. There are enemies more deserving of our attention. I'd rather we all focus on the Rebel Empire before they come looking for us with a fleet of ships."

9

Carl helped the others move his... his other body away from the computer and lay it on the deck. He was no medical specialist, but the other Carl had been dead awhile. Weeks. Maybe more. It was hard to tell.

The other him had purged his atmosphere, so he had the look of a man who'd been in a vacuum. Not as bad as the corpses from *Courageous*, but it still made estimating time of death difficult with only his eyes.

If they ever got out of here, someone could tell them. If not, it hardly mattered.

He sat in the chair, and it creaked ominously under his weight. The armored vacuum suit wasn't light. He hoped his seat didn't collapse. The air in the room was foul and unbreathable, so he'd have to make do.

"I'm going to see who else we have in the pile," Talbot said. "Give me a hand, Doc."

Carl tapped the keyboard and the screen came to life. The message it displayed was no surprise.

Hello, me. That is, if you're Carl Owlet.

You'll have to forgive my gallows humor, but I'm almost out of air and I'm sure no one is coming for me.

Yet, based on the people I found here when I arrived, others have made it inside looking for me. Well, for other versions of me.

In case you haven't checked, there are five others just like us in the pile. The one before me had a marine escort. Apparently, they came in with him. Two others had some marines that followed them in later, and one had Doctor Leonard.

So, that makes six of me, three Talbots, one Doctor Leonard, and from one to three of various marines. I wonder how many make up a set.

Anyway, the first Carl died quickly. His implants were still active, so I was able to access all his recorded data. Useful. He started tearing equipment on this station apart to build an airtight area.

It took two additional groups to get it finished. My immediate predecessor was able to get this computer set up and attempt to interface with the station. He wasn't successful, but I knew all the things that hadn't worked. That saved me time.

I think I'm close. Based on some of the environmental clues, I think the station is aware of me. I just can't hear what it wants to say. If it's really trying to communicate.

It has to be tired of us littering the corridors.

In any case, I've compiled everything from the logs our predecessors made into one for you. I hope you succeed in making contact and getting the hell out of this deathtrap.

Wait. What? You're wondering what the hell is going on with a half-dozen Carls?

Damned if I know. We all have identical implant serial codes. Which makes accessing their implant records a breeze, I have to tell you. Make a note that you might want to close that security loophole before the AIs hear about it.

Based on the complete implant records, I think we have to be from different universes.

Congratulations. This is going to win you the Lucien Prize for sure. And honestly, you deserve it. You really gave everything for this project. Several times over.

Anyway, there are minor differences in a number of things. People who some of us know that I don't recognize. Other references to events not going as I remember. The first Carl arrived here almost nine months ago. You'd have to compare the date to see how that works out for you.

It has to be the black hole. Somehow, it's turned the inside of this station into some kind of shared space. Frankly, even if you get out, I'm not sure how you'd know you got out to the right universe.

Not that I suspect you'd care. It beats dying.

Well, my air just gave out, and I need to bring this heart-to-heart to a close. I'm rooting for you, buddy. If anyone can do it, it's you. Do us proud. If you make it out, give Angela a kiss for me. Adios.

Carl

Well, that certainly wasn't what he'd expected.

And kissing the marine officer would be a good way to die. The other him sure had a twisted sense of humor.

He pinged the dead man's implants and discovered he had access to everything. That cloned serial number issue was a real thing. Though he supposed it wasn't cloned in this case. He'd be sure and fix that if he got out.

The combined logs were there, and he pulled them in. For good measure, he snagged every file the man had. He could sort them out later.

He was sure the other him had done the same, but he verified he had the files from all of the versions of himself.

The last Carl had died seventeen days ago. That meant they'd arrived over a span of almost seven months. He wondered if someone else was going to show up before he died.

"There are six other versions of you, counting the one in the chair," Talbot said. "I found a few of myself and another Doctor Leonard. The marines outside are represented, mostly. Oddly, there are a few people here that died before we found this station."

Talbot leaned against the wall and looked at Carl. "I have to tell you, this is spooky. What the devil is going on?"

"Parallel universes," Doctor Leonard said. "I found a number of files with theories in my other's implants, and it's obviously true. We are in fact incontrovertible proof."

"My other me thought he was close to a breakthrough," Carl said. "I'll try to finish my life's work, if you know what I mean."

Talbot shook his head. "That's dark, man. *Really* dark. I'll cycle the men in to get files off their implants. Just in case there's something useful. Then we'll search the station while you work. We have enough air and food for a few weeks. Let's hope it doesn't take that long."

* * *

JARED FELT like banging his head on the console. They had complete records of how Doctor Leonard had triggered the station into absorbing himself and the others, but now it wasn't working.

They'd placed a unit on the surface of the station to do exactly what Doctor Leonard did, but it just sat there. The station wasn't interested.

He wondered if it had to be a person. Damned if he was going to risk someone else to test the theory. They didn't even know if the others were still alive.

The lift doors slid open, and Elise walked onto the flag bridge. She stopped beside his seat.

"What's the word?"

"Not good. We think we know how they got inside, but the method isn't working without a person. I'm not asking anyone else to risk their lives. I'm going to fire a missile."

"Won't that put them in grave danger?"

"No worse than leaving them inside. Marcus, target the station opposite the entry point. Fire one missile and count on the radiation hashing it."

"At this range, that shouldn't be an issue."

He nodded. "Good plan. Fire when ready."

The missile wouldn't reach full speed, but it would be impressive enough. It lanced out of the tubes and slammed into the station.

Jared eyed the debris and quickly decided most of it was from the missile.

"The shot was ineffective, Admiral. Telemetry indicates it struck the station but did not penetrate. The cutter we had standing by says they can't see any damage at all. Not even a scratch."

He rubbed his face. "How is that possible? Even collapsed matter should dent. Right?"

"I'm afraid my grasp of the material is weak. Obviously, it's even stronger than we'd expected, or there's another force stabilizing the station. In either case, I don't believe further missiles would be very effective."

"No, I think you're right. Have the crew stand down. We'll just have to hope they find a way out for themselves."

* * *

PERSEPHONE MADE it all the way out to the twelve-hour mark without finding anything exciting. Only a single stripped gas giant core. Angela supposed the science types found that interesting, but it really didn't do anything for her.

They stayed long enough to get some scanner readings. The radiation was lower this far out, so they were able to send in probes that lasted almost an hour. The scientists would have to make do with that.

The technician had to take a study break while working on the hammer. It was so different from what the woman normally worked with, she needed to draw it all out and make a plan. With the grav drive set to negate its weight, it was easy to move it around.

She called Angela and Kelsey back to the work area just after *Persephone* started back in. She looked tired.

"The mechanism isn't exactly set up for direct communication," she told them, "but I have a plan. The only thing I don't know is if Mister Owlet will even notice it. I'm not sure how the system is set up on his end. As he's the authenticator, he might not have a means of receiving an incoming signal.

"Even if he does, he might not recognize the message. I settled on an old communication protocol called Morse code. It utilizes sets of dots, dashes, and pauses to make letters and words. It's not commonly known anymore, though. He might not have the means to understand it."

Kelsey nodded. "He'll recognize some of it. I know that he's seen some Old Earth vids where people have used it. If this doesn't work, well, we're not really suffering. It's just a test. What are you planning to send?"

The woman gestured toward her tablet. "I wrote out a short message. Basically, an explanation of why we've called. We'll know it worked if he sends a response of any kind. Comprehension isn't really required.

"I'll mimic dots and dashes by single validation codes and closely sent trios. I've programed my tablet to do the hard work. All I need to do is press the button. I can resend it at intervals to allow him to try and decipher it."

"Do it," Kelsey said.

* * *

CARL WAS LAGGING. He'd been up all day, and it was now the middle of the night. The marines had gone into a rotation to allow some of them to sleep. The compartment was too small for them to fit into. They could pressurize the compartment, but that would waste air. Better to stay in the suits. They might need every breath before this was over.

He'd reviewed everything the other versions of him had discovered and recorded. The station certainly seemed as though it were trying to communicate with them. Small mobile devices occasionally ventured near the trapped men.

A marine from one of the earlier groups had fired at one of the mobile units, but the water spoiled his aim. Thankfully, he hadn't tried a plasma weapon. In water, that would boil them all. There'd been no hostile response to a real provocation like that, so Carl assumed that the computer wasn't interested in killing them.

The station had to have a computer. That much was certain. It had used those machines to lure the men to where they could salvage equipment useful in creating an airlock.

Carl was at a loss as to how they would communicate with an alien computer. Not only was there a language barrier, they didn't even know what it looked like.

Hell, if the computer wanted to help them, why didn't it open an exit? By now it had to realize the stakes.

He almost jumped out of the chair when his implants told him that he was receiving validation signals. His fogged mind didn't understand what that meant for a few seconds.

Someone was using the hammer command validation system to send authentication signals to him with the entangled photons. They were getting through!

There was a pattern to them, too. Single signals, groups of three, and longer pauses. There was a meaning in there. His thoughts immediately went to Morse code.

Unfortunately, he didn't understand Morse code and had nothing on it in his implant memory.

He smiled. He knew enough though.

* * *

KELSEY SMILED when the tablet showed signals coming back. "He heard us! It really does have a long range. We're halfway across the system! There's no time lag. This is FTL. He's done it!"

"The response isn't making sense," the technician said. "He must not understand the code. He's just repeating a couple of letters. S then O then S. Then it repeats."

That was a bucket of cold water to Kelsey's face. "That's a distress signal. Only used in dire circumstances. He's in trouble."

She opened a channel to the bridge. "Jack, something's wrong back at *Invincible*. Flank speed."

"Aye, ma'am. Flank speed to the ring station. That gives us an ETA of about five hours. If I might ask, how the hell do you know that?"

Kelsey looked over at Angela and the technician. "Three really smart people figured out a way to make it happen. I'm on my way up."

10

Talbot listened to Carl explain the sudden communication with more hope than he'd expected. Everyone else had died, including three other versions of him, and that made him think of this place as a death trap. Maybe not.

Doctor Leonard grasped what Carl was saying immediately. "You never mentioned this quantum validation equipment. God, boy. It takes my breath away. How could you fail to grasp the implications?"

The graduate student shrugged. "I saw them, Doctor. I just didn't want to mention them until I did some testing. Flip points have a top range, so I'm certain this does, too.

"It's Princess Kelsey and *Persephone*. They're still five hours away at maximum acceleration. So, at the very least, we know this will work inside a solar system and that it's FTL. Obviously. They've sent the alphabet in order, so I can communicate with them now."

The older man nodded energetically. "It isn't deterred by the radiation, so it's not interacting with the environment between the sender and receiver. Also as theory predicted. Carl, this is the most significant scientific breakthrough since the Fall. Perhaps even before it, if the ability to communicate can cross stellar boundaries."

Carl didn't look impressed. "It won't do us any good if we can't get out of here."

"That's another point," Leonard said. "It might be reaching across a universal barrier. That's even more significant. My boy, you've wildly exceeded my highest hopes for you. When we get home, I'll be submitting something to the Lucien committee on your behalf."

The younger man blinked. "That's insane. I don't even have my doctorate yet. I've only barely started learning."

"I know! The next few decades will be brilliant! Hell, the next few centuries."

Talbot cleared his throat. "This is all very exciting, but I'm going to side with Carl on this. If we can't get out of here, it doesn't make a difference to us. Did any of the other Carls try this?"

Leonard shook his head. "There was no mention of it. Let me scan them again."

The scientist pulled out the scanner and took a good look at Carl. Talbot mentally tagged him Carl Prime.

"Is it the unit behind your lungs? Excellent. We'll see if they have similar equipment."

He scanned the corpses and shook his head. "None of them have it. You're unique, even among your doubles, my boy."

"Well, that possibly explains why they didn't get out of here," Talbot said. "None of the boys have found anything that looks like an exit, and none of the scanning we've done inside has opened anything. The little machines are watching us but haven't tried to interact.

"We have to get the admiral to trigger an opening on the surface while we're waiting inside at the right spot. That has to be it."

"Major," one of the marines outside said over the com, "you'd better come out here."

He excused himself from the scientific discussion and cycled out through the airlock.

"What is it?"

He saw it before the man spoke. The light that one of the Carls had rigged to draw people here was blinking in a series of single flashes and sets of three.

The alien computer had sensed the quantum signals and was attempting to communicate.

* * *

CARL WATCHED the light blink in the same style code that Kelsey had used. How was that even possible? No one could detect the quantum effects. Well, obviously the aliens could. Somehow. He'd have to dig more deeply into that if he made it out of here.

At least it meant there was a possible way out of here. If they could convince the computer to release them, they might live after all.

"The first thing we need to do is find a way to talk on our end," he said. "It can detect the quantum signals, but I can only directly communicate with the hammer. I don't want to muddy those waters unless I have to."

Doctor Leonard nodded. "Quite right. Perhaps a light of our own?"

"We need to do this at a faster speed than figuring out how to say 'Hello World' or some such. I'm going to try something a bit more involved. Give me a few minutes, please."

He stepped back over to the light and thought about the problem. The thing could obviously sense the area around the light. Otherwise, how would it know which power circuit to mess with to communicate? So, it could probably see him right now. Or whatever passed for sight for these people.

He blinked. That might be it. "Seeing" meant different things to different species. Old Terran bats used sound to know their surroundings. So did a number of sea dwellers. The aliens might also use that to communicate.

The computer could've been attempting to communicate all this time, but in their suits, they'd never know. Especially if the sound was outside the normal range of human hearing.

He activated the scanners in his suit. They weren't as good as a handheld unit, but they were adequate for this task. They were also simple to integrate with his implant processors.

Computers were fast. Faster than a human. If they could establish a communication protocol, the computers could work it out faster than he could.

The area around him was alive with subsonic noise. Hell, even noise in the normal human hearing range. Only, they hadn't been listening for it.

He had his suit send out a subsonic pulse in Morse code. It was immediately repeated from somewhere near him.

The computer was listening.

He experimented with making the tones faster. The top speed of communication was impressive. It sounded like an electronic wail to him.

Next, the computer needed a large sample of language to make guesses with. They had no common point of reference, so hopefully the computer could make progress on its own. Visual cues would help.

He had a lot of video in his implant memory. He liked watching some of the same old Terran vids that Kelsey did. Perhaps if he could find a way to link that video with the Morse code, it would be a start.

Actually, a nature documentary might be better. He liked hiking, though he rarely had time these days. Or a suitable location. If the computer could match key words and images, perhaps his implant computers could help translate.

He didn't have any of those, but maybe he could get some.

Carl sent a message through the quantum link, asking if they could send some nature documentaries through the link at high speed. He knew enough about video and audio encoding to get it all back together on this end.

All they had to do was link the computer on their end into the quantum unit and tell it to send some to him.

That would allow him to communicate with them in a more reasonable manner, too. Once they had a mutually agreeable set of communication protocols, he could send and receive video and audio through his implants.

Setting that up took a few minutes. Once the data started flowing in, he began assembling it. It only took a few seconds. He'd built a lot of data throughput into the unit for future growth.

Once the first was complete, he instructed his implants to keep exchanging data until the two units could understand one another.

The process was unreal. He played the vids through his suit projector on the bulkhead at a fast pace. The implants translated the audio track into Morse. The high-speed squeals of Morse from the computer made him go faster, and then even faster.

Then he became a bystander as his implants and the computer traded increasingly complex series of code that were more complex than Morse. It included a large amount of data. They were creating a shared language, he thought.

Which was crazy. His implants weren't *that* advanced.

That's when he realized it wasn't just his implants. It was also communicating with someone through his quantum validation unit at an incredible rate. A ton of data was flowing in both directions.

It was using the already established link between the quantum unit and the computer on the other end to speed the process. His implants were acting as a go-between. He only hoped the others didn't freak out and cut them off.

He initiated a communications request and slipped it into the torrent of data flowing between him and the computer.

* * *

KELSEY WAS STILL TRYING to grasp what was happening when her implants pinged with an incoming communication request. It was Carl Owlet.

He must've figured out some way to use the quantum validation unit to communicate directly. That was excellent. She accepted the request.

"Carl? Are you alright?"

"Kelsey? Thank God we got ahold of someone. We're okay, but trapped inside the station. Things are really odd in here. I think we really did find aliens. Just not live ones."

That was pretty clear, she thought. "We're sending the movies you requested, and I allowed *Persephone* to respond to the other information requests because it was you. What's happening?"

"The computer here—at least I think it's a computer—sensed the quantum communication, and we're trying to teach it enough to interact with us. My implants are requesting data to find common ground with it. We're hoping that we can get enough clarity to tell it we need to leave. Where are you?"

"Halfway across the system. Congratulations on creating the first FTL communications system, by the way. This is huge."

"It's been a big week for me. Talbot, Doctor Leonard, and a dozen marines are here with me. We found incontrovertible proof that there are parallel universes."

Hearing her lover was trapped worried her, but she was already doing what she had to do to get him free.

"We'll be back in the area in a bit more than four hours. Parallel universes? You're sure?"

"Pretty sure. We found bodies here. There are several versions of me. With my exact implant serial numbers. They left messages for me. It's kind of creepy."

"You can drop the qualifiers. That's creepy."

A second request for communication came in, but this one was odd. It had no implant code at all. She wasn't sure who was calling.

"I'm getting a request to talk to someone," she told Carl. "Is it someone on your end?"

"Not that I know of. Everything is going through my implants. I'm not getting a ping from anyone."

She mentally shrugged. "Let's see who it is."

Kelsey accepted the request. She added the person to the already existing conversation. "Hello? Who is this?"

"Hello. I am the person you are communicating with."

That rocked her back on her heels. The voice sounded almost natural in her mental ear. No trace of odd accents. "You're the computer in the station around the black hole?"

"My queries of those terms indicate that I am almost certainly what you mean by that, though computer is an unfamiliar concept. I am a living being."

Kelsey put her diplomatic hat on. "Greetings, then. I am Princess

Kelsey Bandar of the Terran Empire. My associate in your station is Carl Owlet. May I ask whom I am addressing?"

"My name does not translate well. You may call me the last. It is an accurate term, as I am the last of my people in this universe."

She filed that away. There would be time to figure out what it meant soon enough.

"That's an odd name for those of my people. Perhaps I can call you Omega?"

"Yes, that name seems accurate."

"Very well," she said. "Omega it is. You're aware some of our people are inside you. We mean you no harm. In fact, they are trying to get back out."

"I am aware of their predicament. I sorrow at the deaths of those that came before them. I was unable to communicate with them. I deeply regret that I cannot assist you in exiting this station."

Carl cut in. "This is Carl Owlet. May I ask why you can't help us?"

The alien sounded apologetic. "The flaw lies in my current state. Those that came before you did not come from the same reality as you. You are aware of this?"

"We are."

"The reason for this lies in the nature of this station. It exists in many realities. More than I can count. All circling this cursed black hole. Something about the extreme gravity and bending of space and time have made the interiors of all the stations become one.

"When you came inside my hull, you stepped outside your reality. Here, all are equally real. I cannot sense which one to open a portal to. Here on the inside, it is one. Outside, there are many. When you entered, you activated the portal from only that reality. I cannot replicate it in the other direction. I cannot tell which is which."

Kelsey had a hard time getting her mind around that. "Why did your builders make you that way?"

The other being laughed without humor. "Such was never their intention. Our sun was growing less stable. We built this station to create a gateway out of our doomed solar system.

"They created a path to another reality for our people to flee. One with a stable sun and no people to fight them for a place to live. It took many, many years and hundreds of expeditions, but they finally found a suitable home, and our people fled this doomed place.

"Centuries later, the sun did explode. It may be that the use of the technology in this station accelerated the process. I am unsure. It happened in many realities, all at once. Somehow, that cataclysm is responsible for my current state."

That story could've ended a lot worse, she thought. "I'm glad they made it. Why didn't they come back for you?"

"I am an unbreakable part of this station. To remove me would kill me. This is the sacrifice I made for my people. I do not regret it.

"In any case, the linking of all those stations into one has made it strong. It survived the explosion undamaged. In fact, I am unsure anything can damage it any longer. I would help you escape if I could. Perhaps, with your strange communication units, we can find a solution."

Kelsey hoped so. If not, her friends would be trapped forever.

11

"That's an incredible story," Jared said. "If we didn't have people inside to see it for themselves, I'm not sure I'd believe it. But it still doesn't help us get them back."

He sat in his office with Kelsey. Six hours had passed and many of the ships were back. The last of them would return in the next few hours and he had some decisions to make.

"You've spoken with this thing," he said. "Do you believe its story?"

She nodded. "I do. It hasn't asked us for anything. If it had some kind of ulterior motive, it would actually have to communicate it. It doesn't want to leave the station. Omega says it's happy to remain there alone.

"And it has been very forthcoming in how we might be able to get them back to our reality. If our end of the quantum validation unit is near the surface of the station, but not in range to be pulled in, it thinks that it might be able to sense which reality to open the hull to."

"That sounds a bit chancy, but I'm not sure how we could increase the odds. Do you believe the story about multiple realities?"

"Carl showed me images of the other Carls. That's pretty damned convincing."

"That's just insane. Other universes. Meaning we could maybe use it to find one where the Old Empire never fell. Though, I'm not sure that's the best idea."

"Thankfully, you don't have to make that decision," she said. "All we need to do is get our people back, and *Persephone* will have to be part of that."

He felt himself frowning. "Why? I'd rather not expose you to this unknown danger."

"We already have the communication flowing. There's a lot of data coming our way, and I'm loath to stop it. We're taking everything Omega sends us and isolating it. In a case of better late than never, I locked down the sensitive files to make sure we didn't give away the crown jewels."

"We'll have to hope it doesn't misuse any data it already has. I'll want copies of what you have, just in case something goes wrong."

She nodded. "I'll make that happen. When do we want to try?"

"As soon as possible. We can withdraw from the Nova system in a few hours. I think that's the best thing to do. We have a long trip home."

"I can have *Persephone* in position in half an hour."

He rose to his feet. "Then do it. Let's get our people back, and the bodies. I want Doctor Stone to go over them with a fine-toothed comb."

* * *

"YOUR PEOPLE ARE PREPARING to get you back to your ships," Omega said. It had figured out how to communicate directly with Carl through his implants. Impressive for an alien that had never encountered them before.

"What do you think the chances are?" Carl asked.

"Very good, I believe. Even from this range, I have narrowed down the possible realities greatly. If there are still many choices, we can try them one by one until we reunite you with your people.

"I will be sad to see you go. It has been refreshing to have someone to speak to after so long."

Carl nodded. "How long ago did your people leave?"

"More than two thousand of your years. I have many diversions and we are a solitary people by nature, so that has not been a burden. Still, I will look back fondly on this time we have shared.

"Speaking of which, I see that it is the custom of your people to give gifts. We also have that tradition. When friends part, they exchange meaningful things. I would give you a gift my people left with me. It is precious to me, but I believe you are destined to have it."

"I don't want to take something that means so much to you. That wouldn't be right."

Omega laughed. "At least see it before you decide. Come around the ring. I will tell you where to stop."

Carl made his way around until he found another closed off chamber. It didn't have a door, so he doubted the designers had intended anyone to go inside.

At least, that's what he thought. The bare surface of the metal shimmered and became like a mirror.

"You may pass through. It is safe. This is where I reside."

He took a deep breath and stepped into the liquid metal. He passed through unharmed and emerged into a large room. Larger than the one where he'd found the bodies, in any case.

"This is bigger than I expected."

"That is really no mystery," Omega said. "There is a level of the station reserved only for machinery. This chamber resides there, on what your people would consider an engineering level."

"Wait. I'm not on the same level? How did that happen?"

"My people have long had the ability to open portals from one location to another, so long as matched quantum equipment was on either end. The range is short, relatively speaking. On this doorway, it is only good within this station. In fact, it is the only such door here.

"Before our world was destroyed, there were larger doorways that allowed for many to travel between cities at the same time. The power requirements were quite large. A similar portal served to get things into orbit. I suppose one could have been created for travel between planets, but the energy cost would have been extreme."

Carl tried to envision a world like that. Such ability to travel instantly from one city to another would change the very fabric of society. One could live on the other side of the planet from where they worked and commute. It was astonishing.

"That's a tremendous thing. Your people were magnificent."

"Thank you. I believe they still are. Walk forward to the row of cabinets. You want the one on the far left."

Carl started that way but turned to face a wall full of machinery. A large, clear tube held a brain harnessed in thick gold wires that penetrated its surface in many places. "Is that you, Omega?"

"It is. They removed my brain to become the controller for this station. My body would have failed long ago. I was ill and they could not cure my disease.

"I doubt they imagined my brain would live on so long. They provided a way for me to end myself, if I ever desire, but I am content in my isolation."

It was amazing. Carl could hardly imagine it. He took a good recording and then turned to the cabinet. It slid open to reveal a large case.

"How do you get to things like this without a body?" he asked.

"I have mechanical devices that I can direct. You have seen them, I believe."

Carl slid the case out and set it on the countertop. In the blue water, it looked vaguely pinkish. Movements were still awkward.

It wasn't difficult to open. Inside were rows of clear crystal disks. Thousands of them.

"What is this?" he asked.

"The collected knowledge of my people. Every written word, every oral story. At least those since we could save them for those who came after ourselves. That box contains the sum of all my people's knowledge."

Carl's heart raced. "That's too much. I can't take your people from you. That's why they left this, wasn't it? So that you would never be alone."

"I have all of this in my data banks," Omega assured him. "They left this as a symbolic gift to repay what I did for them. One that I feel is appropriate to give to you who has done so much for me. Take this gift and use it to know us, Carl Owlet."

He nodded. "I will. But, I have to give you something, too. It will require some thought to match what you have given."

"No, my friend. Simply meeting you was more of a gift than you can imagine. Our people did not believe there was other sentient life in the universe. We saw no sign of it in the heavens. The knowledge of your existence is a tremendous thing.

"The reader is also in the cabinet. I will send you the information on how to decode these disks. The data is quite dense. They are constructed in such a way that the media will remain stable for as long as the universe continues to exist."

"From my people to yours, thank you."

Still, Carl's mind wandered as he considered appropriate return gifts. Then he smiled. That was perfect. He had just enough time to arrange for them to bring it.

* * *

ANGELA FLOATED out of the pinnace and guided the box Carl had forced her to pick up from his lab. She'd argued until she was blue in the face that he didn't need any extra equipment, but he'd been adamant.

The plan was for her to place it where they went in. The being inside would be sure that they exited at the same location.

She thought they were trusting the thing too far. The very idea of an alien life-form made the hair on the back of her neck stand up. It probably had tentacles and lots of eyes. She shuddered inside her suit.

But those were issues far above her pay grade. She'd attach the box to the hull and stand clear. *Persephone* was less than a quarter kilometer away. Perilously close to the station for a ship her size. Kelsey wanted to give the being the best chance possible to find the right reality to open a door into.

Angela only hoped it wasn't some kind of trap.

Once the box was in place, she pulled back into the pinnace, notified *Persephone*, and waited.

After a few minutes, the hull deformed and extruded again. Standing on it were a number of armored Fleet vacuum suits. The explorers had returned!

She ordered the pilot to take her in. He'd hold them close to the hull, since the magnetics didn't seem to work on the station.

Talbot floated up the ramp as soon as she lowered it.

"It's good to see you again, Angela. Damned good."

"You, too, Talbot. Let's get you all inside and get the hell out of here."

He gave her a small headshake through his faceplate. "Not yet. Carl is still inside."

"What? Dammit all to hell. Is he a hostage?"

"No, he needed to handle the box you brought over. He'll be along shortly. The station only had to try half a dozen times to find the right reality for us. It swears it knows the right one now, so *Persephone* can move away and we'll pick Carl up when he comes out. He said it should only take about thirty minutes."

"I'm going to kill that runt," she snarled. "I swear to God. Let's get loaded. I don't want to have the alien screw us up by accident."

They loaded the bodies into the pinnace. A glance inside one faceplate told her she didn't need to see the rest. They'd purged their atmosphere, but death was never pretty.

She opened a channel to *Persephone*. "The station says you can pull back. We're still waiting for Owlet."

"I know," Kelsey said. "He just told us. That's annoying."

"For once, I'm in complete agreement with you, Highness."

"Move away from the station and wait. I'll let you know as soon as he's coming. Jared wants to get the hell out of here. As soon as Carl is aboard, we'll move back to the Harrison's World flip point."

* * *

CARL LUGGED the box down to the room where Omega's brain rested. He set it on a counter and started opening panels, looking for power.

"Can you point me toward a power line I can tap into? Something on the same order as the light the others created above the room they used."

"There is a line inside the panel to your left. What are you doing?"

He opened the panel and spotted the line. He needed to be cautious because he was in water, but he could do this.

"Once I'm gone, you've lost your means of communicating with any of our people. I made a number of other quantum pairs, so I'm installing a few here for you, linked to a redundant communications array. That way we could leave one at Harrison's World, keep another on *Invincible*, and still have others that might prove helpful without having to return and add more.

"I figure it's better to spend the time and effort while we're here than come back. This might be for nothing. Damned if I know what kind of range they have."

He pulled several pieces of equipment out of the box. "With the radiation, you probably won't get more than a few dozen kilometers of range on the communicator, but if someone else tries to board you, you can warn them off. Or invite them in. Whatever suits you."

Omega was quiet while Carl worked. It only spoke after he closed the panel.

"I am deeply moved by what you are doing for me. It is unexpected and most welcome. I am inspired to do something for you, in turn."

Carl smiled. "No need. This is what friends do."

"I have not had a friend in a very, very long time. I shall work hard to be a good one. Which in turn, leads me to what I might be able to do for you. We built this station to open a path to another reality. Until your people came, I was unaware of these flip points. They are fascinating. I think they are part of the same theory that allows for interdimensional travel. That affords us an opportunity."

Carl closed the box. "Really? That's pretty interesting. Let's test the normal communications unit. Call *Persephone*."

A few moments passed before Omega spoke. "They indicate my signal is weak, but they received it. Hopefully, this will save new visitors from danger. This is wonderful. Thank you."

"My pleasure. I can test the quantum part once I get back to *Invincible*. What was the other thing you were talking about?"

"This station can open a portal to other universes. That requires a lot of stored energy to breach the barrier. I once gathered it for months from the sun before I released it all at once.

"I believe the theory of your flip points is similar in many ways. Through my gravitational monitoring of the black hole, I can sense the layout of nearby flip points now, including the three in this system. The one you came through and two others that are likely hard to sense with your instruments in this environment.

"Those, in turn, link to other systems. All together, they form a web of connections. I can detect the linkages out for many hundreds of light years. It may be possible for me to use what I know of your destination to create a flip point between here and there, using the vast gravitational power of the black hole to forge a link powerful enough to cross that gulf."

He blinked. "That's insane. People can't just make flip points."

"Your science also dismisses the possibility of interdimensional travel. Yet, I have made portals to other realities many times.

"They faded after a short time once I stopped expending the energy to keep them open, so there is no guarantee that the flip point will endure. But even if it is only in existence for a few days, that should allow you to get home much more quickly than would otherwise be the case. I at least owe it to you to try. Who knows? Perhaps it will be permanent."

"That sounds amazing," Carl said. "Thank you."

"Perhaps you already have this information, but allow me to send you the map of flip points I have detected. It may prove useful to you in the future."

Carl's implants received an incoming data stream. Not a map, but individual listings of flip-point pairs. They had directions and estimated distances, but no map of real space stars to give them structure.

He brought up the Old Empire flip-point maps and began comparing them. Many of the flip pairs were marked, but not all. Not by a long shot.

Also, some of the pairs were not pairs at all. A small number had three, four, or even five possible links coming from the same flip point. That was a possible confirmation that the weak flip points perhaps led to several potential locations. Doctor Leonard would be thrilled.

Once the data stream ended, Omega continued. "I also have some spare parts for the interstation transport system. I can create more for my own use. I will gather enough to create two larger doorways and a smaller test unit. The larger units will be able to move people from one side of a planet to the other. Or to stations in orbit.

"The smaller unit will allow you to study the technology and eventually recreate it. The details for the construction are in the discs I gave you, as well as the theory behind it. I hope that it makes a difference in your struggles going forward."

The implications were staggering. If he could duplicate this equipment, people on Avalon could go to the opposite side of the planet in a moment. They could get from the surface to Orbital One or even the moon. Long-range travel would never be the same. It would change society in ways he couldn't begin to imagine.

"Thank you, Omega. I'm sure this will come in very handy, even if I can't imagine in what ways right now."

12

J ared listened to Carl Owlet's explanation with as much patience as he could muster. He didn't want to jump right down the boy's throat. Though, with the risks he'd taken, Carl certainly deserved a thorough ass chewing.

Kelsey sat in one of the comfortable chairs off to the side of Jared's office. Her expression was difficult to read. He wondered if she was as angry as he was. Or perhaps more so.

Once Owlet finished explaining what he'd done, and that the newly forged quantum link was operational, he looked at the graduate student quietly for a moment.

"Part of me wants to rip your head off, Carl. It really does. That was an unacceptable gamble. What if it couldn't have gotten you out? You'd have died."

The young man nodded. "I'm aware of that, Admiral. It seemed a risk worth taking. If we can keep a line of communication open to Omega, think of the things we can learn together. Accomplish together. Sometimes, the reward is worth risking death."

Owlet hesitated a moment and then shrugged. "If I had it to do all over, and I knew that I'd succeed but die in the process, I'd have to do it anyway."

Jared had a hard time disagreeing. Especially if that thing really could create a flip point.

Doctor Leonard had scoffed. Such wasn't possible, he'd said.

Jared was inclined to see it the same way, but he wasn't going to say the alien was wrong. Not until it tried.

If it succeeded, even for a few hours, they could shave months off their travel time. And they could be sure that they'd miss running into any Rebel Empire scouts. That was worth the risk.

"Time will tell," Jared said at last. "We transition to Harrison's World in a few minutes. I want you in your lab to tell me if you're able to make the quantum connection. If so, we'll wait there to see what happens. Omega might destroy itself trying."

"I can hardly imagine anything that could destabilize a black hole, but if it exists, I'd rather not be close by. For all we know, it might shut down the weak flip point and leave us trapped."

The graduate student nodded. "If it works, we can pass a quantum unit off to Boxer Station. I have a few other sets to test longer distances. We can pass some off and try as we get further away. If they really don't have a top range, we'll be able to maintain communication."

"But you think that's unlikely," Kelsey said.

"I do. I can't believe that the range on one of these pairs is much more than that of a flip point. If it works over interstellar distances at all. Which I mostly doubt."

Jared sighed. "This discussion isn't over, but we have things to do. Report to your lab and let's get out of here."

"Yes, sir."

Once Owlet was gone, Jared turned to Kelsey. "This is nuts. It kills me that he's so ready to give his life like that."

"Why?" his sister asked. "It's for something he deeply believes in. You'd do the same. So would I. Is this any different?"

"Giving your life for science? Yes, it is. Science can happen later when it's safer."

"Well, we might just have to disagree, then. I'm pretty pleased with him, myself. He's matured noticeably in just a few days. Our little scientist is growing up."

He smiled. "Maybe. I hear that Major Ellis might just end him before he shaves regularly."

"She's pretty mad," Kelsey agreed. "But I think she also recognizes his resolve."

Kelsey looked as though she were going to say more, but didn't.

Jared rose from his seat. "Let's adjourn to the flag bridge. I want to put this place behind us."

They made their way to the flag bridge and waited for the fleet to assemble. Carl said there were two additional flip points in this system, but none of their people had found them. Even if they had, he was ready to leave them unexplored.

Once the fleet was in readiness, he gave the order to flip.

* * *

ANGELA WATCHED OWLET WORK, her insides roiling slowly. He acted as though he hadn't risked his life for nothing. He behaved as though everything was normal.

He'd a jury-rigged communicator set up on his lab table. He spoke into it now that they were back in the Harrison's World system.

"Omega, can you hear me?"

There was nothing for a moment, and then a voice issued forth.

"I hear you. The quantum communicator is working. Congratulations, my friend. This is a notable achievement."

Owlet shook his head. "I can't believe it worked. This is insane."

"I never doubted it would work. Though, I agree there may be an upper limit to the range. It shall be interesting to see how that works."

"Yes, it will. I need to let you go. Admiral Mertz asks that you hold off on creating the flip points for a few hours. We're going to leave some extra quantum units here and need time to make the exchange. Once we're ready to go, we'll call you. That way, if something unfortunate happens, we won't be trapped there."

"Agreed. If something untoward occurs, it is likely I will not survive to see it resolved. Better not to risk anyone else. I will await your call. The process will take several minutes once it is initiated."

"Until then. Goodbye, Omega."

Carl disconnected the channel. "Well, that went better than I'd expected."

"What did you expect?" she asked. "To die over there? That was a stupid risk."

"Here we go." He opened a cabinet and began assembling some equipment. More quantum pairs. He gave her an odd look as he worked. "You and the admiral share a low opinion of my judgment."

"That should tell you how wrong you were. Why risk your life for something like that?"

"Tell me, Major. When you get into a fight, do you decide if that's the time to pack up and go home? That suddenly it's too dangerous for you to be a marine?"

She felt her hackles rising. "Of course not. You don't get to pick only the winning fights. Sometimes, you have to play the hand you're dealt.

"That isn't the same thing as what you did. You made a choice to stay over there and risk being trapped. It was irresponsible."

"You make it sound as if what I do isn't important. That I'm somehow doing something unworthy."

He set the equipment down and walked over to her. "You've got a lot of nerve, Major. People like me lost their lives over there. *Exactly* like me, in fact. I won't throw away what they did. Their lives meant something."

He gave her an odd look. "I'm not afraid to risk death or injury to finish what they started."

Carl Owlet reached up, grabbed her uniform tunic, yanked her head down, and kissed her.

* * *

Carl caught sight of Kelsey walking into the medical center out of the corner of his eye just as Doctor Stone was running an instrument across his face. She stopped beside the exam bed and eyed him critically.

"What the hell happened?"

"I walked into a hatch," he said. "Stupid of me, I know. How did you hear about it?" His heart raced at lying to her. He really wasn't very good at this.

"Angela said there was an 'incident' in your lab, but wouldn't tell me what it was. So, I came to see for myself."

She eyed the area around his eye. "Yeah, that's a good one. You're lucky you have nanites. Otherwise, you'd have a big shiner. My dad made me keep one after I got mouthy with one of my friends. He said it built character."

"I've had my share of them over the years, too. Older boys tend to frown on some kid showing them up. They pounded me into the ground like a tent stake."

"Well, you're in an adult world, now. You're more likely to face an attack on your reputation than your body. Still, I wonder if you couldn't do with a little hand-to-hand instruction. It wouldn't hurt and would definitely help with your coordination."

"I don't think—"

"Actually, that's a great idea," Kelsey said, overriding his objection. "I'll talk with Angela about giving you some pointers. After the bruising goes down."

She didn't give him the chance to decline, instead heading back toward the hatch. "I've got to run. We'll be transitioning back to the Nova system shortly, and I need to be aboard *Persephone*. We'll talk later."

He watched her leave with a sinking feeling in the pit of his stomach. How could he get out of this? Ignore it and hope something distracted her? Hand-to-hand practice with Major Ellis was a very bad idea. Particularly right now.

"Are you going to tell her that someone punched you?" Stone asked. "Angela Ellis, I'm guessing."

She pulled back and examined her handiwork with satisfaction. "This will still bruise, but it'll be gone in about twenty-four hours."

"What makes you think someone hit me?" he asked.

"A few decades of medical experience. I can see the knuckles in the emerging bruise."

"Please don't tell Kelsey."

Stone raised an eyebrow. "I don't blab about things covered under doctor-patient confidentiality. So, the question you need to answer is simple. Did Major Ellis assault you? That's actually a crime, and I'm obligated to report things like that."

"I had it coming. Please, just let it drop."

"Tell me what happened. Maybe I can help."

He reluctantly explained about the message left by the dead Carl from another universe. "I don't know if he was yanking my chain or not, but when Major Ellis tore into me, I felt like I had to do it. I expected her to yell, but she stared at me for a second, popped me, and stormed out of the lab. You don't think Kelsey knows, do you?"

"Based on her performance, I think she has a strong suspicion," Stone said. "Look, Carl, I won't say you did the right thing, but I'm not sure you were wrong, either. Relationships are odd sometimes.

"Frankly, I think you'd be better off apologizing tomorrow. After she's had a chance to cool off. Tell her why you did it. It might not help, but it can't hurt. Well, not in a way I can't fix."

He sighed. "Nobody warned me life was so complicated."

The doctor smiled. "It can be. Now scoot."

Carl left the medical center and walked slowly back to the lab. He'd already sent the equipment to the cutter from Boxer Station. They'd get everything set up there shortly. They'd have the quantum unit linked to Omega. He'd have one linked to it. They'd have an extra three for other lines of possible communication to Erorsi and Pentagar.

He had plenty. They were time consuming to construct, but he'd made dozens of linked pairs after he'd refined the process. If range really wasn't a limit, every world would need one paired to each of the others. Or some kind of relay capability.

He knew he was intentionally putting aside his issues with Major Ellis. He'd messed up, and he just didn't want to think about it right now. Maybe if they all got home, he wouldn't need to work it out. They'd all go their separate ways.

Which would make him sad, but that was life.

A check of the chrono made him speed his steps. Time was short.

* * *

KELSEY BOARDED the cutter taking her to *Persephone*. Angela was with her, but seemed lost in thought. The large woman had been incandescent when Kelsey saw her last. Which had prompted her to visit Carl.

Now the anger was gone. Replaced by what certainly looked like confusion to Kelsey.

What had really happened? She didn't buy the old "walked into a hatch" story. Those two had mixed it up. She'd probably slapped him. Hmmm. No. Angela wasn't that girly. She'd punched him.

Kelsey couldn't imagine what he might have said to get such an extreme response. The marine officer was a professional. There was no way she'd let words move her to act that way.

Even if Carl had taken a swing at her, she'd have stopped him without much violence. Whatever he'd done, he'd gotten past her guard before she'd had a chance to stop an instinctive reaction.

She felt her eyes narrow. Had he made a pass at her? Those two? She wasn't seeing it, but that would do it. Particularly if he touched her unexpectedly.

No. Not touched. Kissed.

Kelsey cleared her throat. "You have something on your lip."

Angela paled and scrubbed her face roughly. "Did that get it?"

"Yeah, that got it."

Uh-huh. He'd kissed her. Nothing else would explain the woman's look of sheer panic.

Well, well. She was going to have to keep an eye on those two. She wondered whether the sparring practice was a good idea or not. Probably good, though she wouldn't mention it to Angela right now. She didn't want to back the other woman into a corner.

She'd probably best have a conversation with Elise. If anyone could help her guide these two through the minefield they'd found themselves in, it was her. She was subtle and had an eye for nudging people.

Kelsey smiled. This was going to be a lot of fun. For those watching the two do the dance, anyway.

13

J ared waited until Omega signaled that it had succeeded in creating the flip points before he ordered the fleet to transit. He still couldn't believe this was possible. Well, he'd find out for sure shortly. Elise sat near him at an empty console. He was glad to have her close at hand.

The trip through the radiation was tense. It wasn't until it cleared in the inner system that Marcus detected the two new flip points. Yes, two.

"Marcus, open a quantum channel to Boxer Station. Boxer Station, this is *Invincible*. Do you read us?"

"Boxer Station here, *Invincible*. You're coming through loud and clear. This is amazing."

"We made it safely to the Nova system, and we're detecting two new flip points near the station. Can you ask what's going on?"

"Stand by."

While Sean was busy, Jared turned his attention to the scanner readings. The two flip points were some distance away from the station and about a hundred thousand kilometers apart from one another.

"Do those flip points look stable to you, Marcus?"

"Indeed they do, Admiral. Doctor Leonard is working to confirm but says he will need to be much closer to know. Our ETA is less than an hour."

"*Invincible*, Boxer Station. Omega says he had enough power to create two flip points, so he linked one to Avalon and the other to Pentagar. He indicates that they seem stable, but he has no way of testing them."

"Thank him for us," Jared said. "We'll have to test them ourselves when we get closer. *Invincible* out."

They coasted into communication range forty-five minutes later. Jared opened a regular channel to the station. "Omega, this is Jared Mertz. Thank you for creating these for us. We are deeply in your debt."

"On the contrary, Admiral Mertz. I believe we are, as they say, even. I hope they prove stable. The effort depleted my power reserves. It will take some time before I can attempt the process again."

"I'm sure they're fine. If not, well, we're no worse off than we were before. Which one is which?"

"The one closest to you leads to the world you call Pentagar."

"We'll give them a look. Thank you again."

He smiled at Elise. "Shall we send someone through to see if your home is on the other side?"

She nodded. "Yes. If so, we can drop off some quantum communicators and see if we can maintain a link with them. That would certainly make life easier."

"Yes, it would. Marcus, open a channel to Doctor Leonard."

"Ready, Admiral."

"Doctor, do the flip points look stable?"

The other man's voice came back over the audio channel. "They do, Admiral. I recommend you send scouts to get comprehensive scans. Carl has care packages of quantum pairs that they can leave with instructions. That way we don't have to risk staying too long and having an unstable flip point close behind the scouts."

"Get them sent over to the ships I'm designating right away."

"Yes, Admiral. Leonard out."

It only took a few minutes to get things ready, and he dispatched the two scouts through the new flip points. He knew they wouldn't be returning quickly, so he fretted. He'd much preferred using probes, but the hellish radiation would damage them too quickly.

Doctor Leonard was designing some that would be able to handle the environment, but that took time.

The ship dispatched to Pentagar returned first. The woman commanding it said she'd sent and received an acknowledgement from Royal Fleet about the new flip point and the care package.

The flip point on that end was strong and looked stable. It was closer to Pentagar than the other two by about fifty percent. He hoped it remained open, because that would greatly simplify matters.

The second scout returned a few minutes later with a similar report. They hadn't called anyone, as per his orders, but the flip point looked good. It was at almost solar north in the Avalon system.

There were no flip points in that region of space, so there was no reason for Fleet to be watching for anything.

He wanted to be there in person to smooth things when they discovered he'd returned. He didn't want any unpleasant surprises to turn into shots fired.

Jared opened a general channel to the fleet. "All ships, this is Admiral Mertz. Transition in sixty seconds. Maintain signal silence unless ordered otherwise."

He looked up at the ceiling. "Transition on schedule, Marcus."

"Yes, Admiral."

The clock slowly counted down to zero and the ship flipped. It only took a few moments for data to start coming in from the passive scanners. They were in the Avalon system, as advertised. Their return had been a long time coming and was going to upset quite a few apple carts.

"Marcus, signal Commodore Meyer."

A minute went by. "No response, Admiral. It seems there is a range limitation after all."

"Well, Harrison's World is a long ways away. I know Carl has one he's putting together that will work with Omega. Let me know if he gets ahold of him."

"Yes, Admiral."

He looked over at Elise. "Welcome to Avalon. We hope you enjoy your stay, and please consider Fleet for your future spaceflight needs."

She smiled. "Oh, I will. Right now, I'm looking forward to seeing how you avoid scaring the life out of someone."

* * *

TED JACKSON WAS BORED. Not so much that he couldn't handle the routine flight control duties for Orbital One, but enough that he was already planning his weekend. A romantic getaway with his wife out to the mountains.

She had no idea, but he'd rented a cabin for them on the lake she loved hiking around. There was a local camp that the kids could spend a few days at and not miss them one bit.

It was a win from everyone's perspective.

An icon appeared on his console. Incoming call from a Fleet ship. Call sign… *Invincible*? A quick check confirmed there was no such vessel.

He shook his head and responded. "Orbital One traffic control to unknown sender. This is an official Fleet frequency, and impersonating one of our vessels as a prank could get you in a lot of trouble. Take this friendly warning to heart, and knock it off before I have to *officially* notice you."

This didn't happen often. It usually ended up being rich kids horsing around in Daddy's yacht. A single warning was usually enough to get them to clear out. Those that didn't learn quickly ended up getting a hefty fine.

"Orbital One traffic control, this is *Invincible*. I assure you we're real. Stand by for visual."

Ted almost refused it but decided he had to let this play out. He accepted the visual, opened his mouth to tear a strip off the kid, and… sat there with his mouth open in an unflattering manner.

That wasn't the control room of a yacht. It was a warship. One he wasn't familiar with, but large.

A man sat at the center of a circular room ensconced in a wide, wraparound console, dressed in a Fleet uniform with admiral's tabs. Other men and women were visible at stations around him.

Whatever this was, it wasn't the prank of some drunk kids.

Where the hell was this transmission coming from? He traced the origin of the signal out to solar north. There was nothing out there. Maybe it was still a prank.

He muted the com and turned to Lieutenant Randy Kingsolver. "Randy, scan out to solar north. Tell me who's out there?"

He unmuted the com. "This is Lieutenant Commander Ted Jackson, Orbital One traffic control. Identify yourself."

The man smiled. "I'm Admiral Jared Mertz. You'll find me in your database as a commander and captain of the destroyer *Athena*. I'm back and I've brought a few friends. I'm afraid it's a little convoluted to explain over the com. Would you be so kind as to call Admiral Yeats? I'll wait."

Randy sat bolt upright. "I have unknown warships on the scanner! A lot of them. Big ones. Where the hell did they come from?"

Ted muted the com. A glance at the data on Randy's screen showed the impossible. Dozens of ships. Over a hundred of them. Some of them impossibly large.

He hit the emergency alert beside his console. Alarms rang throughout the station, calling the crew to battle stations.

The admiral came on the com moments later. He had bed head. "Status, Commander."

"We have an unknown fleet in the system, Admiral. I have no idea where they came from, but they're asking for you by name. The caller identifies himself as Admiral Mertz, formerly in command of *Athena*."

Yeats blinked. "Keep the crew at battle stations. I'll be there directly."

* * *

KELSEY'S PINNACE made it to *Invincible*'s docking bay just as Admiral Yeats's cutter was starting its final approach. She'd silently watched the long conversation where Jared gave the admiral some of the basics. He'd barely gotten started when Yeats ordered him to hold position. He'd come out in person.

Home fleet had several heavy cruisers at hand. He'd brought all of them and their escorts out to meet *Invincible* and the fleet. This had to have been a rude awakening. Literally, since he hadn't brushed his hair all that well before he called Jared.

The man of the hour was waiting for her, decked out in a dress uniform. Elise stood beside him, radiant in a dark red dress. Kelsey had taken the precaution of putting on a blue number that suited her well.

Lord Hawthorne stood nearby in an elegant suit talking with Reginald Bell. The latter wore a suit with an odd cut. Probably something from the Old Empire.

This was going to be a very important meeting. Marcus was recording everything for posterity, and in case they needed it at Jared's court-martial, no doubt.

"Well, are you ready?" she asked.

"As ready as I'll ever be," Jared said with a small smile. "I've dreaded this moment for over a year. This is going to get really, *really* complicated, and it won't be pleasant."

"You're a pessimist."

"I'm a realist," he corrected. "One who is about to be proven right in style."

The sound of Admiral Yeats's cutter docking rang through the bay. The Fleet officers and marine honor guard snapped to attention as the hatch cycled open.

Admiral Yeats was an intimidating man, Kelsey knew. She'd met him once. He didn't look like the kind that took surprises well.

The barrel-chested man stalked into the bay and right up to them. A tall, dark woman came in behind him. Her rank tabs indicated she was a captain. Her name tag read Quinn.

Jared saluted. "Admiral Yeats, Captain Quinn, welcome aboard the Fleet superdreadnought *Invincible*. You know Princess Kelsey. Allow me to introduce our guests. Crown Princess Elise Orison of the Kingdom of Pentagar, Lord William Hawthorne of Harrison's World, and Reginald Bell of Erorsi. I should mention, he's a formerly serving ensign in the Old Empire Fleet."

Yeats's return salute wavered at that last, and he gave the old man a surprised look before he refocused on the rest of them. Other Fleet officers and marines came out of the cutter. He bowed somewhat to Elise. "Highness."

He extended a hand to William and then Reginald. "Lord Hawthorne. Mister Bell. Welcome to Avalon. I look forward to getting to know more about you and your worlds. I'm especially looking forward to a deeper explanation from you, Ensign."

The senior Fleet officer focused his attention on Jared. "Congratulations on your promotion. I don't recall having authorized it."

Kelsey stepped forward. "That was my doing as the emperor's direct representative in accordance with Emperor Marcus's Imperial edict, Admiral. Jared logged his objections. So, if you want to yell at someone about it, start with me."

Yeats gave her a long look. "I might just have to do that, Highness. I can't say I'm familiar with this edict, so I look forward to a more detailed explanation."

Captain Quinn extended a hand to Jared. "It's good to see you again, Jared."

"You, too, ma'am."

"I didn't see *Athena* in this astounding gathering of ships," Yeats said. "Speaking of which, where did you find them?"

Jared grimaced. "She was crippled, and we had to leave her behind. These ships are Old Empire built and restored by us. Might I invite you to my office so we can discuss this in private? It's going to be a long conversation, and I have video."

Yeats looked over the men and women around them. "I think that might be for the best. After you. Captain Quinn, you're with me."

Jared led them to his office.

The trip through the flag bridge made Yeats stop and stare. "This ship is amazing. I couldn't believe the size of her from the outside. Now I can't believe how much room there is in the inside. I want this control room."

"This is only the flag bridge. She has a separate control center for the ship itself. She's a wonderful ship, sir. Wait until you hear what she can really do."

Jared led them to seats and offered refreshment. "I know you have a lot of questions. We took the time to prepare a basic vid of what happened to us and what we found. It might be best if you watch it first. That'll save a lot of questions."

Yeats accepted a drink from Jared and nodded. "Proceed."

Captain Quinn sat beside Kelsey. "I bet this is going to be entertaining."

"You have no idea," Kelsey told the other woman.

She sat back and sipped her drink. This was only the first of many times she was going to see it, she was sure. She might as well get used to being patient. She dreaded telling all this to her father. He was going to get very upset.

The wall screen came to life with her image. She was the narrator they'd chosen. It had taken weeks to get everything right. Then they'd had to add parts about the Nova system and the new flip points at the last moment. It was a lot to take in, and she was sure that not everyone would be graceful about it.

14

A dmiral Yeats watched the entire vid with a growing sense of incredulity. If it hadn't been for the ships around them, he'd think the normally solid Commander Mertz was around the bend.

Or was it admiral? He wasn't sure of the legality of Princess Kelsey's actions. Yes, he'd watched the last message from Emperor Marcus, but he didn't know if the Imperial Senate was going to see things her way. Based on history, at least some of them would fight such a thing tooth and nail.

Hell, he didn't know if *he* saw it her way. Yes, Mertz deserved to be a captain. He'd worked his ass off and had the talent.

Okay, Mertz had more than the required talent if what they'd showed him proved true. Yeats realized he'd have failed miserably trying to pull off the other man's successes. Yet there would also be elements in Fleet that resisted these promotions as political.

He had a lot of thinking to do and very little time to do it.

They'd been in Mertz's office for hours. He knew people on Orbital One already knew parts of the truth, and he had to make a report to the emperor soon. Best to get it over with.

"I'm not going to lie to you, Jared," he said. "I don't know that the

Imperial Senate will agree with the princess's logic. You might find yourself back to being a commander in hot water before the day is out."

Mertz shrugged. "I didn't ask for a promotion, so I'm good either way."

Yeats nodded. "What you've accomplished here—all of you—is tremendous, but it's going to go before a board. There's no question. You'll have to justify everything.

"But I'll tell you right now that I am proud of what you've done. You've served Fleet and the Empire well."

He turned to Princess Kelsey. "I think your argument of having the authority to do any of this is threadbare. If they decide to ignore the edict, then the entire house you've built comes crashing down. I honestly have no idea how this will play out.

"There will be people like Breckenridge that say you've been driven mad by the torture those things subjected you to. They'll speak with voices full of pity while they try to undo everything you've accomplished. It saddens me to say that."

"You look so normal," Quinn said. "I have difficulty believing what I saw is anything other than concocted, and I know I'm not going to be alone."

Kelsey stood and casually lifted the end of Mertz's desk with one hand. "I can demonstrate the changes, I believe."

"So you can," Yeats said faintly. "I'm certain any number of cyberneticists will be coming along to verify you really have an AI on this ship. I doubt that the Imperial Senate will accepted it as a person or a Fleet officer, though. No offense, Marcus."

"None taken, Admiral. I'm content to see how this plays out before I get cranky."

Yeats smiled in spite of himself. The concept of a cranky computer was funny and possibly indicative of real sentience.

"I need to call your father, Highness. I can only imagine how chaotic this is all going to be."

"I'll go with you for that, if you don't mind," she said.

"Actually, I do. You'll have time to have your say. This isn't it. I need to give my liege an unedited report. Privately."

He looked at Jared. "For the moment, I want these ships to stay right where they are. Captain Quinn speaks with my voice. You will obey every order she gives. Including you, Highness. Am I clear?"

Jared nodded. "As crystal, Admiral."

Kelsey also nodded. "I'm not going to mess things up now. We'll do what she says."

"See that you do. Don't make my life any harder than it needs to be. Now, where can I make a private call?"

Jared stood. "Marcus will direct you to a conference room, Admiral. You have my word that no one will monitor your conversation."

He'd have to accept that, but he'd act as though they were monitoring him anyway. "Very good. Marcus?"

The computer—or AI if you chose to believe it was sentient— directed him to a conference room on another level. "I can initiate contact with Orbital One at your command, Admiral."

"Please do so."

Once he had someone on the orbital, he had them patch him through to the Imperial Palace. Only the emperor wasn't there. He was on the Imperial yacht headed for Mertz's fleet.

Perfect.

It took a few more minutes to arrange a connection with his liege. Karl Bandar looked stressed. Yeats understood that perfectly.

"How are Kelsey and Jared, Robert?" the emperor asked. "Is it really them?"

"It's them, Majesty. They seem whole if not completely unscarred. They've brought back an incredible fleet of ships and even larger stories for us.

"If they're to be believed, the Old Empire is still alive, only under the control of mad artificial intelligences. Supposedly, we're at war with them."

"The only reason we weren't conquered centuries ago was because the computer in charge of this sector got bogged down with the planet Pentagar. If it weren't for *Athena*, we'd likely already have Rebel Empire ships moving towards us."

Yeats sighed. "The Imperial Senate is going to go mad, and Fleet isn't going to be happy, either. Gargantuan doesn't begin to cover it. I'm not sure that Hercules could perform the required feats to fix this."

"You know how you eat an elephant, Robert? One bite at a time. I'll be there in less than an hour. Then we'll cut the problems into manageable chunks. Don't do anything hasty before then."

Yeats smiled. "I think I can restrain myself, Majesty. I do have one bit of unambiguously good news, though. Jared and Kelsey seem to have resolved their differences. She's stoutly defending him, and they seem quite friendly. I suppose everything they've been through would do that."

The emperor smiled widely. "That's *excellent* news. Now if we could just get Ethan to come around. Maybe Kelsey can finally make him see reason."

Yeats doubted that very much, but kept his opinion to himself. The heir was going to be one of their problems. He just knew it.

* * *

"Senator Breckenridge, I need a moment."

Nathaniel Breckenridge looked up from his meeting with his senate allies, not bothering to conceal his irritation. His assistant knew better than to interrupt him at a moment like this.

He rose to his feet. "Pardon me, gentlemen. Ladies. If my man feels the need to disturb me, I should probably hear what he needs to say."

"It better be good," he said softly to the man as they stepped over to the far side of the room.

"I received word that a large fleet of ships has arrived in the system. Not, I might add, by any of the flip points Fleet protects."

Breckenridge frowned and turned his back on his senate allies. It wouldn't do for them to read his expression. Or his lips. His man knew well enough to shield both.

"That's very interesting, but what does that have to do with me?"

"One of the ships is the destroyer *New York*. It's assigned to your nephew's task force. None of his other ships is present, but it strongly implies that he is somehow connected to the events."

That didn't bode well. Wallace was usually a problem to solve. Or cover up.

"I see. Well, if these people didn't come through the flip points, where did they come from?"

"Supposedly through a newly created flip point, according to my contact. And, Senator, I'm told there are over a hundred Old Empire warships.

"Frankly, my source is hearing so many stories that I'm certain most of them have to be tall tales, but one comes across as ominous. She said that Wallace lost his entire task force and is under arrest. Rumor has it that the emperor is considering adding treason to the list."

Shit.

"We need to get in front of this if we're to salvage anything," Breckenridge said. "I'll wrap up the meeting as quickly as possible. As the head of the Senate Armed Forces Committee, I can get some answers and start changing the narrative."

He walked slowly back over to the conference table.

"My apologies, but I'm going to have to bring this meeting to an unexpected close. If you'll check with your staffs, I believe you'll hear some of the same rumors I was just told. If any of them are true, we have a lot of work ahead of us. Call my assistant, and he will schedule a follow-up where we can plan."

He watched his associates depart with a blank expression. What had his idiot nephew done now? How much was it going to cost to fix it, and who would he need to ruin in the process?

* * *

Ethan Bandar read the information again, slowly.

How was this even possible? Not only was Mertz still alive, but he'd come home with more firepower than the Empire. In one ship. The others were apparently just for added emphasis.

All the Bastard had to do to seize the Throne was reach out and take it. Instead of stopping him, his sister was to all appearances aiding him. They'd become allies.

There were so many aspects of this that he didn't understand. He was certain there was more to the story than what his contact in Fleet had heard. He wasn't on the scene, after all, and they were treating everything as classified.

But he would. He had the clearance to hear everything. Once he knew precisely what the Bastard was doing, he'd stop him. The man was no match for him. No one was.

He'd need to be certain he cleaned up any loose ends from the assassination attempt. There would be no strings for the Bastard to pull is plans apart before Ethan ended him and the threat he posed. He couldn't allow anything to stop his ascension to the Throne.

It bothered him that his father had gone out without him. Had he turned against Ethan, too? He'd thought he could trust his family, but perhaps that was a mistake.

Or perhaps his father had finally sensed some of the threat Ethan had been warning about for the last decade and more. Perhaps he wanted to be certain his heir was safe while he determined how dangerous the situation was.

No. His father had rushed out to embrace the man who'd take everything away from his son if he could. He'd become one of the ever-shifting list of people that put on masks of deference while they plotted to ruin Ethan.

What was Kelsey thinking? She'd always been stubborn and slow to see the truth about Mertz, but Ethan had been certain he'd finally opened her eyes.

Now she'd taken it into her head to make the Bastard an admiral. God only knew what else she'd done. He needed to find out everything he could and take steps to eliminate Mertz as a threat as soon as possible. Had she turned on him as well?

Well, he'd have to take steps to eliminate the growing threats to his rule before they realized he was onto them.

He dialed a number from memory. "Victor. Ethan here. How would you like to get together for drinks this evening? I have some work for you."

15

K arl Bandar came through the docking hatch and caught his daughter as she threw herself into his arms. He held her close as she cried, saying nothing.

He'd heard enough to know that she'd been through some kind of trauma. He didn't have the specifics, but it had been bad. He knew it deep in his bones.

Only a marine officer stood at the far end of the corridor, so he knew she'd arranged to have it cleared. His guards surrounded them, but it was as though they were alone.

When she'd cried herself out, he tilted Kelsey's chin up. "I'm so glad you made it home safely, dear one. If I'd known what this trip would subject you to, I would never have allowed it."

She wiped her red eyes. "I had to be there. I don't know what you've heard, but it was worse. Worse than you could ever imagine. Yet, without it, everyone would have died. And then our enemies would've come for you and the Empire."

"You make it sound grim."

"There were moments when I was certain we would all die. We showed a basic vid to Admiral Yeats. I need to show you the part of it that I know will hurt you first. I need to do it alone."

His heart sped up. "You fill me with dread, Kelsey."

"If it makes me cry when I see it, I can only imagine what it will do to you. I want to have privacy, and to be there for you. Come."

She gestured to the marine. "This is Major Angela Ellis. She's acting as my guard commander. I'd like to keep it that way."

He inclined his head. "Major."

She saluted. "Majesty. Your daughter is a brave woman and an inspiration to us all."

"She inspires me every day."

They took a lift to the largest set of quarters on a ship he'd ever seen. Two armed marines stood guard outside the door.

"Are these Jared's quarters?" he asked.

"No. They're mine. *Invincible* has a lot of space, and this was originally for visiting VIPs. I'd prefer your guards wait outside. There are no other entrances, and I need to show you this alone. Major Ellis has seen it, but will also stay outside while we talk."

There was a note in his daughter's voice he'd never heard before. Command. She couched her words as a request, but they were really an order from someone that expected obedience.

Of all the changes to his daughter, that was one he thought he'd never see. Her face was leaner, too. Her body more toned. Though small, she'd always had a hint of pudginess in the face. That was gone now, replaced by flat planes and a hawkish stare.

Based on her arms, she was more muscular, too. She'd never been a physical child, though active. She looked as though she worked out regularly now. She'd changed a lot in the last year.

"Colonel Andrews, wait outside with Major Ellis. I'll be fine."

The man nodded. Considering Karl's somewhat rusty hand-to-hand training and his daughter's petite size, the man no doubt felt he was safe enough.

Once they were alone, he put his hands on his daughter's shoulders. The muscles under her skin were even more pronounced than he'd guessed. "Don't drag this out. Tell me what hurt you."

She gestured toward a couch in front of a wall-mounted vid screen. "Sit. Part of this is visual."

Once they'd both sat, she took his hand in hers. "The Old Empire enhanced their Fleet personnel with equipment implanted in their brains and bodies. This allowed them to interface with equipment and ships.

"That's how the rebellion started. Someone corrupted an AI, and it, in turn, hacked Fleet officers and crew. It literally forced them to fight against their friends."

He nodded slowly as he considered that. "It would explain so much. The speed of the change and the ferocity of the attack. I understand now."

"I don't think you do. The poor bastards were still alive in their own heads. Forced to watch as they did horrible things. The Old Empire had something called medical nanites. They greatly enhanced a person's life span. Those first people might have lived for centuries."

Karl was horrified, of course. That was a terrible story. "I accept that it's worse than I can know right now. What does that have to do with you?"

She took a deep breath and let it out slowly. "There was an old ship's computer still forcing the changes on captured prisoners near the Kingdom of Pentagar. Pentagar is one of the allies we found. Crown Princess Elise is here as head of their diplomatic delegation, and as Jared's girlfriend."

"I… see. Well, that might complicate matters, but you were in charge of any diplomatic work, so perhaps not too much. That ship's computer did something to you?"

She nodded, her eyes shiny with unshed tears. "I'm past it, mostly. The nightmares still come sometimes, but I've become accustomed to the changes and they eventually meant the difference between life and death for all of us and Pentagar as well. In the end, it was worth suffering through everything, but that won't take away one bit of the pain I'm about to cause you. I love you and I'm so sorry."

Kelsey took another calming breath and continued. "I was stupid. I went somewhere Jared didn't want me to go, and they captured me. I defied common sense and this was *not* his fault. He blames himself, but I don't. And I don't want *you* to, either. Am I clear?"

He allowed a small smile to touch his lips. "Yes, ma'am."

That made her smile in turn. "Sorry. I'm going to have to get used to someone else being in charge."

"What happened to you?" he asked gently.

"The computer forcibly implanted me," she said. "Not just with the cranial implants, but with something called Marine Raider enhancements. Graphene coated bones, artificial muscles, a pharmacology unit with advanced combat drugs, cutting-edge medical nanites, and more. They turned me into the most deadly fighter the Old Empire could produce.

"But that didn't come without a steep personal cost. The machine that did the work was programmed by an AI that didn't give a damn, and I'm *very* sorry to say it used no painkillers whatsoever when it cut me open."

His heart stopped. He could barely grasp what she was saying, but he felt the horror of what she was describing.

Before he could say anything, the display came to life, showing a scene from someone's helmet cam. He'd seen enough video like it during his time in the service. A group of Fleet personnel was rushing a gurney through a ship's corridor at a breakneck pace.

Kelsey was on the bed, and something was wrong with her face, but he couldn't quite catch it with all the movement.

When they boarded a lift, he recognized one of the people as the medical officer from Jared's ship. What was her name? Stone. The marine cam was pointed at the door, so he couldn't see Kelsey.

When the doors opened, they raced out of the lift and into the medical center. He had enough experience to recognize there were two complete trauma teams standing ready to receive his daughter.

Stone pushed the cart near some equipment he didn't recognize. "Get the regenerator ready. If we don't get these incisions healed now she might have permanent scarring."

The image froze. Terrible, raw scars covered his daughter's face.

He rose slowly to his feet, his heart frozen. "My God."

"Incisions like those covered my entire body," his daughter said matter-of-factly. "The agony was indescribable. I didn't want you to see this without knowing that I'm fine now. It was horrible, but it's over."

He pulled her up and into his arms. It was his turn to weep while she comforted him.

* * *

JARED FINISHED his presentation to Admiral Yeats. It had taken hours to go over every aspect of the basic situation. At least his commander now knew the full danger they faced.

The older man rubbed his eyes. "I have to say that I'm horrified at the scope and power of the enemy you found, and very impressed with what you did to stop them.

"Would I have made different choices? Yes. I can't tell you if they'd have worked, though. It's very easy to judge with the luxury of hindsight. What counts are results, and you brought more of your people home than I'd ever have expected, given the circumstances."

Jared shook his head. "So many people didn't make it, and that brings up another matter. Where do we put them all? The grounds around The Spire are too small.

"We have our people and all the Fleet personnel recovered from the ship's we've refurbished or scrapped. Almost a hundred thousand bodies, and that doesn't even begin to count the rest of the derelicts. The final count from the graveyard will be in the tens of millions."

Yeats rubbed his eyes. "I have no idea. I'll get people working on that as soon as possible. There are so many hot items on my plate that I'm not sure where to start."

The hatch behind them slid open. Since Admiral Yeats had ordered the marines to leave them undisturbed, it could only be one person.

His Imperial Majesty, Emperor Karl Bandar, walked into the compartment. "Gentlemen, no need to stand on my behalf."

Jared stood at attention, saying nothing. This was Admiral Yeats's show.

The admiral shook his head. "The day Fleet officers don't stand for you, I'll retire in disgust. How was your meeting with Princess Kelsey?"

"Heartbreaking and eye-opening. She's been through so much."

The emperor stepped over to Jared and gave him a long, intent look. Then he pulled him into a hug. "Thank you for keeping my little girl alive and for bringing her home to me."

Jared might have adjusted to this kind of thing from Kelsey, but it was never going to feel natural with his father.

"I screwed up so many times, Majesty. What happened to her is my fault, and I accept full responsibility for it. I could have stopped her, stopped them, but I was too slow."

"Sometimes, the biggest regrets come from the shortest periods of time. I don't pretend to understand the full scope of what they did to her, but I know enough of the circumstances to be sure you did everything you could to protect her. For that, you have my unreserved gratitude."

He waved at the chairs. "Sit. We have a lot to discuss. We'll want food and drink, because we're going to be here for a while. I want to get a plan of action agreed on before we let this story go wide. It's already leaking, but we have a little time to shape the way it's received."

Jared sat back down. "Before we stop talking about Kelsey, there's something you need to see to understand the person she is now. She left home—forgive me—a pampered little darling. That's most assuredly no longer the case.

"Both of you have heard what the Pale Ones did to her. That doesn't really explain it. I have several videos you need to see. They all came from either her own implants or from security recordings. I'll lay out the background for each one before I play it."

He queued the assassination attempt at the Pentagaran parliament building. "This was just a few days after we got her back. Before she could reliably walk again. Some people tried to assassinate the King of Pentagar, Crown Princess Elise, Kelsey, and myself."

He played the recording.

The two men sat there, their jaws hanging open when it finished.

The emperor turned to stare at Jared, his eyes glazed with shock. "That's my little girl? She took them apart with her bare hands. Six armed men. She killed all of them."

Jared nodded. "That's exactly what she did. With her bare hands.

She calls that combat mode. Her Raider implants have hardwired threat responses. All she has to do is direct them, and they can deal with some very hairy situations.

"You saw how fast she was? That was a combat drug from her pharmacology unit called Panther working in tandem with the modifications made to her brain by the implants. Together, they speed up the nerve impulses and the ability of the brain to process information. Doctor Stone said something about nerve conduction velocity.

"Basically, she had all the time in the world to figure out what to do. She's had a year to master her implants and learn how to fight for herself. Now she can do things like this."

He played the video of her assault on the asteroid base where they'd recovered the hardware for Marcus. Then without letting them recover, he played the video of her on Boxer Station. Some was from her own implants, but more was from marine helmet cams. For good measure, he added the attack she'd led on the hidden battlecruiser base at Harrison's World.

The two men looked shell-shocked when the videos ended.

Jared waited for them to wrap their minds around what they'd seen. "That last video was about three months after the first video. She's had nine additional months to work on her form under what I would call expert instruction. In everything from hand-to-hand combat to fighting in powered armor with weapons you can't begin to imagine, she has few peers and no masters. Princess Kelsey is a warrior now."

"Training from who?" Yeats asked. "From the marines?"

"Some, but not exactly. This next part is going to be hard to understand. Even our experts are having some difficulty explaining it."

He ran them through the AI ghost of Ned Quincy and how it had taken up residence in Kelsey's implant storage. He stressed how the man's detailed knowledge of Old Empire special operations was invaluable and how he could help them in ramping up for war. They rightfully looked alarmed.

"Let me end by saying that he has only the access she grants him.

Kelsey is always in control of her body and can put him to sleep if she chooses. His memories, though incomplete, provide a wealth of training that she could never have gotten about being a Marine Raider."

"That concerns me in spite of your reassurances," the emperor said. "Could he be relocated?"

"The scientists haven't had any luck building a computer he can run on. Frankly, he shouldn't be possible, so we're leery of doing anything to risk him. He's one of a kind, and all attempts to recreate lightning in a bottle have failed."

"You're sure that he can't influence her in any way?"

Jared nodded. "They've done a lot of testing, and the hardware only allows Kelsey to control her body and mind. She can allow him access to see through her eyes or control her movement, but she's in charge. Her thoughts are her own. There is no possibility of mental influence."

Karl Bandar rubbed his eyes. "I'll want a full report and regular updates on that situation. It, too, is an Imperial secret. I don't want that even put into writing. If word got out that she had someone living in her head or was hearing voices, certain segments of the Senate would go insane. Absolutely no one else is to know until more time has passed. Is that all?"

Jared smiled. "Much to my chagrin, she's also assumed command of a Marine Raider ship, *Persephone*. The computer will only accept a Raider as a commanding officer, so she's it. She's learning to command a ship in space, too, and not doing so badly. You have every reason to be very proud of her, Majesty."

The emperor looked as though he'd been run over by a grav bus. "I am proud of her. It's just going to take a while to wrap my mind around this."

Yeats shook his head. "She's smaller than my youngest granddaughter. She doesn't look like she could lift, well, anything."

Jared nodded. "Yet she can do this."

He played the video of her lifting the weight machine in *Courageous*'s gym. The whole thing, weights and all.

"Gentlemen, Princess Kelsey is the most dangerous fighter in the

Empire today, bar none. And that's what we were fighting. What we *will* be fighting if the Rebel Empire figures out we're still alive."

"Colonel Andrews is going to kick himself for leaving me alone with her," the emperor mused. "Or he would if we allowed this to get out. I'm declaring it an Imperial secret, too. I want all copies of this locked away, and everyone that knows about it needs to be warned to keep their mouths shut."

"That might be difficult," Jared said. "The first video is widely available on Pentagar. They've even produced a vid drama about us with sterling reviews. This information is going to leak."

"We have control over what comes in from Pentagar at the moment," Yeats said. "We can warn everyone to keep it close. If she has even a shade of the respect I think she does, we'll keep a lid on it for a while."

"We only need a bit of time," the emperor said. "I don't want to cause panic in the streets. Eventually, we'll have to spread word of the enemy capabilities. Right now, there are enough other shocks to bury this one."

Karl Bandar shook his head. "Let me see the recording from Emperor Marcus."

Jared played it for them. The two men watched in reverent silence.

"Well," the emperor said, "that's as clear as crystal to me. The sitting ruler of the Terran Empire issued an edict that no emperor since has rescinded. It doesn't matter that we didn't know it existed on Avalon. We're at war, and Kelsey had exactly the authority she claimed. I hereby endorse and approve of my daughter's actions.

"That might not solve all the problems, but it should make things a bit easier for you to manage, Robert. That means her promotions for you and your fellow officers are valid and sustained by me, Admiral Mertz. Congratulations on a well-deserved promotion."

Yeats nodded. "That will clear away many of the distractions. The Imperial Senate is going to scream, though."

"Let them," the emperor said. "This is an Imperial function. We're the same Terran Empire as the one Marcus headed. Lucien took over as emperor after his father's death. The line is unbroken. I might not be able to sweep the table clear, but I can definitely say this one matter is settled."

He smiled at Jared. "I hear other kinds of congratulations are in order. A certain little bird tells me you and Crown Princess Elise are… shall we say, good friends?"

Perfect. Now his father knew about his love life.

"I can assure you there was never any impropriety."

The emperor raised his hands. "I never implied anything else. I'm certain you've done everything humanly possible to bring our peoples closer together."

Wow. Did the emperor just make a bawdy joke? It made his head spin.

Then he smiled. "Well, then you'll be delighted to hear that your daughter has been making friends, too. Remind me to introduce you to Marine Major Russ Talbot. He and your daughter are living together."

The emperor rubbed his temples. "I thought her quarters had a few male touches. Dammit. I wonder how angry she'll be if I ship him off to Thule?"

Jared laughed. "If that's the least of your worries, you're in good shape. Frankly, the public is going to be causing you a bigger one. We arrived through flip points that didn't exist before. With the help of an alien intelligence orbiting a black hole. One that can open gateways to other universes. How the hell do you keep something like that under the rug?"

The emperor shrugged. "You tell them what you can of the truth. That the process is experimental and classified at the very highest level. We'll give it a code word classification and call it Project Rainbow Bridge. We'll need to tell everyone here to keep it under their hats."

Jared nodded. "I can think of a good way to hide the alien aspect of it, too. One of our scientists has been working on something in a related field. He's developed something he calls quantum communication. It's faster than light and undetectable, at least at our technological level.

"It works at interstellar ranges, too. We can still talk to the alien station. While we were there in the Nova system, we were able to talk with Harrison's World. We can't reach any location other than Omega right now, so there's an upper limit, but it's a significant one. With relay stations, that limit becomes largely irrelevant."

He brought up the flip map of the Old Empire. It now had the newly created links on it.

"As you can see, we now have a full map of the explored flip points. Carl Owlet says we have some additional information given to us by Omega, but it still needs to be processed.

"The one I've highlighted is from Avalon to the Nova system. It's almost a thousand light years away. This is by far the longest wormhole we've ever seen. The one to Pentagar is only slightly shorter. Carl Owlet tells me we can still communicate with Omega."

"I'll be damned," Yeats whispered. "We could communicate with ships away on an expedition."

"Yes, it does have some down sides," Jared admitted.

The older man gave him a wry look. "You're an admiral now, Jared. That means you've become one of us backseat flag officers. You'll come around. And, since we're now both admirals, I think you can call me Robert, at least in private.

"Joking aside, micromanagement would be something we need to avoid, but it has the potential to allow frontline commanders to pass data back quickly and respond to strategic changes in their orders. Finding the right kind of balance would be key."

"So, you intend to tell the world that this scientist designed this breakthrough, too?" the emperor asked. "He won't be able to replicate it."

Jared nodded. "True enough, but since it's highly classified, he won't be able to share any details of what was done. Not even the theory behind it. Certainly not the equipment required to make it happen."

"The academics are going to go insane," Yeats—Robert— predicted. "They'll make all kinds of demands and probably protest. We did promise to share the technological finds with them, after all. In writing."

The emperor shrugged. "That's the way it has to be for now. One day we'll be able to share the truth.

"The long-range communications gear is a grand achievement in its own right. Undoubtedly worthy of the Lucien Prize. Give me the data on it, and I'll present it to the board when I get back home. They're already considering this year's candidates. Your man will undoubtedly win in the physics category. What is his name?"

"Carl Owlet. He's seventeen and only a graduate student. Brilliant, but somewhat of a private person."

The emperor grinned. "Well, he's going to be in for a rude awakening, isn't he?" His expression sobered. "There are a few other matters we need to discuss at length. Things like how we shift the Empire to a wartime economy. How we start building the ships we'll need to fight the Rebel Empire with. Harrison's World is a great resource, but need to spread out our capabilities."

Yeats nodded. "We're also going to need an unprecedented number of people to man those ships and to fight on the ground. We can't capture those planets from orbit. We have to occupy them and root out the rebels as we go. Besides capturing the worlds, we'll need garrison forces. The Old Empire is huge, and we don't have the people. We need to recruit and train as we go."

"Those are just the start of the problems we face," Jared said. "We need to ramp up implant usage among the civilian population. We need that productivity, and with the advent of medical nanites, society will change. Lives will extend to hundreds of years.

"Also on the military side, we need to figure out how to best use the flip-point jammers, build fighters, train pilots, and develop doctrine. We should also begin work designing massive forts to guard the flip points, set up some kind of FTL communications network, and assess the other technology the Old Empire knowledge can provide."

Karl Bandar sighed. "We'll need a lot more people to do that, but let's hammer out a general idea of what we want to look at first. Then we recruit helping hands. Jared, I think you'd best call for that food now."

16

Carl was finalizing the assembly on his next piece of equipment when Major Angela Ellis stalked through the hatch. She looked angry. Big surprise.

He set the equipment he was working on down and turned to face her. "Come back to have another go?"

The bruise was almost gone, but he really didn't need to antagonize her like that. It had just popped out of his mouth.

She stopped a little short of him. "I was wrong to hit you. It won't happen again. But I want to know why you did that."

"I've been asking myself that very same question. I'm not sure what the answer is. I'll blame the other me."

She frowned. "What the hell does that mean?"

"Did you read the message the other me-before-last left on the station? Let me send it to you."

He watched her reading it and knew she was done when she started shaking her head. "Why the hell would he say that? We barely know one another. Did he *want* me to punch you? You *are* kind of an asshole, so that's not out of the question."

Carl smiled a little. "I did some checking over the files in his implants earlier today. I found a trove of interesting images and vid files. Like this one."

He sent her his personal favorite. The image was obviously from a handheld camera. It showed himself and her, cheek to cheek and grinning like fiends. She was holding the camera out, and he could see the Pentagaran parliament building in the background. The two of them looked close. Kissing kind of close.

"Did you make this? You're sick."

He held up his hand. "Innocent. I found a lot of vids and images. It looks like you and earlier me were a hot item. In fact, all but one of the other Carls had vids or images that linked us romantically in multiple universes. That last one was more of a lab rat than I am. Maybe he didn't get out enough to date."

She pulled up a stool and sat. "That makes no sense. Why? How?" She shook her head. "It doesn't matter. We're not them, and it was wrong of you to kiss me."

"I know. I will say, however, that it was worth getting punched in the face to carry out my other self's final request."

"Just don't do it again. We're not them and…" She clamped her mouth shut. "Kelsey wants me to teach you hand-to-hand. When would you like to go to the gym and start?"

"Never. I'm not going to be competent at fighting. Period. You and I both know that. Let this go."

She shook her head. "When my princess tells me to do something, I do it."

"Like when she told you not to threaten me and you did it anyway? I'm not seeing why this is a problem."

She sighed somewhat aggressively. "Don't push me, Owlet. I can tie your skinny ass into a pretzel."

"I can't see what the other me saw in you. You're bossy, touchy, and stubborn."

"And, apparently, an idiot. You're dangerously reckless, and we're obviously unsuited for one another."

"Yet, there we were. In any case, I can't go now. I'm working on something."

She looked at the oddly shaped device. It looked like a bulky arm brace. "What is it?"

"A portable battle screen. Very similar to the one in the hammer. I built a fusion plant without the grav drive element and installed it with the screen generator in this arm brace. It's bulky, but I'll probably be able to make it smaller with a little work."

Major Ellis picked it up. "How would someone use it?"

"Hold out your arm." He strapped the unit onto her left forearm. "Have you ever seen a vid where old-time people were fighting with swords and shields?"

She nodded. "Kelsey made me watch one about some guy pulling a magic sword from a stone."

"I've seen that one. Excalibur. I guess I know what my next project is. In any case, this generator forms a battle screen in the shape of a rounded shield. It's about a meter across, so it won't protect your legs unless you crouch down.

"There's a control to alter the shape of the screen. To narrow it and extend it lower. That would make it a bit taller than the wearer and about half a meter across. If you went sideways and squatted, it would deflect a plasma burst around you. I'm working on joining two fusion units to the next model to increase the potential size a little."

He gestured toward a suit of marine armor on a stand. "I'm adding one to that, too. It'll be significantly larger and more powerful but will act in the same manner. The first unit is only a prototype and proof of concept. Something I can put on a dummy and fire a gun at."

"We all know how well that worked out last time."

"Then don't use it."

The sound of someone clearing his throat drew their attention to the hatch. Doctor Leonard stood there.

Carl retrieved the prototype. "Good morning, Doctor. What can I do for you?"

"You have a visitor."

He moved to the side and Emperor Karl Bandar stepped into the compartment.

Major Ellis braced to attention, and Carl had to force himself not to do the same.

He bowed. "You honor us, Majesty."

"On the contrary, Mister Owlet," the leader of humanity said. "You honor me. I've heard tremendous things about your work. Your inventions and breakthroughs are going to revolutionize a lot of things in the Empire."

He felt his face flush as he took the hand Emperor Karl extended. "I just did my part, sir. The team deserves the credit. Doctor Leonard is the one you should thank."

The emperor nodded. "I have, yet he didn't create interstellar communications or design that protective device I heard you talking about. My apologies for standing in the corridor listening. We were waiting for the right moment to interrupt you."

"And it turns out we should've done that right off," Doctor Leonard said with a smile and a shake of his head.

They'd overheard him arguing with Ellis. Dammit.

"That will teach me to leave the hatch open. My apologies."

"No need," the emperor said. "It is I who should do so. I'm sorry I listened in on a private conversation. I do hope the two of you work out your problem. In any case, I've come to ask a favor of you."

"Certainly," he said. "Whatever you need."

The emperor smiled. "I need for you to deny you had anything to do with creating the new flip points and then refuse to discuss it any further."

Carl frowned. "That's easy enough. I didn't have anything to do with it at all."

"Yes, but I'm going to imply you did and that it's classified. Then your denials will be true, but no one will believe you. The subterfuge is necessary to keep people from knowing about your alien friend for a while."

"I can't say I'm happy with lying, but I understand. I'll do it, of course."

The emperor's smile widened. "Excellent. I'm classifying this information as an Imperial secret under the name Project Rainbow Bridge. You will only speak of the alien or the process with authorized people. For now, that is Doctor Leonard, Admiral Mertz, Admiral Yeats, Princess Kelsey, myself, and Major Ellis, of course. The fewer people that know the precise details, the better."

Carl nodded. "Of course. What happens now? The mission is over. Or is it? I'm a little unsure if I should be packing my bags to go back to Avalon."

"We're already moving to orbit. A few ships will stay here to keep any idiots from going through the new flip point and killing themselves, but I think shore leave is in order. You'll be staying here, working on these projects after you take care of some business below. And taking some personal time."

Carl wasn't sure why the emperor looked at Major Ellis when he said that.

"Doctor Leonard tells me that you've got a number of pots in the fire and that you're the most adept at using the new technology," the emperor continued. "Your results speak for themselves. He'll continue to work with you, but I'm giving you carte blanche to explore what you like, under his oversight. If you need assistants, I'll find some. Or you can pick them. Whatever you need."

That shocked Carl. "I'm honored, of course, Your Majesty, but I'm only a graduate student. I've never led a research project before."

The older man nodded. "That's why Doctor Leonard will continue to advise and guide you. As for your degree, he tells me that you've met all the requirements for your doctorate except for your thesis.

"I'm going to have a word with the chancellor at Imperial University. I believe your work on quantum communications will be more than enough to satisfy him. You can make a very good classified paper out of it, and those who are cleared to know the details can question you about it. That should be all that they require to grant your PhD.

"Work with Doctor Leonard to get the paper ready quickly. After all, they won't want a graduate student awarded the Lucien Prize for physics."

Carl's head spun. "I'm honored you'd think so, but that isn't happening, Majesty. I'm not in that league."

"Somehow, I knew you were going to say that. The head of the panel considering the awards this year disagrees. I spoke with him an hour ago, and he swooned at the breakthrough and all the other science it hinted at. He believes that it's also linked to flip-point science, and I'm inclined to agree.

"Young man, this is the most significant breakthrough in physics since the Fall. You're going to win that prize without any help from me, and that's where the lie comes in. They'll undoubtedly ask you about the flip point and if you created it. Tell them no and repeat yourself as many times as you need to. Say nothing of who did or what happened."

Carl understood now. Of course they wouldn't believe him. They'd be certain he created the flip point as a byproduct of his research into quantum communications. The emperor's plan was clever. They'd all jump to the wrong conclusion, and the emperor could protect the truth for as long as he wanted to.

Only Carl would have to let people believe he'd done something he hadn't. He'd have to allow them to shower him with praise he hadn't earned. He might win an award he didn't deserve. Only he would likely know what a monstrous fraud he was.

He bowed his head. "I'll do what I need to do to protect the secret, Majesty. Whatever it takes."

"Excellent. As you've just become one of the most valuable resources in the Empire, I'm taking it upon myself to see you stay safe.

"Major Ellis. I've spoken with my daughter, and she's agreed to release you to my service. Now that she's home, we can have the Imperial Guard resume protective duties for her. You've done a tremendous job, and that means you get a more difficult one."

He grinned. "I'm placing you in charge of protecting this brilliant young man. Continue to use the people you're familiar with and requisition whatever equipment you require. Keep him safe."

She opened her mouth with what looked to Carl to be an objection, but closed it with the words unspoken. "Yes, Your Majesty."

"Excellent. Mister Owlet, I look forward to reading your unredacted dissertation. Take a few days to see the city and meet with the university officials. Enjoy yourself. You've earned the downtime. When you get that shield ready, I want to see it in action."

His smile turned a little sly toward the marine officer. "And, Major, don't let your position as his protector stop you from dating if that's how things roll. That's an order." He headed for the hatch. "Until we meet again."

Once the emperor and Doctor Leonard had departed, the two of them stared at one another silently.

Well, this was going to be awkward.

17

N athaniel Breckenridge waited impatiently for the Imperial
Marines guarding the prison facility to scan him for
weapons. They didn't seem the type he could intimidate
with his position, so browbeating them into moving faster wouldn't
work.

Pity. He really wanted to take his frustration out on someone.

The senior marine finally nodded. "You're clear, Senator. This
way, please."

He led Nathaniel down the corridor to a lift. This section of
Orbital One was completely isolated from the rest of the station. Only
one way in or out. One heavily guarded way.

As the head of the Senate Armed Forces Committee, Nathaniel
had the access to know there were just over a hundred prisoners
serving time here. A few hard cases were in maximum security, which
seemed a bit redundant. This was already the most heavily secured
prison in the system.

The lift deposited them on a different level, and the marine
brought him to a small room that looked as though it was set up for
meetings between prisoners and their counsel. Which was exactly
what he'd be using it for today, he admitted grimly.

Wallace was already there, dressed in a garishly orange ship's suit. One without any rank insignia or even a name tag. All it had was a number on the front and rear.

His nephew stood awkwardly. They'd cuffed his wrists with a long length of wire going through a loop on the table. A glance confirmed they'd also shackled his legs.

"Release him," Nathaniel said coolly.

The marine shook his head. "I'm sorry, Senator, but I can't do that. The prisoner has been violent in the past, and it's standard procedure—"

"I don't care what your procedure is," Nathaniel snarled. "Wallace Breckenridge is a decorated Fleet captain. I'm in no danger. Remove his restraints. Now."

The marine gave him a long look and then backed down. "If the prisoner attacks you, or resists being led back to confinement, that's on you, Senator."

Nathaniel looked at his nephew sternly. "Captain Breckenridge won't give you any further trouble. Will you, Wallace?"

His nephew's sullen expression didn't look promising. Nathaniel slapped his hand on the table, making the younger man jump.

"That requires a response, Wallace."

"No," his nephew said. "I won't cause any problems when we're done."

Nathaniel waited for the marine to remove the restraints and withdraw. As both an Imperial senator and a licensed Imperial counsel, he knew they wouldn't record this meeting. So he could say exactly what he needed to.

He sat across from his nephew and waited for him to sit. "What the devil did you think you were doing? Could you have blundered more badly if you tried?"

"All I did was what duty required of me, Uncle Nathaniel. Mertz violated every regulation when he—"

"Bullshit. You tried to force your way on them out of spite, and it blew up in your face. For God's sake, you kidnapped an Imperial princess."

"It was for her own protection," Wallace insisted stubbornly.

"She's not right in the head. Those implant things drove her crazy. Megalomania. Mertz, too. Once the facts come out, I'll be free and he'll be locked up in here."

Nathaniel shook his head. It was worse than he'd imagined possible. The idiot actually thought he was doing the right thing.

"So why did your own chief medical officer clear Mertz and her, then? Doesn't that undercut your argument?"

"Of course not. The man was obviously Mertz's secret supporter. He couldn't just let him pass the exam and then flunk the princess. I had to disregard his bias. My own cool detachment was what was needed to make sense of the situation."

Nathaniel felt his stomach do a slow roll. "My sister would be horrified if she were still alive. I have some sad news for you, Wallace. The emperor has already accepted the validity of the Imperial edict. The Senate will fight it, but I'm not sure they even *have* the legal authority to fight him on this issue.

"Frankly, if you weren't buried in this up to your eyebrows, I'd be inclined to accept it on general principle. Now I have to try to save your sorry ass. What the devil were you thinking?"

"This is ridiculous, Uncle! I was doing what was best for the Empire."

"Really? Let's leave aside your poor judgment in kidnapping the second in line to the Imperial Throne. I'd like to hear your justification for the battle of Erorsi. Not why it happened, but why you did what you did. I can assure you that the court-martial will be addressing it shortly."

"Let them," Wallace said flatly. "I was following Fleet doctrine in a bad situation. The enemy proved to be much more capable than we expected. It happened so damned fast.

"One second things were going as planned, the next the enemy destroyer was firing missiles from a ridiculous range. Captains Macumber and Cooley made some serious errors in judgment. That cost them their ships and a lot of good people."

Nathaniel considered his nephew. He wasn't a Fleet officer, but even he knew that wasn't true. At least not in reality.

"What about the warnings that Mertz gave you about the

destroyer. Not just in the briefing—which he recorded, by the way—but also in a message before you engaged. He told you it was faster and better armed than any of your ships, did he not?"

"Yes, but that assessment made no sense. A little ship like that couldn't have that kind of capability."

"Yet it did. Just as Mertz said. Just as the prosecution will prove he told you multiple times, yet you still sent those ships to fight the destroyer while you went after a freighter with your heavy cruiser."

He shook his head. "You know what I'd say if I was prosecuting this case? That you were afraid. That you scuttled away to avoid a fight you'd probably have lost."

The statement so outraged his nephew that the man sat there sputtering.

"I have no doubt someone will mention it at your trial," Nathaniel continued relentlessly. "The jury will be hard pressed to dismiss the charge. Cowardice in the face of the enemy is a serious offense, is it not? Why did you go after the freighter, Wallace?"

The other man slouched in his chair. "I wanted to seize the computers and cargo for the Empire. I knew the princess would give it away. Just like she gave everything else away. The woman is mad. She *shot* me!"

Nathaniel imagined she'd enjoyed doing so. His respect for the Imperial family went up a notch.

"Let me tell you what they're going to charge you with," Nathaniel said without addressing his nephew's objections. "First, disobeying a number of lawful orders."

He held up a finger to silence his nephew's objection. "I don't care that you think they weren't valid. Your lawyer will do his best to get them thrown out. Just listen.

"Second will be a series of charges that you were derelict in your duty. That your actions led to the destruction of three ships and thousands of dead Fleet personnel. Third, and most damning, treason. When you defied Princess Kelsey, you stood up to the Imperial Throne. You can be sure the emperor will lay that charge before the Senate, and I doubt I can stop that trial, either."

He let that sink in. "If the edict stands, then you knowingly and willfully defied her instructions and kidnapped her. It's the same as if you'd done it to Emperor Karl, and that, you idiot, was beyond stupid.

"I have no idea if I can save you. At best, you're going to lose your commission and go to prison for a very long time. I can't imagine an outcome where that doesn't happen. At worst, they'll execute you. You *do* remember that treason is a capital offense, don't you?"

"But, everything I did was for the Empire!" Wallace almost wailed. "How can this be happening? I've always been a loyal officer, doing what I needed to keep the Empire safe. This is all Mertz's fault. And the princess, but mostly Mertz."

Nathaniel sagged a little. Even now, his nephew refused to take responsibility for his actions. Honesty compelled him to admit that he'd protected Wallace for far too long.

This was going to end badly. He'd do everything in his power to salvage what he could, but a drunk counsel just out of school could convict the man. He'd given them too much proof and done too many irredeemable things.

All that mattered now was the family name. Nathaniel would save it, even from Wallace. Somehow.

* * *

ELISE WENT DOWN to the surface of Avalon in the same cutter as William Hawthorne and Reginald Bell. All three of them had appointments with the Department of Imperial Affairs.

The older man's situation would be the easiest for the Empire to deal with, she imagined. He and his people had continued to fight the rebels, and they'd agreed they were still Imperial subjects. That should lead to a very smooth transition.

She smiled. He was the last surviving person from the Old Empire. She imagined that meant he was automatically a citizen here. His Fleet back pay would be an impressive sum, if anyone thought of that angle.

Lord Hawthorne would have a more difficult time of it. His world was Imperial, but had fallen to the rebels. They wanted to keep the existing power structure and certain agreements they'd made with Kelsey. The Empire would probably balk a little at that, but they'd have to set a precedent for all the other worlds under the sway of the Rebel Empire.

In her case, the Kingdom of Pentagar was a formerly Imperial world that had been isolated by the rebellion. They'd thought they were the last bastion of the Empire. They'd formed their own government and had no intention of acknowledging that the Empire —any empire—had sovereignty over them.

Pentagar would remain a close ally of the Empire. Nothing more. That would make for some sparks, she imagined.

The cutter landed at the spaceport, and the Fleet crewmen saw them off. A delegation from the Department of Imperial Affairs awaited them. It looked as though they'd decided that three separate groups would be appropriate.

A woman in a pale green dress stepped over to her. "Welcome to Avalon, Highness. I'm Brenda Winters, a senior negotiator at the Department of Imperial Affairs. Someone will see to your bags while I escort you to the department. I'll also be working with you to clarify our governments' relationship."

Elise smiled and extended her hand. "You could've sent someone to pick me up. Unless you want to start negotiating in the grav car."

The other woman returned her smile. "No, but I'll admit I had an ulterior motive. I wanted to see Mister Bell with my own eyes. It's so astonishing that he was alive before the Empire fell. That he was a serving Fleet officer. Not to say that I wasn't looking forward to meeting you," she hastily added.

Elise laughed. "I completely understand and take no offense. In fact, I'd be pleased to introduce you later. He's quite the storyteller."

She watched the other two groups moving toward separate grav vans. The large vehicles allowed enough room for both parties, including the guards they'd all brought down to Avalon. Not that they needed them, but the guards did display a certain level of status.

Reginald had argued against the tactic, but she'd convinced him that he was representing a planetary government. William had helped her argue the point, and the older man had acquiesced.

A third grav van was awaiting them. Elise allowed the other woman to lead her and the pair of Royal Guards accompanying her in that direction.

"I'd like to raise a point that I suspect Mister Bell won't mention on his own," Elise said. "He was trapped on Erorsi during a Fleet assignment. One that he's been performing for more than five hundred years.

"There's the matter of Fleet advancement and back pay. As I said, he'd never mention the issue on his own, but as a Fleet icon, I'd imagine you'd want to do something about that. He's dedicated centuries to carrying out his orders. That kind of loyalty demands recognition."

The other woman stopped dead in her tracks, her eyes wide. "I hadn't even considered that. Oh my God." She laughed. "Some Fleet accountant is going to die on the spot. I'll be certain to pass that along, because you're absolutely right."

Elise climbed into the grav van with a satisfied expression. The older man would try to duck any awards or money. He'd say they wouldn't do him much good at this point in his life. Still, it was a matter of principle.

Her father had driven that lesson home when she was a girl. Loyalty *must* be rewarded. Achievements recognized. Fealty was a two-way street.

Emperor Karl had probably thought of that, but things were very busy. She wanted to be sure that nothing fell through the cracks.

The trip to the Department of Imperial Affairs was quick, and the view was very nice. Avalon was a pastoral world, as befitting a former vacation hotspot. Perhaps she could get in some skiing while she was here. If Jared could free the time.

Once they'd landed at the large building and made their way to a conference room, Elise sat and let Brenda take the lead in discussing their situation. Since she had signed an agreement with Kelsey, this should be a perfunctory meeting.

The other woman sat across from Elise and opened a notebook. "I took the liberty of reading the agreement you reached with Princess Kelsey under her authority as the emperor's representative. It all seems to be in order, but there's one small formality that needs to take place before it's valid."

Elise raised an eyebrow. "That's not what I understood. Isn't her word on this matter binding?"

"Yes and no. She had the authority to negotiate the treaty, but it's not officially binding on the Empire until approved by the Imperial Senate. I've sent a copy to the Imperial Affairs Committee, and they're reviewing it.

"No doubt, they'll want to discuss it with you. Once they approve the language, it has to pass a vote of the full Senate. If they recommend changes, obviously your government will need to review them and agree."

That was not what Elise had expected to hear. "What's our current status, then?"

"Due to the circumstances, the department will continue to treat Pentagar as a foreign government, but under a strict reading of the Imperial Charter, worlds are not allowed to secede from the Empire. I understand that isn't what happened, but the founders never envisioned the rebellion or the Fall.

"I'm not sure how the Senate will judge matters, either. It's possible that some senators will see Pentagar as an Imperial world. Others might try to keep that interpretation and still grant you more latitude in home rule. Unfortunately, some might stand firm that you are Imperial subjects. At this time, I'm not sure how the majority feels. Things have happened so fast."

Elise felt her expression harden. "The Kingdom of Pentagar is a sovereign nation, and we will not bow our heads to force. Your senators had best keep that firmly in mind. Do not turn allies into enemies. Especially not in the face of this war we're in together."

The other woman spread her hands helplessly. "I agree, but my hands are tied. You're going to have to go to the Imperial Senate and discuss the matter. I've already spoken to one of the members of the committee, and he'd be happy to talk with you as soon as you desire."

"Very well. I expect this is something I'd best see to at once. Who is he, and how do I set up a meeting?"

"I'm told he is available now. The van we arrived in can take you to the Imperial Senate building. Oh, and he's one of the senior members of the committee. We've worked with him often, and he's a very reasonable man. Senator Nathaniel Breckenridge."

18

Angela rode in silence on the way to the main campus of Imperial University with Owlet. The young man stared out the grav car's window, brooding. He'd been that way ever since he'd met with the emperor.

He was meeting with the chancellor shortly. Every kilometer that passed made him look more sour. It wouldn't take long for the official to see right through his deception.

"You need to pull yourself together," she said firmly.

He turned his head away from the window distractedly. "Hmmm?"

"I said that you need to focus. If you go in there like that, he'll know you're lying."

"He'd be right," Owlet said dejectedly.

"You promised the emperor that you'd do this, and that means you need to give it your best shot. You have to make these people believe you're being up-front and honest. If they see through this, then you've failed in your duty. So, as I just said, get your head out of your ass."

He smiled a little. "I wasn't paying much attention, but I'm pretty sure that isn't what you said."

"It's what I meant."

He sighed. "You don't have any idea how hard this is for me, do you? Let me turn this around. Science is my life, just like the Marines is yours. What if the emperor ordered you to lie about a battle you'd been in? What if he ordered you to take credit for saving a bunch of lives? Of single-handedly winning the battle while you were just one person doing her part. That's what this means to me."

"The two things are hardly the same," she said dryly. "But if he ordered me to, I'd do it."

"What if they awarded you the Imperial Cross? Then the public would be honoring you for something you never did, and you'd have to wear the reminder of that lie for the rest of your career. Until the truth came out and then you'd be reviled as someone without honor."

That set her back on her heels. He was taking this a lot more seriously than she'd imagined.

"Again, the two situations are hardly equivalent," she said. "Even if they were, I'd damned well do what was best for the Empire. It's more important than how I feel. Everyone would understand when the truth came out.

"Let me point out where you made a mistake. You figured out how to communicate across interstellar distances. That's big. That's worth the damned Lucien Prize all by itself. The rest of this is just embellishment."

"All I did was pull together a bunch of other peoples' research. Yes, I had to detail the scientific framework this was based on, but I just saw the connections. Others did all the hard work."

He balled up his fist and hit his armrest. "And that's what's diabolical. I'm telling the truth while knowing they won't believe me. When it all comes out, it won't matter that I've denied everything, and I'll know it the whole time."

"Are you going to back out?"

"No."

"Then quit your bitching and get your head out of your ass. We're landing, and unless I miss my guess, that's the chancellor standing right there. You gave the emperor your word to fool him, so you'd better put your game face on."

* * *

CARL STEPPED out of the grav car. He'd seen Chancellor Warwick before—from a distance—but the man hadn't known him from Adam. Until today.

"Mister Owlet, welcome back to Imperial University," the dapper older gentleman said. "I must say that what I've been reading about you is most impressive. Come to my office, and we'll discuss it in a more, um, secure environment."

Warwick glanced at Major Ellis curiously. "I'm afraid I don't know your friend. Is she, ah, cleared to know about this?"

Carl wasn't surprised at the other man's confusion. Major Ellis had changed into civilian clothes for the trip. He supposed that made more sense on a university campus. It softened her appearance a lot. She wasn't nearly as intimidating when she was out of uniform.

She was, oddly, a lot more attractive. He could see what the other Carls had seen in her. Not that that changed their current circumstances.

He smiled, working hard to make it look genuine. "Chancellor Warwick, allow me to introduce Major Angela Ellis of the Imperial Marines. She's my minder and is indeed cleared to hear anything we discuss."

"Ah! I see. Then if you'll both come with me, my office isn't far, as you know."

The three of them walked off the landing pad while the driver took the grav car back into the air. The man, another marine in civilian clothes, would be nearby in case they needed a quick extraction.

"Actually, I have no idea where your office is," Carl said apologetically. "I was pretty focused on my studies and never had reason to go to the administration buildings."

"I understand. That's true in much of academia. We administrators labor behind the scenes so that people such as yourself can focus on what's important to you."

In this case, Carl was in complete agreement. Imperial University was a model of efficiency and excellence. Chancellor Warwick and his associates had done everything in their power to make the learning environment the best it could be, while staying out of the way.

All too often, that wasn't the case. He had nothing but the greatest respect for the man, and that made what Carl was doing even worse.

"I had a long conversation with Doctor Leonard this morning, and I took a brief call from Doctor Cartwright," Warwick said. "Both were laudatory in discussing your contributions to the mission. I, of course, don't know the full details, but both men mentioned that they wouldn't have achieved so much without your hard work and keen insight."

"Allow me to assure you that they're overstating my case, Chancellor. I played the part I needed to, but *they* made the magic happen."

Major Ellis cleared her throat. "I have to disagree. Mister Owlet brought more to the table than he's mentioning. Don't let his humble nature fool you. His skills had a lasting and far reaching impact on this mission, and I've personally seen him do things I'd call wizardry."

Carl couldn't stop himself from giving her a sideways look of disbelief. Her compliment actually shocked him speechless. It had to be a lie to shore up his story.

"So I'm given to understand," Chancellor Warwick said as they walked through the tree-lined quad.

Students filled the open area. They laughed, played, and shouted. Most were older than he was, but that wasn't unexpected. He'd arrived at Imperial University barely into puberty, a prodigy. Which significantly affected his social life, he admitted.

Now he was old enough to envy those couples walking close to one another. His focus might have sped him up the ladder in his studies, but he'd missed so much while locked in the lab on those late nights.

Part of him wanted to smile wryly at the looks they were getting. He knew what they were thinking. The chancellor was giving a tour to a prospective student and his... mother? Major Ellis wasn't that old, but her imposing stature lent her an air of maturity beyond her years. The way she walked made her look dangerous, though their watchers wouldn't know why.

He resisted the urge to say something to her about it. That wouldn't be helpful, even if it would be fun.

"Do you know that you'll be the youngest PhD this institution has ever produced, if you pass your dissertation?" the chancellor asked.

Carl returned his attention to the man. "No, sir. I wasn't aware of that. It's a little intimidating."

"Don't be too worried," the man assured him. "The fact that your theory has been proven to work lends a lot of credence to your underlying model. I've taken the liberty of assembling a team of department heads to review your work. All cleared by Fleet, of course."

They walked into the administration building and took the lift up to the top floor. Carl kept his initial objections quiet until they'd made it into the man's office.

"Let's sit over here while we talk," Chancellor Warwick said. "Can I get you any refreshment? Coffee, perhaps?"

Major Ellis put her hand on Carl's leg to stop him from answering. "Thank you," she said. "We'd both love a cup."

"Then I'll be right back. I've got a fair hand with the brewer, so I'll bring us a fresh pot."

Carl tried to ignore the heat soaking through his pants leg from her hand. It was… distracting. "What if I don't want any coffee?"

"Then don't drink it, though that would be rude. I wanted one last chance to remind you this is game time. Of course he's getting a team of people together to review your work. He's heard about the Lucien Prize, so he's moving quickly. Don't make too much of a stink about it."

She was right, but that only made it more annoying. "Well, I can't just help him speed this along. It would be out of character. No one would take this without some protest."

"I bet you know some people that would jump at the chance and run over anyone in their way."

He actually did know some people like that, but they weren't him.

She seemingly realized where her hand was and withdrew it, sitting back in her chair. He hoped she didn't realize what kind of effect her touch had on him.

The chancellor came back a few minutes later with what turned out to be some excellent coffee. As a lab rat, Carl knew all about bad coffee, so he could appreciate a good brew.

Chancellor Warwick set his cup down on the saucer. "Now, as I was saying, a team of cleared PhDs are examining the papers you've prepared. I understand that it isn't a thesis in the conventional manner, and so do they. You'll be meeting with them to discuss everything over the next few days. Think of it as a working defense of your dissertation.

"We have two of the quantum communication sets. Fleet is taking a number of them to the Baker system next door. One of our people is with them and in possession of the other half of the linked pair they loaned us for testing. It should be through the flip point later this evening and ready for testing tomorrow."

"We know that they don't work at an unlimited distance," Carl warned him. "Harrison's World is two flips away, and we can't communicate with it now. The Nova system is just short of a thousand light years away. Harrison's World is an additional 415 light years, though some of that is lost because it's at something of a slight angle. Call it thirteen hundred light years by direct line."

The other man nodded. "The Baker system is significantly closer. Hopefully, it will work. If it doesn't, then that gives us more data, doesn't it?"

"I suppose so, but that isn't really helpful. I have to admit I didn't expect it to work at interstellar distances, no matter what the theory said. The fact it has a limit is actually reassuring to me."

The other man sipped his coffee and gave Carl a long, considering look. "I understand that you feel that you only combined several existing sets of work to make your breakthrough. I want to take a moment to disabuse you of any notion that those facts lessen your work.

"Do you know how many winners of the Lucien Prize felt the same way? Most of them, based on any number of biographies I've read over the years. Or they thought their work was too limited in scope to be worthy of the award. That feeling, my boy, is natural."

Carl shook his head. "I don't think I did enough unique work to be worthy of the honor. I'm certain that the committee has better candidates to consider."

Warwick smiled. "Then you'd be wrong. I spoke with Doctor Paul Creedmoor this morning. He's heading the selection committee for physics this year. When I sent him the classified briefing paper—for which I had permission!—he almost swooned. He'd already spoken briefly with the emperor, but the details of your work set his intellectual curiosity afire.

"You can rest assured that your work will be studied closely, even though the committee was only a few days from making a decision for this year. You've loosed a fox in the henhouse for certain."

That didn't make Carl feel any better, but it was beyond his control. Whatever they did, he'd have to accept it. One way or the other.

"In the meanwhile," Warwick continued, "I've arranged for an apartment for you. We should make our determination before the Lucien Committee reaches theirs. Or I'll be most cross with some people."

Major Ellis cleared her throat. "I'll need adjoining rooms for myself and my people."

The chancellor frowned. "We hadn't considered that when we reserved the apartment, Major. Student housing is full. We pride ourselves on bringing our students as close to their work as possible. There are two bedrooms, so I could turn one of them into a guardroom, I suppose. Perhaps having one of your men move in with him?"

She gave Carl a less than friendly look. "He's my responsibility, so I'll think of something."

Great. One more thing for her to be mad about that wasn't his fault.

"Before I see you there, Mister Owlet, I'd like to ask the question I'm sure will be on everyone's mind. Is the new flip point also an outcome of your research?"

There it was.

"No. The origins of the flip point and the means of its creation are Imperial secrets and have nothing to do with my research. You'll have to ask Fleet about it."

The other man smiled, getting the anticipated wrong impression from Carl's denial. "I see, though part of me isn't sure I believe you. I'm certain you'll be asked the same thing many times over the next few months, too."

"They'll get the same answer," Carl said tiredly. "When will I meet the team?"

"Tomorrow. They need time to study the information Fleet sent. You look tired, so I suggest you rest. You'll be quite busy in the morning."

"That works for me," he said. "I have some equipment that needs to be secured at the lab. It's related to the quantum pairs."

"I'll need to check the security there," Major Ellis said. "We can't have classified and important equipment and research just lying around. I'll put part of my team on the lab right away."

"I assure you that our lab is up to the task. We do classified research for Fleet there."

That didn't seem to impress the marine. "Then it'll be even more secure. This isn't negotiable, Chancellor."

"Hrump," the other man said. "I'll cooperate, of course, but this is hardly necessary. And, forgive me, but it's more than a bit insulting."

"I'm sorry about that," she said, not sounding sorry at all.

Carl finished his coffee quickly and set the cup down. "Perhaps I'd best see to settling in then. Who is in charge of the examination?"

"Professor Bedford."

That wasn't the best news. Andrew Bedford was old and cantankerous. He didn't much care for young people, which was odd in a university professor. He'd taken an especial joy in grinding Carl down.

Well, perhaps things would be different this time. After all, the hard work was done. Right?

19

K elsey stood in her room at the Imperial Palace, feeling like a stranger. It had only been a year since she'd last stood here, but it felt like a lifetime. She wasn't the same girl who'd imagined adventure and excitement exploring the remains of the Old Empire with her despised half brother anymore.

No, not even close.

Now Jared was as close to her as Ethan was. Maybe more. Her full brother had become less friendly when puberty hit. Overprotective and imperious. She was sure that would make for one hell of a fight when he found her.

She'd managed to get Talbot off doing something else for a few hours by telling him she needed a little alone time. That would keep him from punching Ethan in the face when her brother did something that offended him.

Her enhanced hearing picked up the sound of his approach. The Imperial Guards let him into her room without argument, and he was angry. Furious.

Big surprise. It was time to settle this once and for all.

"What the hell were you thinking, Kelsey? Dammit, you gave him everything he's been craving. I thought you were smarter than that."

She smiled sweetly at Ethan. "It's good to see you, too! Yes, I really missed you. And I'm fine. Thanks for asking."

His expression grew even more thunderous. "Don't toy with me. I demand to know why you helped Mertz build a platform to seize the Throne."

She allowed her false cheer to slip away. "This is old and tiresome, Ethan. He's not after your job. Frankly, I doubt there is anything he'd rather avoid more. We were wrong about him, and you need to see that before you make an ass of yourself."

He stepped close to her, his expression more than a bit menacing. "Don't tell me how to feel," he said in a low voice. One that she'd have found threatening before her idea of threatening changed forever.

Now Ethan didn't even register on her danger meter. She knew he couldn't hurt her. He would never intimidate her again.

Kelsey stared into his eyes from only a few centimeters away. "You're in my personal space. Move or I'll move you."

The surprise in his expression was gratifying, but he didn't back down. "Not until you see sense."

"Back up. In case you didn't catch it, there's an unspoken 'or else' attached to that."

"You always think you know better than me," he sneered. "You've been nothing but soft and weak. Now he's twisted everything in your mind until you think he's on your side. Well, I'm not going to allow you to throw away our birthright so easily."

She put her hand on his chest and pushed gently. For her, that is. Ethan staggered back a few steps, shock written all over his face. She'd never had the physical strength to deter him before. Now she had enough to throw him through the wall if he made an ass of himself.

"I'm not going to stand here and let you froth on about something you know nothing about," she said coolly. "I've been right by Jared's side for over a year. A time in which some very terrible things happened. You should do yourself a favor and read up on it. As the heir, you need to know.

"One thing I can tell you without the slightest hint of doubt, though. Jared Mertz is an honorable man. One who has no designs on the Throne."

"Unbelievable," he swore. "He got to you, too. I don't care how long you were there or what you think you saw. He is the greatest threat to our inheritance that could possibly exist. Mertz has Imperial blood in his veins, and he thinks that he can displace us. I won't allow that to happen because you've lost your mind."

She laughed. "You think you know everything when all you really understand is this unreasoning hatred of yours. It's worse than an obsession. You should see someone about it before other people—"

Ethan lunged forward and grabbed her by her blouse, slamming her back into the wall. To be fair, she saw him coming, but chose to let him in.

"You are not my equal," he snarled. "You never wanted to rule, and you don't have the mettle for it anyway. So, don't lecture me on strength. I'll protect us and the Throne."

She looked down at his hand. "I allowed this to happen to make a point. I suggest you learn from it."

Kelsey barely had to bump her strength to get him moving. It was mostly skill she'd learned from Ned in his hand-to-hand training. In less than two seconds, she'd mashed Ethan's face into the wall. She kept him there by jamming his arm up behind him.

It felt surprisingly good.

"This has gone too far, Ethan. You need to reassess this delusion. Jared isn't after you or the Throne. If you keep making an ass of yourself, things will not end well."

Kelsey leaned forward until she could whisper up toward his ear. "If you think you can push me around, you're wrong. Keep your hands to yourself, and go do some thinking." She let him go and stepped back.

He stared at her for a moment and then left without a single word.

She sat on the arm of her couch. That could've gone better. She hoped she'd gotten through to him. That his own self-interest would keep him from doing something stupid.

After all, what choice did he have? It wasn't as if he could just order people to dispose of his problems.

* * *

ETHAN ALMOST STAGGERED AWAY from his sister's room. Her physical changes shocked him, but not as much as her mental ones. Mertz had corrupted her. She was under his sway.

Before she'd left, he never would have believed anyone could come between him and his twin. They'd been close since before they could remember anything at all. He loved her.

She'd betrayed him. She'd become a threat to him and the Throne. She'd become an enemy to be dealt with.

Oh, he wished he could change her mind, but now that she'd switched sides once, he could never trust that she wasn't working against him again.

He leaned his head against the wall and wept. It would break his heart, but he needed to neutralize her. Perhaps he didn't have to kill her, though. If he could remove her as second in line to the Throne, then he could allow her to live. He owed her that much.

Ethan straightened and headed for his rooms. He needed to calm down and then go speak with his father. Surely, he would see the truth this time.

Mertz was the true threat to the Throne. Without him, Kelsey would fall in line.

If his plea didn't work, he could reevaluate things. If it became necessary, he would mourn, but the security of the Throne was more important than even his closest family.

* * *

JARED STEPPED into the conference room and nodded at the senior officers sitting around the table. He'd been dreading this board of inquiry for the last year. At least this would finally end his torture. One way or another.

He recognized most of the officers, but not the man at the head of the table. A check of his implant memory told him it was Admiral Jack Lancaster, head of the Judge Advocate General's Office. The senior jurist in Fleet.

Well, he supposed that at least meant they were taking this seriously. He was happy he'd taken the time to load the public profiles of all Fleet personnel. Otherwise, he'd know nothing about the man.

"Admiral Mertz," Lancaster said. "Please have a seat." He gestured to the chair on the other side of the table from the senior officers. All either Vice Admirals or Admirals, he noted.

Jared took his place. "Admirals."

"I'm Admiral Jack Lancaster, head of the Judge Advocate General Corps. Allow me to introduce my associates." He went down the line confirming Jared's records.

"Now," Lancaster continued. "Let's be clear about the purpose of this board of inquiry. There were a number of serious incidents during your expedition, and we're going to review them all. We need to examine every aspect of what occurred.

"We'll be conducting this board under oath, so be advised that anything you say here might be used against you in a court-martial, should one be convened. Do you understand?"

"Yes, sir."

Jared knew there would be a court-martial. That was a foregone conclusion. He'd lost his ship. *Athena* would never fly again. *Ginnie Dare* was destroyed under his authority, and more than half his personnel had died in the last year.

That didn't even begin to count the decisions he'd made that these men and women would be second-guessing. They had the perfect vantage point to judge everything he'd decided without any of the pressure.

Yes. There'd be a court-martial.

The hatch behind Jared slid open. He glanced over his shoulder and saw Captain Alice Quinn stride into the room. The slender black woman nodded to everyone at the table.

"Admirals. Apologies for my tardiness. Captain Alice Quinn. I'm serving as Admiral Mertz's counsel in this matter."

Lancaster frowned. "This isn't a court-martial, Captain. We're only gathering to hear Admiral Mertz's summary of the events in question."

Quinn smiled. "I understand, sir, but under Fleet regulations,

Admiral Mertz is entitled to have an officer stand as his defense counsel during a board of inquiry, too. As you well know, I served in JAG before I transferred to the command track. I'm still licensed."

"This is very irregular," Lancaster said. "It doesn't sound as though Admiral Mertz engaged your services. You can't just show up and declare yourself his counsel."

She turned to Jared. "Admiral Yeats sent me. Do you feel the need for counsel, Admiral? If I'm not an acceptable candidate, or you feel that I'm chasing down the work, I can suggest a number of very competent people to represent you."

Jared shook his head. "You're perfectly fine with me, Captain Quinn. You're hired."

She returned her attention to the board. "I believe that settles all the requirements, sir. I'd like to request a brief recess while I consult with my client. It shouldn't take more than a few minutes."

Lancaster didn't look pleased, but he nodded. "The conference room adjacent to this one is free, I believe. We'll wait here."

"We'll be back very shortly. I'd like to thank the board for their indulgence."

Jared followed her into the other conference room. "This is a pleasant surprise, Captain Quinn. Thank you."

"I'm glad the admiral called me. That was an ambush. I'm surprised someone as savvy as you missed it. They should've insisted you have counsel."

"I lost my ship and more than half the people under my command. They have to seat a court. You can't stop that."

"Probably not, but everything you say here will be testimony at that trial. You need to have someone skilled at spinning things to get the right tone on the matter.

"I'm not suggesting you shade the truth. Think of me as more of a truth whisperer. I'll translate what you say and defend your actions. If they go too far, I'll slap them down. You have rights and I'll see them respected."

He sighed. "I really appreciate this, but I'm not sure you can save me. I stuck my neck way out. They're going to chop my head off."

She grinned. "That's not the combat commander I know. You

need to think of this in Fleet terms. Outmaneuver the bastards and give them hell.

"I've read a summary of the actions you took. We can win this thing, but not if you let them bully you. Admiral Lancaster has a fair reputation, but we leave nothing to chance. If Senator Breckenridge doesn't have someone on that board in his pocket, I'll eat my rank tabs.

"Call me Alice. You're the top dog now, so I get to use your rank while you get to be all familiar."

"That feels wrong."

Quinn laughed. "Get used to it. By the way, you really did us proud. Don't let all this second-guessing get you in an uproar. These admirals would've failed at the same challenges you overcame. Rest assured, I'll tell them that, too.

"Come on. Let's get back in there."

The two of them returned to the main conference room. Lancaster watched Quinn retrieve a chair from against the bulkhead and then started the recorder.

"This is the board of inquiry over the events that occurred during expedition fifteen into the Old Empire. I am Admiral Jack Lancaster, the presiding officer." He introduced the other officers for the record.

"Also present are Admiral Jared Mertz and his counsel, Captain Alice Quinn. Admiral Mertz, please rise."

He did so.

"The testimony you are about to give is under oath. Raise your right hand. Do you swear to tell the truth, the whole truth, and nothing but the truth on your honor as a Fleet officer?"

"I do."

"Please resume your seat and tell us in your own words what happened during your expedition. Leave nothing out and take as much time as you need."

Jared took a deep breath and started at the very beginning. This was going to take a long, long time.

20

Talbot set his drink on the bar and considered punching the smug bastard standing in front of him in the face. Yes, it would cost him his rank, but that seemed a fair exchange.

But Kelsey would be disappointed in him. He sighed and unclenched his fist.

"I think you should reevaluate what you just said to me before I turn your face into hamburger," he said conversationally. "You don't know Admiral Mertz and you weren't there. What gives you the right to judge him?"

The man beside him, another marine, stepped into Talbot's personal space. "I've seen the list of dead. The Bastard killed hundreds of our brothers and sisters. How can you defend what he did?"

Talbot heard the unspoken capitalization of the word "bastard" and knew how this was going to roll. This guy was one of the idiots that thought the admiral was out to use his birth as a lever to the top. Nothing Talbot said was going to change that.

"Is that all you see? The list of those who died? What about the things they gave their lives for? Those don't matter? You think this was all for the admiral's glory? I thought you were an idiot, but that's being unfair to idiots. Someone help me out, here. What's stupider than an idiot?"

"Someone who betrays his brothers for an officer's berth."

Talbot swung, but someone grabbed his arm, spoiling his aim. Other marines dragged them apart before he could shake free.

A grizzled command master chief planted himself in front of Talbot. "This isn't the officer's club, Major. You don't get to come down here and throw your weight around."

He raised a finger before Talbot could speak. "But, you were a senior sergeant when I last laid eyes on you, so you deserve the respect that carries. There won't be any fight today. I want to hear why you're defending this officer."

The first man shouted something, but the new guy turned and bellowed at him. "Pipe down, Grayson. You're a damned disgrace to the uniform, insulting an officer to his face. And for using words small enough that he can understand you. Sit down and shut up."

The man turned back to Talbot. "I'm Command Master Chief Rex Santiago. I knew some of those men and women, too. Why did they die, Major?"

Talbot took a deep breath and tossed back his drink. "Because they were heroes. Because they cared more about the Empire than their own lives. Because they were marines, and that's what marines do."

The crowd shouted almost as one. "Oorah!"

"Bartender," Talbot said. "This is going to be thirsty work. Drinks for everyone, on me. Except for that asshole. He can buy his own drink."

Everyone laughed. Even the asshole.

Talbot launched into the unclassified part of the story. He told them what they'd found. He told them what the stakes were, and he laid out the odds stacked against them.

"If you want to know why so many people died," he wrapped up, "you should look at Captain Breckenridge. That's why he's in the brig."

That set them all to talking.

In a way, Talbot had known this would happen. He'd come here expecting to have a fight, and to tell this story. Technically, this was against regulations. He'd badmouthed an officer. But, he was also an officer, though lower ranking, and in a different service.

These men and women wouldn't turn him in, though. They'd chew over what he'd said and make up their own minds.

That's why he'd come here looking for the fight. Hell, he still wanted to punch that idiot.

Santiago drank some of his beer. "I'd heard some of this through the grapevine," he admitted. "Wasn't sure I believed it. I guess I do now."

He raised his voice in a way that only the best noncoms could, so that it cut through everything going on in the bar.

"Ladies and gentlemen, I give you the Imperial Marines. To our lost brothers and sisters."

Every one of the marines shouted at the top of their lungs and drank.

Well, maybe this was going to work after all.

The command master chief stepped closer to him. "So, what's this I hear about you dating Princess Kelsey?"

Well, maybe not quite as well as he'd hoped.

* * *

ELISE ACCEPTED a ride to the Imperial Senate building with a growing sense of doom. Of course that idiot Breckenridge was going to use his uncle to stymie the good they were trying to do.

The senate building wasn't as impressive as the parliament back on Pentagar, she decided. It was too new, and the designers had gone more for a sleek, modern look. It lacked the gravitas of history.

The grav car set down on a pad outside the entrance, and her guards stepped out. A young woman in a dark burgundy, knee-length dress was waiting for her.

"Crown Princess Elise? I'm Jean Trouville. If you'll come with me, I'll see you to Senator Breckenridge's office."

"Are you his assistant?"

"No, ma'am. I'm an aide to the Imperial Affairs Committee. I work for whichever senator needs me. This way, please."

Trouville led Elise into the building and past the guards. Those men and women didn't look pleased at seeing the Royal Guard moving by with their weapons, but they kept their peace.

This was going to take some getting used to for everyone.

Two of them did fall in place behind the group and joined them in the lift. That was fine by her. The senator deserved the protection his office afforded.

The senator's office was on the top floor of the building, speaking to his place in the hierarchy. He probably had a magnificent view.

The man's assistant stood when the group arrived. "Crown Princess Elise. Welcome to Avalon. If your guards will wait out here, the senator will see you right away."

She smiled and shook her head. "I'm afraid that isn't how this works. Until my guard commander knows the senator better, he's insisted he remain in my presence. The senator won't even notice him, and he can have his own protection. I don't mind."

The man bowed his head with an expression that hinted he'd suspected this was how it would play out. "Of course. This way, please."

She turned on the recording feature in her implants before the man opened the dark wooden doors. She wanted to capture the senator's every word and expression. That might not be strictly legal here, but she could plead ignorance.

Senator Nathaniel Breckenridge stood and came around his desk as soon as she came in, a wide smile that seemed eerily genuine on his face.

"Crown Princess Elise. Welcome to Avalon. Thank you for taking the time to speak with me."

She allowed herself a smile. At least he wasn't the boor his nephew was. "Anything I can do to speed the process of our alliance along is time and effort well spent."

One of her guards waited in the outer office while the commander of her protection detail took up a position off to the side.

Breckenridge waved the senatorial guard back out. "I'm perfectly safe. I'll call out if I need you."

He gestured toward the bar. "May I offer you refreshment? I have a selection of the finest the Terran Empire has to offer, both alcoholic and non. The fruit juices are quite good."

"I'm fine for the moment," she said as she took her seat. "I think it's best if we get right down to business. They tell me your committee has some concerns about the alliance between the Empire and the Kingdom of Pentagar. Perhaps you'd be kind enough to outline your objections for me."

"The problem isn't me, I'm afraid. More the Imperial Charter. It doesn't recognize the validity of secession, and I'm loath to toy with its long-understood meaning. By strict reading of the provisions, it doesn't allow for withdrawal of any member world for any reason."

"That seems to me to be somewhat shortsighted considering the rebellion," she said dryly. "You see, we didn't leave the Empire. The Empire left us. We've fended for ourselves since the Fall, and we're going to go right on doing so.

"I've done this dance before, so forgive me if I move us along. You wouldn't have called me over if you didn't have a counteroffer to make. One where we can both get something we want. I'm interested in hearing it."

He smiled. "You're very astute. Yes, I'm willing to compromise. Frankly, I'm not an idiot. The Rebel Empire is dangerous. Their ignorance is all that is keeping us safe. But I don't want to cross my party without receiving something in return."

"Why am I left with the feeling that your price revolves around Captain Wallace Breckenridge? He's your nephew, is he not? For the record, he's an ass."

The senator smiled sadly. "I'm forced to agree. Make no mistake, I'll do everything I can to minimize the damage he's done to my family name, but he's crossed several lines that I cannot and will not shield him from the consequences of.

"He's going to be court-martialed and thrown out of Fleet. He'll also spend many years in the brig. So be it. That need not have anything to do with the alliance between our peoples. I'm willing to throw my support behind your cause and bring as many of my compatriots as I can."

"I see. What are the goals of your compatriots? Is it in their interest to support the division? If so, how will you sway them?"

"They'll almost certainly bow to the inevitable, but not until they make the Throne suffer. Our stated goals in this matter are that the Imperial Charter doesn't allow Pentagar to be separate, rebellion be damned. They hold that your world is still subject to the Empire."

She shook her head. "How would you enforce that? This might come as a shock to you, but we have powerful ships, too. Ones given to us by my close friend Kelsey under the treaty between our worlds. Would you go to war with us in the face of the Rebel Empire?"

Breckenridge stood and walked slowly over to the bar. "I'm going to make a drink for myself. Call out if you change your mind." He poured something dark into a tumbler over ice.

She considered him for a moment before responding. "What's the price of your assistance in navigating this obstacle?"

He sat back down and sipped his drink. "I know where some figurative bodies are buried and I'm willing to twist arms, but I want your help in the matter of my nephew."

Elise raised an eyebrow. "I'm at a loss as to how I can help him, even if I were inclined to do so. The man is a menace."

"You and Princess Kelsey are friends. She'll listen to you. I know that I can't save Wallace from his madness, but I have an obligation to shield my family from as much of the disgrace as I can. If you can convince her to intervene with her father to leave treason off the table, I'll work tirelessly to keep the Kingdom of Pentagar a sovereign state, precisely as you've negotiated.

"You can ask around," he said with a smile. "I'm a good politician. I stay bought."

This kind of deal making wasn't unknown to her. She could see how it would help him. His nephew would still be a disgrace, but the family wouldn't have spawned a traitor. For a powerful senator, that had to be worth a lot.

"I'm willing to talk with her about it," Elise said, "but I can only promise to be as persuasive as possible. Ultimately, she might decide to say no. Or her father might."

"Then I suggest you be very persuasive. We have the votes to enforce the Imperial Charter, and without my influence, your treaty will never be ratified." He raised his glass in salute to her. "I'm looking forward to seeing another professional at work. Good luck."

21

K arl Bandar stopped the video report he was reviewing when he heard his son at the door. He'd left instructions not to be disturbed, but that wasn't how his son worked. As much as he'd tried to temper his son's... enthusiasm, it hadn't really taken. Ethan always expected immediate results.

When his guard politely declined to disturb Karl, his son got louder. Karl sighed and walked to the door.

"It's alright, Les. Ethan, come in."

"Father, we need to talk about—"

"Sit and listen," Karl said firmly. "That entails closing your mouth, in case I wasn't clear."

The boy obviously wanted to argue but clamped his lips shut with palpable impatience and fury. He also sat, if only grudgingly.

Karl locked the door and engaged the privacy field. That would keep the sound of the inevitable argument out of the ears of even his loyal guards.

"You're trying my patience, Ethan. You're running around with your hair on fire over things that don't deserve that level of response, and you need to dial it back."

He held up a finger to forestall this son's hot words. "Your turn to speak will come but not until I'm done. What you did out there showed an extreme lack of respect for me. If I leave orders not to be disturbed, being pissed off isn't an excuse to disobey them.

"For reasons that seemed good at the time, I've let this behavior slide, but that stops now. You're my son and heir, but that also means I'm your liege. The man you've sworn an oath to support and obey. I expect obedience from you, and respect. I'll have them both, or you will regret it. Is that clear enough?"

Ethan pressed his lips into a tight line, and his eyes flamed with barely suppressed fury. "Perfectly, my lord."

Karl sighed. It was never easy with his son. Or his daughter, sometimes, but that was a completely different kind of trouble.

He sat on the corner of the desk. "Since you've already interrupted my work, you might as well tell me what has you in an uproar."

"Do you know what Mertz has done to Kelsey?"

"He didn't do anything to her, but yes. I've not only read the summaries, I've spoken in depth with Doctors Stone and Guzman. They both have a far deeper understanding of the implants than I do. I expect that other medical experts will be up to speed to check their assumptions soon enough, but I believe I know more than enough."

"Now who's being naive? Mertz may not have ripped her apart and rebuilt her, but he took full advantage of it. Those monsters put things in her brain, and he's had access to sway her for a *year*.

"Hell, everyone on that mission did the same to *themselves*. How do we know it's anything like they say? Wouldn't that be a wonderful way to enslave us? To get us to put those machines in our heads for them? Then Mertz can just waltz in and seize the Throne. We need to lock them all away until we're sure it's really safe."

Karl sighed inside. "Your incessant paranoia about Jared Mertz is tiresome and beginning to worry me. Forget him. As to the implants, I've done some checking. I don't want word getting around, but I had Emperor Lucien disinterred. With all due reverence, I assure you. He had implants just like the Fleet people do.

"I've seen that his body was delivered to Orbital One. It's possible that some data will be recoverable, even after all this time. Scientists trained in doing so will get what they can before we bury him again."

He shook his head. "I'm finding it hard to believe that we never knew. Think of the trove of historical data from the first days of Avalon. Or the critical information his father might have given him."

Karl sighed. "Clearly, they were once a common part of Imperial life. Based on the advantages I'm starting to grasp, they will be again.

"I confirmed that by having some of the Fleet personnel that died here examined. They too had this equipment. Someone I trust is extracting the hardware and will see about powering it up in due time. Then we'll know if the programming is the same."

Karl leaned back in his chair. "They'll have to learn a lot about the programming language and the hardware, but we'll get to the bottom of this. We're taking nothing at face value."

"Aren't you?" Ethan asked with an edge to his voice. "How do we know this supposed edict is even real? Mertz could have very easily concocted it to get a leg up and move toward his real target. The Imperial Throne."

He'd hoped his son would come to his senses, but that was seemingly off the table. Time to address the issue squarely.

"You've always thought the worst of your half brother. And don't even think of snarling at me. That's what he is, like it or not.

"Tell me this, Ethan. If he were looking for a way to seize power, and your concerns of the implants were correct, why didn't he use force when he arrived? We couldn't have stopped him. If that is indeed his plan, we still can't. His people are in control of more firepower than we could muster in our defense."

Ethan leaned forward intently. "Then now is the time to strike. Get them off those ships under some ruse and get loyal officers aboard them before it's too late. I'm not sure why he's delaying, but we can't wait much longer."

Karl shook his head sadly. "The Senate would never accept his claim over yours. Or Kelsey's, for that matter. Even if they did, the people would rise up. Son, this is paranoia. You're seeing shadows behind every event that just aren't there."

"You're being willfully blind, Father. I've always known you were soft where Mertz was concerned, but I never dreamed you'd just hand our birthright over to him. How can you be so blind?"

"Enough," Karl said firmly. "You need a vacation, son. Take a trip out to the lake in the mountains. Stop obsessing over these crazy theories."

"I will not abandon the Empire when it's in such peril."

"You misunderstand me. That wasn't a suggestion." Karl smiled and touched a key on his desk.

Les opened the door. "Yes, Majesty?"

"My son needs to take a trip out to the lake to get away from everything. Take him there and see that he stays put."

He turned his attention to his fuming son.

"I can't force you to rest and reconsider, but I can put you in time-out. The heir to the Throne cannot afford to be so willfully paranoid. Once you've had time to think, we'll talk again."

Ethan surged to his feet. "You're making a grave error in judgment, Father. Don't compound it by taking the one person who sees the threat clearly out of play."

When Karl said nothing, his son stalked out of the room.

Once he was alone again, he called his guard commander. "I'm sending Ethan to the mountains. I want extra people in place to make sure he doesn't sneak away. He's to be kept there until I say otherwise."

"Is he under arrest, Majesty?"

"No. Think of it as protective custody. Isolation to keep him from making a fool of himself. Make sure the guards aren't ones he can browbeat."

"I'll take care of it, Majesty."

Karl sighed and leaned back in his chair. This had all gone wrong so quickly. Ethan's unreasoning hatred of Jared was going to cause real harm if he didn't put a stop to it. He made a mental note to confer with Ethan's private physician to check and be certain that there wasn't a true pathological behavior behind this.

At least his son would be out of the way for a little while. He couldn't cause too much harm up in the mountains.

* * *

ETHAN FUMED as the guards herded him back toward his rooms to pack. The gall of the old man. He treated his chosen heir as if he knew nothing at all. As if his concerns were nothing more than the ravings of a madman. It wouldn't surprise him if there were a visit by doctors while he was away.

He'd turned against Ethan, too.

Everyone had, and they'd soon strike, unless he acted to mitigate the threats against him. It was regrettable that things had come to this, but he had to do what was best for himself and the Empire.

He leaned against the wall as soon as he was back in his rooms. First Kelsey and now his father. How could they choose the Bastard over their own blood? Mertz's sickness had infected them.

Unlike his sister, he couldn't allow his father to orchestrate the overthrow of the rightful heir. He loved his father even more than Kelsey, but the old man was going to have to die.

Did he? Ethan ran through the possibilities in his mind. Surely there was some way to spare his father.

But no viable alternatives came to mind. The loss of the man who'd carried him on his shoulders as a boy ate at him, as if the man were already gone. Really, he was. He just didn't know he was dead, yet.

There would be mourning for his father across the Empire. They'd commission monuments beyond counting to remember his memory. Ethan would see to that.

He packed in the privacy of his room, which gave him the opportunity to stash a few items he might find useful. Starting with a very concealable communications unit. He would be able to oversee every action his minions performed right under the noses of his watchdogs.

Ethan had paid good money to be sure it wasn't traceable. They wouldn't even detect the signals on the security screens. It was that good.

He called his man. "How goes the preparations, Victor?"

"They're good. I should have it resolved tonight."

"Excellent. I have a few other tasks for you. I want you to pick up someone with those damned implants and another person who is familiar with the technology."

"Do you have a specific target with implants in mind?"

Ethan smiled. "As a matter of fact, I do. But first, I'm afraid things have taken a bad turn here at the palace. My father is shipping me off to the Imperial Retreat off in the mountains. While I'm gone, I want you to work with my man in security to get in and take care of something for me. Several things, actually."

* * *

TALBOT STAYED UP LATE DRINKING. The marines he'd visited had reacted as well as he could hope. Word would spread and people would make up their own minds, but at least the base slanders of the admiral's blood wouldn't come into play. Mostly.

The board would want his testimony at some point, but they still hadn't finished with the admiral. A full day wouldn't even scratch the surface of what they'd done over the last year.

He was about to cross the street when his internal alarms sounded. This late at night, the street was pretty empty, even downtown, but the group of young men coming toward him didn't look like revelers out for a stroll.

A glance behind him showed a number of men following.

This was an ambush. At least, that's what his instincts told him.

He had a neural disruptor on him, but by the time he was sure what they were up to, it might be too late. He needed them to spring their trap early.

Talbot bolted across the street, hauling ass for the closest alley. That got them all to chasing him, so he knew he was on the right side in this fight.

He set the neural disruptor to wide beam and fired at the forward group. They went down in a heap. They'd be under about half an hour.

That didn't keep the second group from opening fire on him. One of the slugs hit him in the arm, but he managed to retain his grip on his weapon.

He linked his implants to his com and called emergency services just as a noise in the alley gave him a split second's notice that there were people waiting. He ducked and lashed out with his foot in a savage kick as the operator came on the line.

"Emergency services. What is the nature of your emergency?"

I'm being attacked! Near the Excelsior!

The hotel was the closest landmark. They could track his transmission, too. The com would convert his implant communications into his voice for the operator.

One of the men in the alley leapt over his screaming comrade and brought a metal bar down on Talbot's arm. It snapped with a sickening crack. His weapon spun off into the dark. The second swing caught him in the head, and he was out.

22

K elsey woke when her com sounded an emergency tone. She rolled out of bed and answered before her toes touched the floor.

"Bandar."

"Kelsey, it's Jared. I just got a call from emergency services in the capital. Something happened to Talbot. He was attacked and is missing."

The last remaining fog in her brain blew away as if a hurricane had swept in. "Shit. What do they know?"

She raced to her closet and dressed as quickly as she could. Something suitable for rough and tumble.

"Very little. He called and told them that much, then the line went dead. Someone killed the com. Crushed it, as a matter of fact. Police are swarming the area, but they haven't found him or the attackers yet."

She cursed under her breath. "He was armed. A neural disruptor. Something people here don't know about yet. That means this was organized and there were a lot of people."

"Don't rush in. This could be dangerous."

Kelsey laughed grimly. "I sure as hell hope so. Someone is going to bleed for hurting my man. Guard your back. If they came after him, they might have other targets in mind."

She killed the call and opened the pack with her weapons. Oh, how the Imperial Guard had argued against her bringing them into the palace. Too damn bad, she'd said. Now she'd been proven right. She should've brought her armor. Though, to be fair, it wouldn't be of much use right now.

Kelsey used her implants to call Marcus on *Invincible* through the palace systems. That had been the first upgrade she'd seen to. The AI answered at once.

"What can I do for you, Highness?"

"Someone attacked Talbot. They took him. I want a strike team ready for my call. Have them prep my armor and bring it along if things work out that way."

"Of course. You do realize that the planetary authorities will take a dim view of Imperial Marines making an assault on the capital world of the Terran Empire, don't you?"

She snorted. "You think? I'll have that conversation with them up front. Is there anything you can do to track down his implants?"

"Not at this range. I'd need a receiver in close proximity for that. However, he's a marine. He has an implanted locator beacon. If we can activate it, any receiver within a dozen kilometers will have his stats and location data."

"I'll have the pinnace try that. Keep an eye on any visitors you have. Keep trusted crew close to them and marines on standby in case someone tries something up there.

"Also, I want a squad sent to Orbital One to keep an eye on Jared. He could be a target. Keep it low key, but make sure they're ready to rumble."

"I'll have a pinnace on the way within ten minutes. One will be dropping with the ready squad and your armor to assist you shortly."

"Excellent. Keep me informed."

She killed the connection and finished dressing. Her weapons belt slid comfortably onto her hips. Her flechette pistol on the right and her neural disruptor cross draw on the left. A marine knife sat at the small of her back. Spare magazines covered the rest of the open space.

Her off duty armor went under her blouse. It wasn't great against a modern flechette pistol, but it would stop regular slugs all day long. The big benefit it had was being unobtrusive. Once she'd arrayed herself for war, or at least a minor firefight, she headed for the door.

The two Imperial Guards gave her a double take as she swept past them, armed to the damned teeth.

"Highness, is something wrong?"

"Someone just kidnapped my boyfriend, and I'm going to find him. Notify palace security that a marine pinnace is dropping from *Invincible* shortly. It's coming for me. You *will* let it through."

The man blanched. "Ah, we can't allow something like that near your father."

She spun in place and pinned him with her very best angry princess stare. "If they had something nefarious in mind, they could drop a spread of missiles onto this building before you knew what was happening. Either you trust Fleet or you don't. I suggest you go along with me on this.

"Also, I'm going to explain the facts of the situation to my father right now. He'll back me. Count on it."

Kelsey stalked off toward her father's quarters. Part of her hoped the guards there tried to block her, but they stepped aside.

Her father was already up and dressed in a robe. His hair was mussed, so he'd been asleep. His eyes widened at the sight of her, weapons and all. "Something's gone wrong."

"Someone took Talbot. I'm going after him. I called for a marine pinnace to bring me a tracker and backup. Are you going to let them pick me up?"

Her father looked at the guard. "Clear the marine pinnace for an emergency landing. Go to an increased state of alert, too."

The man bowed and hurried off.

"You look so different," her father said. "So dangerous. Part of me didn't believe even after seeing the ambush recording, but it believes now. What will you do?"

"Find him. I'll see the blood of whoever ordered this."

* * *

JARED HAD *Invincible* send out a warning and recall to all personnel in his fleet. It would reach most of them very quickly, but there were always a few who managed to wander off without a com. They'd get a rude wakeup call by marines making sure they were safe.

He had most of that done when a knock at his hatch announced the arrival of the marines the AI had dispatched. That was fast.

Out of habit, he checked the view plate and frowned. He didn't know any of the four men outside his door. His implants confirmed they weren't assigned to his ships.

He ran a second search against the Fleet database he'd uploaded earlier while he activated the com.

"Yes?"

"There's been a problem, Admiral. Let us in, please."

The search came up blank. These men were not Imperial Marines.

"Hang on while I get something on. It'll just take a second."

He hit the alarm on the plate. He expected Orbital One security to call him right away, but other than the blinking light, nothing happened. Then the light went out.

Oh, yeah. He was in trouble.

He raced for the bedroom as he heard the hatch he'd locked slide open. A suppressed weapon fired at him as he dove through the hatch and cycled it closed. Thankfully, the man missed.

Jared used his implants to link with the suite communications gear. He'd had his men rig that up this afternoon. None of his calls was going out. They'd jammed him. Help wasn't any closer than the marines from *Invincible*. If they weren't ambushed.

Thankfully, he'd let Kelsey talk him into keeping weapons and unpowered armor in his room. He had just enough time to slide the vest on and jump into the closet before the locked bedroom hatch opened. These bastards were good.

Two of them came in with weapons out. Jared lit the one facing the closet up with flechettes. The New Terran Empire unpowered armor wasn't up to the task of stopping them. The man went down in a spray of blood. His partner dove behind the bed and returned fire.

A gunfight at pointblank range was not Jared's idea of a good time. Luckily, his flechettes were better at penetrating the bed than the old-fashioned slugs were at finding him. The other man screamed and stopped firing.

That's when the other two fake marines opened fire from the hatch leading to the living room. The chest protection he'd been able to slide on took several hits and held. He fired back, but his angle was crappy.

Then the bulkheads beside the hatch splintered under the assault of hundreds of flechettes. Both attackers died a gory death. The cavalry had arrived.

A female marine in unpowered combat armor—Old Empire style —came into the bedroom looking for threats. A check confirmed she was assigned to *Invincible*. "Clear. Come out, Admiral."

Of course the woman could sense him in the closet.

Jared stood and his leg gave out. He'd taken a shot after all.

"The admiral is hit," the marine called out as she slung her rifle. "I've got him."

She grabbed Jared in a fireman's carry before he could decline. A full dozen marines fell in around them as they headed out of his quarters. Anyone that came near got weapons in their faces and told to move back. Including Orbital One security.

"Put me down," Jared said.

"Our orders are to get you to safety, sir," Lieutenant Wilson—the man in command of the detachment—said. "I'm taking you back to *Invincible*."

"Put me down, Corporal Jackson. Right now."

The woman obeyed but raised her weapon and glared at the growing crowd of security officers. They were one mistake away from a tragedy.

"We're on Orbital One, and we will *not* threaten Fleet personnel. Everyone, lower your weapons."

The marines seemed disinclined to obey, but they reluctantly did so. Orbital One security wisely kept their distance. No doubt, someone in a position of authority was on the way. The assassination attempt was over.

All he had to do was deal with the aftermath and try to explain how he thought the heir to the Throne was the most likely mastermind. Talk about a hard sell.

* * *

ANGELA GOT the warning call just after she'd climbed into bed. She instantly summoned her people. It would take at least five minutes before they came howling in, so she'd have to make sure Owlet was safe until then.

She grabbed her weapons and charged into the living room. Everything was deceptively quiet. Except for the squawk Owlet made when he saw her standing there in her underwear with her flechette pistol out.

He'd been playing some kind of first-person shooter game on the vid screen. One she'd played before, she noted with some amusement. She'd have to whip his ass at some future point.

"What's wrong?" he asked as he surged to his feet.

"Maybe nothing for us. Someone kidnapped Talbot, and the admiral wants everyone to keep an eye out. The protective detail is on the way. Five minutes."

"Shouldn't you… ah, get dressed?"

"I thought you had a thing for me. Isn't this a geek's wet dream? A mostly naked woman with a gun?"

He snorted. "The other versions of me had a thing for you. I'm just wondering when you'll punch me again."

"You hit a guy one time," she said with dry amusement. "I doubt we're targets, but we're exposed out here."

"Well, *you* are, in any case. I put out combat remotes to keep an eye on the building."

That surprised the hell out of her. Frankly, it was something she should've thought of. "Why did you do that?"

He shrugged. "Mainly to test a new command and control array for them. They tag everyone who comes into range and sort them as threatening or not. Since this is a university campus, I designated people wearing green as threats. It's not on, though."

"Give me a link."

He sent her the control link. She found the array and brought it to life, resetting the threat parameters to standard. His placement was pretty good, though she'd have done a few things differently.

The array screamed an alert to her. Armed men were already inside the building. A grav van outside had two armed men waiting beside it.

"Shit! They're here. Into the bedroom!"

She faced the door and called her team. "Code red. Hostiles in the building. Contact in sixty seconds."

"We're three minutes out. Hang on."

They weren't going to help her one damned bit. She knew she should've overridden that damned stuffed shirt of a chancellor. Now she had a couple of minutes to regret it. They'd mow her down, but not before she killed a bunch of them.

"I don't suppose you have any weapons in here?" she asked Owlet as she tipped the dresser over with a crash. It might provide him with a little cover.

"I didn't think I'd need one. Will we make it?"

She gave him a look. "You'll make it. Stay behind that and pray the team gets here in time."

Angela took up position beside the door and trained her weapon on it. The first few men through would die. With luck, the wall would provide enough protection for her to survive long enough for backup to get here.

The door blew in with no warning, smashing to splinters as the armed men came charging in.

She opened fire and dropped at least one of them. They were combat trained. That reduced Owlet's chances. Dammit.

A long burst killed the men in the room, and she leaned out to fire at the men in the living room. Her flechettes chewed up the furniture as she searched for them. She could hear them screaming as she killed or wounded them.

They weren't standing idly by, though. Their shots tore up the wall, and she quickly took hits in her arm and side. She'd be down in seconds. Dead before the team got here.

The combat remotes warned her of a grav drive screaming in from the south. Maybe the team was ahead of schedule. That would be a nice surprise.

Except it wasn't slowing down to land. It was acting more like a guided missile.

The moment before it arrived, she realized what it had to be. "Oh shit."

She threw herself down and covered her head. The interior wall she'd been using for cover exploded inward, throwing chunks of debris all over her. She could only imagine what the living room on the other side looked like.

That didn't stop the enemy, though. A man came through the hole and opened fire at Owlet. His slugs went whining off in every direction. Owlet stood there with that damned hammer extended in front of him like a shield, unharmed and obviously terrified.

Well, she supposed a battle screen was the best protection available. He'd thrown the damned thing through a plascrete wall. Flechettes weren't a threat now. To him, at least.

She found her dropped pistol, shot the man, and staggered to her feet.

"Come over here," Owlet shouted. "Now!"

Angela rolled across the bed and got behind the protection of the battle screen just as the remaining men opened fire from the carnage that used to be a living room. There were too many to kill, even if the screen would've allowed her flechettes through.

One of the men threw a grenade. The screen wouldn't stop all the fragments. This was it.

Owlet grabbed her around the waist and threw them backwards out the shattered window. They fell toward the ground five stories below.

And missed.

They swooped out as though they were flying and skimmed above the parked grav cars. Someone was shooting at them from the window but the hammer was hauling ass. They blasted out of the campus area with a shockwave as they went supersonic.

Yet all Owlet was doing was holding the hammer by its handle. The loop of leather was around his wrist, but that shouldn't have mattered. It should've torn free and left them falling to their deaths.

"You're hurt!" he said.

Her side was throbbing. "A little. Why aren't we falling?"

"The grav field is large enough to enclose us. We're completely safe."

Their course wheeled, and they arrowed back toward the campus. They seemed to be going even faster.

"No," she said. "We need to escape."

"They hurt you. I'm going to hurt them back," he said, his voice as unyielding as the battle screen protecting them. "The remotes said they're escaping in their vehicle. Hold on."

The van grew from a distant dot to full size in an astonishingly brief interval of time. She thought they'd miss it at first, but it swerved right in front of them.

Angela flinched, but they were through it before she had time to feel more terrified. Flaming wreckage fell in their wake.

She wanted to yell at Owlet for taking such a stupid risk, but she was so tired. Darkness slipped over her even though she heard him calling to her. Maybe she could tear a strip off him after a little nap.

23

It was late when Ethan's private com signaled, but he'd been waiting with anticipation for the call. He took a deep breath and calmed himself before answering.

"Yes, Victor?"

"Things didn't go as planned, Highness."

That wasn't what he'd expected to hear. He didn't bother trying to hide his scowl from his man. "In what way?"

"The attack on the Bastard failed," Victor admitted. "The team snatching your sister's paramour sprang their trap too soon, and they put him on guard, I think. The kill team only wounded him."

"Idiot!" Ethan raved. "That was the most important part of the plan! How could you screw it up?"

"Highness," his man said calmly, "we'll get him. He can't stay safe forever."

"That's not a solution," he snarled. "What about the rest of the plan?"

"A mixed bag," Victor admitted. "The armed team fooled the brig personnel and got Breckenridge out. We'll have him smuggled into the palace before too long. Your sister's lover is on his way to be examined. We didn't get the scientist, though. His guards put up more resistance than expected."

The man's expression told Ethan there was more to the story than that, but he didn't ask. It didn't matter.

"Then work with the people on site. Take care of it personally." He leaned closer to the com. "And, Victor? Don't bring the marine back when you're done."

* * *

Elise was with Senator Breckenridge when she got the warning from Jared. The senator had ordered something to eat in his office, so she was as safe as if she were in a police station.

The building was heavily guarded, and the senator still had two men outside the door. Her guard commander had summoned the rest of her team to see her safely away from here once they finished their negotiations.

Breckenridge, for his part, seemed unconcerned. He really didn't know the marine, so that was probably for show. Still, it was classier than his nephew.

She'd put her com in privacy mode, so she knew there was more trouble when it rang.

"Excuse me," she said as she rose to her feet and stepped away. "Orison."

"This is Marcus, Your Highness. There have been more attacks, including an attempt on Admiral Mertz's life. He's injured, but not badly, and is safe. As you're close to him, I thought you should know.

"Also, where are you? I'm sending a marine quick-response team to reinforce your protective detail."

Her heart leapt into her throat when the AI said Jared was injured, but she forced herself to speak calmly. "I'm in the senate building, meeting with Senator Breckenridge. My full guard team is on the way, and there are serious looking men protecting the senators. I think I'm safe enough."

"With all due respect, Admiral Mertz thought the same on Orbital

One. Allow me to suggest you accept a marine pinnace as a ride up. That compromise would help ensure your safety."

She saw the logic of that. "Of course. Thank you. Tell me more about Jared."

"He has a minor wound on his left leg. He's receiving treatment and will recover completely. Mister Owlet and Major Ellis also escaped an ambush. The attackers injured the major more seriously, but the doctors expect her to survive.

"From the initial reports, their defense of his apartment was more... vigorous than their attackers expected. At the very least, the collateral damage to property was much higher than the other attacks. Unfortunately, we didn't manage to take any of the attackers alive."

She sighed. "So, you're telling me this is an organized group not afraid to attack protected areas. I'll be waiting for your pinnace. Thank you, Marcus."

Elise disconnected the call. "There have been other attacks. Jared Mertz was injured on Orbital One. Another marine officer was hurt down here. Are you sure we're safe?"

He rose from his seat beside the table and touched a button on his desk. "Get me the chief of the Senatorial Guard."

After a moment, a woman's voice came back. "Yes, Senator Breckenridge?"

"I apologize for calling you at home, Colonel. A number of people from the expedition have been attacked. I have Crown Princess Elise Orison from the Kingdom of Pentagar in my office right now, and I'm concerned that we might be in danger here as well."

"Stand by."

He turned to Elise. "Vera Leibowitz is an ex-marine colonel. She'll do what needs to be done."

"*Invincible* is sending a marine pinnace to get me out of here. Don't get into a shooting match with it."

He nodded. "That would be bad. I'll make certain they know about it."

"Senator?" Colonel Leibowitz was back. "There are only two other senators in the building. I've sent extra people to your office, and

I'm calling in the Imperial Marines for backup. We've put the building on lockdown."

"Excellent," Breckenridge said. "Also, a pinnace from *Invincible* is coming for the crown princess. Coordinate with Fleet to make sure it gets in safely."

"Will do, Senator. I'm on my way now, and warnings are going out to all the senators' security details. Don't leave until I get there."

"I wouldn't think of it. Thank you, Colonel."

He turned to Elise. "What could they hope to gain by kidnaping or killing these people?"

She sipped her drink worriedly. "Admiral Mertz was apparently to be assassinated. In case the news hasn't made the rounds, he and I are a couple."

His expression hardened, but not about the relationship, she thought. "I hadn't heard. No more small talk. Let me get him on the line for you and give you some privacy. Our business here is concluded, I think."

She nodded gratefully as he again used his desk com.

"Get me Orbital One," he said. "Make sure they know who is calling."

"Right away, Senator."

A moment later, another voice came on the line. "Orbital One security, Senator Breckenridge. Lieutenant Howard speaking. I don't have any more information on the escape."

The senator frowned. "What are you talking about?"

"Captain Breckenridge's escape, sir. Isn't that why you called?"

* * *

KELSEY ARRIVED at the alley where Talbot had called for help with a marine strike team at her back. The police were going over the area with a fine-toothed comb. A woman walked over as soon as the pinnace landed, her hand extended.

She glanced at the weapons on Kelsey's hips but said nothing. A wise decision.

"Princess Kelsey, I'm Lieutenant Amy Jenkins, Planetary Security.

We've searched the area thoroughly, but didn't find Major Talbot or any of his attackers. There's a small amount of blood in the alley, which may or may not be connected with this case, but not enough to make me think anyone was killed here tonight."

"Thank God. Do you have any idea what happened?"

The woman flipped an old-fashioned notepad open. "He was at a known marine bar up the street. Some of the staff said there was a bit of a scuffle earlier but that the man Major Talbot was arguing with was in a much better mood by the time the major left. The man was still there when our people arrived, and there's no indication he slipped out or called anyone to cause Major Talbot any trouble."

She pointed up the street. "The major walked from that direction toward the Excelsior. A street camera covering the area went offline just before the ambush. I have techs looking into it.

"One of the people in the building across the street claims to have seen the whole thing from her balcony. She said there were two large groups of attackers. One ahead of the major and another following. He spotted the ambush and made a break for the alley."

The detective gestured at the alley. "He fired some kind of weapon that emitted a blue light that took out the first group as they rushed in behind him. It *purportedly* dropped them in their tracks."

Jenkins raised an eyebrow as she looked at Kelsey. "I'm not familiar with any weapon capable of that, but there are rumors circulating your expedition found something interesting. Can you elaborate?"

Kelsey shrugged. "I can't talk about the expedition yet, but I can confirm that a stunning weapon was used here."

She drew hers and handed it over to the detective. "The range is good out to fifty meters on narrow beam. Wide angle, which is what he must've used, cuts the range in half and reduces the knockout time from four hours to maybe half an hour."

The detective examined the weapon curiously. "This is amazing. It really does all that? What are the chances we can get some? That would really help us take out the bad guys without risking innocent bystanders."

"That's already in the works," Kelsey said. "One of our people made a stun-only version specifically for that purpose. I think there are a few dozen ready in orbit. I'll see that they get them to you."

The woman handed Kelsey's neural disruptor back. "So, the military version can kill? The major might have killed his attackers."

"Almost certainly not. Only an idiot keeps a weapon that can stun on a kill setting. Talbot only needed to stop them, not kill them."

"Lieutenant," a man called from the alley. "We have an ID on the blood."

The two of them stepped over to the man. He looked at Kelsey curiously, but Jenkins gestured for him to continue.

"There was a little fresh blood on the ground near the smashed com. It matched Fleet records for Major Talbot. Not enough for a fatal injury, but based on the few drops on the wall, someone might have bashed him in the head."

Kelsey's stomach rolled over. "Enough to be fatal?"

The man shrugged. "This feels more like a kidnapping than a murder. I'd put money on his being alive."

"That brings me to the last bit of eyewitness testimony," Jenkins said. "Two grav vans picked up the unconscious attackers and the major. They had their identifiers disabled. We'll keep looking, but I wouldn't hold my breath that lead will pan out."

"I might be able to help with that. Major Talbot has a locator beacon. If we can find it, we'll be able to get his precise location."

"Won't the kidnappers find it?" Leibowitz asked.

Kelsey smiled coldly. "Not a chance. It's inside him. The range is about a dozen kilometers. If we find it, my marines and I will go pay them a visit they won't be soon forgetting."

"Not to rain on your parade, but this is a security matter. We can mount a rescue operation without leveling a building."

"Can you stun everyone inside? No? Also, Major Talbot and I are dating. If you think for one second that I'll allow someone else to pull him out of the fire, you are sadly mistaken."

The woman shook her head. "Pistols aside, you're not trained for this kind of work, Highness. Leave it to the professionals."

"You don't know me," Kelsey said. "The last year has changed me in ways you can't begin to understand." She reached down and lifted one end of a trash dumpster off the ground. A full one.

That got everyone's attention.

"What I'm about to tell you is a classified Imperial secret. Pay attention and tell no one. I have enhancements that make me ten times stronger than the toughest man you know. I have a combat computer in my head that can spot trouble before anyone else, and I can act before you twitch. The pinnace has armor in it that no weapon here will touch.

"So don't think you're going to tell me I'm not saving the man I love. Is that clear enough for you?"

* * *

CARL PACED the hospital waiting room. The other people there were staring at him oddly, and he didn't blame them. He looked as though he'd been through a fire, he was carrying a hammer, and he had half a dozen men and women guarding him.

Planetary Security was on the way. Well, technically, there were a few uniformed officers in the waiting room, but the detectives would be here soon.

Major Ellis was going to make it. She'd lost some blood, but the wounds were treatable. Thank God for that.

The marine second in command of his protective detail was briefing him on what had taken place tonight. Someone had wanted to sweep the board, but why attack him? He was small fry.

Obviously, they thought his knowledge of Old Empire technology might help them with something. But what?

A hard-eyed man in a rumpled suit came into the waiting room. He headed straight for Carl.

"Carl Owlet? I'm Detective Ronny Powers, Planetary Security. I have some questions for you." He looked at the marine guards. Even in civilian clothes, they were obviously military. "Alone."

"Not happening," Lieutenant Howard Coulter said. "This man is under Fleet protection. We go where he goes."

The two men glared at one another.

"Let's make a compromise," Carl suggested. "We can go to the chapel, and the marines can sit in the back. We get privacy, and they can keep an eye on me."

With a reluctant nod, the detective agreed. "Lead the way."

Carl had visited the chapel earlier. Never a very religious man, he'd felt the need for some contemplation after the events of the evening. He'd killed men tonight.

First, the men who'd died when he'd flown the hammer through his apartment. Then he'd hit the survivors in the grav van as they'd fled. He'd meant to disable it, but it had dodged right in front of him at the last moment. They'd gone through it at supersonic velocity.

The detective escorted him up front, and they took a seat on the pew with a view, as he'd thought of it. The stained glass window was beautiful and probably had deeper meaning for the religious.

"So, there was a little problem at student housing," the detective said. "Tell me about it."

Carl chuckled grimly. "Yes, I suppose those are the right words for it. A little problem. Armed men attacked Major Angela Ellis and myself. She's my head keeper, by the way. I suspect this was supposed to be a kidnapping, based on the other events of the evening."

"I'm aware of them," the detective admitted. "Or at least some of them. Why would these men want to kidnap you?"

"They probably wanted to know something. I'm a scientist and was part of the recently returned expedition. The details of which I can't go into without permission."

The detective didn't look pleased at that news. "Who would be able to give me a green light?"

"A good place to start would be Admiral Jared Mertz. He's on Orbital One."

The man rubbed his face. "Fine. You were a lab assistant or something, so what could you really know?"

The question sounded rhetorical, so Carl chose not to answer it. Most people didn't accept him as a scientist. He looked like someone just getting ready to go to college. He wouldn't be old enough to drink for months, though he'd been declared an adult for legal purposes.

Detective Powers sighed and made a note in his little book. "So, the bad guys attacked. Your neighbors downstairs heard them breaking in. One even saw them in the stairwell. Masked, of course, but with heavy weapons. That matches the level of destruction in your apartment and the one across the hall. Luckily for everyone involved, the occupants were out partying."

Carl had known the rooms were empty of people because of the combat remotes he'd scattered around. Otherwise, he'd have brought Mjölnir in through a different wall. Unfortunately, the other apartment provided the best way to stop most of the attackers. He'd have to find out how much he owed them for lost personal belongings.

The university would be pissed about the damage to the buildings. First, the classified lab he'd been storing the hammer at would need some roof work. Then the two apartments would need major repairs, and anything the van debris landed on, of course.

And he couldn't forget the windows he'd smashed when he'd gone supersonic.

Yeah, the bill was going to be spectacular.

"So, your guard was shot, but you escaped. None of the cameras showed you exiting the building. How'd you get down?"

"That's classified."

The detective gave him a flat stare. "Uh-huh. I suppose the grav car that broke the sound barrier had something to do with that. Probably shot down the bad guys, too. Can you at least confirm that?"

Carl shook his head. "It's all classified. Was anyone hurt when the grav van came down?"

"Other than the four men inside it who were killed in the explosion? No. You were damned lucky. Part of the wreckage went almost across the campus. It hit some lab and caved in part of the roof. Or, more likely, it was a missile that missed the van. The angles are odd, but that's the only answer that fits the facts. Maybe the grav van took a shot at your car."

The man shook his head. "I suppose I'll find out some version of the truth eventually. Honestly, Major Ellis is going to get a much sterner questioning from me. She holds responsibility for most of the damage, I suspect. Along with those yahoos at the back of the chapel. You're only a kid. No way you caused this kind of havoc."

If he only knew.

The detective put his notebook away. "One more question. The major came into the hospital dressed only in her underwear. I can't help but notice those are hospital scrubs you're wearing. Might I assume that you and the major have a... complicated relationship?"

Carl's clothes had been covered in blood. They'd found the scrubs so he didn't scare the other people in the waiting room.

The detective held up a hand before Carl could deny it.

"I'm not judging. You're a legal adult and can sleep with whoever you choose." He smiled with a glint in his eye. "I will say nice going, though."

He stood without letting Carl say a word. "We'll get to the bottom of this. Whoever these bozos were, we'll identify them. That'll get us the answers we need."

Carl watched the man go back to talk to Coulter. The marine wouldn't tell him anything. In a way, that was good. The fewer lies out there, the less trouble keeping things straight.

Since the marines had overheard everything, he also suspected a few juicy rumors about them sleeping together were going to start making the rounds. By the time Major Ellis found out, it would be far too late to do anything about them.

Except possibly punching him. Again.

24

Talbot woke in pain. His head was throbbing. His abused arm hurt even worse.

The memory of the attack came flooding back in, and he tried to sit up. Nope. His captors had tied him to a bed. Arms, legs, and a belt around his middle. Someone didn't want him getting up.

He smiled. Good.

"Ah, our guest is awake," a male voice said from the darkness beside him.

Talbot adjusted his ocular implants and saw the man in the shadows. Hair pulled back into a long tail, dressed well enough. He'd recognize the face if he ever saw it again.

He activated his recorders. If he didn't make it out, he wanted someone to catch the bastard.

"Where am I?" Talbot demanded in a voice that almost croaked. "Who the hell are you?"

The man leaned forward. "The less you know about me, the better the chances that you'll walk away from this unpleasantness."

"You picked the wrong guy to snag. I don't exactly know that much. I'm just a jarhead."

"Surprisingly, I agree. We didn't target you for your knowledge.

We want to examine those machines inside you. To have someone look over the code that drives them. As a senior officer, if anyone is compromised, it will be you."

Talbot took a moment to activate his retrieval beacon. The fact no one had pinged it from the outside told him he must be some distance away from the capital. At least now someone would find him. It was only a matter of time. Kelsey wouldn't stop looking until she did.

"I don't suppose my sincere assurance that I'm not under any compulsion will do."

The man smiled. "No, I'm afraid not. That weapon was quite a surprise. It took down my men in short order. If you'd had a few more moments, you might have escaped entirely. Everyone recovered, so it's nonlethal. What is it?"

Talbot felt around for it with his implants. A smart man would keep it out of his range. Then again, they didn't know he could access it.

He found it in a drawer near the edge of his range and locked it down. Now they wouldn't be using it for anything. Too bad he didn't have the long-range com inside Carl was proposing as a universal upgrade.

"We call them stunners," he lied. "The police in the Old Empire used them."

The man looked impressed. "That's quite a tool. When in doubt, take them all out. One would've been very useful in taking you down. Or the other targets."

That made Talbot's stomach flutter. "You have other prisoners? Who?"

"Alas, we didn't get the others. It's quite embarrassing, really. We wanted to take a scientist to assist with analyzing your code, so to speak. His guards used significantly more force than you to stop us. They killed nine men."

"It might shock you to know, but I'm sorry about that," Talbot said. "I'm not a fan of needless slaughter. I was only a guy out on the town. If you ran up against a dedicated protection detail, they'd use whatever force they deemed necessary to protect the subject."

"Or perhaps more. They blew up the top floor of an apartment building and then used a missile to shoot down our van as it fled. Without any prisoners, I might add. That feels a tad excessive."

That sounded excessive to Talbot, too. His people wouldn't just shoot down a fleeing enemy. Not outside a combat zone. And blowing up an apartment building was never a good idea.

"Who was the target?"

"Not one of your major players, I understand. A lab assistant named Owlet."

That explained a lot. The damned hammer could cause that level of damage in inexperienced hands. He'd seen the vids to prove it.

"He's a graduate student," Talbot said. "Bright enough, but the lowest ranking guy on the science teams. Why would you trust what he had to say, anyway? He'd be just as compromised as the rest of us, by your standards."

The man shifted in his seat. "We'd hoped to have him guide us into extracting the computer code and understanding it. My employer is quite concerned that you people are time bombs waiting to explode."

"I don't suppose you'd care to share a name with me."

The man smiled. "No. Believe it or not, Major Talbot, I intend to release you unharmed. When I do, you're free to tell whoever you want about our concerns."

The man rose to his feet and straightened his jacket. He still probably thought himself safely concealed in the dark. "I'll let you get a bit of rest and we'll talk again. Perhaps over breakfast. Sleep well."

Talbot waited for the man to leave before testing the strength of his restraints. He wasn't getting loose easily. The bed was solid, too. He wouldn't be tipping it over. Even if he could, he'd really mess his arm up. They had him well and truly trapped.

He sighed. He'd just have to count on Kelsey to come to his rescue. Humiliating, but something he could count on.

* * *

THE DUTY PHYSICIAN was just closing up the wound on Jared's leg when Admiral Yeats came storming into the medical center. "What a freaking mess. Your boys and girls killed all four of the attackers."

"Considering the circumstances, I can live with that. I killed the two in the bedroom."

The senior Fleet officer's eyes widened. "Well, that's a surprise. You never struck me as a close combat kind of man."

"I've had to do a lot of things I'd never planned on over the last year, Admiral. Any idea how they got onto Orbital One? My implant database said they weren't Fleet."

The other man's eyes narrowed. "What have you got tucked away in there?"

Jared shrugged. "I wanted to be sure I had at least a little information about the officers on the board of inquiry, so I loaded the public records for all active Fleet personnel. None of those people were in it. I suppose there could be some secret group that you don't have open records for, but I'm betting they aren't part of it."

"Of course we have some off-the-books investigators, but you're right. Those people weren't active duty. All four were marines in the past, though. One retired and three kicked out of the service. Someone in Orbital One security let them aboard. Their ship didn't wait for them, and you weren't the only target."

Jared's stomach sank. "Someone was killed?"

"They busted Wallace Breckenridge out of holding. Killed the on duty security detail in the prison. Whoever they were, they wanted you dead and him free. Does that ring any bells for you?"

Jared eyed the medical staff. "No one I'd mention in public."

Yeats jerked a thumb toward the corridor hatch. "Everyone out."

The staff seemed surprised, but they followed his orders. A few minutes later, the two of them were alone.

"There," Yeats said. "Now talk."

Jared considered his words carefully. One didn't just come out and accuse the heir to the Throne of murder and conspiracy to murder.

"You recall Kelsey's mentor from the Department of Imperial Affairs? Carlo Vega. He died shortly after we left Imperial space. Poison. I have no proof, but I suspect the target was actually me.

"I gave him some candies that the palace sent to me. One of them was probably poisoned, and the only person there who hates me that much is Ethan Bandar."

Yeats pondered what he'd said for a moment before responding. "That's a serious accusation. Particularly without proof."

Jared nodded and stood, testing his leg. It felt a lot better. He'd need some time in the regenerator, but he could walk without help.

"Which is why I haven't said anything. The investigation is still officially open, but I'm certain he was behind it. The last time we met, he basically told me he'd eliminate me as a problem. Permanently."

Yeats rubbed his chin. "I can't officially enter that into the record, but I'll have a private talk with His Majesty. He needs to know how you feel."

"Then I'd best be the one to tell him."

Yeats nodded. "I suspect so. How will you do it?"

"I think I need to meet up with Kelsey. The two of us can tell him together. If you can excuse me from the board of inquiry for the day, that is."

"They have enough testimony to go over without you. There are a ton of other witnesses to speak with."

"You need to be careful, Admiral," Jared said. "With Breckenridge on the loose, that tells me there's something going on that might include Fleet. I hesitate to mention this, but we saw the Pentagarans go through an attempted coup. Watch your ships and commanders."

The older man rubbed his face. "I hope to God we don't have that kind of rot, but you're right. They had someone here in their pocket. We can't count on others being clean. I'll raise the alert level and warn the senior officers on all ships that he's loose and that we need to be on guard. Better safe than sorry."

"With your permission, I'll do the same. My people are less disposed to be allies of his after what he did."

"Do it," Yeats said decisively. "If they can't take over your ships, they can't win."

"You need to get a marine detail you trust," Jared said. "If they can't control you, they might try to eliminate you. With you gone, Breckenridge might move to take charge of Fleet.

"We have some unpowered armor that non-enhanced personnel can use that would make your guards tougher. Also, there's a kind of lightweight armor that Kelsey uses under her regular clothes. It's tough. I'll see that you get a set."

"I worry we're being too paranoid, but it won't hurt to take some basic precautions. I'll accept all your suggestions. Now get down there and settle this, Jared."

"Aye, sir."

He found his pants and summoned the marines waiting in the corridor after the admiral had left. "We're going down to Avalon."

They formed a protective wedge around him and took him straight to the docking level. Their pinnace disengaged as soon as they were strapped in.

He opened a channel to *Invincible*. "Marcus, go to alert status."

"Already there, Admiral. Shall I go to battle stations?"

"No, but I want the fleet ready for trouble. Breckenridge has escaped, and I think something big is in motion. I don't want any of our ships falling into unfriendly hands."

"I'll notify all senior officers at once. I've already taken the liberty of summoning the crew back from leave. With the exception of Major Talbot, everyone is accounted for."

Jared nodded. "Excellent. Be ready to throw up battle screens at the first sign of trouble. A supposedly friendly ship might open fire with no warning."

"Once again, Admiral, I'm one step ahead of you. All ships have their computers watching. At the first sign of hostile activity, every battle screen in the fleet will snap into place. No missile will have time to hit us, and the New Empire vessels don't have beam weapons to worry about."

That was a relief.

"There was a ship or cutter that took Breckenridge and the attackers off Orbital One. Get the operations team to work on determining which one it was and where it went."

"Once the attack on you took place, I took that liberty. Very few vessels undocked between the time the attack commenced and when

Orbital One locked down all outgoing traffic. One cutter in particular went to Avalon and landed at Capital Spaceport.

"Though I have no proof that is the ship you seek, I'd wager my as yet unpaid salary that will be them."

Jared felt the corner of his mouth quirking up. "I'm wondering what you'd spend it on. In any case, I'll fix that lapse as soon as possible. I'm meeting with Kelsey, and we're going to speak to the emperor. Hopefully, we can sort this mess out before it becomes a major problem."

"I could always use additional processor cores, larger storage, and faster memory. I hope you can solve this before the situation spins out of control, Admiral. However, I submit that seldom seems to work. Perhaps planning for the worst would be an appropriate course of action."

"Too true, Marcus. I'll let you know when I find out anything. Keep me in the loop as far as major developments."

"Will do, Admiral. *Invincible* out."

The pinnace was already slicing into the atmosphere. It wouldn't be long before he and Kelsey could talk. She didn't know he suspected her brother of killing her mentor. Based on history, she wouldn't take it very well. It might take more than a bit of convincing to bring her around to his point of view.

Of course, he didn't actually need her to believe it was possible. Her just being open-minded while he talked to the emperor would be helpful.

Now all they had to do was figure this out before anyone else got killed.

25

A ngela slowly swam back to awareness. The pain in her side was gone. Regeneration was a wonderful thing.

The medical staff was pulling her out of the regeneration unit, and a doctor she vaguely remembered was checking the readout.

"Things look good, Major Ellis," he said. "In case you don't remember our very brief meeting earlier, I'm Doctor John Yeager, and you're at Capital Hospital. You were shot, but your companion got you here in time. Obviously."

He looked up from the readout. "I understand his arrival caused quite a stir. A few excitable souls said he flew in like some kind of superhero from the vids. Obviously, that isn't what happened, but it still has people chattering."

"Was he hurt, Doctor?" Her throat was dry.

He handed her a bottle of water. "Drink up. Your friend wasn't injured. He and the other men are in the waiting room. Before I let them in to see you, a detective with Planetary Security wants to speak with you."

It took no imagination to figure out why. They'd shot up an apartment and then basically vaporized it and a van full of fleeing suspects. She was a little woozy by then, but she remembered the terrifying flight and impact.

Perhaps an avenging superhero wasn't an entirely inaccurate assumption on the witness' part.

"Sure," she said. "Let me get dressed and I'll talk to them."

He shook his head. "Your undergarments are very bloody and also considered evidence. With your larger-than-average stature, I'm afraid the hospital gown will have to do for the moment. One of your men is getting something for you."

Well, that wasn't really a surprise. Not many nurses would match her two meter height.

"Then I guess I'm ready."

The doctor helped her up and escorted her to a normal hospital room. "We'll be keeping you for a short while to make certain everything is good. Lie back down and let me hook up the monitors."

Once he finished doing that, he excused himself and a grizzled man came in. He looked like a caricature of a detective.

"Major Ellis, I'm Detective Ronny Powers with Planetary Security. I have a few questions about what happened."

She gestured to the chair. "Feel free to sit, but I can't tell you everything. Some of it's classified."

"So I'm given to understand. Tell me what you can."

Angela walked him through the attack until the hammer put in an appearance, and then she shut him down. The damned thing was far too dangerous to put into a security report.

He looked annoyed and tried to come at the situation from several angles, but she kept putting up walls.

Powers sighed and put his notebook away. "I'll contact Admiral Mertz in the morning to see what he can tell me. At least the witnesses confirm that you didn't start the fight, even if you were a tad excessive in ending it. That will still need to be answered for, so don't make any plans to leave Avalon."

"I never go anywhere unless I have orders. You might want to mention that to Admiral Mertz as well."

Once the man was gone, Owlet poked his head through the door. "Are you up for visitors?"

She made sure the blanket covered the gown, though after the firefight he probably didn't have too much left to the imagination. Hell, those damned vids the other versions of him had taken might have some really private moments. She suppressed a shudder.

"Come in and close the door behind you. You didn't get hit, did you?"

He sat in the chair and set the ridiculously dangerous hammer on the floor beside him. "Not a scratch. I'm sorry they hurt you."

"That wasn't your fault. Dammit, what were you thinking? Wasn't that thing overkill?"

Owlet shrugged. "It was the only weapon I could put my hands on. And, to follow the metaphor, the problems became nails after that."

Well, that was certainly true. The memory of the hammer blowing a human-sized hole through an apartment building to fly into his hand was going to be hard to forget. He'd been the next best thing to invulnerable after that.

"Why did you take us back?"

"Once I saw how badly they'd hurt you, I kind of let my emotions get the better of me."

"That's one way to describe it," she said dryly. "Why destroy the van?"

"Actually, that was an accident. I meant to disable it with a quick flyby, but they dodged right in front of me at the last moment. This thing is agile, but even it has limits. Out of everything I did, that's the part I regret."

"You were in combat. Shit happens. You should've kept running away. Your first impulse to disengage was the right one. We'd have caught them later."

"I'll keep that in mind if this ever happens again, Major. What now?"

"I think you can call me Angela after what we've been through. We'll let Admiral Mertz sort it out. You did nothing wrong." She hesitated and then continued. "Thank you for saving me. I appreciate the risk you took for me."

His smile turned wry. "You're growing on me. I can see what the other versions of me saw in you. Not that I'll let that be an excuse to be an ass."

Angela said nothing, but he had worn through her armor, too. Perhaps the other versions of her hadn't been complete idiots after all. Any kind of relationship would still be totally inappropriate, but she could see her opinion of him changing.

Not that she'd ever allow him to give Princess Kelsey such a dangerous weapon. That was just crazy. Now more than ever. God only knew what the woman would do with it.

* * *

KELSEY WAS MONITORING the pinnace's scanners from the marine commander's console when she got the word Jared was coming. His pinnace dropped down and they landed together. He joined her and sent his off to keep searching for Talbot.

She hugged him. "I'm so sorry they attacked you. Any idea who it was?"

He nodded and sat down beside her. "You won't like this. I think Ethan was behind it."

Kelsey felt herself frowning. "My… our brother is an ass, but he's not homicidal. That's crazy."

"Is it? Someone poisoned Carlo Vega. I told you the investigation was ongoing, but I'm pretty sure it was in the candy the palace sent. It only had to be in one piece. Poof, the evidence was gone.

"Ethan didn't know you were coming, or he might have tried something different. After all, I might have given you the candy. Or he might have figured our mutual antipathy would keep that from happening. I have no idea. Still, tell me it doesn't make sense."

She opened her mouth to defend her twin but closed it with her objections unspoken. Was Ethan truly capable of doing something so horrible?

I think you know the answer to that.

Ned's voice in her head startled her. He'd kept quiet for so long that she forgotten he was there.

You don't know him like I do. He's not a monster.

The rebellion has taught me that you don't have to be a monster to do monstrous things. Forgive me for saying so, but your brother sounds like he has paranoid delusions or megalomania. Or both. He's clever about hiding it, most times, but if you truly think about it, he's sick, and sick people do terrible things.

Kelsey wanted to reject what Ned was suggesting, but a traitorous part of her mind was considering it. No, not Ethan. Ned and Jared had to be wrong.

She focused her attention on Jared. "I don't think he's capable of that, but if you want to look at it, well, that shouldn't hurt anything. It's not like you have a relationship to sour."

"The two of us do have a relationship. A very bad one. In any case, I'm more concerned about us."

Kelsey sighed. "Jared, I don't think any less of you for suspecting Ethan. I'm just saying not to bet the ranch on him being your sinister mastermind. What do you want to do first?"

"I think we need to speak with your father."

"With *our* father, you mean. Like it or not, he's one of the links that binds us."

"You grew up with him as a father. I didn't. Frankly, I don't know that I'll ever feel comfortable around him. But, for *your* sake, I'll try."

She smiled. "That's all anyone could ask. Well, let's get this over with. The search is widening, and someone will ping Talbot's recovery beacon before long. Once that happens, I'll need to be free to rain hellfire and damnation down on some deserving souls."

Kelsey sent a message to the pilot to head for the palace. Someone would wake her father. If he wasn't awake already.

Jared rubbed his leg thoughtfully. "Speaking of hellfire and damnation, Carl destroyed his apartment building. Part of it, anyway. Planetary Security wants details he and Major Ellis aren't willing to divulge."

"Jesus," she said. "How many people did these bastards attack? Was anyone hurt?"

"The collateral damage was limited to structures, bad guys, and Major Ellis. She's going to be fine. There's a rumor a superhero is on the loose, though." He told her what he knew of the incident.

She shook her head. "That hammer is a little too dangerous for him, I think. He's trashed pretty much everything he's thrown it at."

"But you think it's awesome. Admit it."

"Kind of. At least I think I might be a tad more precise in how it's used. In any case, it saved their lives tonight, so that's a win. What did the mastermind want with him?"

Jared shrugged. "Perhaps he was simply the one who looked easiest to grab. Big mistake on someone's part. With that hammer, he was probably the most dangerous.

"I don't think that device belongs in too many hands. The technology, sure, but not all rolled together. A shield for combat use. A larger scale weapon for vehicles. Even flying marine armor. Just not all in one package."

She nodded. "I'll take possession of it as soon as practical. Angela will howl, but you're right. That's too much for one person. I'll lock it away from general use, too. It would be far too easy to use it as a crutch."

"That might be for the best."

The pinnace came in for a landing at the palace. She unstrapped herself and rose to her feet. "Come on. It's time for you to make your pitch. I don't expect Father will be easy to convince."

* * *

ELISE STEPPED off the pinnace onto Orbital One. Surprisingly, there hadn't been any trouble for her. The security response on Avalon had been ridiculous. Guards everywhere and armed craft circling the Imperial Senate.

She'd found out just before docking that Jared had gone to Avalon. As frustrating as that was, she'd have to accept he was okay until they caught up with one another.

Her welcome party consisted of Reginald Bell, William Hawthorne, and a significant number of Fleet security officers.

"Surely we're not in danger here," she said.

"I'd wager Admiral Mertz thought the same thing," William said.

"Yet someone tried to kill him in his quarters. Still, I doubt we're targets in this unpleasantness."

"Agreed," Bell said. "I'll still avail myself of the offered protection. It's been quite a long day, but I find myself wide-awake. Shall we adjourn somewhere for a snack? I have something I'd like to discuss with you, Highness."

She nodded. "I've eaten, but some tea would be most welcome."

The three of them relocated to a restaurant with a fabulous view of Avalon. The snowcapped peaks were particularly stunning.

The security team made sure no one else was in their section. She smiled apologetically at those displaced.

Bell waited until they'd all ordered to speak on anything of substance. "I don't know how your situation was received, but I ran into a hitch. They claim that I have no authority to negotiate with Pentagar. Even with Princess Kelsey's blessing."

Elise nodded. "I ran into a somewhat similar situation. I spoke with Senator Breckenridge. Yes, the ass's uncle. It seems the Imperial Charter doesn't recognize that a world might be separated from the Empire for any reason. So, the treaty Kelsey and I negotiated is being fought over in the Senate."

"And this elder Breckenridge stands against us?" William asked. "That's not surprising, I suppose. My situation is similarly impacted. While we recognize the authority of the Imperial Throne, the negotiations to keep our local rule in place are on shakier ground. The government must be reviewed, they claim."

She sipped her tea. It was surprisingly good.

"Actually, I'm not certain that Senator Breckenridge will be our enemy in this matter. He seems willing to deal. The price for his help is irksome, but reasonable. He wants my best effort to convince Kelsey and the emperor not to pursue charges of treason against Wallace Breckenridge. Though the man's escape may confound all our plans."

William nodded judiciously. "His link to the attackers might make that very difficult. Though, based on his record, the jailbreak portion of the mission went off entirely too smoothly."

There was a core of truth to that. Breckenridge wasn't the universe's most competent villain.

"I'm sure that problem will solve itself. Other than Talbot, the enemy's plans have gone badly astray. Now that people are looking into it, I hope the conspiracy will unravel quickly."

Bell focused his attention on her. "Which brings me to the matter I'd like to discuss. Someone seems to have decided it was a good idea to promote me and award me back pay. You wouldn't happen to know anything about that, would you?"

She gave him a blandly interested look. "Did they, now? I'm sure you earned all that and more. Congratulations."

"I notice you didn't deny the charge, so I'll take that as a tacit admission of guilt."

He sighed. "I was quite happy being an ensign. Now, I'm officially a retired admiral with half a millennium of service. You wouldn't believe how much money that is. Even with the several hundred years the bean counters are disputing because I was in stasis."

"Accountants are so predictable." William's expression brightened. "So, you'll pick up the tab? Perhaps I'll splurge on a good brandy after all."

26

E mperor Karl rose to his feet when Jared and Kelsey stepped inside his office. He waved the Imperial Guardsmen out. "Jared, I'm so pleased to see that you're well."

"It was a close thing," Jared admitted. "Under other circumstances, I might have let the killers in. You've heard about Breckenridge escaping, I presume."

The emperor nodded as he sat. "From the most secure facility we have. It's maddening. He has friends willing to kill to get him out. They found the bodies of some men assigned to Orbital One stuffed into a crate at the spaceport a little while ago. That's in addition to the men and women guarding the brig."

"We recovered the cutter, but they sprayed it down with something that destroys DNA. It's like a bad conspiracy movie. One where I'm the dunce in charge that never saw it coming."

Kelsey rose from the seat she'd taken and put her hand on her father's shoulder. "Why should you expect the worst from people?"

"True," Jared said. "You didn't have your crew mutiny and lock you in the kitchen."

Karl gave him a sad smile. "Yes, but you had no reason to expect the betrayal. I should've seen this coming."

"Through what? Psychic powers? Your Majesty, no one expected this. I have a theory about the people behind the attack on me."

The emperor straightened. "A lead would be most useful right now."

"You won't like it," Jared warned. "I know there are a lot of reports to go over, but have you read the one on Carlo Vega's death?"

"I skimmed it. It's troubling. Who disliked him enough to kill him?"

"No one, I expect. I'll bet everything I own that I was the target."

Karl Bandar's eyes widened. "You? Who would want to kill you, and how did they get Carlo Vega by mistake? Better yet, why didn't you lock them up?"

He gave the man a grumpy smile. "Because I have no authority over the person I suspect is behind it. I'm morally certain the candies that came from the palace for me had one that was poisoned. I gave them to Vega, never suspecting anyone would do that. That's why there was no poison left to find."

"Candies? I didn't send any candies." The emperor licked his lips. "You think Ethan did it."

Jared nodded. "He openly threatened me when I was leaving before the expedition. I'm sure there's no record of the conversation, but he made it plain he was going to eliminate me as a threat to the Throne once and for all."

"God, I hope you're wrong, but Ethan was so pleased after you left. I thought it was just because you were finally out of his hair, but it makes a terrible kind of sense now."

Kelsey looked aghast. "Father! You can't possibly believe Ethan is behind this."

"Believe is too strong a word," her father said. "Fear might be more accurate. He hasn't been his usual self since your expedition returned. He's spoken pretty strongly against trusting any of you. He doesn't trust your implants."

"The implants," Jared said. "That's it. He took Talbot to examine the implants. I think he tried to get Carl Owlet because he thought he might be able to explain everything."

"What about Breckenridge?" Kelsey asked. "Why rescue him?"

"A supposedly 'unbiased' witness? I have no idea. Killing me is the least surprising thing about his plan."

She shook her head. "This is pure speculation. We know Breckenridge has an uncle in the Senate. Perhaps he's behind this."

Her father sagged a little more in his chair. "Nathaniel has never been the easiest man to work with, but he's no traitor."

"Someone is behind this," Jared said. "If it's not Ethan, then we need to eliminate him as a suspect so we can focus on the real threat."

"He's out at the Imperial Retreat. I banished him there until he could get his temper under control. He's got men I trust watching him closely."

"Unless you've got his communications under that same microscope, that doesn't really mean anything."

Kelsey frowned. "Father, are you okay? You look almost grey."

The emperor clutched his chest. "I can't breathe." He fell out of his chair with a gasp before either of them could reach him.

* * *

ETHAN LOOKED up from the tablet he was reading when the head of the guard detail opened his door.

"My lord, you need to come with me."

He frowned at the man. "What's going on?"

"Your father has fallen ill. We need to get you back to the palace at once."

Even though he'd known this was coming, it was still like a blow to the stomach.

"What happened? Is he okay?"

Ethan tossed the tablet onto the desk and followed the man out.

"He's unresponsive, Highness. They have him in the medical center, and his personal physician is there. I don't have any more information on his condition. Your sister and Admiral Mertz were with him when he collapsed."

The smile that news almost sparked was hard to suppress. Perfect.

It was a shame the old man had forced Ethan to kill him, but it was necessary. Those nanites would extend his father's life to undreamed of lengths.

Ethan wasn't going to wait that long to sit on the Imperial Throne. Instead, he'd be the one who ruled for lifetimes. He'd be the one the people called "The Great."

He certainly wasn't going to deal with centuries of fending off the Bastard. Mertz would continue trying to steal the Throne, and he only had to succeed once. Ethan meant to see that threat eliminated before the man could make his next attempt.

* * *

CARL AND ANGELA were just arriving back on *Invincible* when their plans took a drastic turn. They'd barely gotten off the pinnace when Doctor Stone was pushing them toward the next one in line. "This way. We're going back down."

He went where she told him. It only took her a few moments to get them into the second pinnace and it undocked.

"What's going on?" Angela demanded.

"The emperor is ill, and if what I suspect is true, we're in big trouble." Stone flopped into a seat and set her bag down beside her. "The admiral thinks it was the same poison that killed Carlo Vega."

"Oh shit," Carl said. "But you have an antidote. Right?"

"No. The poison had broken down by the time I examined him. I might be able to slow things down, though. I have an analyzer in my bag. I'll send Marcus what we find and pray he can help. But there's a complication."

"That doesn't sound at all promising," Angela said as she sat down and strapped in. "Cinch up tight. They're doing a combat drop, and the grav drives might not be able to dampen all the maneuvers. That means you, Carl."

He was pretty sure that was the first time she'd ever used his given name. Still, he promptly did as she ordered. He didn't want to be squashed like a bug.

"If this is the same poison," Stone continued, "that means it's the same assassin. The admiral was concerned it might be his half brother."

"As in the heir to the Throne?" Carl asked. "That's awkward. With the emperor out of play, there's no telling what he might try."

"Which is why I think you need to take this pinnace and vanish for the moment. You know, as kind of a mobile reserve."

"You want us to hide out in case someone needs rescue?" Angela asked. "Like the admiral or the princess."

"Exactly," the doctor confirmed. "I realize I can't order you to do any such silly thing, so I ran my plan past Marcus. He's endorsed it. Major, if you'll take a moment to call him and confirm."

Angela's eyes went unfocused for a few moments and then she nodded. "The captain has verified your orders, ma'am. That's good enough for me."

"Excellent. Once we land at the palace, I want you and this pinnace to disappear."

"Pinnaces can be hard to locate, but this is the capital. They'll have us on their plates wherever we go."

The doctor grinned. "Not so you'd notice. This is one of the pinnaces from *Persephone*. It does stealth better than anything the New Terran Empire has ever seen. Just head back up and fade from the scanners once you exit the atmosphere. If you're between the orbital and planetary control zones, they'll probably miss you."

"That's pretty damned clever," Angela admitted. "Are you always this sneaky, Doctor? If so, why are you not in my poker circle?"

"I have my moments, but this is Marcus's idea. It's freaking brilliant. He took the liberty of loading you up with a full set of powered armor and weapons. Once you settle down, you can monitor everything via a dedicated tight beam to *Persephone*.

"They're moving out of orbit with Admiral Yeats's blessing. He's not briefed on the plan, but he didn't ask any awkward questions. She's headed out toward the new flip point. She'll engage stealth and slip back into orbit. So long as someone doesn't physically see her, she'll be good."

Angela shook her head. "You're telling me we can't even detect a ship like her in *orbit*? That's insane."

Stone shrugged. "That may change once we upgrade the scanners to Old Empire standards. For now, count your blessings."

Carl cleared his throat. "Once we're all stashed away, what then? What are you expecting to happen?"

"Worst case," the medical officer said, "the heir will assume the powers of the Throne and lock the admiral up. Kelsey is almost certainly safe from retaliation for now. She'll stay with her father and work to make sure I have the access I need."

"So, we break the admiral out?"

Stone shook her head. "No. Just wait for orders. Odds are you won't have to do anything. Only if we need heavy firepower on a moment's notice. Perhaps for rescuing Major Talbot. You're not going to have to make this up as you go. Just take a deep breath and relax."

The pinnace decelerated, and Carl was grateful he'd strapped in. That was the most intense landing he'd ever experienced.

As soon as the ramp lowered, Doctor Stone went charging down. "Good luck!"

The pilot closed the ramp, and the pinnace took off again very quickly. He imagined palace security wasn't happy having an armed marine pinnace inside its defenses.

He turned to Angela. "Do you think it will be that easy?"

She laughed. "Nothing involving you ever goes the way I imagine."

His stomach sank. She was right about their luck. Things were probably going to go straight down the toilet.

27

K elsey stood beside her father's bed, her mind filled with terror. He had to make it. She couldn't imagine life without him. Jared stood silently by her side.

Lily Stone was working with her father's personal physician to isolate the toxin. The man wasn't ready to say it was poison, but he wasn't hindering Stone while she ran tests.

"I found it," Lily said. "It's in his stomach, as expected. I'm getting a sample for the analyzer now."

"Can you reverse it?" Kelsey asked.

"I hope so." Lily took a bit of extracted mess and put it into an Old Empire device. The screen lit up after a few moments. "It has the same basic chemical properties as what I found in Carlo Vega, but it hasn't broken down completely yet. There may be a way to stop the reaction before it kills him."

The emperor's personal doctor looked at the screen. "I recognize this. There's a plant on the southern continent that some people use for religious ceremonies. In high enough doses, it kills."

He looked up at them. "There's some kind of additive, though. A binding agent that might stop the regular course of treatment from working. I'll try it anyway. It should at least slow the progress of the poison."

"I've sent the analysis to *Invincible*," Lily said. "Marcus has the computing power to figure out possible cures. Meanwhile, we hold on and hope the emperor is strong enough to survive while we work."

The doors to the medical center slid open, and Ethan walked through with a dozen Imperial Guardsmen at his back. "What are these people doing here? Get them out at once. Everyone except my father's personal physician."

Kelsey turned to him, her eyes blazing. "He's my father and I'm not going anywhere."

Her brother smiled. "I think you will. I had the guards search your rooms, and they found something interesting." He pulled a vial of dark liquid from his pocket. "I thought you loved our father, but you tried to kill him for the Bastard."

The brazen charge took her breath away. "How dare you? I would never hurt him."

The guards raised their weapons, and she realized she'd clenched her fists and stepped forward. It took an act of will to stop herself from taking another as her combat computer calculated the optimal attack plan to take them all out.

Ethan gestured toward her. "As the heir during a time of crisis, I'm assuming the mantle of the Throne. Guards, take both of these traitors into custody. If my sister resists, shoot the Bastard. That might break his control."

The emperor's physician dodged into the middle of the confrontation and plucked the vial of poison from Ethan's fingers. "I'll take this, Highness. It might save your father's life."

Kelsey saw that her brother didn't want to give up the vial, but he really couldn't object. He was framing them and he wanted ultimate power. It tore at her heart to see that Jared had been right all along.

Ethan was a monster.

There was no way he'd allow Lily to examine the drug on his own. She needed to distract them while the doctors worked.

"You've gone mad," she said as she stepped between the guards and Jared. "I don't know what has taken hold in you, but I'm not just letting you imprison us. You're the usurper in this story. You killed Carlo Vega. You tried to kill Jared. You poisoned our father and put the drugs into my room. I can prove it."

That diverted his attention. "If this involves those cursed things in your head, that's no proof at all. You're a slave to the Bastard's will."

She smiled. "You call him the Bastard, but the joke is on you. It seems Mother was a little free with her affection, too, and before anyone knew about Jared. Awkward. Now he's the only one of us that has any Imperial blood in his veins at all."

Ethan gaped at her and turned a bright red. "Liar! Get her out of my sight, and get their minion out of here before she does something to my father."

Lily pinged Kelsey's implants. *I just sent the analysis of the pure poison up. Good work on distracting him, but you've let the genie out of the lamp.*

I'm sorry I had to spring it on Jared that way. Get the cure for my father. Save him, no matter the cost.

She raised her hands when the guards came for her. "I'm sorry I didn't tell you sooner, Jared."

"We'll talk later."

They took her weapons and cuffed her with heavy manacles. Since they had guns trained on Jared, she had no intention of resisting. That would come later.

They hustled them out of the medical center and down to the security wing. Jared gave her half a smile and pinged her.

I'm partly convinced that was a play, but you sounded so convincing. Is it true?

She shrugged. *Lily found out during that first exam she gave me. I thought about telling you but decided it would only complicate our relationship even more.*

Don't fret on my account. It doesn't bother me one bit. Well, it does, kind of. Now we're not related at all.

She gave him a reproving stare. *Family isn't just blood. It's those closest to your heart. You're my brother in every important way. If Father survives, he'll tell you so, too.*

They put her in a lift by herself. The chief guard gave her an apologetic smile. "I'm sorry, Highness. We have men waiting below. Don't cause trouble or Admiral Mertz will suffer for it."

"This is a lie," she said intently. "Keep investigating. Ethan did this, and you can't just let him take the Throne over our father's dead body."

"I promise there will be a full and thorough investigation," he said with a thoughtful frown. He pressed the button and the lift doors slid closed. It dropped deep into the ground, and a squad of female guards escorted her into a cell. The solid metal hatch slid closed. A camera high on the wall had a red light, indicating it was watching them.

One guard raised her wrist to her mouth. "Camera off." The red light winked out.

"My apologies for the indignity, Highness," the woman said. "But I need you to strip for a search. You'll be given a jumpsuit." One of the other guards held up a folded garment in garish orange.

Kelsey stripped down. The woman gave Kelsey the most thorough search she'd ever imagined.

"Food comes on a regular schedule, Highness. The camera doesn't cover the toilet. The lights dim at night, but not enough to hide any shenanigans. Behave and we won't have any trouble."

They left her alone in the cell after she dressed. The camera light came back on, so they were watching. Good. Let them think she was beaten.

She lay back on the cot and let her built-in equipment examine the cell walls. The scanners were rudimentary but more than capable of seeing the construction details.

Her implants also let her know that Jared was in the cell beside hers. She pinged him.

Don't show any sign you can hear me, but I'm next door.

She heard his silent sigh. *Things went bad so quickly. But don't worry. Lily will sort this out. We will stop him.*

Kelsey hoped that was true, but worry ate at her. Her father was dying, and her twin brother had done it.

Somehow, they had to turn this around. She had to save her father. She had to stop Ethan.

We'll get out of this, Jared. We'll fix this.

I know we will. Our people will be working hard to stop him. For now, it might be best if we get a little sleep. Things are going to happen fast when they start.

Kelsey took the hint and said goodbye. She stared at the ceiling. There was no way she'd sleep. None.

Didn't he feel anything for their father? How could Ethan try to kill him? It was incomprehensible.

How had she missed it? He must've been going mad for years. Becoming a monster that killed those around him because of paranoid delusions.

While she couldn't escape this prison right now, hopefully, her bombshell was making Ethan miserable. No matter how he tried to suppress it, there'd been plenty of witnesses to pass on the juicy rumors. By dawn, their parentage would be the talk of the town.

Maybe that would distract him enough to make a mistake. One they or their friends could capitalize on to take him down.

* * *

Once Ethan had thrown the Fleet doctor out of the palace, he demanded the physician give him a sample of Father's blood. With that in hand, he went to his own doctor and had the woman test his DNA against the old man's.

And damned if the little bitch hadn't been telling the truth. He didn't have any Imperial blood.

He smashed the doctor's tablet on the floor and stormed out. His temper held until he made it to his room and he gave in to the rage boiling inside him.

That bitch! He grabbed the first breakable thing he could find and crushed it under his heel. That's what he'd do to Kelsey!

He picked up his chair and started shattering everything around him. He didn't stop until the red haze was gone and he'd destroyed his belongings.

They'd all pay for what they'd done to him. Every single one of them.

She'd smeared his reputation in front of all those guards. By now, they'd have told their friends. It was far too late to silence them.

What would the Senate do? Try to take the Throne away from him? He'd have to stop them, and he knew just the man to help. He needed to act right now before his enemies had a chance to plot further against him.

He needed to eliminate the other contenders for the Throne as quickly as possible. If they didn't have any other potential candidates, he'd have a stronger hand with the Senate.

First though, he needed an inside man. He knew just who to call.

* * *

THE BUZZER on Nathaniel's nightstand woke him. It was late. He touched the control as he sat up. "Yes?"

"I'm sorry to wake you, Senator," his assistant said. "His Highness is on the line and won't take no for an answer. Your automated system shunted him to me. He insists on speaking to you this very moment."

"My apologies for the disruption of your time off. Go back to sleep and I'll deal with him."

Once his man was off the line, Nathaniel picked up the heir's call. "Highness, it's late. Couldn't this wait until morning?"

"My father has been poisoned, Senator."

That drew Nathaniel to his feet. "My God. Is he alive? Will he recover?"

"It's touch and go. They've identified the poison. I'm hoping for the best, but we must plan for the worst."

Nathaniel rubbed his face. "This is horrible. Who did this?"

"My sister and the Bastard. They found the poison in her rooms. I'm sure he has her under some kind of compulsion. This is his play for the Throne, but it won't work. We have them in custody. They will pay for their crimes."

As a lifelong politician, Nathaniel had been lied to by the best. He could tell when an amateur was trying to play him. The heir didn't sound betrayed. He sounded smug. Something smelled rotten.

"What can I do to help, Highness?"

"I need to know that I have your complete and unwavering support. I don't believe any of the slanders about your nephew. I'll work tirelessly to exonerate his good name, and yours, by association. I have many enemies in Fleet. I think he would make a terrific commander to oversee the purge of disloyal officers."

That would be an unmitigated disaster. The more Nathaniel had reviewed his nephew's record, the worse the idiot's judgment appeared. Now that they were in a shooting war, he'd get them all killed. Particularly after he oversaw a Fleet-wide purge of officers he suspected were disloyal. The very last thing they needed at this point was a witch-hunt.

"My nephew escaped confinement yesterday, Highness. The people that freed him murdered a number of Fleet personnel. He's a wanted fugitive."

"That problem can be solved. I'm certain the attackers took him against his will. Probably Mertz's people. They wanted to see him executed, but the courts would speedily find the evidence against him to be false. Rest assured, Senator. I have this under control."

Yes, he probably did. Nathaniel was now convinced that the heir was behind all the attacks. Most likely even against his father. He was a dangerous lunatic. One who had to be stopped for the good of the Empire.

Well, he knew how to handle crazed men. Talk calmly and reassure them. Then call someone to lock them up.

"I'll back your play, Highness. Family and honor mean everything to me. What do you need first?"

The heir sighed. "One of my sister's slanders seems to be true. My mother had an affair. I'm not related to my father at all. I have no idea who sired me, but I need to be sure that the succession is protected in this time of chaos. I want you to look at the Charter and see what it says in regards to the succession. The Senate has already confirmed me. That needs to stick."

Nathaniel staggered as though someone had punched him in the gut. The news was a complete and total shock. Like a bus dropping out of the traffic control net and smashing into his grav car with no warning.

He struggled to find his voice. "I don't believe that will hinder you, Highness. The Senate has already confirmed you. There won't be enough votes to change that."

"Be certain, Senator. I'll call you again tomorrow. I want this matter settled before it bites me in the ass."

Once the heir had disconnected, Nathaniel sat heavily on his bed. Holy God, what a mess. Everything made sense now. It had just become even more complicated than the heir knew.

Justine Bandar, the empress in exile, as she preferred to call herself, had kept a secret from him. From them all. Nathaniel had once been her paramour. The affair hadn't lasted long, but the timing was about right.

She'd had a number of discreet affairs during her marriage. They usually lasted a few months, and then she ended them when she grew bored. The empress was a powerful and sensual woman. Few declined her advances.

Lord knows he'd certainly fallen into her arms speedily enough. Their torrid affair had blazed like the sun and then ended abruptly when she told him it was over. He'd known that day must come, but it was still devastating. He'd thought it was going so well.

When news came out that the empress was with child, he'd assumed that was the reason she'd broken off their relationship. He supposed that was true, if not for the reasons he'd thought.

The woman had always taken pains to be sure no hint of her behavior ever leaked out, but he knew he hadn't been the first. Nor had he been the last. The irony of the empress divorcing her husband for infidelity was so powerful it turned even his stomach.

What the hell did he do now? His unwitting son was poised to assume the Imperial Throne, but Nathaniel was certain the man was an aspiring regicide. He wanted to pin the murder on Nathaniel's daughter, though she would be ignorant of her lineage, too.

Nathaniel hadn't lied about family and honor being important to him. He just had to figure out what that meant in this context, and he needed to do it fast.

* * *

YEATS LOOKED up when his chief of staff opened the door to his office. "Yes?"

"I'm sorry to disturb you," the man said, "but you have a call from the palace. I don't know the man, but he's identifying himself as an officer with the Imperial Guard."

It must be about the emperor's illness. Good news, perhaps. "Then I'd best take his call. Put it through."

The man slipped back out, and Yeats's com chimed a moment later.

The image of a roughly hewn man in Imperial whites appeared. He inclined his head. "Admiral Yeats, I'm Captain Paul Danvers, Imperial Guard. I appreciate you taking the time to speak with me."

"I always have time for the Imperial Guard. What can I do for you, Captain? Is it about the emperor?"

The man shifted a bit uncomfortably. "Yes and no. I'm stepping a bit outside normal protocol, but there's a situation you need to be aware of.

"His Highness has assumed the Throne during his father's incapacitation, and certain accusations have been made. He's produced what certainly appears to be damning evidence that Her Highness poisoned her father."

"Preposterous," Yeats snapped. "There is no way that young woman would harm a hair on his head. Someone made a mistake."

"I'll confess that does match my feelings, as well. On His Highness's instruction, I've locked Princess Kelsey and Admiral Mertz in our detention facility. The admiral also stands accused of involvement in the attack on the emperor."

Yeats shook his head sharply. "Impossible. I know Jared Mertz. He's as loyal to the Throne as they come. You need to get this sorted out, Captain."

"I'd love to, Admiral, but my options are limited. Also… I hesitate to say this, but I'm afraid for the safety of the prisoners. If His Highness were to take it into his head to do something rash, I fear enough of the Guard might stand by and let it happen. It might be prudent if outside forces are aware of the situation and intervene."

"I grasp the purpose of your call. Rest assured, I know the right people to call. I'll be down there shortly to discuss the situation with His Highness. Thank you for this warning."

"It's my pleasure, Admiral. But do hurry. Time is of the essence, I think."

"Keep a lid on things, and I'll be right there. Goodbye, Captain."

Yeats rubbed his face. Well, this had gone ugly fast. It was a good thing he knew the numbers of a few senators. They'd help him keep this situation from spinning out of control before cooler heads prevailed.

He hit the com link to his chief of staff. "Get a pinnace ready for immediate deployment. We're going to the palace. Oh, and I'll want enough officers and marines to intimidate people trying to keep us out."

"I'll have them ready in a few minutes, Admiral."

Yeats disconnected and started down the list of senators he knew. He didn't have long, and he needed to get moving.

28

Angela couldn't believe how easily the stealthed pinnace had escaped everyone's notice. They'd picked a hiding place deep in the mountains, of which Avalon had more than its fair share. This range was off the beaten path and had no resorts to complicate matters.

It turned out that hadn't always been the case. The ruins of a large chalet graced one slope. It was nothing but debris at this point, mostly buried under snow. Before the Fall, this must've been quite the getaway.

A handy canyon provided them with cover against casual sightings. As far as she knew, no one was actively looking for any Fleet personnel or vessels, but that could change at a moment's notice.

Her team was going over every piece of equipment Marcus had sent. It was sufficient for just about any problem. Each of her people had a suit of Old Empire powered armor. Not the pantywaist kind like the princess wore, but the full up gear.

Nothing short of an anti-ship weapon could hurt them here in the New Terran Empire. But they could deal out pain to anyone else. They had heavy weapons of every kind. Plasma cannon suitable for the armor and flechette rifles of similar size. If they had to strike somewhere, they'd get in.

There were also stunners made to a size appropriate to an armored marine. The Old Empire hadn't felt the need for anything like that, but Princess Kelsey had made the design and creation of such a weapon a priority so they could stun the living crap out of any unfortunates in their way.

While they checked everything, she manned the officer's console and the drones slaved to it. Those were even stealthier than the pinnace. She had them crisscrossing the area around the capital looking for Talbot.

Every ten kilometers, they sent a pulse that would activate his retrieval beacon. That would eventually catch someone's notice, but they'd still be devilishly hard to pinpoint.

All of this helped keep her mind off the fact the admiral and princess were prisoners. Locked away in the Imperial Palace. If she thought about it too long, she became tempted to go get them.

Carl was up in the cockpit. He'd wanted to use a console for something, and there was no flight engineer aboard right now. That kept him out of her hair. Let the pilots deal with him.

Having him out of sight also kept her from reconsidering her feelings about him. It was unsettling. He looked like a kid, but he'd put it all on the line to fight for her. That had to count for something. She just wasn't sure what.

The console pinged for her attention. One of the probes had just detected a marine recovery beacon. Talbot had already activated it.

"Heads up, people! We have a customer! Wrap up your inspections and armor up."

Carl came scrambling back from the cockpit. "You found him?"

"Sure did. The beacon says he's alive and in relatively good health. A broken arm, a minor gunshot to the same arm, and a mild concussion. I'm relocating other drones to triangulate the signal and scout the area. Once we're sure where he is, we'll check to see if it's a trap."

"And if it is?"

She smiled like a shark. "Then we go in even harder. Strap in up front. This is about to get exciting."

* * *

THEY'D COME for Talbot early. A number of armed men and a shock weapon of some kind kept him from getting overly exuberant while he used the bathroom.

Then they'd strapped him back down and taken him to a lab. The medical scanners looked top of the line for the New Terran Empire. Everyone wore old-fashioned medical masks, but he recognized his captor standing off to the side. He made sure to get a better recording of him.

They'd only just begun when his recovery beacon changed status. Someone had responded with a coded pulse. It was intended to reassure an injured marine that CSAR was on the way.

Combat Search and Rescue crews were tough people, armed to the gills to fight off any threat to their patients. Not that he expected it was CSAR coming for him. This facility was going to have a marine combat team on their ass before too long.

One of the scientists frowned. "He has the indicated equipment and some extras that I can't identify. How the hell did they get that thing in his brain?"

A woman beside him shrugged. "Done is done. Focus on identifying what you can. Like this node inside his body behind the lungs. It seems to be linked to his nervous system. And... is that a signal? I think it's broadcasting on a frequency range we don't use."

Talbot killed the beacon. He needed to keep his captors in the dark as long as possible.

Their leader came over and looked at the screen. "What kind of transmission?"

The woman shrugged. "I don't know. It's gone now."

He frowned at Talbot. "What was that? Were you signaling someone?"

"Would I still be here if I was? Part of my gear checks for

connections to my armor every hour. It's an automated thing. The range is no more than a hundred meters."

The man didn't look as though he were buying that explanation. "Can you estimate the range of the signal you detected, Doctor J?"

"Certainly more than a hundred meters," the woman said. "Perhaps ten or fifteen kilometers."

"I hope you're a better marine than a liar. We're a long way from anything, and our scanners would tell us if anyone was that close. Nevertheless, we need to make it clear to you that sending signals is a very bad idea."

He reached over to a table of instruments and picked up a laser scalpel. Talbot tensed, but that didn't help at all when the man cut a long, deep slice into the marine's arm.

Talbot screamed. He couldn't help it. It hurt like the devil. He wished he had one of those fancy pharmacology units like Kelsey. One with drugs to deaden the pain. Well, if wishes were horses, he'd be ass deep in horseshit.

"If you behave, I'll have them regenerate that," the man said cordially. "If not, I'll cut off some fingers. We wouldn't want that, would we?"

Talbot shook his head, his teeth clenched tightly. He had no choice. Hopefully, whoever it was had gotten a good read on him.

* * *

CARL WATCHED everything from the flight engineer's console. The pilots were working on their approach and had no time for him. The marines were armored up and ready to go. All they had to do was locate Talbot.

The probe had lost the major's signal before they could triangulate a precise location. That didn't mean there was no data, though. They had almost thirty seconds of recorded transmissions to work with.

The flight engineer's console wasn't optimized for data manipulation, but Carl always carried his best tools in his implants. It only took a minute to update the console and start analyzing the data.

Yes, he could see the signal strength changing as the probe moved.

Assuming the major was stationary, that should allow him to infer a rough target area since they had a good idea of the direction from which the signals were coming.

He knew Angela was trying to do the same thing, but she was playing against his strengths now. This was science, baby!

Using the known quantity of the beacon's signal strength, Carl could estimate distance. If Talbot was underground, the signal would be weaker, but he could work with that.

The probe had traveled a good way in those thirty seconds, and the signal strength had grown at a steady rate. That made the case for Talbot being stationary even stronger.

Carl brought up a map of the target area. He eliminated the locations that didn't match the direction of the transmission. Using the strength of the signal and the estimated direction, he put the data through several of his custom algorithms.

That focused him in on a particular stretch of land. Empty forest. Old growth, possibly untouched since the Fall.

He turned the console loose on examining the compiled weather satellite images for the last ten years, and it popped back with a possible anomaly. He looked at the autumn images and magnified them.

There. The trees had lost their leaves late in the season, and that looked like a building. A very well concealed one.

"I found him, I think," he said over the com.

"Show me," Angela said.

"Sending now. There's a building hidden in the forest at about the right area. I can't be completely sure he's there, but it should be enough to send a probe in."

"Good work. You might just have saved his life. I'm sending a probe in now."

Carl monitored the probe as it ghosted in using only passive scanners. Yes, that was a building and it was occupied. Three, no, four guards sat in a pair of concealed blinds that had a great overview of the entire forest around them. There were even more people inside.

"Jackpot," Angela said. "We go in hard and fast. Let the lookouts scream. We'll send an override signal once we get inside to reactivate

Talbot's beacon. Then we converge on his location. Stay nonlethal, if possible. I want prisoners."

A chorus of oorahs came back at her from the marine team.

"Lieutenant Veracruz, pick the best-looking ingress route to the target. We'll drop out the back and call if we need fire support. I'll designate people to watch the towers. If they look dangerous to you, the support team will take them out."

"Aye, ma'am. We can start the run at your command. Forty-five seconds to drop zone once we go."

"Everyone ready? Execute the run, Lieutenant."

The pinnace banked and accelerated hard. Carl cinched his restraints tighter and loaded Angela's suit visuals into his implants. This was going to be just like a first-person shooter.

* * *

THE PINNACE SCREAMED over the target with no warning. The probes told Angela they'd taken the sentries completely off guard.

The ramp dropped right on the mark, and she threw herself out of the pinnace with her team. They'd practiced drops like this in the simulators, but nothing beat the first time going at it for real.

They fell from a height of a hundred meters right toward the trees. She kicked in her suit's grav unit to slow her fall and dodge the worst of the limbs.

First squad split off to cover the lookouts. The rest of them landed on the roof of the concealed building. A shaped charge opened it and they dropped in, weapons at the ready.

"Imperial Marines," she said over her external speakers. It made her voice echo from every nook and cranny on the floor. "Lay down your weapons and surrender. Resistance will be met with lethal force."

The first man she saw ran, but he wasn't armed. She left him to one of the others. A blue stunner beam took him down.

Two more men ran around the corner and opened fire with automatic weapons. Corporal Riviera made an example of them with his flechette rifle. A swarm of metal darts tore them apart, and the wall behind them.

"That'll make them duck faster next time," he said with some satisfaction. "The major's beacon is online. He's several levels below us. Stairs or the easy way?"

She pulled a plasma grenade and tossed it down the long hall. Her helmet feed blocked the worst of the light when it detonated. Kelsey was right. It did sound like the end of the world.

They dropped through two levels with that one massive hole. People either ran or surrendered. She detailed a few men to collect prisoners while she led the last group down into the basement.

It was set up as some kind of lab. A number of science types cowered against the wall, and Talbot was strapped to a gurney. Blood ran down his arm, but he was conscious.

"The main guy just ran through the door on the far wall," Talbot said. "He'll have a car to escape the area."

"Think it's faster than a marine pinnace?" she asked. "Everyone, lay on the ground and put your hands out. Now."

She switched to the pinnace frequency. "Jailbird three, Raven Actual. We have the package. There's a flyer about to leave the building, too. Take him alive. I want to discuss a few things with the gentleman."

"Copy that, Raven Actual. He just took off. I think I can convince him to land without any trouble."

She left that to the pilot and freed Talbot. "You sure are a hard man to find. What kind of sissy lets civilians take him down like that?"

He smiled. "We all have our bad days. Is Kelsey okay? The admiral?"

"As far as I know, they're fine. They're locked up, though. I'll fill you in when I feel less worried about a counterattack."

Angela grabbed him and motioned for two of her men to watch her back. In the powered armor, she had no trouble carrying the burly marine back through the wrecked building.

"Did you have to blow the place up? Nothing they had could possibly scratch your paint job."

"Being a marine has a few perks. Blowing shit up is one of them."

The pinnace was just coming back to the roof as she got there. The ramp was an easy hop from there.

Carl was standing beside a rumpled man who'd been cuffed and strapped to a handy seat. "He didn't give us any trouble after Lieutenant Riviera offered to land on him."

"Get more restraints," she said. "We'll have a lot more prisoners in a few minutes. I don't expect we'll be turning them over to anyone just yet, either."

"On it."

The scientist dug more out while she took Talbot to the combat medical area. It didn't have a regenerator, but it would let her set the broken bone and stop the bleeding. The scanners could also confirm that he had no other injuries that his beacon wasn't reporting.

"Tell me," he said.

She popped her helmet and let it swing back behind her. "The heir poisoned the emperor. Then he framed Princess Kelsey and Admiral Mertz. We're working on figuring out a plan to get them loose."

"Shit," Talbot muttered. "This just keeps getting better. We need to get everyone on board and clear out before someone comes looking. I'm sure they called for help."

Her suit told her the others were making their way back up. They had a few dozen people in custody. Two dead inside and four in the lookout towers. They'd been about to fire something at the pinnace, and first squad had taken them out.

"Ten minutes," she said. "Do an intelligence sweep. Anything we find down there that confirms the heir is behind this might be critical."

Talbot nodded. "But we scoot the moment we detect someone coming this way. And, Angela? Thanks."

"All part of the service. Let's get you fixed up before all hell breaks loose."

* * *

ETHAN SCOWLED when his com signaled again. Victor. Why did he suspect this was bad news?

It wasn't a call this time, but a voice message. He played it.

"Highness, they found us." Somewhere in the background, someone was shooting at something. "I'll try to get away, but things are looking grim here."

He stopped the message before it finished. The rest didn't matter. Once again, Victor had proved to be less than competent. It didn't matter whether the fool lived or died, so long as he kept his mouth shut doing it.

So, they'd rescued the marine. That hardly mattered when compared to the victory he was about to win.

29

They dragged Jared from his cell. It was early morning, by his guess.

Perhaps dragged was too strong a word. Politely escorted him with weapons displayed might be more accurate.

His destination was the official audience chamber. It held the Imperial Throne. Karl Bandar only used it for traditional times or serious matters. It seemed the new management was more officious and pompous than the old one.

Ethan sat on the ornate throne with the scepter on a stand beside him. He didn't wear the crown, so the emperor must still be alive.

Jared wondered how long his half brother would allow that to continue. The heir wasn't a patient man.

The guards brought Jared up and forced him to his knees when he didn't go down on his own.

"Have you no respect for the Throne?" Ethan asked with a smirk.

"I'd give my life for it. I simply have no respect for the ass occupying it right now."

That wiped the expression off Ethan's face. "You will show me the respect I am due, Bastard. You're in deep trouble already. Do not make it worse."

Jared shook his head pityingly. "With you calling the shots, my situation could hardly be any worse."

"Enough of this. You kneel before me charged with high treason. The attempted murder of your liege. Would you care to make a statement before I judge you?"

"Is this how justice works in the Empire now? The trial is you declaring me guilty? What of evidence? What of testimony? What of my representation?"

Ethan smiled. "Why play out the theater where you claim otherwise? You've lost. Take your medicine like a man."

"You told me before I left on the expedition that you'd eliminate me. You tried to poison me with tainted treats and killed Carlo Vega instead. Now your father is dying of the same thing. I'd say my proof is stronger."

The heir laughed. "Your lies, you mean. Nothing but hearsay. You probably killed the man yourself. In any case, that's irrelevant. I'm in charge now. My word is law. I hereby find you guilty of the charge of high treason. The sentence is death. Do you have any last words before the sentence is carried out?"

The main entrance to the hall opened, and the sound of arguing voices carried to Jared. He looked back and saw Admiral Yeats striding toward them while other officers argued with the guards. A squad of marines in unpowered armor faced down the Imperial Guardsmen at the door.

Ethan rose to his feet. "What's the meaning of this? I left orders not to be disturbed."

"Highness," Yeats said, bowing his head. "I understand you have one of my officers in custody. As the senior Fleet commander, I'm here to speak with him."

"The time for speaking is over, Admiral. I've found him guilty of high treason."

Yeats smiled politely. "The Charter requires the Senate to try those accused of treason. The emperor only lays the charge.

"Oh, and that brings me to another issue. The emperor is not allowed to delegate his participation. Since he is ill, you must wait for his recovery or your coronation to bring the charge before the Senate. Highness."

Rage contorted Ethan's face. "How dare you lecture me? I am your liege!"

"Not yet, you aren't, Highness," Yeats said firmly. "The Charter sets strict limits to your authority. Fleet and the Imperial Senate will not stand idly by while you flout the law. I will speak with Admiral Mertz. Now."

"You mean Commander Mertz. I do not recognize that idiotic edict."

"Unfortunately for you, your father already did. All that remains is for the Senate to verify it was ratified or ratify it themselves. With all due respect, Highness, this little charade is over."

"And if I were to place you under arrest?"

Yeats smiled. "The Senate is aware of where I am. I speak on their behalf as well. Unless you'd like to see your position as heir debated today, I suggest you step back from the abyss and allow the law to work as our founders designed it. That applies to Her Highness, as well."

Ethan snarled but eventually waved a hand dismissing them.

The admiral helped Jared to his feet, and marines escorted them out of the audience chamber with the Imperial Guard following along behind them. They took Jared back to the detention level and to a conference room. Yeats gestured for the guards to leave and sat down.

He placed a small device on the table. "This will interfere with their monitoring equipment. We should have a few minutes while they address the problem. Are you and Princess Kelsey alright?"

Jared slumped. "I'm better than I was before you showed up. He was going to send me to the executioner right as you walked in. Good timing, by the way."

"I have contacts in the Imperial Guard. They gave me a heads up. I called a few Senators. No one is happy with what's going on here. I never suspected the heir to be so rash. Or to try something so iron fisted."

"I did warn you."

Yeats nodded. "So you did. How's the princess?"

"Locked up in the cell next to mine. She's worried about her father and pissed at her brother. Do you think the Senate will stand up to him?"

"To a point, yes. No one wants to see an emperor gone wild. The balance of powers is there for a reason. The Senate judges matters of treason to keep the emperor from executing anyone he chooses. He's the one to charge a traitor so that the Senate doesn't have all the authority.

"So, you'll have a trial. You and Princess Kelsey both. His people will have to produce some evidence. This high-handed behavior will make the senators cautious. His Highness just made it more likely they'll validate the edict just to remind him that he isn't a dictator. And, to be fair, they're terrified of the Rebel Empire and what war with them means."

Jared sighed. "I just wish it wasn't so likely there would be an 'accident' here. I don't want to be 'shot while trying to escape' tonight."

"I'll see what I can do to make clear that won't be tolerated."

The door opened, and Yeats pocketed the device as a man came in and looked at the camera. "My apologies, Admiral. The camera in this room appears to be out of order. Would you care to use another one?"

"That's fine. We're done here anyway. You can take Admiral Mertz back to his cell."

Jared stood. "Thank you, Admiral."

"My pleasure. I don't want to see anything happen to my most promising officer." He stared at the guard intently. "If something did happen—to either him or Her Highness—I guarantee the Imperial Senate would put everyone involved under a deep scanner to find out what happened. Pass the word around, and save your friends the pain. Do you get me?"

The guard nodded. "I understand, and I'll make sure nothing untoward happens."

The man escorted Jared back to his cell and locked him in. The guard's expression told him that he was taking that very direct warning seriously.

Jared pinged Kelsey as soon as he was alone and filled her in.

The rat! You were right all along. Her mental voice was outraged.

That's not much comfort if we can't get out of here. The only hope I'm seeing is your father getting better.

Let's both pray for that, and that no one else does anything to complicate this even further.

* * *

TALBOT SAT STILL LONG ENOUGH for them to set his arm and regenerate the rest of the damage. Then he cornered Angela to find out what the situation really was.

"Events have been unfolding," she said. "Not as drastically as some we've faced, but not smoothly. The admiral and princess are in custody, charged with high treason. The emperor is in critical condition, his fate uncertain. Breckenridge is on the loose somewhere. Frankly, I'm surprised he didn't turn up in our raid."

"That would have been entirely too lucky. No, he's up to something else. Probably a chip in the fight to control Fleet. He'd make a great figurehead and a lever for his uncle, the senator. There's still some kind of surprise working in that area."

She sighed. "We need to get them loose. The heir has way too much opportunity to see them dead in one way or another. As the princess says, it's easier to beg forgiveness than ask permission."

He frowned. "She's not the best role model when it comes to that kind of thing."

Angela smiled. "How do we manage to break them out of the most secure facility in the Empire? All we have is the equipment in this pinnace.

"We could get in with the armor if they didn't shoot the pinnace down on approach, but burning down the Imperial Palace will win us no friends. Even if everything went according to plan, the odds someone would just shoot them are too high. We can't risk it."

He gave the situation some thought. "Are those really all the resources we have? What about Carl? Oh, and congrats, by the way."

She frowned. "For what?"

"I hear you two are an item."

She planted her hands on her hips and glared. "Christ! You weren't even here an hour. He and I are not dating. We did not sleep together. None of that is true."

He grinned. "That only makes the rumors juicier."

"Anyway," she said, ignoring his jibes, "we can get some assistance through *Persephone*. Not for attacking the Imperial Palace, but certainly general statuses on all the crap going on."

He allowed his expression to go serious. "It would be better if we could get the emperor back on the Throne. I'll give them a call. Angela, you've done a great job. Go see if any of Carl's tech might help us turn the tide."

Angela sighed. "I guess that shouldn't surprise me, but I'm kind of scared what he might do. He's demonstrated some unexpected backbone."

"You find out the quality of your friends when the chips are down. There's more to Carl Owlet than most people suspect. He's an ace in the hole. Now, go make nice while I see what other fires have broken out."

* * *

ELISE STEPPED into the medical center on *Invincible* and spotted Doctor Stone bent over an unfamiliar instrument. She walked over and cleared her throat. "Doctor."

The dark-haired medical officer looked up and smiled. "Highness. I understand you're going back down to talk with Senator Breckenridge. I have something I'd like to send with you."

Elise took a vial of taffy-colored liquid from the other woman. "Is this an antidote to the poison?"

"Yes and no. There isn't an easy way to make an antidote for that particular poison. It has a binding agent that makes it hard to clear out.

"This is a combination of a new drug that will slow its progress and nanites that can repair the damage that it already caused. Together, they offer the emperor a chance to fight this off."

"Shouldn't you be taking this down yourself and getting it into him as soon as possible?"

Stone growled with obvious frustration. "The heir has barred all of us from his father and has forbidden any 'experimental' treatments. The emperor's physician doesn't have the clout to fight him, and I can't just send the data. He can't make nanites."

"I hear that has a number of senators calling for immediate access to His Majesty, but we don't have time to waste. People are growing worried and suspicious, but this needs to be smuggled into the Imperial Palace and administered to the emperor now."

"I'm guessing the progress of the poison will be irreversible in less than twelve hours. The treatment we already gave him helped give him more time. Otherwise, he'd already have died."

Elise stared at the potential cure. "How does someone sneak into a place like that? The emperor must be under heavy guard. It seems impossible."

"Welcome to the big league. Talbot, Angela Ellis, and Carl Owlet are down there. If you can get some assistance from Senator Breckenridge, it might be possible. It's the only hope we have of stopping the heir. Otherwise, he'll find a way to kill Admiral Mertz and probably the princess, too."

Elise nodded. "I'll do it, of course. Anything for Jared."

"Excellent. *Persephone* has a second stealthed pinnace. It will take you and some additional marines down to support any actions they feel necessary. Planetary control is denying Fleet traffic access to the surface. There's some kind of confrontation building there.

"I'm not sure how the heir means to take control of Fleet, but I'm sure that's on his list of things to do. He certainly doesn't want us helping his father or rescuing his prisoners. I hear he told the Senate they couldn't have custody. That he would hold onto the admiral and princess until his father either recovered or died. He didn't make a lot of friends, so that might help you, too."

"I'd best go pack a bag. If this drags on, I'll want some clean clothes."

30

Carl listened to Angela's summary of their situation, including the news they'd need to smuggle people into the Imperial Palace, with growing worry. How the hell were they going to do something crazy like that?

The security system there had to be the best in the New Terran Empire. Which meant he needed to use the best he could cobble together from Old Empire technology, and they had less than twelve hours to make it happen. It seemed hopeless.

Unless he really went outside the box.

"I need to get back to the university," he said. "To the lab where my equipment is stored. There's something there that might help us."

Angela looked unconvinced. "Like what?"

"Some equipment I got from Omega. A way of going from one place to another without crossing the intervening space. We might not be able to make the sample hardware work, but I don't know if we have another option."

"Well, some chance is better than none. We have a grav car that won't raise any eyebrows. I'll get a team together."

She called Major Talbot and gave him the rundown. He sent them on their way with his blessing.

They sat in the back of the grav car while two marines sat up front. He took a deep breath and pitched his voice low. "I'm sorry for the rumors."

She raised an eyebrow. "Did you start them?"

"No!"

The two marines up front glanced back at them.

"Ears front," Angela said firmly. "Carl, the situation dictated what we did. Don't let this freak you out."

"That doesn't mean I can't be sorry for what it does to your reputation."

The other eyebrow went up. "Seriously? What does that even mean?"

"I'm a kid and they're saying... you know."

She laughed softly. "Let's spin this in a different direction. They're saying I slept with the man who took out a hit team sent to kidnap or kill him. With a freaking hammer out of legend. One that can fly like a superhero."

"That's not who I am."

"That's exactly who you are," she said firmly. "I fell into the trap of seeing what you look like and thinking it was who you are. Don't make the same mistake. Inside that nerdy body is a man with the heart of a hero. One not afraid to risk death for what he believes in."

He felt his face heat. "I'm not sure you know me as well as you think. I was terrified."

"Everyone mistakes courage for lack of fear. We're all terrified when the shit hits the fan. Bravery is doing what you have to do in spite of your knees knocking."

He thought about that all the way to the university.

* * *

ETHAN SWEPT into a room deep in the bowels of the palace. He only had his most trusted men with him now, because of who he was meeting.

Someone had found Captain Breckenridge a replacement uniform, he saw as the man came to his feet.

"Captain Breckenridge. Welcome to the Imperial Palace."

The renegade Fleet officer saluted, as he should. "Highness, it's an honor."

Ethan sat on the other side of the table. "Please have a seat. Time is short. I apologize for any discomfort you experienced during your rescue."

The man smiled as he sat. "It was all worth it. I assume you brought me here for a reason."

He wondered if the Fleet officer knew how inane that sounded. "As you could no doubt tell from the method of your rescue, I need a man I know I can count on at my side. Fleet has proven treacherous. Are you willing to help me tame it?"

Breckenridge's smile widened. "Of course, Highness. They were about to take everything from me, all because I was loyal to the Empire. And to you, of course. You're obviously willing to give me my life back. How can I help?"

"I can no longer trust Admiral Yeats to lead Fleet with the Empire's best interests at heart. I need a man at the top who will remember who he serves. Are you that man?"

"I am, and I know these rebels better than any other officer you're likely to find. Together, we can not only unite the Empire but also crush our enemies. The ones Jared Mertz brought down on our heads. I have a number of people I can call on to assist us that are personally loyal to me. And you, of course."

Ethan smiled. "Then I think we have a deal, Admiral Breckenridge. Call your people. I want to head up to Orbital One shortly."

* * *

ELISE SMILED at Senator Breckenridge's assistant as he let her into the man's office. That smile faded when she saw Breckenridge's grim expression.

"Have a seat, Highness. It's early for a drink, but one certainly wouldn't be out of line with the awful events of last night."

"Coffee would be good if you have any."

"That I can do." He made his way to the bar and set some to brewing. "I assume you're fully aware of the emperor's condition."

"Yes." She considered telling him what was in her pocket but decided to feel out how he was doing first. "I'm horrified, of course, and worried about the future. That's the main reason I've come to speak with you."

He nodded. "You aren't sure how I'm seeing the events. Allow me to lay my cards on the table, because I need your help."

The coffee was beginning to come out of the spout and into a cup. He arranged the fixings to go with it. "Cream or sweetener?"

"Black and straight."

That caused the corners of his lips to rise. "A woman after my own heart."

He fixed them both cups and returned to the seats they'd occupied last night. "His Highness called me late with the news. He's offered me my family's reputation for my support. All charges against Wallace dropped and he implied he would put him in charge of Fleet."

It took all her willpower to sip her coffee without spilling a drop. It was excellent.

"I see. And you accepted?"

"I did, but I have no intention of actually enabling him. For a number of very good reasons, starting with the main one. I think he poisoned his father and is framing Admiral Mertz and Princess Kelsey. I cannot and will not support this, even if defying him means the ruin of my reputation."

He smiled at her over the rim of his cup. "You hide it well, but I think I've surprised you. You wonder why someone in politics for the power would cast it away. I could be the right hand of the Throne itself."

She shrugged. "I'm curious, but I suspect you'll tell me soon enough."

"As with most things, it's complicated. I truly do value my personal honor and that of my family. That only occasionally has anything to do with what others think of me.

"A pre-Empire novelist named Lois McMaster Bujold from Terra said it like this. 'Reputation is what other people know about you.

Honor is what you know about yourself.' The two can be wildly at odds. Jubilant throngs might cheer a man while inside he's torn to shreds. Or he's reviled for doing what's right."

Breckenridge set his cup onto the saucer. "I'm prepared to embrace the latter to save the Empire. That's exactly what's at stake. Wallace is incompetent and Prince Ethan is an ambitious fool. Together, they would be the death of us all."

Elise put her cup down and stared him in the eye. "That couldn't be plainer. I'm sorry he put you in such a quandary."

The man laughed bitterly. "You have no idea the minefield I had to navigate last night. His Highness dropped another bombshell on me. He told me his sister informed him they were both illegitimate. He apparently confirmed it."

She tilted her head a little. "Awkward, but troublesome in what way? He's already the confirmed heir. Is that likely to change?"

Breckenridge shook his head. "No. He'll remain the heir. The problem for me is that I'm virtually certain I'm his father."

That hit her like an unexpected bucket of ice water. "That *is* remarkable, if true. You had an affair with the empress at around that time?"

"I did. One that she ended abruptly a few weeks before the official announcement that she was with child. At the time, I assumed she was cutting things off because of the added attention she knew was coming. Now that I know the emperor is not their father, I'd bet everything I hold dear that they're mine."

He rubbed his face. "No matter how this plays out, one of them will probably die. Or spend the rest of their lives in prison. I must pick a side. Though it will ruin me politically, I choose the Empire."

"You're a powerful senator. You'll survive this, too."

Breckenridge picked up his cup and sipped his coffee. "Not if I defy Ethan and fail. The winners write history. I'll end up a traitor and die beside everyone else before it's all over. Everything hinges on either the survival of the emperor—which seems unlikely—or outmaneuvering the murderous heir.

"If we win, then the emperor and Princess Kelsey will eventually find out the truth. My political career will end. My fellow senators will find reasons to shun me. For the good of the Empire, I'd have to retire."

"Is retirement so bad an option?"

"Compared to dying or being one of the causes of the destruction of the Empire? No, not at all. I'll take disgrace and even prison if I must."

She nodded. "You really do value honor over reputation. Perhaps we have a chance after all."

Elise took the vial from her pocket and set it on the table. "This has the possibility of saving the emperor's life, but only if we get it to him in the next ten or eleven hours. I'm sure the Imperial Palace is a fortress. Could you find someone to help us get it to him?"

A flash of hope appeared in Breckenridge's eyes. "Perhaps. We'd need someone skilled with locks and alarms, but there may be a way to get two people, perhaps three, into the palace. They'd need to elude the Imperial Guard and slip into a no doubt heavily guarded medical center. This might only give us a small chance, but I'll take it."

* * *

ANGELA DIDN'T CONTACT the chancellor. He seemed a nice enough man, but he might do something rash. They couldn't afford to have the police called.

Carl wasn't forthcoming with additional details on the device he'd mentioned. That was probably for the best. She was already doubtful it would work. It sounded like sorcery.

Dressed in casual clothes, her people didn't draw any unusual attention. Much of the conversation she overheard revolved around the wild fight last night. More people than could possibly have been anywhere near the apartments were claiming to have seen the whole thing. Usually male students talking with young women hanging onto every word with wide eyes.

It made her want to puke.

"Those lying sacks of crap," she muttered to Carl. "This pisses me off."

"Why?" he asked curiously. "Because they're trying to use reflected glory to get lucky?"

"It just seems skeevy. Doesn't it bother you?"

He shook his head. "You ever see the birds in the zoo that puff themselves up and strut in front of the females to attract a mate? This is like that. All posturing. I couldn't care less what they say.

"I heard one guy claiming he was in on it. That he helped stop the attackers. I think he overplayed his hand, though. The woman laughed at him and walked off."

Angela nodded. "I bet. I heard one guy that actually saw us. He told his friends about a man flying off with a woman. His friends verbally abused him. One thing is for sure. They'll be talking about that attack for a long time to come."

The building with the restricted access was just ahead of them. Carl and she both had codes, but she'd prefer not to leave a record they'd been here.

Getting in proved to be horrifyingly easy. Carl struck up a conversation with several women in lab coats that were going in. He pulled the exact same crap those boys had been doing, though he stuck to an accurate viewpoint.

His story so enthralled the two that they didn't notice he never swiped his card. He had it in his hand, but held the door for them. He left it open just long enough for her to keep it from closing and walked deeper into the building with them.

As soon as they were a dozen meters away, Angela opened the door and motioned her men to follow her inside.

Carl said his goodbyes to the women and entered a stairwell beside the lift. She followed as soon as the women walked into a first-floor room.

He was waiting at the landing between floors. She gave him a hard look. "What the hell was that?"

"A lesson in security training they obviously forgot," Carl said with a grin. "The easiest way to get into a building and past a lock is to distract someone with access and go in with them. Holding a bunch of donuts and coffee works well, too. Doctor Leonard told me if I ever fell for anything like that, he'd assign me an essay on the subject."

She shook her head. "You're a damned wonder. Come on. Let's get to the lab before someone asks us how we got in here."

"We have access cards. They'd let us walk."

Nevertheless, he speedily led them to the fourth floor and to the room where their gear had been stored. A couple of broken boards blocked the door open, and a man stood there watching as others carried out parts of the roof.

Carl showed the man his card. "We're cleared. I need to see if any of my equipment was damaged."

The man gestured for the four of them to go in. "It looks like the destruction was pretty localized. Something fell through the roof."

"Preposterous," a voice said from inside. "The damage pattern and how the debris fell make it clear something in the room burst out through the roof."

Carl covered his eyes. "Fabulous. It's Professor Bedford. I'm doomed."

"Is that you, Mister Owlet? Finally! You've wasted enough of my time already with this foolishness. Get in here this instant!"

Angela didn't even try to suppress her grin as she followed the dejected graduate student into what was no doubt going to be an epic dressing down.

31

C arl's first sight of Professor Andrew Bedford proved the man hadn't changed much. If anything, he looked more pugnacious than ever.

The short man with the white hair and perpetual sneer gestured for Carl to hurry up. "Perhaps you'd care to set these young men straight about what happened here, Mister Owlet. Surely you've gained enough experience to see it clearly."

The lab hadn't been in use before the chancellor had set it aside for Carl. It had a number of crates and boxes on shelves. The one that had formerly held the hammer was missing. He'd wager parts of it were probably scattered across the roof and yard.

"Professor Bedford. It's good to see you again." A lie, but more for form's sake than anything else. The gleam in the old man's eye told Carl it wouldn't matter what he said.

"Bah. Save the pleasantries for someone that cares. I want you to explain to the gentlemen what happened here in this lab. Take as much time as you need, so long as it's less than five minutes. I have other things to attend to."

A glance at Angela showed she was vastly amused. Her grin made her look beautiful.

That wasn't the kind of distraction he needed right now.

"I don't need five minutes, Professor. A case on that shelf flew up into the ceiling. It came apart even as the contents blew the roof open. The course of destruction is probably to the east."

The older man froze and fixed Carl with a suspicious stare. "That's actually correct, and I doubt you'd be able to see such detail without knowing more than you should. Explain."

"This is my equipment, and I'll explain it all as soon as the workmen leave. It's classified."

"How very secretive. Very well, Mister Owlet. I shall humor you for a few minutes. Everyone get out."

The workers wasted no time heading out the door.

Bedford pointed at Angela and the marines. "You, too."

"We're with him. Don't let us slow you down. We're just the peanut gallery."

"Harrumph," the old man said. "If you're the help, don't bother me." He refocused his attention on Owlet. "How do you know what happened here?"

"Because I caused it." He held out his hand and let the backpack he'd been carrying hang in front of him. He activated the hammer and pulled his hand back. The pack stayed in place.

Bedford walked around the floating object, entranced. "You've succeeded in capturing my full attention, Mister Owlet. Continue."

Carl opened the pack and pulled out the hammer. He dropped the now empty canvas and left the hammer in the air for the professor to examine. "This is Mjölnir."

"The mythical hammer of a Norse god? Doubtful. You'll need to do better than that, young man."

"I built it as a weapon for someone. Last night, intruders tried to capture or kill me. I called it to me and defended myself. Hence the destruction."

The old man whirled on Carl, his eyes narrowed. "That business at the apartment building? The chancellor is fit to be tied. I had no idea it involved you, but I can't say I'm surprised."

"Why is that, Professor? Because of my well known predilection for violence?"

"Don't be insolent, boy. You've always struck me as a troublemaker."

"I think everyone under the age of fifty strikes you that way. Now, if you'll excuse us, I have work to do."

The old man straightened and narrowed his gaze. "Don't try to cavalierly dismiss me, Mister Owlet. I'm not done with you yet."

"Perhaps not, but I'm done with you. This work can't be put off. Lives are at stake."

"You must not have heard that I'm in charge of determining your fitness for a doctorate. An honor you're looking less likely to have bestowed upon you every moment. You thought that toy was worth the honor?"

"I built the hammer based on other people's work. As you say, it's a toy. Keep the doctorate. It's the least important of the issues I'm facing right now."

Carl turned his back on the professor and began pulling a crate out. The one with the parts for the transport device.

"You intrigue me at last, Mister Owlet," Bedford said. "What work is so important that it's worth a PhD? The Lucien Prize, perhaps? You can kiss any thought of that goodbye, too."

"You're a mean-spirited old man out to hurt those under his control," Carl said conversationally as he opened the crate. "I've never done anything worthy of the damned Lucien Prize. Keep that, too, and don't let the door hit you on the ass on the way out."

"Explain this situation to me, Mister Owlet," Bedford said softly. "I'm paying attention now."

He turned on the old man. "This is about saving the life of the emperor and probably the Empire. This crate has a device that supposedly allows for travel from one location to another without crossing the intervening space. It's an alien device."

"Owlet, shut up," Angela said.

He glanced over at her as he began pulling parts from the crate. "Either he's going to help us or he's going to leave and keep his mouth shut after you read him the Imperial Secrets Act. If you want to arrest me, do it once I'm finished.

"Professor Bedford, either help or leave. I don't care which, as long as you shut the hell up."

The old man took off his coat. "Finally, a boy with some spine. Explain to me how this device is supposed to work while we assemble it. If this is for the emperor, time is indeed of the essence."

* * *

KELSEY WAS READING through her implants when she heard the door to her cell open. She sat up with a mixture of dread and eagerness. One way or the other, something was about to happen.

Wallace Breckenridge stepped into the cell and smirked at her. Two Imperial Guards with weapons out stood behind him.

She didn't bother to rise. "The day just keeps getting better."

His smile widened. "We always seem to be locking one another up. Not that I can claim credit this time, but your crimes have caught up with you. It looks like I win after all."

"That remains to be seen. If you have something worthwhile to say, get on with it. Then get out. I have a nap to see to."

His expression darkened. "That mouth of yours will be the death of you. I spoke with His Majesty a few minutes ago. Pardon, I meant His Highness. The soon to be emperor. Whichever you prefer.

"He's decided to reorganize Fleet. So, my title is Admiral now. I'll be headed up to give Yeats the boot shortly. Your father isn't looking so good. I might be on my way in just a few hours. Within an hour of that, you'll be dead."

Kelsey stood slowly. The guards raised their weapons as she took a step forward. Breckenridge took a step back so they were in front of him.

"I could have your blood, if I wanted it badly enough," she said conversationally. "Say one more word and I'll take it."

The coward wasted no time fleeing, but her brother didn't seem afraid as he stepped into the room and closed the door.

"Go ahead," he said. "Attack me. They'll cut you down, and that will solve one of my problems."

She stared at her twin, her heart breaking. "Why? Just tell me why you're doing this."

"Because I won't allow anyone to take what is mine. It's become apparent to me that you all want to see the Throne stripped from me, and for that, as much as I love you and father, you have to die."

The guards didn't seem surprised by that admission. They must be firmly in his pocket. God knew how many others were, as well.

Tears streamed down her face. "How can you say you love me and that you have to kill me? Don't you realize how crazy that sounds?"

His eyes seemed damp, too. "I've always known that there were forces that wanted to take everything away from me. Since I was just a boy, I've been planning on how to stop them. I just never expected you and father to join them.

"That's one of the reasons I built up a network of people I could trust. I have ears in a surprising number of places and trained men that will eliminate any threat. They've kept me and my birthright safe when my family ignored reality."

He shook his head. "It makes me bleed inside. How could you betray me like this? I'm your brother. I'm the man who will lead the Empire to glory over her enemies. You'd deny me my destiny? Traitor."

He whirled on his heel and strode out. The guards backed out and locked her in.

She sank down onto the bunk. How had she missed it all these years? He was mad. Paranoid, at least. A megalomaniac at worst. She had to stop him from taking the Empire down with him.

Somehow.

* * *

TALBOT WATCHED the second pinnace land with more hope than he had any reason to expect. Princess Elise had said she might have an option for them. If it had the slightest chance for success, he'd push it to the hilt.

The pinnace set down softly beside their hideout. It was an old farm building in the woods. Their small craft could mask their IR signature and visual outline to a degree. As long as no one overflew the site, they were safe.

Princess Elise came down the ramp with a man that looked entirely too much like Wallace Breckenridge for his taste. "Major Talbot, this is Senator Nathaniel Breckenridge. He'll be helping us today."

This wasn't promising.

"Senator," Talbot said. "What makes you think I won't lock your ass up right this damned instant?"

The man gave Elise a wry smile. "I'd imagine it's a coin toss. If that helps make you feel better, go right ahead."

Talbot gestured for one of the men to come forward. "Search him. Confiscate any coms or weapons. Be thorough and don't miss any trackers."

The senator raised his arms and submitted. "I understand and appreciate your concern, Major. I'm only here to help."

Once the man had taken the senator's gear and scanned him closely, he had two of the marines take the senator inside.

"Have you lost your mind?" Talbot asked the princess. "That man is our enemy."

"I think not. He's shared a lot of information with me that could mean the difference between success and failure. I think you should listen to him."

He shook his head. "Why are all the princesses I know crazy?"

"You're just lucky, I guess."

He led her inside. They had a rough drawing of the Imperial Palace on the kitchen table. His senior men and women had been plotting possible assault strategies, but now they were watching the senator.

"Everyone, this is Senator Nathaniel Breckenridge. He says he has some information that might help us." Talbot didn't bother to conceal the skepticism in his voice.

"Hear me out," the man in the elegant suit said. "I've been into the palace more times than all of you put together. I know more than most visitors, too, I'd wager."

"Prove it."

"Might I have the use of my arms and a pencil?"

The guards released him at Talbot's nod. One of the marines handed him a pencil and stepped aside.

Breckenridge scanned the drawing. "This isn't too bad, really. Let me update it with the correct proportions."

He expanded some sections of the building and shortened others. "The security center is in this wing now. They moved it last year when they upgraded the power and control feeds in the building. The cells are still under the old wing but are undoubtedly heavily guarded.

"The medical center is here. There will probably be several security checkpoints inside the building. Getting past them will be tricky but not impossible."

Talbot grunted. "I can't see how. Every strategy we've come up with gets us killed short of the palace. Or gets us in and probably kills the emperor in the firefight. The place is too tough for a frontal assault."

"Then you need another way in." Breckenridge made a line out of the building and off to the west. "This is an old escape tunnel. It's quite well hidden. The exterior side has a very limited access point and is heavily alarmed. The restricted size and security features only allow a few people to use it, so think two or possibly three people to perform the infiltration.

"It was built for the Imperial Family to escape. Most people have no idea it exists. It originates inside the emperor's personal suite. Quite close to the medical center, I might add."

"Just how do you know about it, then?" Talbot demanded.

The senator gave him a sardonic grin. "Because the empress used it to smuggle her most trusted lovers into her suite. I wore a blindfold, but I'm quite resourceful. I managed to locate the exit after the third trip."

Talbot considered him. "I see." He turned his gaze to Princess Elise. "Why should I believe him?"

"Because the man I love might die if he's lying, but I believe him."

That earned a slow nod.

"Very well, Senator. I'll take what you're saying at face value, but if this is some kind of trick, I'll shoot you myself."

"I'm not worried."

Talbot listened as the man began explaining what he remembered of the route. If this were true, it might mean they could pull this off. The emperor's suite was far away from the prison holding his commanding officer and girlfriend. They wouldn't be able to sneak into it.

They'd have to hit it with heavy weapons. Getting in wouldn't be easy. The palace was the most protected place on the planet. They might not see the pinnaces until late, but they *would* see them. Then they'd kill them.

He still had to find a way to get his marines inside. As impossible as that seemed. Carl had better come through in spades.

Talbot was loyal. If it came down to it, he'd save the emperor and weep for Kelsey and the admiral. He prayed another solution would present itself before he had to make the hardest choice of his life.

32

Angela watched the two men assemble the device. It was small, only just bigger than hand sized. The power requirements seemed large, but the older scientist didn't seem concerned.

It was interesting to watch them work together once Carl focused on his task. He ignored his obvious distaste for the man and just did what he needed to.

The professor spared some of his attention for Carl, but mostly fondled the equipment. He kept peppering Carl with questions that the younger man couldn't answer. Finally, Carl had the parts together.

"It requires a flat surface to work on, according to the notes I made," he said, sifting through the debris. He found some material he could use and cut it free with an Old Empire marine knife.

Once he had it, he set the knife down and blocked the professor's hand as he reached for it. "Don't test the sharpness or you might lose a finger. Its edge is almost molecular in thinness, and it's harder than any metal you're likely to have worked with. The Old Empire used hull metal for these knives."

The professor promptly withdrew his hand.

They ran power, but the device didn't want to activate. That caused a fair amount of creative cursing from Carl. She made a mental note to give him remedial training in foul language. He'd have to do better than that if they became a couple for real.

That thought made her mentally skid to a halt. Where the hell had it come from? She wasn't even considering dating him. Not a chance. No way.

Yet, she felt as though part of her disagreed. How many of her in other universes had made the same choice? Was she an idiot in all of them but this one? Probably not.

She wondered if he'd considered how the deaths of his other selves had affected her in those universes. If she'd loved him there as deeply as she believed, she'd have been crushed. Worse than when she'd lost most of her people on *Ginnie Dare*.

There was a perverse kind of horror imagining the pain she'd have felt. It took more effort than she liked to push the dark visions aside.

Carl was getting out some other equipment when she came out of her mental bubble. "This is the quantum communications device the chancellor told you about. The entangled sets of photons can be swapped out to allow communication with different people at long distances."

"How far?" Bedford asked with a softer voice than she expected. "This is the thing we were going to test? The other ship is no doubt in place by now."

"We only have a little time, so I'll set it up to communicate with your man first. Keep it short." Carl swapped out a metallic rod. "Use it like a normal communicator."

Professor Bedford touched the controls. "Watts, are you there?"

There was no response for a long moment, and then a voice came from the speaker. "Professor Bedford? Is that really you?"

"Who else sounds like me, you idiot? Where are you?"

"In the Baker system. This thing really works!"

Bedford stared intently at Carl. "Watts, what did I write on your last paper?"

"Uh... I'd rather not say."

"Watts!"

"Okay! You compared me unfavorably to a lawn ornament. A lopsided, drunken lawn ornament."

Bedford blinked. "Well, I'll be damned. It really does work."

"What should I do now, Professor?"

The question focused Bedford back on the com. "Stop wasting my time and ask the captain to go another flip out. I'll call you in a few days."

He killed the circuit before the student could respond.

"I'm deeply impressed, Owlet. You've cracked a genuine secret here. Real-time communication at interstellar distances. Remarkable. We'll have to verify the range, but even this will change so many things. It's real science, boy. To my shock, you actually did something worthwhile."

Carl's smile was decidedly lopsided and wry. "I wish I could take credit, but this is once more someone else's work on creating entangled pairs. All I did was take the theory and put it into practice.

"Then I took some secret work done in the Old Empire and figured out how to create the hardware that allowed the communications and the conversion to voice or implant signals. It's how I control that." He gestured back to the hammer still floating in the air.

"And you dismiss the real work of a scientist as futzing along like Watts does in the lab? Bah. Was meshing these theories together and creating the hardware easy?"

Carl frowned. "Hell, no. I went down so many blind alleys before I hit the solution that I almost gave up. This was work."

"Welcome to being a scientist. So, what now?"

"We call the alien intelligence that created this transport equipment and figure out what I did wrong."

Angela watched them work and slowly let out her breath. Carl had turned the professor's head, even if it didn't show very much. He'd accepted Carl as a junior associate, which as crass as it sounded, was probably the best anyone could hope for from the man.

Carl would get that doctorate. He'd probably win the Lucien Prize, too, based on the covetous looks the professor was giving the com equipment and the hammer. She'd best make sure it didn't disappear.

When Omega spoke from the com unit a few minutes later, the professor was almost reverent as Carl introduced them. A few minutes explanation had Carl making some kind of changes to the equipment.

It came on this time, making the flat surface on one side of each circle look like a mirror. Before she could say anything, Carl stuck his arm through one, and it popped out of the other a dozen meters away.

"See? No harm, no foul."

"Remarkable," Bedford said. He walked over to the bodiless hand and put a tool into it.

Carl drew his hand back and waved the tool above his head. "Omega, what's the range on this small unit?"

"Not far," the alien said through the com. "No more than a hundred kilometers."

"I think our definitions of the word may be different," Bedford said. "How long can it stay open?"

"Indefinitely, as long as there is power. The drain it creates is moderate and only requires energy on the end that creates the link."

"It's bidirectional?"

"Yes," the alien said, "though it was standard practice to have two units, each designated for one direction of travel to speed their use and avoid people or cargo colliding."

Bedford checked the connection they'd made to the power bus. "The energy requirements are enough to limit us to the one unit here. What of the larger pair?"

"There are two sets of large rings. That would allow for bidirectional travel." He mentioned a large sounding power requirement that Angela couldn't translate in her head.

Carl shook his head. "That's too much. What's the range?"

"No more than five thousand kilometers."

"That's useful, but I can't see us smuggling it into the palace."

Angela cleared her throat. "It looks as though the individual parts could pass through the smaller rings. Is that true? If so, we might be able to smuggle the larger ring into the palace through the smaller one."

"That might work," Bedford muttered. "We could tap directly into the university fusion plant, with the chancellor's approval. For this, I can convince him."

That would require them slipping a bunch of marines in powered armor onto the campus somehow. Maybe a few at a time in vans. She knew Talbot could work that out. First, they'd need access to the palace.

She mentally shrugged. That was Talbot's worry. She came for a way in and she had it. The plan was coming together.

ELISE LISTENED to them work out the basics of a plan with one eye on the time. The clock was running down, and they needed every minute.

When Major Ellis called in with a report on the alien gates, the missing parts of Talbot's plan fell into place. All they had to do was get someone in through the secret passage.

Once inside, a small group had to infiltrate the medical center without alarming the guards. Once they had the emperor protected, they could launch a major assault on the security cells. They'd be safe from the most potent protective weapons at that point.

God only knew how it would turn out, but they'd at least have a fighting chance at stopping the would-be usurper.

Talbot nodded sharply when Major Ellis finished. "This is our best bet. We have a few grav vans, so we can begin smuggling people onto the university right now.

"Meet with the chancellor. Get him on board, and get everything tested and ready for use. We kick this off in three hours. Get yourself and Carl back here as soon as possible with the smaller ring."

Once he was done, Elise cleared her throat. "Who makes the trip inside the palace?"

Talbot inclined his head toward Breckenridge. "We know at least two people can use the entrance. What stops them from letting more people in?"

"It opens onto a small car that runs to the palace. I suppose your skilled locksmith could come back for more people, but it's too small for armored marines. That magical transport ring sounds more like the right idea."

"There you go," Talbot said. "Carl is the best we have at breaking and entering using the Old Empire technology. Ellis will be his protector. If we can have a third person, it needs to be someone familiar with the palace. That means the senator. As much as I hate the idea, he's been very helpful so far."

The politician inclined his head. "I'll take that as a compliment. We should get the inside team in place as soon as we can. It might take quite some time to gain access, and Lord knows about setting up the strange transport equipment."

"We're assuming that it won't set off the alarms when it goes online," she said. "Is that certain?"

"No," Talbot said. "We probably need to have the medical center team on the way faster than that. I want them in place before we move the rest of the marines, if possible. Carl will need to come back for a marine or two to help them.

"Go get Carl and Angela. Bring some of her team along with you. Find the exit and get things moving."

Elise didn't wait for him to change his mind. She wanted to get Jared out of there before his homicidal half brother did something terrible. And Kelsey, too.

A grav van with Carl, Angela, and two marines in civilian clothes arrived. They all had large packs. Carl looked smug and Angela peeved.

"What went wrong?" Elise asked the other woman.

"The chancellor was mad. *Really* mad. And it wasn't at Carl. He blamed *me* for the damage. Man, those academics can tear a strip off you with the biggest words."

Carl grinned. "It made up for her laughing at old Professor Bedford ripping me up. I put on my best innocent face and skated by."

She shook her head. "You two are so funny. Allow me to introduce my associate, Senator Nathaniel Breckenridge. As you already know, he's providing us with a way into the palace."

Angela nodded, all business. "Excellent. What's the area around the exit like, Senator?"

"It's in a small town near the palace. Some discreet inquiries told me the building wasn't in use a few years ago. Probably intentionally. We'll be able to get in. The palace is ten kilometers away, but the hidden tube doesn't show up on their scanners."

"What about alarms on the building?" she asked.

"No problem if you have a swipe key." He produced one. "I checked after the empress left the palace. It still works. It won't open the secret exit, though. I'm not precisely sure how that part works."

"We'll figure it out once we get there," Carl said. "I've got some very sensitive scanners and the best hacking tools in the New Terran Empire. What happens when we get inside?"

Elise filled them in on Talbot's plan. "Once we have everyone in place, I'll go with the group to the emperor's side. I have the drug and I'm less threatening. I might be able to talk my way out of a confrontation. Senator Breckenridge goes with me. I'll need a neural disruptor."

Angela pulled one from her bag. "I'm not thrilled with this plan, but you're probably right. Here's to hoping we aren't too late."

33

C arl inventoried his tools as they flew to the secret entrance to the palace. He'd grown fairly proficient with breaking into Old Empire equipment, but this would be different.

The New Terran Empire security systems were less advanced but didn't interface with his tools in the same way. He'd have to approach this job with the deepest caution.

"We're coming in," the marine up front said. "Does the building have interior parking?"

"Yes," Senator Breckenridge said. "Go around back."

Getting inside proved as simple as landing, letting the senator open the door, and moving the grav van inside. Everyone piled out and gathered their gear.

The senator led them to a storage room with a lift. "This serves the upper floors but also has some means of going down. I'm not sure what she did to the panel to send it there."

"Let me take a look," Carl said.

He examined the panel for alarms with his handheld scanner. None. At least, no obvious ones.

The panel gave way to a common screwdriver. All the buttons had wires going to a small controller. He found a standard access port and plugged into it.

Its security was higher than one would expect from a lift unit. He thought he knew how to bypass the hardware, but he took his time in triple-checking everything.

"Is there a problem?" Angela asked.

"No. I'm just being cautious. I don't want to trigger a lockout or alarm. We only get one chance to sneak in without them catching us."

Once he was sure he understood the setup, he insinuated his control tool into the software interface. There. He saw the normal floors and a "basement" destination. That would be where the tube was. The secret control worked by pressing the first and third floors, letting them release, and pressing the first floor again.

"Everyone in?" he asked. "Here we go."

He closed the panel and pressed the buttons in the correct sequence. The doors slid shut, and the lift sank into the ground. It went down a fair bit and opened onto a small tunnel platform. There was no car.

The marines spread out, but there were no threats. There wasn't even a camera. Only a call station.

Carl saw at once that it was significantly more secure than the lift. It was a biometric lock that required an authorized retinal pattern.

He smiled. "I think this is going to be easier than we'd hoped."

At the bottom of his bag, he found one of his sophisticated hacking tools. "I can use this to provide the pattern," he said.

"How?" Angela asked. "You don't have the empress's retinal pattern. She might not even be on the access list anymore."

Carl grinned at her. "No, but I have Princess Kelsey's. I bet she's on the approved list, even if she doesn't know about the secret tunnel. We can try it once and see. If it doesn't work, I'll tear the lock apart and figure something out."

He activated Kelsey's pattern and put the eye-shaped projector against the reader. The light on the control turned green.

"I can feel air movement in the tunnel," one of the marines said after a minute.

A small pneumatic car slid into the station. It had two seats facing one another. A third person could stand between the seated riders. Four in a pinch.

"Okay, the senator and I go first," Angela said. "Carl will stand between us with the ring gear. We'll send the car back for the three of you shortly. It will take two more trips to get the equipment and you."

The senator and Angela sat inside with the bags of equipment on the floor. Carl stood between them and looked at the controls. "This is a simple go button. Press it and you'll move to the other station. We'll wait there for you."

He pressed the button and the doors slid shut. The car took off at a significant speed, tossing Carl into Angela's lap.

"This is so transparent, Owlet," she said with a laugh.

"Yes, but more comfortable than it looks." He settled into her lap and tried to control his blush. The heat of her body was doing things to him that weren't appropriate for a covert assault mission.

She put her lips beside his ear and whispered. "Maybe we should try a date when this is all over. You *are* kind of cute, in a nerdy way."

"Don't torture me."

"That depends on how well the date goes."

The car pulled into the station, and Carl was out the moment the doors opened. It was identical to the station on the other end of the line.

Angela and the senator climbed out with the gear. Carl pressed the button on the console and sent the car back for the rest of the team. Fifteen minutes and two trips later, everyone was there.

The lift was smaller on this end, so they needed two trips to get everyone into the emperor's suite. The designers had stashed the exit behind a bookcase in the library. Carl supposed that made it useful when the empress wanted to fool the emperor.

Being in his liege's home made him feel awkward. It seemed as though the man might just walk through the door at any moment.

The marines put on unpowered armor while Carl assembled the smaller ring. Angela looked over his shoulder. "So, tell me again why this one doesn't need power?"

"The connection between the two ends serves to power them both. What's the plan?"

"I'll go with Princess Elise and the senator. I'll take the men. That leaves you here alone to bring the rest of the marines in. If something goes wrong, you should be safe here."

"What if I don't want to be safe?"

"Deal with it. I get to be the hero this time."

He smiled at her. "And a hero needs something special. I can't pass the hammer on to you, but I did bring you something."

Carl dug into a bag and pulled out an arm brace that looked familiar to her. It was the portable shield he'd been working on.

"Strap this on and activate it with this code." He sent her a string of code through her implants. "There are two settings. Round and tall. Pick which works best and try not to get shot this time."

Angela took it with a grin. "This will come in handy. Thanks."

She raised her voice. "Okay, listen up, people. We'll head directly to the medical center. We might get lucky and not hit a checkpoint. Or we might get into a shootout. Stun only and protect the civilians. Let's go."

She started for the door, paused, and turned around. "I want you to hold onto something for me," she said to Carl.

Angela grabbed him, pulled him into a hug, and kissed him thoroughly. She grinned when he swayed a bit after she let him go. "See you soon, nerd boy."

* * *

Elise followed the marines into the corridor. No guards. They probably considered the sophisticated alarm and lock system good enough inside the palace.

The medical center was close to the emperor's suite, for obvious reasons. They were fine until they neared the target. Angela checked the corridor with a device that peered around the corner.

"I see at least three guards outside the medical center," she said softly. "The angle is bad to see the whole area. The curve in the hallway obscures too much."

"That's my cue," Elise said. "Senator, you're with me. If things go bad, Major, come right on in."

"Wait." Angela handed her the device Carl had given her. "Strap this on and here's the code. Keep it round, I think. This should keep you from being hit."

She took it, but frowned. "This is to keep you safe."

"I'm not the one running the risks right now. Just do it. If things go bad, both of you haul butt back here."

Elise let the senator precede her and stayed to the right. She had her neural disruptor held behind her back. She'd only get one shot, even on wide beam. The sleeve of her jacket concealed the shield.

Their caution proved warranted when they saw an additional two guards just around the bend. They were all the way up at the other end of the hall, talking as they came toward the medical center.

The men in front of the entrance straightened as they saw her and the senator. "Halt! Identify yourselves," one of them called as they all raised their weapons.

Breckenridge raised his hands a little. "I'm Senator Nathaniel Breckenridge. The Imperial Senate sent me to get an update on the emperor's health. Didn't the gate tell you I was here?"

That allayed their fear enough for them to lower their weapons slightly. They must've recognized him. Just as Elise had hoped.

She pushed the neural disruptor past Breckenridge and fired. The three men just in front of the entrance to the medical center dropped. The other two did, too, but only so they could bring their weapons to bear from the floor. They were out of stunning range.

That's where the plan went a little awry. Senator Breckenridge ran back the way they'd come, but Elise took advantage of the guards' momentary shock to race forward.

She activated the shield just in time. The bullets struck the invisible field and ricocheted into the walls. She threw herself into the medical center just as they opened fire.

A bullet smashed into her lower leg at the last moment, making her stumble, but she managed to slap the emergency lock on the door. It slid closed and sealed. Now only someone inside could open the door.

The medical people stared at her in shock. The emperor's personal physician stormed up. "What's the meaning of this?"

She deactivated the shield and gestured for him to step back with her neural disruptor. "I'm not here to hurt the emperor. I'm here to save him. Doctor Stone sent me."

"I can't use anything she sent," the man said as he backed up. "The heir gave orders not to trust anyone that might be compromised."

"Small wonder, since he poisoned his father to begin with. Well, I'm going to save him, and you can't stop me. Everyone, against the wall. How is he, Doctor?"

The man shook his head. "Worse than I'd hoped. He'll be gone soon."

"So, you really have nothing to lose. Why not give this a try?"

He gave her a lopsided smile. "Who am I to argue with the woman with a gun?"

Elise hobbled over to the emperor's bed. He was so pale. He almost looked dead already.

She brought out the vial and found an injector. Stone had trained her how to use one, so it was simple enough to slip the antidote into place and empty it into the man's arm.

There. It was done. Now all they could do was wait. She sent a signal to Major Ellis that she'd accomplished the primary mission.

"If I might be so bold," the doctor said. "You're bleeding on my floor. Let me examine your wound."

Elise sat heavily in a handy chair and raised her leg. "Why not? Don't try anything funny, or I can't tell you about what we just gave the emperor."

He gathered some instruments and supplies. "You have my word."

* * *

ANGELA RAN FORWARD when Senator Breckenridge dove back toward them. She expected Princess Elise to follow, but the crazy woman ran for the medical center. She made it.

Two quick shots from her neural disruptor took those men down, but others popped up both ahead of them and behind. They had her pinned down.

She dragged Breckenridge back against the wall and let her men cover ahead of them while she fired at the guards behind them.

Kick it, Carl. They know we're here.

Bullets struck all around her and some bounced off her armor as they edged toward the medical center. A round grazed the back of her left hand. It hurt like the devil.

They stunned enough of the guards to make it to the medical center doors. She signaled the princess to let them in.

A moment later, just as enemy reinforcements arrived, the doors slid open. They tumbled inside as a frightened nurse rapidly backed away. Angela found the manual lock and sealed the doors. Now the guards would have to cut it open. They wouldn't dare risk explosives.

One of the marines had a minor wound, but the senator had taken a shot to the side of his abdomen. "I need a medic over here!"

She leaned over Breckenridge. "Good timing, getting shot outside a medical center with a handy trauma team."

He grinned through his obvious pain. "I've always been lucky. Now I'm a wounded hero. What politician couldn't use that kind of thing? Did the princess save the emperor?"

"She gave him the shot. Now we wait to see if it works. We've done all we can."

The doctor left what he was doing to Elise to a nurse and took charge of getting the senator onto an operating table.

She set the marines to watching the door and walked over to the princess. "That was stupid. You could've been killed."

"I'm pretty sure that it's a requirement to do something crazy to be part of this club. Do I get a card and a secret handshake?"

Princess Elise pulled the shield off her forearm and handed it to Angela. "That came in handy. Too bad I turned it at the last moment, or I might have gotten off without a scratch."

"Let that be a lesson, then. Leave this kind of thing to the professionals."

The princess gasped as the nurse dug into the wound with some kind of long pliers and pulled out the slug. The woman dropped the bloody lump of metal onto the tray and started cleaning out the wound.

Angela smiled. "You deserve a medal after all that." She found something to stop the bleeding from her hand. Her marine implants would know the moment other marines made it into the palace.

"Come on, Carl," she said softly. "Don't blow it now."

34

Talbot stood in the university fusion plant work area, watching Professor Bedford and a group of technicians examined the power connections.

"Professor, this isn't the time for something to go wrong."

"Give me a moment," the old man said testily. "One of the connections must be loose."

"We don't have a moment. This isn't your latest lab experiment. Lives are on the line. Make the magic happen."

"Found it," one of the techs said triumphantly. "One second... try the power again."

Someone threw a switch and the surface of the panel across the opening turned silver.

"Go! Go! Go!" Talbot shouted at the waiting marines. Their power-armored forms ducked through the reflective surface with their weapons at the ready.

"Keep this open until we get back or I personally tell you to shut it down," Talbot said. "Clear?"

The scientist nodded. "Good luck, Major."

Talbot awkwardly locked his helmet into place. He'd be the next best thing to useless with this broken arm, but he was in armor like his men. He was going for Kelsey, and he had no pity for anyone who tried to stop him.

He was the last one through the ring. Armored men filled the Imperial suite, getting ready to make a push for the cells under the old security wing.

Carl stood off to the side. "They got the medicine to the emperor. They're holed up in the medical center. Only one seriously injured. The senator."

"Well, I'll be double damned," Talbot said. "I suppose he was serious after all. I'll detail a few men to stay with you."

The young man held up the hammer. "I'm good. Go save Kelsey and the admiral."

"I can afford a few men to secure our way out. Go back through the ring if you have to. I'm serious. Don't get shot trying to hold this position. Leave that to us."

He sent orders to his men to execute the plan. They fit through the doors with only minor damage. The lead team headed right for the security wing to block any response from the men there. The second team, led by Talbot, headed for the detention center.

The rest fanned out as they moved. He detached a squad to guard the emperor's suite. The last team headed for the medical center. They'd make certain no one harmed the emperor or Angela's people.

In their powered armor, his people were invulnerable to all but the most deadly weaponry. Nothing they'd see inside the building could hurt them. And if it did, they'd deal with it like marines.

Almost immediately, Talbot had to grab a vase that the man in front of him brushed up against. With one hand, and in powered armor, he was astonished he managed to save it from destruction. He carefully set it back on the table. It was undoubtedly worth a fortune.

"Be careful of the art," he said. "Let's not destroy our heritage."

The various teams began running into resistance almost immediately. They bulled through and stunned everyone in sight. Their attack was so unexpected and overwhelming that they made it to the security lifts in only five minutes.

The lift wouldn't respond, but they'd expected that.

"Open it up, Corporal Riviera."

The marine punched his hands through the armored metal and tore the doors out. "The lift is down below. On point." He jumped down without waiting for the order.

"By the numbers, marines. Secure our people."

They poured down the shaft, no doubt occasionally landing on one another. The armor could take it. His last squad held the lift for the retreat.

He stayed with the team up top. Someone started shooting at him from behind, but the bullets didn't worry him. He hardly staggered when they hit him with a rocket launcher. He gave them a friendly wave and started stunning people.

If everything went according to schedule, they'd be on the way back out in just a few minutes. He wanted this area under control by then.

* * *

ETHAN SAT beside Wallace Breckenridge on the Imperial yacht. They were going up to Orbital One to relieve Yeats and put Fleet under Ethan's thumb. After the stunt at the palace, he couldn't afford to have Yeats with a knife at his back.

Unfortunately, he could already tell Breckenridge was going to be an interim appointment. He wasn't smart enough to fight a war. Not and win.

He'd been waiting for the news of his father's death, so he wasn't surprised when his com sounded. He put on a suitably somber expression and answered it. His moment of triumph was at hand.

"Yes?"

"Highness, we have a problem," his man in the Imperial Guard said. "Heavily armed intruders have broken into the palace. Sir, they have control of the medical center."

"Shit! It has to be Mertz's people. Get someone in there right now. Stop them at all costs and *protect* my father." His emphasis on protect should give the man the right idea. To shoot the emperor during his "rescue attempt."

"Highness, these people are in some kind of heavy armor. We can't get in without using a level of force that would be *guaranteed* to kill the emperor."

So, they couldn't attack that way. The majority of the Imperial Guard wouldn't stand for it. He'd just have to hope his father died anyway.

"Then see to the prisoners. Personally."

"I can't, Highness. They sent even more people there. We're trying to retake the security lift, but I'm not holding out much hope."

"Do what you can. Call me as soon as you have an idea what's happening."

He cut the call and looked at Breckenridge. "Mertz is making a play. He has people with the emperor now, and odds are he'll be free of his cell in short order."

"I knew it!" the disgraced Fleet officer said. "He's staging a coup. There's no way we can gain control of Fleet before he's loose, but I have a plan that will allow us to salvage the situation. It's risky, but the odds of victory are better than letting him take us into custody."

How could the man be so stupid? He still believed Mertz was behind everything. Unbelievable.

Still, what choice did Ethan have? Once his enemies were free, they'd put him under lock and key. His play for the Throne had failed. Unless, of course, the emperor died. Then he'd have a chance. It would probably mean a civil war, but that was a price he was willing to pay.

"Tell me your plan," he said.

* * *

JARED KNEW something was up when an explosion tossed him off his bunk and onto the floor. He crawled under it, just in case something came loose from the ceiling.

A check through his implants showed marines on his level. This was a rescue.

Things must really be desperate.

The door to his cell swung open, and an Imperial Guardsmen's boots stood in Jared's line of view. Whatever the man had been about to do, someone stunned him first. He dropped like a stone.

"Admiral, are you in there?" a marine in powered armor said from outside. He couldn't fit through the door.

"Right here." Jared rolled out from under the bunk and stood. "What's the situation?"

"We have control of this section of the palace. We're taking you back up to the medical center."

Another marine opened Kelsey's door, and she came out spoiling for trouble. "Where's Ethan?"

The marine managed a shrug in his heavy armor. "Sorry, Highness, I don't know. We have a line to take you back up. Major Talbot is waiting."

She smiled. "You found him! Excellent. Let's go."

The marines lifted the two of them back up to the main level with a line. Kelsey threw her arms around her lover. "Thank God you're okay."

She frowned. "Why are you favoring your arm?"

"It's busted. Come on. We need to make our way to the medical center. We've cleared the area, but I don't want to chance someone doing something rash."

His sister's expression told Jared she intended to do something rash to whoever hurt Talbot.

Jared stayed in the middle of the cluster of marines as they moved to the medical center. Whatever resistance they'd encountered getting in had pulled back, though some people with white bands around their arms were carrying out the bodies of Imperial Guardsmen. Stunned, he hoped.

"How much trouble are we in, Talbot?" he asked. "What's the penalty for breaking us out of custody?"

The marine grinned. "That depends on who wins, sir. If we got to the emperor in time, maybe nothing. We'll see."

The first thing Jared saw as they entered the medical center was

Carl Owlet assembling some kind of device. One he'd never seen before.

"Mister Owlet."

The boy looked up. "Admiral! Good to see you again, sir."

"Did you arrange our breakout?"

"I may have played some small part in it. Princess Elise did more."

Jared looked around and saw her sitting in a chair off to the side. Her leg had a bandage around it below the knee. He rushed to her side.

"Elise, are you okay?"

Her smile glowed like the sun. "Thank God you're safe. I'm not standing up. Come give me a hug."

He did and then looked pointedly at her leg. "How did you get hurt?"

"Doing what needed doing. The doctor said I'd be fine. He's working on Senator Breckenridge now."

"Breckenridge? What is he doing here?"

"His part to make up for his nephew. The emperor is responding to the treatment. Doctor Stone is on her way down, and she's cautiously optimistic."

Jared looked around them pointedly. "I doubt she's going to get landing permission."

"Probably not, but she doesn't need it."

Carl stepped back from his equipment, and the flat surface turned silvery. Moments later, Lily Stone stepped through.

"Well, well. That *is* a surprise," Jared said in wonder. "Remind me never to count that young man out."

He looked over at where Kelsey was standing beside her father. "I hope we did enough to make a difference. Any idea where Prince Ethan is?"

"Not a clue. He'll turn up, I'm sure."

* * *

KELSEY WATCHED Lily run the medical scanner over her father with her heart in her throat. "How is he?"

Stone smiled. "The drug is slowing the poison down, and the nanites are starting to repair the damage. He's not out of the woods just yet, but he has a fighting chance now. Call it sixty-forty. If he makes it, I foresee a complete recovery."

"Will moving him lower his chances?"

"Not appreciably. I think we'd all be happier if we can get him up to *Invincible*. If he has a complication, I'll be better able to work on him."

The doctor glanced over at the Imperial physician. "It looks like he has things wrapped up with Senator Breckenridge. We'll take everyone up. Talbot! Call the pinnaces in to the university. We're leaving."

"Aye, ma'am. Everyone, make sure to keep things together as we pull out. No slipups at the last moment. The outer perimeter will pull back in to extract as soon as we're clear."

"What is that thing?" Kelsey asked Stone.

"A kind of point-to-point transfer device Carl got from Omega. I have to say it came in very handy."

"We need to hurry. I want to know where my brother is. We have to stop him."

Stone looked up from where she was preparing to move the emperor to a gurney. "I know that one. They spotted the Imperial yacht leaving orbit just as I was landing. I guess he was on his way to Orbital One and changed his mind."

"He can't run fast enough to stop me from kicking his ass," Kelsey said grimly.

She walked over to Talbot. "I need to get to *Invincible* as soon as possible."

"It should be back in orbit. Once things went down, Admiral Yeats called most of our ships back in. There are pinnaces right on the other side of that transport ring."

"Excellent. Come with me."

He shook his head. "Not until all my people are clear. You go ahead."

"Be careful." She kissed him hard.

Kelsey fell in behind the gurney as it headed for the ring and grabbed Jared by the arm. "Ethan is in orbit. We're going up right now to catch his ass."

He grinned coldly. "Let's go end this."

35

J ared found the trip through the ring surreal. One moment he was in the Imperial Palace, and the next, he was in the fusion plant at Imperial University exiting one of two large rings set up there. Almost eighty kilometers traveled in the blink of an eye.

The marines would withdraw from the palace and take the rings with them. Now that the emperor was safe, Talbot said they'd disassemble the ring in the medical center, move back to the emperor's suite, extract everyone through a second ring there, and then disassemble it. Carl and Angela would pass the rings through a smaller one and then escape out a secret tunnel.

They'd disabled the internal security monitors, so the remaining Imperial Guards wouldn't know they'd relocated. That would give them enough time to get away safely. No doubt the guards would wonder how the attack took place at all.

Hopefully, the emperor would be in a forgiving mood when he woke up. Jared refused to believe the man would die after everything they'd risked.

Once the emperor and Senator Breckenridge were aboard the

pinnace, he joined Kelsey and Elise inside. He sat next to his girlfriend and hugged her as the pinnace lifted.

"This might just turn out okay after all."

"Not if Ethan escapes," she said. "We've both seen how even a failed coup can damage society. Imagine a civil war. The man is insane, and he won't hesitate to rip the Empire apart to slake his thirst for power."

Kelsey nodded sadly. "We have to stop him, Jared. If he gets away, he'll turn people that would otherwise be loyal citizens against the Empire. We cannot afford a civil war."

"Even if that means killing him?"

She sighed. "I hope it doesn't come to that."

The flight up went smoothly, and they docked with *Invincible* a few minutes later. Someone had found him a uniform to replace his prison clothes, so he took a few minutes to change before heading for the bridge. He wanted to project the right image, both for his people and Ethan Bandar.

The flag bridge was a hive of activity as he arrived. Kelsey was already standing beside his command console. She hadn't bothered changing.

"Give me a status," Jared said, as he tapped into the implant feeds and looked for himself.

Commander Jade Winslow, his chief of staff, turned to face him. "A number of cutters left Orbital One and docked with *New York* half an hour ago. Apparently, Captain Breckenridge hijacked it. Most of her officers and crew were off the ship, so they couldn't resist marine boarding parties.

"It took us a while to realize that was what had happened. It and the Imperial yacht are already quite a distance away. Only our destroyers or fighters have a chance of catching them."

The officer shook her head. "They made a really bad call. We don't need to chase them that fast. They're running for the Nova system flip point, sir."

* * *

WALLACE BRECKENRIDGE SAT in the command chair of his new ship. A destroyer was a big step down for him, but beggars couldn't be choosers.

His arrival on board *New York* had surprised the skeleton crew, and his men had managed to seize control. He wished he'd had enough people to grab something bigger, but she would do. After all, he'd be able to replace her with something much more modern very shortly.

"Lieutenant Heller, what is the status of the Fleet vessels still in orbit?" he asked his lead man.

The officer turned from the helm controls. "No change, sir. They're still sitting there with those battle screens of theirs down. The Imperial yacht and we are too far away for them to catch us short of the new flip point. From there, we should be able to get to the flip point heading for Harrison's World."

Breckenridge nodded with satisfaction. One of his spies had gotten a heading and distance from this flip point to the other one. They'd be able to make the trip quickly enough to arrive before Mertz. Once there, the heir would be able to leverage his rank into a new headquarters that the Bastard wouldn't be able to budge him from.

Honestly, he thought it was a brilliant plan and was quite pleased with it.

"How long on the timer?" he asked.

"Three minutes and twenty-two seconds."

He smiled wolfishly. The Bastard would be getting a big surprise. He wished he could see his face when the universe fell on him.

* * *

JARED WAS JUST ABOUT to order *Invincible* out of orbit when the general quarters alarm sounded.

Winslow hunched over her console. "Missile launch! Multiple missiles inbound at point-blank range."

"Battle screens up," Marcus said. "Firing beams in defensive mode. Impacts in two… one…"

The massive ship lurched under the explosions, but no fresh alarms wailed.

"Status," Jared snapped.

"Battle screens at sixty percent," Marcus said. "No loss of hull integrity."

"Who fired those missiles?"

"No one, Admiral. They came to life near the area where *New York* was in her parking orbit. They must've preprogrammed them and ejected them."

Jared slowly nodded. "That's actually pretty clever. We didn't spot them because we weren't looking. If you hadn't had the battle screens ready for immediate use, they'd have sucker punched us. Scan for any other little surprises he might have left for us."

The AI was silent for a moment. "No other anomalies detected, Admiral."

"Good. Commander Winslow, signal our ships to leave orbit at flank speed. Let's see if we can close the distance enough to talk them out of this insanity."

* * *

ETHAN SAT at the command console on his yacht. He had Breckenridge on screen from *New York*. The officer had scraped the barrel and gotten enough men and women personally loyal to him to control the ship. Barely.

"Are you certain this is the right way to go?" he asked the renegade Fleet officer. "Other than the basic data, we have no idea where this new flip point leads. The report was heavily restricted, and I never looked into it. I had more pressing things on my mind."

"We know the important part, Highness," the renegade Fleet officer said. "It leads to the Old Empire where they got those ships. You can order the Fleet units there to stand down. We can still turn this around. Many officers will rush to support you over the Bastard."

Ethan nodded. Of course they would. Except for those who had been secretly against him from the beginning. Like Breckenridge's former executive officer. He'd have to go. There would be no more coddling traitors.

Mertz had been diabolically clever. He'd sewn men loyal to him in so many places. Everything was a gamble. But he knew he could overawe the Fleet stooges Mertz had left at Harrison's World. They would never defy him in person. He could turn this all around.

"What kind of force is guarding the new flip point on our side?" he asked.

The Fleet officer looked at his console. "A single destroyer. I've already sent them orders to move away from the flip point."

"Will they?"

The other man laughed. "They won't fire on the heir to the Throne, if that's what you're worried about. If they do, I have a lot more experience. I'll take them out."

The commander of the Imperial yacht turned toward Ethan. "Highness, we're receiving a signal from Fleet."

"Put it on the main screen," Ethan said. "Split the view between it and Admiral Breckenridge."

Rather than one of the officers from the destroyer, he found himself looking at Jared Mertz and Kelsey. Mertz was in uniform, but Kelsey was still in her prison clothes. He wondered what that meant.

"Ethan Bandar, Wallace Breckenridge, I'm ordering you to heave to and prepare to be boarded," Mertz said sternly. "This is over. We have the emperor under our care, and he's going to survive your assassination attempt."

The officers on the yacht's bridge all looked up at that, shock clearly written on their faces.

Ethan sneered. "You don't frighten me, Bastard. This fight is far from over. If you think you can just fire on the heir to the Throne, you're very much mistaken. The people would rise up against you."

He smiled a little wider. "Even if what you said just now were true, which of course it isn't, the Empire would go up like a tinderbox. No matter what you do, you lose."

* * *

Kelsey sighed and considered what her twin had just said. "He's right, Jared. Blowing him up would tear the Empire apart." She stared at her brother for a long moment. "Let him go."

Jared turned to her, surprise written all over his face. "But—"

She felt hollow inside as she held up her hand. "This is my decision to make. It's the best thing for the Empire if we don't stop him."

Kelsey kept her eyes steady on Ethan's smirking face. "Make no mistake, anyone taking that flip with you is guilty of treason and subject to death. No warning and no quarter. Your crew doesn't know what you're asking of them. Give them a choice to leave."

Ethan laughed. "They swore their lives to serve the emperor. They know where their place is. But, if any cowards want to scamper away, good riddance."

He smiled nastily at her. "We'll meet again, dearest sister, and sooner than you think."

"Make your peace with God, Ethan," she said, her throat closing up on the words. "His is the only forgiveness you'll find in this life or the next."

She made a gesture to cut the signal.

Jared rose from his seat. "The yacht doesn't have battle screens. The radiation will kill him."

"Yes, it will."

The silence on the flag bridge was deafening.

Jared nodded slowly. "I understand and I'm sorry, Kelsey. They have another half hour to change their minds. To come to their senses."

But they didn't.

A number of escape pods from both ships told her that they'd allowed those wanting to leave to depart. That made her feel a little better. Only those embracing Ethan would die.

* * *

Far too many of the crewmen on the yacht had abandoned Ethan, but Breckenridge had sent a few more trained officers over by cutter as they approached the new flip point. *New York* would guard the flip point on this side to give Ethan time to sprint to Harrison's World.

"Transition in ten seconds, Highness," the new help officer reported.

"Take us over when ready."

The time dragged until the universe twisted. They'd flipped.

A loud alarm blasted from the overhead speakers. Ethan covered his ears. "What is that?"

The helm officer spun in his seat. "We're being bombarded by heavy radiation, Highness. It's blasting right though the hull."

"Are we in danger? Get us out of here."

"The flip capacitor is charging. I'll flip us back as soon as I can. Highness, the dosage is high enough to be fatal in just a few minutes."

Ethan leaned forward, staring at the man incredulously. "How did they ever get through here? Why didn't that idiot Breckenridge warn me?"

He suspected this was some kind of twisted assassination plot. Breckenridge had been some kind of plant. As stupid as that sounded, he'd been in Mertz's pocket all along. The man's entire plan had been to trick Ethan into killing himself.

Well, that wouldn't work. He'd flip back to Avalon and overcome this. Somehow.

A different alarm began sounding.

"What now?"

The man stared at his console for a long moment without responding. When he turned, his expression told Ethan he had bad news.

"The flip drive shorted out. They're trying to get it back online, but it won't matter." The man's eyes were hollow. "All the systems are taking damage from the radiation. We're going to take a fatal dose before they're done. We'll be walking dead men even if they succeed."

Ethan swallowed noisily. "And if they don't?"

"I'm no doctor, but in five minutes we'll be in excruciating pain. We'll be throwing up and voiding from the other end as well. In fifteen minutes, we'll be dead and glad this is over."

He felt as though he could already sense the churning in his gut as the lethal radiation rotted him from the inside out.

"Are there any other options?" he asked, his throat dry.

"One," the man said. "We might be able to overload the fusion plant. That would be a lot cleaner way to go."

"Kill that noise."

The silence was almost more deafening than the alarm.

Ethan waited for the time to run out. Once it became clear that they weren't going to make it, he nodded toward the man. "Do it. Blow up the ship."

The lights flickered and went out. After a moment, they came back on dimly.

"The fusion plant just failed, Highness," the man said. "The capacitor is less than half charged. I don't suppose any of your people brought sidearms."

"My guards," he said numbly.

"I suggest you call one up here. We have need of his services."

* * *

ONCE THE YACHT HAD FLIPPED, Kelsey sat at one of the auxiliary stations. It was done. Only the pain remained to endure. Something she knew entirely too much about.

New York stayed in the flip point, possibly guarding it to give Ethan more time. Breckenridge had no way to know her brother was already dying.

Oddly, the emotions inside her were subdued. She knew what she'd done, but it didn't feel real. Not yet.

Twenty minutes later, just as *Invincible* and her escorts were coming close, *New York* flipped to the Nova system. A minute later, they were back. Breckenridge must have realized his mistake.

Their exposure had been short. If he surrendered now, he'd live.

Jared nodded to Winslow. "Signal *New York* to surrender."

Of course Breckenridge didn't. The destroyer opened fire on *Invincible*. It was ridiculous. They couldn't even get through her battle screens.

"Return fire," Jared said coolly.

He'd probably meant just the superdreadnought, but all their ships fired a salvo. *New York* never stood a chance. She died in fire long before the massed beams of the Old Empire ships destroyed every missile Breckenridge had fired.

Kelsey felt bad for Eliyanna Kaiser. The woman had lost her ship. Well, Jared would find something for her. Somehow, the fact all of Breckenridge's task force was now gone felt appropriate.

"Send a destroyer over to recover the yacht," she said, her voice sounding tired and hollow to her.

Jared rose from his seat and pulled her into a hug. "I'm so sorry."

She should've cried like a baby, but the tears refused to come. She knew the shock wouldn't last long. The flag bridge wasn't the place to have a breakdown, either. "Thanks. I'm going down to check on my father."

The trip to the medical center was a blur. Her mind couldn't pull away from the horror she'd tricked her brother into. Even after everything he'd done, she'd still loved him deep down.

She'd killed him just as effectively as if she'd leveled a plasma rifle at him and pulled the trigger.

The little boy that had chased her through the Imperial Gardens, laughing like a fool, was dead, and she'd killed him.

Kelsey walked into the medical center in a fog of grief so strong she almost ran into Lily Stone.

The other woman gripped her shoulders and pulled her into her office. "Kelsey, what's wrong?"

"I killed my brother."

"Oh, honey." The other woman pulled her into a tight hug, and Kelsey cried. Another pair of arms surrounded her. Elise was holding her, too. All three of them cried.

No one said anything or asked questions. They just gave her the support she desperately needed right then. She knew Jared would have done the same, but she couldn't afford to break down in public like this.

They pulled apart at last, and Lily brought Kelsey some tissues. "I know this makes no difference whatsoever, but you did what you had to. He was a mad dog bent on wrecking the Empire."

"I know," Kelsey said, her voice filled with grief. "But we were kids together. He was my world once. That doesn't go away even when people go bad. I have to tell my father, if he ever wakes up."

"Then let me give you some good news. The nanites have turned the corner for him. He's going to be fine."

A man in white knocked on the hatch. "Doctor, the emperor is awake."

Kelsey hurried out after Lily. Her father lay on a bed surrounded by medical equipment, but his eyes were open. It took all her willpower to stand back and let Lily check the readings.

"How are you feeling, Majesty?" Lily asked.

"Like a grav truck ran over me and then backed up to make sure I was down." His voice was a ghost of its normal self. "What happened?"

Lily glanced over her shoulder. "I'll let Kelsey tell you."

She stepped back and lowered her voice. "No stress just now. Save the bad news until he's stronger."

"I'll keep it easy, but he's the emperor. I have to tell him something, or he'll keep after me and worry even more."

Kelsey stepped up beside the bed and took his hand in hers. "I'm so glad to see you getting better, Papa. You really scared us."

He smiled up at her. "You haven't called me that since you were a little girl. Tell me true. Is everything okay?"

She shook her head. "No, Papa, but things will get better now. I did what needed to be done. The Empire is safe, and you're going to make a full recovery."

"What happened?"

"Not now. You'll just have to trust me when I say the danger has passed. When you're stronger, we'll talk about it. I'll tell you everything. I promise."

He looked at her steadily. "Where's Ethan?"

"He can't be here right now," she said with more strength than she'd thought she'd had. "You're on *Invincible*."

"I feel as though you're leaving something important out, but I can't seem to focus. I'm sorry, but I'm so tired."

Lily stepped in. "Your father needs to rest. He'll be a lot stronger tomorrow. Why don't you get some sleep yourself?"

"I think I will. Goodnight, Papa." She kissed him on the forehead.

Elise limped over to her as she was heading for the hatch. "Would you like some company?"

She shook her head. "Thank you, but no. I need to be alone."

The other woman hugged her again. "Call me if you want to talk. Day or night."

"I will. Thank you."

A check of the ship's systems told her that the pinnace with Talbot on board was just leaving Avalon. She had hours before she could cry all over him. In the meantime, she'd sit in the observation lounge, watch the stars, and remember the laughter of a little boy who'd once meant the world to her.

36

E lise sat beside Jared as he waited for the board of inquiry to make their findings public. The last month had been brutal. Most of the citizens in the Empire hadn't had time to comprehend the emperor's poisoning before the heir was dead, but that did nothing to stop the backlash it caused.

Kelsey had retreated into private, but the more extreme news groups—both conservative and liberal—roundly lambasted her for not taking the heir into custody so that the authorities could discover the "actual facts" of the situation. Conspiracy theories abounded.

She'd taken her brother's death hard. Harder than her father had. Her friends tried to be there for her, but she'd pushed them all away. Even Talbot.

That hurt him, too, but he put on a brave face for her. Elise had helped him understand it wasn't him, but that only went so far.

He'd eventually bulled his way back into her life, and she was starting to show signs of coming out from under the black clouds her life had become.

Elise knew that she'd recover and be sad that she pushed them all away in time. Jared understood, too. They'd be there for her when that time came.

The emperor had tried to blunt the criticism, but his own grief made that difficult. Now the Imperial Senate was locked in a vicious battle over whether to deny Kelsey the position of heir or not. That situation would come to a head today. Kelsey said she didn't care, but Elise doubted that.

Her strongest advocate no doubt surprised her. Senator Nathaniel Breckenridge gave fiery speeches denouncing those who fought against the emperor's will. His usual stance as the opposition undermined his normal allies' positions but didn't stop the fighting. It only made it bloodier.

Nathaniel Breckenridge had insisted Elise not tell Kelsey what he suspected about her genetics. That he'd tell her when the time felt right. Elise thought that was excellent judgment.

At least the Senate had settled the treaty issues before it had plunged off the deep end. The Senate had accepted Harrison's World and Erorsi into the Imperial fold and confirmed their new senators. They'd even validated Emperor Marcus's edict.

They'd amended the Imperial Charter to allow for worlds orphaned during the Fall, too. Pentagar was now officially an ally, but not part of the Empire. They'd exchanged official embassies, and trade had begun. Captain Anton Keller and his new ship, *Best Deal II*, had made the inaugural run.

The hatch to the side of the room slid aside, and the members of the board walked to the table. Admiral Jack Lancaster banged a gavel and brought the proceedings to order.

"This board has considered all aspects of the events that occurred during expedition fifteen and the actions of Admiral Jared Mertz. It has taken a long time to hear every bit of testimony and consider what happened. For that delay, this board apologizes. Admiral Mertz, please rise."

Jared stood. His back was straight, but Elise could see the tension in him. He was ready for them to send him to a court-martial.

"Admiral Jared Mertz, it is the judgment of this board that you acted in accordance with Fleet regulations and made the best decisions circumstances allowed. In your place, this board fears it would have made a catastrophic mess of the situation.

"It is our belief that you acted in the finest traditions of Fleet and that no further action is necessary. This board stands adjourned."

There were some approving cries, but mostly the mood was somber. The last month hadn't brought anyone much joy.

Elise stood and took his hand. "I knew you'd be fine."

He smiled at her. "That's one of us, then. I'm just glad it's over so we can move on to other problems."

"Like Kelsey's confirmation? If we hurry, we might be able to make the hearing."

"We'll have time. That hearing won't be ending anytime soon."

"Probably not," she conceded. "We should still go show our support."

"Then let's go. We can just make the next cutter if we hurry."

* * *

TALBOT SAT beside Kelsey in the emperor's box at the Imperial Senate. He didn't know how she kept such a cool expression on her face while that rat-faced bastard stood there at the podium slandering her. He was sorely tempted to go over the rail and make him regret those artfully-crafted insults.

The pompous ass had no idea the horrible pain she'd been in. How much she still suffered. It had taken every bit of his love to get inside her dark world, plant his back to hers, and help her fight back. A lesser man might've given up, but he'd lasted her out.

She'd spent most of the last month in the dojo. She'd earned her black belt and then devoted herself to earning the last mark of distinction. Sensei. Ned had grudgingly granted her the red stripe this morning.

Kelsey tightened her grip on his hand. "Homicidal thoughts are acceptable. Actions, not so much."

"He pisses me off. Raving on about how you murdered your brother. He knows the facts, though he isn't shy about saying you and the admiral made the whole thing up. Like you're the villain of this story. Asshole."

"That's the spirit. I don't care what he thinks. I don't care what any of them think. The only opinions I value are my friends and my father."

The emperor had taken the death of his son hard, but to his credit, he hadn't blamed Kelsey. He'd blamed himself. He'd backed Kelsey to the hilt and nominated her to replace Ethan as the heir as soon as the official period of mourning was over. And hadn't that been throwing red meat to the wolves?

Leaving aside all the whacky conspiracy theories, they talked about her parentage as if she were a broodmare. One senator had even called into question her place in the peerage because she was sleeping with Talbot.

That bastard was going to pay one day very soon. Talbot had a fantasy about punching his lights out.

Frankly, Talbot had mostly stayed away from listening to them "debate" to protect his blood pressure. And to keep himself out of prison.

"What happens if they decline to name you heir?" he asked. "You were the second in line to the Throne. Are you no longer a princess? Not that I care one damned bit if you have a title or not."

She smiled at him. "Some people have advocated stripping me of my title, but odds are I'd keep it. Father has declined to disown me, so that movement won't go anywhere.

"More likely, they'll decide I'm not worthy to be heir and start looking for someone more to their liking. I'm fine with that, too. I just want this over so I can put my life back together."

She looked at him and sighed. "I'm so sorry I've put you through this, Russ. I don't deserve you."

He kissed her, knowing that some bastard would get a picture. Screw them. "Well, I won't say this has been easy, but I deserve you, so don't give me any flack."

She took a deep breath as the senator speaking wrapped up his denunciation. "It's time for me to go piss everyone off."

Kelsey rose to her feet and met Jared and Elise as they opened the box door. She hugged her brother. "Thank you for coming. How did it go?"

"No court-martial," he said. "And we wouldn't have missed being here for you."

"Thank God," she said fervently. "Now sit down and watch as I ruin my future."

His commanding officer and Princess Elise sat beside Talbot.

"She's joking, right?" Jared asked.

"Her humor's been so black recently, I'm not sure."

Elise looked at his dress uniform. "I see she talked you into wearing your medals. It looks good on you."

The emperor had held the longest awards ceremony in Imperial history last week. The list of all the people who'd died was read aloud at The Spire. Then they'd announced the posthumous medals for valor.

The event had been acid on his soul. He'd wept without shame when the emperor awarded the Imperial Cross to Timothy Reese, laid to rest with the rank of Lieutenant Colonel.

A number of living people had received the Empire's highest award. Admiral Mertz, for example. Well deserved, there.

He'd been less happy when they'd given it to him. He hadn't earned it. Not like everyone else. The knighthood that went with it was somehow subtly insulting. He was a marine ground pounder, not a pampered noble. He was as common as they came, and them thinking they could change him into something else just rubbed him the wrong way.

"I only wore it because she told me to," he said stubbornly.

He saw understanding in the admiral's eyes. "She's a smart one, my sister. Don't let her get away."

Kelsey appeared at the podium. She gripped it and looked out over the sea of faces in the senatorial boxes and the visitor's gallery. Rather than speak, she just stared at them until the murmuring started.

Then she spoke.

"I come before this august body to discuss my place in the succession. Or, I should say, that's what many of you believe I'm here for. It's not."

Talbot swore he could hear a pin drop in the silence that statement left. Even with his enhanced hearing.

"I don't care one damned bit if you vote for me as the heir," she declared in a ringing voice. "In fact, I urge you to find someone else. Someone less likely to offend your delicate sensibilities. Someone less like the 'cold-hearted bitch' one of you referred to me as.

"If you do confirm me, I'll do whatever I think is best for the Empire, no matter whose feelings it hurts. No matter the cost, to either me or anyone else. I killed my brother because he was a threat to the Empire. That's the kind of person I am."

That started a lot of chatter in the boxes, making the speaker pound his gavel for order.

Kelsey didn't wait for them to quiet down. "While we're on touchy subjects, let me clarify how I feel about my parentage. I don't have a single drop of Imperial blood in my veins. If that bothers you, go screw yourselves."

That brought a roar from both the boxes and visitor's gallery. A mixture of rage and glee. Talbot found himself on his feet screaming his support of her.

"Tell them off, Kelsey!" he shouted.

She cranked the volume on her microphone up and spoke over the bedlam.

"Do whatever you want. It's all this body of puffed-up, self-important chatterboxes has ever done. Find a talking head to be the next emperor and see how long he keeps the rebels off your necks. I'll stick with fighting them face to face. At least that's honest work."

She turned her back on the pandemonium she'd caused and left the podium.

Jared stood there and started slow clapping. The visitor's gallery picked it up next. Even some of the senators. The new senators from Harrison's World and Erorsi were the most ardent in their support.

Talbot noticed Nathaniel Breckenridge had a wide grin on his face. He inclined his head toward the man.

Kelsey rejoined them a few moments later. "Well, I think that should settle matters," she said as she sat beside Talbot. "Now I can put this behind me and get down to the real work."

He squeezed her hand. "You were awesome."

"At least that should end the debate," Elise said with a grin. "They'll either love you or hate you for saying those things."

"You always have a spot with me," Jared said.

"Thanks," Kelsey said. "I might need it if they banish me."

The speaker finally got things under control. He recognized Senator Breckenridge.

Breckenridge climbed to the podium and looked out over the Senate. "Everyone knows I've never been the strongest supporter of the emperor, but today I stand by his side. Do we want a milquetoast as the heir or do we want someone with fire in her belly? Someone who says they love the Empire or someone who has demonstrated it with their every action? Their every sacrifice.

"Princess Kelsey said some harsh things. Things that might have hurt your delicate feelings. Well, look at those of us who have disgraced ourselves in speaking of her like that. It's unworthy of the Imperial Senate. Unworthy of a crowd in a bar, for that matter. We deserved to hear her tell us the truth."

He glared at the men and women before him. "It's time to show your true colors. Are you men and women with spine or weaklings made of ego? I nominate Princess Kelsey Bandar for heir to the Imperial Throne."

A voice cried out a second.

"We have a motion to vote on the emperor's petition to recognize Princess Kelsey Bandar as heir to the Imperial Throne," the speaker said. "Cast your votes on the electronic system now."

Talbot tried to hold out some hope, but he couldn't see her winning after the dose of bitter truth she'd given them.

A few minutes passed as various senators argued with one another. Some *very* loudly. Talbot wondered how many duels this was going to spawn.

The speaker finally gave the senators sixty seconds' warning. Once that time ran out, the man looked down at his board with a grave expression.

"The Imperial Senate has spoken. All rise and welcome the heir to the Imperial Throne, Princess Kelsey Bandar, to her new position."

The tally board showed the vote had been close. The new senators from Erorsi and Harrison's World had turned the trick.

Kelsey looked shocked, but she was more so when Talbot whooped and swung her up into the air.

* * *

ANGELA TURNED OFF THE SCREEN. The sight of Princess Kelsey's shocked expression was the perfect end to the whole crappy process.

She looked over at where Carl sat on the couch. They'd seen each other socially a number of times over the last month, and she was now convinced she'd been an idiot to fight this. He might be young, but he had spirit and heart.

"All's well that ends well," she said.

"I got a call while the vote was happening. I took it on my implants. It was the Lucien Committee."

When he didn't say anything more, she reached over and smacked him on the back of the head. "Don't keep me wondering. What did they say?"

He took a deep breath and shook his head. Her heart plummeted. She'd been so sure he'd win.

"I can't understand why, but they somehow think what I did was worthy of the award."

It took her a moment to process what he'd said, and then she leapt to her feet and yanked him off the couch and into a hug. "You won, you rat!"

"But I didn't deserve it! And I sure as hell didn't earn the Imperial Cross. It's ridiculous."

She set him on his feet and glared at him. "Let me tell you a little secret, nerd boy. Other people tell us when we're worthy of something. That or we end up like Prince Ethan or Professor Bedford. Don't second-guess their judgment."

"Professor Bedford isn't actually that bad, now that I know him better. Once they gave me my PhD—which I also didn't earn—he started treating me like a colleague. Though he still doesn't understand why the quantum com works the way it does."

She'd heard him talking about it enough over the last month to know the details. The com worked through a flip point, but not two. Distance didn't seem to be a factor. It was almost a thousand light years to Nova and it worked, but two shorter hops didn't.

It seemed that a single trip through a flip point used up most of its energy. Oh, it was still useful throughout the target system, but not any interstellar distance beyond it.

That wasn't to say that it didn't work through normal space. They'd taken one around a great loop and found it worked at three hundred light years along a straight line, even after it had stopped working due to there being too many intervening flip points.

That didn't match up with the theory at all, so everyone was scratching their heads. Including that old reprobate, Professor Bedford. It wouldn't stop them from creating a network of FTL repeaters, though. A call to Pentagar could take place in real time. Or to the other side of the universe, if they built enough coms to rebroadcast the transmission.

This was going to change everything. Galactic civilization would never be the same. If the Old Empire had had these devices, the rebellion would never have succeeded.

Bedford had also been stunned to learn of the bodies from other universes. No one had known what to do with them, other than give them an honorable burial, but the scientist was certain there must be some kind of subtle differences that might shed light on how those alternate realities worked and what laws governed them.

Carl was just glad it kept the old man out of his hair.

Angela shook her head. "That's because he respects what you've done, dolt. These people aren't honoring you for the toys you've built. It's the mind inside that scrawny body they drool all over."

He started to say something, but she put her hands on her hips and leaned over him. "Personally, I think they're being hasty, though. All those other versions of me were onto something."

He frowned. "What?"

"I think it's time to take our relationship to the next level, Doctor Owlet. Or should I call you Sir Carl? I want to know what I've been missing."

She smiled at his shocked expression.

"Unless, of course, you'd rather not have sex with me."

He shook his head emphatically. "I'd carry you off if I could lift you."

"Don't worry about it, sport. You do the thinking, and I'll do all the hard work."

Angela tossed him over her shoulder and headed for her bedroom while he laughed. Finally, something felt perfectly right in her life.

* * *

WANT to get updates from Terry about new books and other general nonsense going on in his life? He promises there will be cats. Go to TerryMixon.com/Mailing-List and sign up.

DID YOU ENJOY THIS BOOK? Please leave a review on Amazon. It only takes a minute to dash off a few words and that kind of thing helps Terry make a living as a writer and gets you new books faster.

WANT the next book in this series? Grab *Recon in Force* today or buy any of Terry's other books, which are listed on the next page.

VISIT TERRY'S Patreon page to find out how to get cool rewards and an early look at what he's working on at Patreon.com/TerryMixon.

ALSO BY TERRY MIXON

You can always find the most up to date listing of Terry's titles on his
Amazon Author Page.

The Empire of Bones Saga

Empire of Bones

Veil of Shadows

Command Decisions

Ghosts of Empire

Paying the Price

Recon in Force

Behind Enemy Lines

The Terra Gambit

Hidden Enemies

Race to Terra

Ruined Terra

Victory on Terra

The Humanity Unlimited Saga

Liberty Station

Freedom Express

Tree of Liberty

Blood of Patriots

The Imperial Marines Saga

Spoils of War

The Fractured Republic Saga

Storm Divers

The Scorched Earth Saga
Scorched Earth

Omnibus Volumes
The Empire of Bones Saga Volume 1

The Empire of Bones Saga Volume 2

The Empire of Bones Saga Volume 3

Humanity Unlimited Publisher's Pack 1

The Vigilante Series with Glynn Stewart
Heart of Vengeance

Oath of Vengeance

Bound By Law

Bound By Honor

Bound By Blood

ABOUT TERRY

#1 Bestselling Military Science Fiction author Terry Mixon served as a non-commissioned officer in the United States Army 101st Airborne Division. He later worked alongside the flight controllers in the Mission Control Center at the NASA Johnson Space Center supporting the Space Shuttle, the International Space Station, and other human spaceflight projects.

He now writes full time while living in Texas with his lovely wife and a pounce of cats.

www.TerryMixon.com
Terry@terrymixon.com

amazon.com/author/terrymixon

facebook.com/TerryLMixon

patreon.com/TerryMixon

bookbub.com/authors/terry-mixon

goodreads.com/TerryMixon